METACOSM CHRONICLES
—— BOOK TWO ——

N.A. SOLEIL

Copyright © 2024 by N.A. Soleil

All rights reserved.

No part of this publication may be reproduced, distributed, or transmitted in any form or by any means, including photocopying, recording, or other electronic or mechanical methods, without the prior written permission of the publisher, except as permitted by U.S. copyright law. For permission requests, contact N.A. Soleil at either NASoleilAuthor@gmail.com or via the contact form on Metacosmchronicles.com.

The story, all names, characters, and incidents portrayed in this production are fictitious. No identification with actual persons (living or deceased), places, buildings, and products is intended or should be inferred.

Book Cover by Lance Buckley [lancebuckley.com].
Cover symbol design by N.A. Soleil.

Warning

This book is not appropriate for children, because it contains gore, murder, attempted molestation and rape (though both are brief, implied, not graphic, and the perpetrator is rewarded with a grisly, immediate, screaming death), slavery, and violence.

Why? Why write about the worst depravities of sapientkind? Because, this is the story of Justice. And though we can't see it, Justice is present with every evil act.

Though we tell a tale that contains some horrors, you must remember one thing: in this metacosm, Justice always has the final say.

Throughout this work we will place content notations in bold on the right side of the page where there are potentially particularly triggering sections, like this:

(Warning)

If you choose to skip the section, look for the second bolded right-aligned note, like this:

(Continue here)

Note:
No part of this book was algorithmically generated (commonly known as "AI"). What you hold in your hands is simply the result of hundreds of hours of human blood, sweat, and tears. We actually broke Google Docs *twice* and had to make backups because there were too many edits, which is a thing I didn't know could happen til it happened to us.
(I can't freaking believe I have to say this.)

Dedication

This book is dedicated to those who can't fight for themselves.
To those whose voice was taken. To those who are only just now finding their voice.
To those who have been screaming so long they aren't certain they have a voice any longer.
To those who were never allowed a voice.
We are here. We see you.
You matter.

As always, thanks to my wonderful and talented mom for being there to support us
in more ways than I could write here.
To Sara, Sarah, and Aimee, for kicking my ass and being Metacosm's biggest fans.
It means more to me than you will ever know.
To our little goblin and our not-so-little cybernetic artificial lifeform.
You're getting too clever. Stop it.

MY DEAR CHILD.
I HAVE NEVER CREATED ANYTHING LIKE YOU,
AND NEVER WILL AGAIN.
SHOULD YOU CHOOSE TO SERVE,
YOUR SHOULDERS AND HEART WILL BE EVER-HEAVY.
HOWEVER, KNOW THIS:
AMONG ALL MY CREATIONS,
YOU COMMAND THE UNDIVIDED ATTENTION
AND DIRECT INTERVENTION
OTHERWISE FORBIDDEN.
AND YOUR SERVICE
WILL HELP USHER IN THE CHANGE NEEDED
TO FIX
WHAT WENT WRONG
IN
THE
VERY
BEGINNING.

What say you?

PROLOGUE

Spiraea awoke.

Something had changed.

She cast her 'gaze' over the Creation, seeing and experiencing all planes and times, the in-between spaces and the in-potentia, as her given slice of Creator's power afforded her.

She picked through the overlapping stimuli with the delicate precision of a spider plucking its web — and came to the source of the problem.

The life-streams *and* soul-streams were shifting.

All of them.

While in this form, Spiraea was only a consciousness with power, but having spent much time with sapients, their reactions were ingrained in her. She paused in shock, not sure how to react to or even fathom what she was seeing.

She, shepherd of souls and caretaker of the streams, watched it happen …

Without her.

A pressure built up, incalculable, within and without, directionless and everywhere. The weight of trillions of new souls flooding the new streams settled on her, eliciting a shiver.

Triumph chased the shiver, cutting sharply through the miasma of her chaos-riddled mind.

Finally, she thought savagely. *The time has come.*

ONE
Zero Point

With a guttural scream and one last push, a child was born.

Of the few birthing-room occupants, none gushed enthusiastic congratulations or offered assurances of love. There was only morbid silence, punctuated by the mother's panted half-sobs.

A man looking out the nearby window listened but didn't care enough to turn and look. His posture screamed impatience; arms behind his back, feet spread wide. One hand tapped a pipe against the fingers of his other hand.

A nurse brought him the child, and it took only one glance to explain the unnatural quiet and the nurse's obvious horror.

Now bundled in a white cloth, the child stared up at him with big, dark eyes. Plastered to its head from the remnants of birthing fluids, was a smear of jet-black hair.

Immediately the man knew he had failed.

The child *watched* him with an unnerving awareness.

With a quick flip of his hand, the man turned back the folding of the cloth and surveyed his latest experiment with growing disgust.

One of the child's arms ended in an overly-large claw and rather than soft hominin skin, the appendage was covered in bumpy red scales. The other hand, while more hominin in shape and texture, was also clawed. The child's feet were similar to primate feet, and it lay on two leathery black flaps that looked like wings — none of which had been part of the plan. It was as though the disparate genetics the man had used had fought to the death in the womb. Finally, though barely worth noticing as it was a natural variant, there were no genitals at all. However, the child also had no anus; it was entirely smooth from stomach to rear.

Rage rose.

He'd expertly curated every single strand of DNA, personally handcrafted every single cell. *None* of that painstaking work showed in the child that lay before him.

Throwing the cloth back over his latest and most bitter failure, the man turned around once again, the tapping of the pipe against his fingers now the only sound in the room.

This one was supposed to have been the culmination of all his research — the birth of a perfect being.

"Take it away," he barked to the nurse, and waited until the room was silent again of her puttering before turning to the woman lying exhausted in the bed.

"We're done here," he said, and she flinched. He stabbed a forefinger at her. "You failed me for the final time. Our contract is null. I expect you to be gone by tomorrow."

He took a step towards her. She launched herself at the bedside table and yanked open the drawer. The gun she leveled at him wavered with her trembling hands, though it was unclear whether the movement was from her recent exertions or fear.

"Now where did you get that?" he asked, momentarily amused.

Another step made her jerk.

"Don't come near me!" she shrieked, then took a deep, shaky breath. "Give me my money, and I'll go."

"I expect you didn't hear me," he said through gritted teeth. "Let me attempt to restate, in a manner you might comprehend. You broke our contract; the only possible reason for … that … was failure by the incubator." He waved a hand in the direction of the door. "Therefore, you don't get one goddamned cent. Get out. Or I can always send you to the slave pits with your abomination. I'll be magnanimous and leave it as your choice."

She lowered the weapon, her mouth open. Her whole body was shaking, tears streaming from her bloodshot eyes.

"Well. Good night, then." Pipe now clenched between his teeth, he clapped his hands together and strode out of the room. He paused outside the door to steel himself against the resurgence of anger. A clear head was needed to consider his next step.

He strode down a lushly decorated hallway. Priceless furniture and paintings lined the walls, which were sparsely lit by antique sconces specially fitted with electrical wiring. An agonized scream echoed from behind him, followed by a gunshot.

He snorted but immediately put it out of his mind. The staff would deal with that mess. He opened the door to his study, then made his way to the bar on the far side of his sanctuary.

Bottles of all shapes and sizes and composition were lined up on the shelves, no two alike. He didn't drink most of the liquids contained in those bottles — some were even lethal to his species — but he did his best work while surrounded by the finest things from around the metacosm. It was only befitting his status as the greatest genius sapientkind had ever known.

The rest of his study fit with this self-important belief: in between the shelving units holding his vast collection of knowledge from all over the universe were his prized pieces, on prominent display. A Deimmortalizer sat just next to his desk, the tortured face of its former incarnation leering in a death mask. Similarly, the heads of endangered species spanning the galaxies hung on the walls, and on another pedestal near one wall was a small, stoppered bottle labeled 'Godslayer poison.'

Selecting a plain bottle from his liquor collection, the man poured a splash of the glowing, sky-blue stuff into an old fashioned glass.

Cradling the glass, he approached a pedestal in the middle of the room, as conspicuous as the prized trophy exhibited on it. In protected containment on the top of the pedestal was a single page — an ancient but pristine slip of some unidentifiable material covered in strange symbols that, despite all his research, he could make very little sense out of.

He'd only managed to decipher two phrases in over three hundred years: 'all species' and 'ultimate being.' His difficulty in translation was partially due to the nature of the script itself. It shifted as a living being, ghosting in between there and not, bright and dark, crawling across the page to sometimes disappear if not caught at the right moment. As far as he knew, the symbols that had disappeared had never returned. It was also written interspersedly in languages both ancient and modern, as well as a few yet to be discovered (that revelation had been a shocker).

Shaking his head, the man made his way to his desk and moved aside some papers to set the glass of liquor on its marble top. The desk looked like the aftermath of a tornado: papers, notes, binders, books, and all manner of detritus from his ongoing research littered the surface.

He stared at the 'input needed' message on his computer monitor, then pulled the keyboard toward him. Files opened as his computer awoke, reinstating what he had been working on before being informed of the birth. He set his pipe down in its special ivory tray and took a sip of his drink.

After a moment of brow-furrowed contemplation, he pushed the keyboard away and leaned back in his chair, rubbing his temples. No, it was no good. He couldn't concentrate. The image of that damned *mistake* was persistent. He needed to deal with it before he moved on.

Picking up his phone's receiver, he punched in numbers and waited while it connected.

"Yes, sir?" came a voice, respectful with a touch of fear.

"I have a new specimen for you. Come get it."

"Affirmative."

"I don't care what you do with it, but *do not kill it*."

"... As you wish, sir."

He slammed the phone down, caught up his drink, and downed it in a single gulp. As the liquid fire burned the back of his throat, he grimaced, and forced himself to relax.

He couldn't hear his staff as they bustled around like the little ants they were, but knew that by tomorrow morning that particular room of his impressive mansion would be pristine.

And the damnable child ... he'd never see it again.

He sighed and allowed himself a very small smile.

A setback, that's all it was.

The phone trilled.

Frowning, he snatched up the receiver. Unexpectedly the vid screen lit up, sans command. Only one caller could force him into a video call.

He went cold and bit back the sharp rebuke that had jumped to his tongue.

A man's shadowed face, hidden under a wide-brimmed black hat, filled the screen. Behind him was another individual: a blonde man with wings.

He was briefly stunned. *Wings*? Could it possibly be an angel? But ... they'd been extinct for *three hundred years!* Even the sample of angel DNA used for his perfect specimen project had taken the sacrifice of the kind of assets most agencies would never even see.

"Report," the man in black said, snapping him out of his abstraction. Mildly spoken, but a command nonetheless.

How it rankled.

"I sent my most recent summary of the work done on the translations last — "

"The specimen."

"We are ... still awaiting the birth."

"A lie. Your presence on this project is not a necessity; any greedy fool would jump at the chance to slit your throat personally and take over your position ... and your perks."

The receiver shook in a grip made suddenly unstable by terror.

"I ... I understand. Of course. The specimen was a failure. I sold it."

The man in black did not respond. The vid feed cut off abruptly, leaving the rattled man on the other end struggling against his tremors to get the receiver back into its cradle. He surged from his seat.

Pacing the room in agitation, he ran his fingers one by one over the most prized pieces in his collection, filling an urgent need to prove that they were still there, still his. After a full revolution of the room, he'd calmed enough to sit at his desk once more. He gave the Deimmortalizer a sardonic, if shaky, smile.

"If he thinks he has me against a wall, he's more the fool than he considers me to be," he muttered, starting his computer up again. "My brilliance will prove blinding even to the likes of him, once this project is completed. I just need to start again, and I can rid myself of that imbecile's blustering and shed the odious yoke of his master."

He had all of time, and more than enough resources. One day, the secrets of the universe *would* be laid bare to him and him alone. And then, he'd make them all pay for humiliating him.

TWO
Violet Eyes

Five years later …

The child curled up in his too-small cage with knees to chest, parts of his wings and other bits of him sticking out of the minuscule gaps in between the bars simply because there was no other place for them to be.

The cage clattered down with a teeth-jarring thump on a marble table.

They'd taken him from the slave pens and down hall after hall, finally ending in the largest room he'd seen yet. It was full of shiny, complicated things — but somehow empty at the same time.

The child took in five individuals. He knew how to count. He knew a lot of things — things the other slaves had taught him, things he'd overheard.

Three of the people in the room were the slavers he saw everywhere: helmeted, wearing black armor. These had more objects attached to their armor than the ones he commonly saw, though the child wasn't sure what that difference signified. One was a pointy-eared person with dark skin and red eyes. The final person in the room was a grey-skinned man. This one leaned down to look into the boy's cage, a greasy smirk spreading across his face.

"So this is the one they call Pheo-nix, because he's too stupid to die, eh?"

He wore no helmet, and had the most things on his armor, which was bigger and more complex than any of the others the child had ever seen. He was totally hairless and his eyes were completely black. The hand that reached to unlatch Pheonix's cage was abnormally long and thin.

The three helmeted men behind the grey man erupted in raucous laughter. One nudged the red-eyed man, who gave a twitch of a smile. The sense in the room was one of thick anticipation.

They were all armed. But that wasn't unusual; all the slavers were armed.

Pheonix stayed in the cage.

(Warning: attempted molestation, but the perpetrator dies horribly before he can accomplish it.)

"Come on, boy. Out," the grey man said, and grabbed Pheonix, who tumbled out of the cage, his lanky, undernourished body sprawling on the bare floor with a loud thump. The grey man still had a grip on his arm and hauled him up roughly. The others snickered behind him.

"You've gotten to that special age where you've earned a special visit to my quarters, slave. And since you're *very* special, I'll enjoy this *very* much. Maybe even my boys, eh? It'll be a party! And you're our *special* guest!"

The others cheered behind him.

Still holding Pheonix by one arm, he undid his trousers and dropped them, revealing stiff genitals. That hand then latched onto Pheonix's face roughly, wrenching his mouth open.

His heavy breathing and that of the others was the only sound in the room for a few moments — then an ear shattering scream.

The grey man's severed meat still in his mouth, Pheonix surged upwards, led by what they called his demon claw. The claw guided his body and Pheonix let it, a mild observer in all things. It grabbed the grey man's throat and tore it out, cutting off the tortured screaming. Then, the demon claw reached inside his gaping tracheal cavity, and into his ribcage. When it emerged, covered in blood, it was gripping the grey man's heart. The organ gave a couple of weak pumps, spurting purple blood — which at this point, everyone and everything was soaked in — then went flaccid.

Pheonix chewed the meat he already had in his mouth, then swallowed it. He tucked into the heart next.

Meat was food, and food was food when you were a slave.

(Continue here.)

The body fell back, convulsing only once.

The other slavers were too shocked to move, the silence sudden and heavy. Then three of them piled on Pheonix, who did not resist, while the red-eyed man screamed shrilly for an 'MPT.'

They held him down with rough hands, though Pheonix wasn't resisting. Oddly, these large, armed men were trembling and reeking of fear. Pheonix knew that smell. Slaves always smelled like that, and one had explained to him what it meant when he'd asked:

"Fear is when you don't want something to happen, but you are pretty sure it will. Or it is happening right then and you want it to stop. It feels bad."

Pheonix didn't understand the explanation, though. He didn't think he could 'feel.' At least, not in the way he'd observed in the people surrounding him. No thing was 'bad' or 'good.' It just was. And he didn't 'want' things. His body did things sometimes — like killing the man, or the compulsion to eat the meat — but he, himself, didn't have an opinion on it.

A stronger smell than fear arose. One of the slavers holding Pheonix had soiled himself. Pheonix idly wondered why.

After a while, the door opened again, revealing a pale and sweaty man holding some kind of bladed contraption. It roared to life and the blade began to spin. They forced Pheonix's mouth open again and the bladed thing pressed against his naturally sharp teeth.

Food goes in mouth, he thought, and bit down again, only to end up with a chunk of metal that he couldn't chew. He spit it out.

Not food.

The machine shuddered and sparked, then catastrophically died.

Swearing and now sweating profusely, the pale man tossed that machine away and picked up another, similar-looking bladed contraption.

The door slammed open and the machine-wielding man was gone.

More accurately, he became dust.

Chaos erupted. The other slavers rolled off of Pheonix, yelling and grabbing at their weapons, before becoming dust as well. Pheonix sat up, coughing with the sudden clouds of particulate matter.

A man in black entered the room, weapon leading. He wasn't just wearing black clothes; it was as if he stood in perpetual deep shadow. The silhouette Pheonix saw was of a broad-shouldered person wearing a wide hat. A flash of glowing green dots that Pheonix could only assume were eyes froze Pheonix in place.

The man pointed to the cage. Pheonix managed to crawl inside and the door slammed shut behind him.

The man in black picked up the cage and carried it, Pheonix inside, purposefully through the halls, turning anyone who crossed his path into dust.

Pheonix was confused. There had been too much input in too little time; he couldn't process.

That changed when a door opened next to the man in black and he whipped to face it. A slaver was swiftly turned to dust, though the person behind him — a female slave — had enough time to look up and meet Pheonix's gaze.

She had the brightest violet eyes Pheonix had ever seen.

Watching her suddenly crumble to a cloud that hung in the still air, the afterimage of her piercing eyes still burned in his vision, made Pheonix feel something.

The first something he'd ever felt.

A hot pressure built in his stomach and spread to his limbs, and all his senses screamed for him to release it, though he didn't know how.

The slavers becoming dust didn't create this hot sensation, yet it compounded with every slave the man in black leveled his weapon on. Pheonix didn't know what to make of it and it had physically paralyzed him, so his mind went into overdrive to analyze it.

To a degree, he was well-inured to horror. He'd been with the slavers since he was a few days old, after all. They would often beat a screaming enslaved person until the noise stopped and all that remained were the sick wet thuds of the blows. Sometimes they left the body; sometimes they dragged it out. They didn't always take someone to a 'special' room as they'd done for Pheonix. Sometimes they broke them right in front of the others.

Pheonix had witnessed it enough on the faces and in the actions of those around him to instinctively recognize pain, fear, grief, anger, shame, desperation — and many more emotions he didn't seem to possess. Maybe he couldn't name or relate to them, but he knew them by sight.

Pheonix knew what death was. When a body stopped moving. When eyes went blank and staring. When breath stopped. As if whatever was inside the body that made it move had left.

But these things had always remained a distant curiosity that happened to others and not him, as the child called Pheonix had no context for them in his own life.

As though something had passed from those violet eyes to Pheonix, he suddenly found himself with understanding. His young mind did a rapid series of calculations.

"It feels bad," rang in his head.

So, he thought, *this is what 'feeling bad' is.* He had an instinctual aversion to that heat filling him. For the first time, he wanted something to stop.

The slavers were the cause of the bad, so they too, were bad. A cascade of context clicked into place. The things the slavers did: bad. The man in black: bad.

After passing through an airlock and into the tiny, crowded cargo room of a second vessel, the man in black slammed Pheonix's cage down. The airlock sealed and the man in black stalked into another part of the vessel beyond Pheonix's field of view, leaving him alone. Through the large viewports on either side of the small ship, Pheonix could see that they had disengaged from the slaver ship and were rapidly traveling away from it.

When the slaver ship was no larger than a dot, just before it passed out of view completely, it exploded.

The burning sensation resurged and seized control of Pheonix's muscles. Caught in its grip, he attacked the bars of his cage, throwing his body around in the restrictive space.

Faces flashed before his eyes — slaves that had talked to him, slaves who told stories to the children when they were scared, slaves that had passed him half of a nutrient pill when the slavers had stopped feeding him, hoping he'd die.

All dust, now.

"*You killed them all!*" he yelled. It was the first time he'd ever spoken. His voice was rough.

There was no response.

THREE
The Vow

After Pheonix had exhausted himself from the throes of his newly-birthed rage, the man in black stuffed Pheonix into the smallest cage yet while the ripples of the slaver ship explosion were still visible in the distance. Pheonix's lackluster accommodations only got tighter as the child grew, until, eventually, he couldn't move at all.

Pheonix didn't spend much time with the man in black after being abducted. He was swiftly passed over to the owner of what Pheonix later learned was a casino/pleasure ship, a greedy blowhard who took every opportunity to show the unusual Pheonix off like a trophy.

Unlike the slavers who rarely said anything of substance, the casino owner and his ever-rotating crowd of wealthy clientele talked incessantly. Pheonix quickly learned to listen.

And he listened for two years as the owner paraded him around to every event and gathering, and often on the casino floor itself. Pheonix took in a lot of data in that time, but it, too, remained bereft of context.

Two years later ...

Another day, another party.

Pheonix's cage hung suspended over a long gilded table at which sat some of the casino's most frequent and wealthy patrons.

Delicate golden goblets filled with hot coals had been placed beside every set of plates, into which a long golden poker rested its nose. Occasionally someone seated around the table would poke at Pheonix with the red-hot end to watch his dark skin split open and almost instantaneously recover.

Pheonix's blood was an almost-black which, like oil, shone with an iridescent sheen. The poker-wielders marveled at it when one of them managed to get it on the end of their implement, and tittered in delight as the droplets were sucked back into his body.

Pheonix ignored them. They'd get bored soon enough.

Then one individual jammed the poker into his demon arm — which reacted on its own, snatching the metal rod and whipping it back with such force as to bury it several inches deep in the forehead of the unfortunate sod.

This sparked an uproar. Screaming, wailing bodies threw themselves away from the table in a disordered jumble, knocking over plates and hot coal bowls and each other. Several fires started, adding to the chaos.

The man in black took that opportunity to enter.

"The Death Dealer — " someone shrieked, but their cry was cut off as they became dust.

The man in black leveled a weapon at the owner of the casino, whose eyes were bulging out of his head with fear. Though before the man could even open his mouth in protest, he was dust. Pheonix stared, processing, as each person in the room quickly became dust. The dining hall was empty except for Pheonix and the man in black almost as soon as the first shot had been fired. The man in black strode through the billowing, crawling fires and cut Pheonix's cage down.

Sick embers settled in the pit of Pheonix's stomach, as though he'd swallowed the contents of one of the goblets. Confused, he studied the sensation.

He was a creature of the here-and-now. Memory and the other trappings of time, both time gone past and time still to come, held no meaning for him at all. He was barely aware of its existence, and even then, only in how it affected others. The other slaves got hungry, thirsty, slept, or died. A lot of the ways that others judged 'time' weren't things Pheonix experienced himself.

So when he reacted, it was to a memory he couldn't consciously recall. The reaction came first, and it took digging to realize what the catalyst was. It was counterintuitive to *remember*. What had already happened was gone forever.

But he had a nagging feeling that a certain past thing was important in the here-and-now.

And Pheonix was, above all, a creature of instinct.

It hit him as the door of the man in black's ship sealed behind them and another hatch opened, this one too small to lead into another room. Inside was an unknown, dark space.

The demon arm lashed out, parting the bars of Pheonix's cage through sheer force, to close its claws around the man in black's arm.

"You're going to kill them again," Pheonix hissed. It was the second time he'd ever spoken.

The man in black whipped out a violet, crystalline rod, which he brought around in an arc that neatly sliced Pheonix's demon hand from its arm. The hand spasmed, released its grip, and dropped with a thud, where it skittered noisily with further convulsions until the man in black kicked it into a corner.

Pheonix froze, staring at his arm. The pause allowed the man in black to toss his cage, with him in it, into the dark opening. The cage skidded onto its side and clanged against a wall Pheonix couldn't see with jarring force.

Then the man in black spoke for the first time, though his voice was more mechanical buzzing than speech.

"You are an utter failure. Since none of these buffoons can seem to manage to kill you, I'm taking you to the one place guaranteed to do so. Whatever bedamned magic keeps you alive, it will not interfere there. This will be the end of the line. If you manage to survive the trip."

He slammed the hatch shut and Pheonix heard it seal, leaving him in complete darkness.

His brain was still struggling to parse the monumental amount of data that had just been rapidly thrown at him, so he stayed silent and still, reflexively holding his severed arm. Some unknown amount of time passed, with the only sensory input being the random sounds of the ship's inner workings echoing through the small chamber.

The only warning Pheonix had for what was to come was a ramping-up of the noises around him. Then — sudden movement — and *cold*.

The cold snatched everything out of his lungs. His insides felt like they were suddenly too big for his skin. He looked around, blinking away ice crystals, and found himself surrounded by the vastness of space.

He'd been fired out of the man in black's ship. Somehow, despite the lack of oxygen and pressure differential and cold (and despite having lost a hand), he was still alive. Naked, in a metal cage, hurtling through space with nary a protection. But alive.

He craned around to see the man in black's ship rapidly retreating. In the distance, an explosion. It was so far away it was barely visible, but he recognized its significance.

In space, no one can hear a scream, but that didn't stop him from trying. The attempt froze his tongue, mouth and throat — and then, with his battered body at its limit, he sunk into unconsciousness.

An unpleasant warmth woke Pheonix from his brief nap.

He staggered to his feet, shedding burning clumps of metal and raining sand. There seemed to be noise all around him, but his frazzled brain couldn't identify if it was rushing in his ears, an outside sensation, or some combination of both. His eyes wouldn't focus, so visual input was no assistance.

He stood in place while his eyes and ears cleared sluggishly. He'd landed in the sand pit at the center of a giant bowl-shaped building lined with empty seats. The building didn't seem to have a ceiling, though the lights shining into the sand pit were garishly bright, so he couldn't make out what was beyond it.

He'd survived.

With that bit of data tucked away, he looked around. There seemed to be no easy way out of the sand pit — a giant wall surrounded it at all angles, with four heavily gated, large entrances at evenly spaced intervals. His body was stiff from two unmoving, caged years, but he still managed to shuffle towards one of said gated entrances. He hit his toe on something underneath the surface. Bending down, he brushed away the sand.

A severed arm. He instinctively looked down at his own arm, and found that the hand the man in black had cut off had grown back while he'd been unconscious.

He looked back at the half-buried arm. That explained the patchy color and chunky consistency of the sand. And the smell. This was a place of death.

He approached one of the only other landmarks in this austere place: a giant column, one of two, caked with the grisly ancient remnants of many bodily fluids. There was movement and he stopped. An unidentifiable bulbous skin of something — open, wailing maws; disconnected eyeballs; wiggling fingers; a helplessly flapping half of a wing —

writhed, chained and somehow morphed together, all around the column's base. A quick glance confirmed the other column was similarly adorned.

The writhing thing repulsed him on a level he couldn't quite comprehend. He'd seen enough gore and death — been the perpetrator of some of it himself. But this ... this was disgusting in a whole different way. It made his skin crawl.

He wanted the sensation to stop, so he balled up his demon fist and bashed the column nearest him until it crumbled, pulverizing the thing/things attached to it. As they died, the buzzing under his skin lessened. He shuffled to the other column, his feet catching on the uneven ground, and reduced it to rubble as well.

The nearest entrance opened with a loud grinding. Out poured individuals he was all too familiar with: slavers.

The sick burning rose in him again.

Slavers: bad.

The first line of them to come at him, yelling, succumbed to a rake from his demon arm, slashed to pieces.

The second wave was more hesitant. One intrepid individual edged forward and shot a weapon at him that trailed thin wire leads sparking electricity, which buried in Pheonix's chest. Pheonix wrapped the wires around his normal hand, ignoring it cutting in, ignoring the tremors of the electricity pulsing through his body (which did little more than tickle), and yanked the gun out of its wielder's hands. Several more leads pierced him, but the pulsations only threw fuel onto the fire driving him. He was dimly aware of more bodies pouring out of the entrance, then four more slavers jumped at him, stabbing him with long metal prods. He cut down everything and everyone that got too close, driven by a mindless, wild rage.

Eventually, the bodies stopped coming. Panting, he peered through hazy and wavering vision. Another group was approaching, marching with slow purpose. Hysterical crying reached his ears, somehow penetrating the pounding in his head. He forced his eyes to focus. In the arms of each slaver was a child — living meat shields — naked, skeletal, and wild-eyed with fear.

The burning feeling leached from him and his demon arm sagged. When he was in danger, the demon arm had always reacted and dragged him along for the ride, protecting him somehow. But with the children in the line of fire, the arm refused to engage further.

The slavers piled on him and beat him. But this, he was used to. He couldn't feel pain, so he awaited the beating's end.

He didn't resist being dragged off through hallways that his brain automatically recorded and filed away. The journey lasted a good few minutes. Whatever this place was, it was huge. They stopped at a series of grates in the floor. Indecipherable moaning filled the air, coming from everywhere and nowhere, punctuated by the occasional scream. The smell was terrible.

His captors pulled aside a grate and tossed him inside. A long drop — at least triple his height — ended abruptly, somewhat cushioned by amorphous muck that came up to his mid-shins.

The grate rasped back into place, and the echoes of the slavers muttering curses followed the sound of boots clomping away, leaving him in muffled silence.

Drained, he crawled through the gunk to find slightly higher ground, curled up with his back against the wall, and closed his eyes.

His respite was brief.

The grate slid noisily open.

A bucket on a rope lowered. Pheonix stared at it until shouts came for him to hurry up and climb on. Awkward and precarious, he stuffed his feet in the bucket and, holding onto the rope, was lifted out.

Five of them dragged him (unresisting) down a hallway that echoed with vocal suffering and into a side room. A battered metal table with straps dangling from all corners was the centerpiece here. They secured him onto it, a seven-year-old the size of most hominin teenagers.

His five escorts hovered nearby and a person who wasn't dressed as a slaver approached. This person's form was marred by machinery attached haphazardly to every square inch of skin that wasn't otherwise clothed in robes, and one of their arms appeared to have been repurposed from some much larger robot. They had perhaps been a hominin to begin with, but with half of their face whirring gears and wires and pulsing tubes and the shapeless cloth sack they wore studded with random bits of technology and tools, any remaining species traits were unrecognizable to Pheonix's limited knowledge of such things. As the person came into the circle of light around the table, they removed a tool — an ugly three-pronged fork arcing with electricity — from the upper part of the robotic arm and attached it to the part where a hand normally would be. Their organic hand held a collar.

Pheonix's immediate reaction was a violent refusal to be collared.

His demon arm tensed and ripped out of its strap, grabbing the collar and jamming it around the machine-person's neck in the same motion, where it snapped into place. The slaver-guards were apparently too stunned to act, and the machine-person was fighting with the collar, which gave Pheonix time to rip his other limbs out of the straps.

He launched at the machine-person, landing with one knee on their chest, the other on the non-robot arm to pin it down. Pheonix's demon arm shifted to grapple with the robot arm while Pheonix's other hand pressed into the person's face to keep it down despite the thrashing of their lower half.

Apparently, despite all the machine-person's augmentations, the monstrous seven-year-old was stronger still.

Pheonix's demon arm pivoted the robot arm around and bullied it down until the sparking fork at the end came into contact with the collar. The collar constricted, searing into flesh, the sickening sizzle heard even over the machine-person's pained screaming. A burnt smell filled the room.

Pheonix held pressure on the collar until the machine-person's body convulsed uncontrollably and blood poured out over the ring of damaged flesh, staining their robe. The screaming choked off into a wet gurgle, and the body ceased its flailing.

Panting, Pheonix stood —

— just in time to see another group of slavers rush into the doorway. They piled on him.

While they were hitting him, his mind wandered. Another smell tickled his nose, one that woke long-dormant memories in the same way seeing the man in black had stoked his anger.

The smell: fear.

Again.

Something clicked into place in his mind.

They were terrified *of him*.

They were beating him *because they were afraid*.

The last time he'd brutalized an attacker, there had been this same effluvium of fear. The repeated experience nagged at him, though he didn't know how to question it.

When the beating ended, with his contusions and cuts already healing, the slavers forced him down the long main hall. Back to the sand pit.

The gate loudly ground open and they tossed him past it, to tumble unceremoniously into the dirt. It closed again. He stood, brushed himself off.

"It's the arena for you, kid. Have fun," one of the slavers grunted sardonically from behind the gate and his heavy helmet.

They clomped off.

Pheonix turned.

The noise hit him. An overwhelming wave of sound that nearly bowled him over. He looked up, into the seats that had been, at his last visit, empty.

They were not unoccupied any longer.

He kept turning.

The amount of input froze him — species he had never seen, had no name for, individuals uncountable, all with oral orifices gaping open to add to the din, appendages gesticulating with wild abandon. He finished his revolution facing the opposite gate from the one he'd been shoved through — where, similarly, a man emerged, prodded by slavers.

He was hominin-looking, though even from this distance, Pheonix got the sense that something was wrong. The man twitched, scratched at the huge collar burned into the flesh around his neck, rolled his eyes until just the whites showed, and stumbled on weak legs away from the electric prods of the slavers. He wore what could have been a harness and kilt in another life, though they were only tatters now. One hand clutched a rusty dagger.

The man weaved closer, somehow advancing despite the disordered zigzag gait. And as he neared, Pheonix could see his lips moving and hear from them a gibbering that wasn't any speech pattern he recognized. A new layer of data.

Pheonix hadn't moved a step since being shoved into the arena, so in short order the man loomed over him. Foaming spittle spilled down his chin. The arm with the dagger reared back.

A hush of anticipation fell over the crowd.

There was a thud, a bone-jarring shock that rippled through Pheonix's body. Without pain, it wasn't immediately apparent to Pheonix what had happened. The man slumped over him, bowling the two of them gracelessly into the sand. The man stood up; Pheonix tried to and couldn't.

The man turned his back on Pheonix, raising his arms to the sky in a pose of victory.

Pheonix looked down at his chest — at the dagger, buried hilt-deep therein.

He laid his head back on the sand, contemplating the stars barely seen through the glaring lights of the arena. The crowd murmured, confused.

Blood seeped from the wound, but it seemed to pool just at the surface as though cupped by invisible hands. His heart struggled around the blade. But still, it pumped.

Annoying, Pheonix thought of the feeling.

His demon hand curled around the dagger and removed it, tossing it carelessly to one side, before he could fully make the decision for himself.

He stood. The audible, palpable, shock of those in the stands was data he wanted to study, but he had no time to ruminate on it.

The demon arm lashed out, taking Pheonix with it, and punched through the man's back, through his spine, shattered bone chips and blood spraying. It grasped his heart, and withdrew in a grisly geyser, to hold its quivering prize aloft.

The stands erupted.

Pheonix ignored the noise; there was something more interesting to focus on. New data.

The demon arm, quiescent once more, dropped the heart. Pheonix crouched down to inspect the man, who had toppled forward with only part of his face visible: gaping mouth twitching, one wide eye bulging from its bony compartment. Pheonix knew enough about anatomy to wonder how the man was clinging to life. The eye rolled to focus on him, the intensity of its gaze startling.

"Thank … you …"

Somehow, Pheonix heard the man's whispered words clearly over the tumultuous roaring of the crowd. He nodded once, unsure of what else to do. The man sighed, and breathed no more.

Pheonix stood again and looked around at the chaos in the seats above him. He decided, then and there, that he would do what it took to make it out of the arena.

These people — they were all just like the man in black and the slavers. Bad.

All he needed was time — to observe, learn, and plan.

And then ... he would kill them all.

FOUR
No Touchy

Eight years later ...

Pheonix had matured into an extremely tall, lanky teenager, wiry from near-constant physical activity. And he'd become a celebrity in the arena.

A freak of unknown provenance; his physical appearance the monstrous mockery of a hominin; immortal, unable to feel pain, with near-instantaneous healing; a fast learner with strength as unnatural as his appearance. These were the things they knew about him, the ways he'd heard himself described. He had a couple of other tricks up his metaphorical sleeve they hadn't seemed to really pin down yet — one being the demon arm's intuition, and another being an ability he'd realized he had innately as he grew, to 'see' past the physical. He wasn't exactly sure *what* he was seeing, but he'd sometimes catch shadows or spots of light that indicated places he could attack or acted as a 'tell' when an attack was coming.

Because he never lost a match and they couldn't seem to be able to get rid of him, they had found a way to use him: wringing high bets out of newcomers too drugged or arrogant to take note of the cold look in his cobalt eyes and the easy confidence with which he stood.

The promise he'd made to himself eight years ago, that moment covered in someone else's blood, was ever on the forefront of his mind. He watched, listened, and obeyed — for now.

He didn't have enough data yet to finalize his plan. They were cautious around him — far more so than his previous 'owners.' Only the heavies (remorseless, entirely-armored slavers) escorted him to and from the arena; and in fact, he'd only ever been to his cell, the arena floor, and the winding hallways connecting them. However, listening gleaned him much. They thought him stupid, or mute, because he never spoke, never acknowledged them. A conscious ploy. Things slipped. Slavers were nothing if not egotistical.

But aside from that, why should he talk? They never allowed him around other slaves unless it was to face them in the pit.

And he had nothing to say to slavers.

There were no good people on the entire arena ship, with the exception of *some* of the slaves. The foes he faced in the arena were mostly captured pirates, disgraced dark elves, merchants who thought they were smart enough to play the game and were proven wrong, creatures that supped on sapient flesh or mana, even the occasional goblin. However, Pheonix's most common opposition were beasts.

He'd also learned that his demon arm was a sort of tuning fork for truly malicious intent. It would react of its own accord when he was threatened. He relied on it implicitly so his brain could be always open, gathering the information he needed.

Today was another day, another fight. They opened the gate and he strode through.

The static of the crowd in his ears was a constant.

As he passed out of the shadows, he heard someone saying, *"Certainly this mutant child couldn't defeat a hydra, right? Ahahahaha."*

This 'hydra,' already in the arena as Pheonix came through the entranceway, was a scaled, four-legged creature with a long tail. The walls of the arena were about half again Pheonix's height, but as this thing reared back to fix its gaze on him, its tallest head was just shy of eye-level with the top of the walls. Three necks — each topped with blunt heads bristling with teeth — emerged from roughly the same place on its wide chest, making it extremely forward-heavy.

The shackles around the hydra's necks dropped and the creature, in a frothing rage, scrambled at Pheonix. He allowed it to come close, then dove to one side and slashed at it. Today they had given him a sword — a rusty thing that caught in the hydra's scaly hide and fractured like a rotten carrot.

No matter. He was as often weaponless as armed.

He waited for the hydra to turn, then leapt onto one of its thrashing heads and drove the broken sword between its eyes.

The hydra screamed in agony and the crowd screamed in delight.

Pheonix threw himself backwards and the teeth from another head snapped closed where he had just been. Pheonix's wings, black and deformed, opened as far as they could to soften his landing.

He lost his footing on the humped and loose sand and the hydra snatched him up in one claw to bring him close to the nearest head.

Pheonix's demon arm buried itself bicep-deep in its eye socket, and the hydra roared with such force that it shook the seats closest to the wall around the arena floor. Milky jelly from the pierced eyeball ran down, acid-hot, over Pheonix's bare chest.

The claw that still held him squeezed with the creature's histrionics of pain. It flung itself into the side of the arena, knocking some of the closer viewers into the bowl. An intentional design: the crowd loved when someone from the stands fell in, as long as it wasn't them.

Those unlucky members of the faceless masses that had been just moments before cheering the grotesque violence of the fight with almost sexual lust, now scrabbled at the walls, ran back and forth like cornered rats, or sat and blubbered. The hydra turned towards them with predictable inevitability and cast Pheonix aside. Those still secure in their seats screamed "Kill them!" and "Get them!" to the doomed former spectators.

That was the thing about the people that populated this damned place; they used something only as long as that thing's usefulness outweighed the fun of destroying it.

Now sated with senseless death and carnage, the audience — and the hydra — turned their collective attention back to Pheonix.

He dodged and feinted and struck out at the hydra in turn as it lunged at him again and again in an ugly dance of death.

Pheonix stumbled and a clawed foot blindsided him. He smashed into the wall and slid down like a ragdoll, momentarily stunned. The hydra was on him in an instant.

It snatched him up in triumph between razor-sharp teeth and lifted him high as if it, too, knew its part to play in this nightly debacle. The crowd fell silent, drunk with anticipation. The vice tightened, teeth covered in rot and gore puncturing his body — but the hydra was unable to close its mouth completely. It struggled with an unknown force, blood-flecked foam issuing forth from its gurgling maw.

Pheonix, regaining his senses, wrapped his arms around one of its longer fangs and, using all his strength, wrenched it out. Blood sprayed. The hydra dropped him, screaming and thrashing. Now he had a weapon.

And now it was time to end it. Pheonix was done being on display.

Caked in sand from its latest seizure of pain, the hydra rounded on him once more. This time, he ducked under it, jammed the tooth into the place where its heads joined — the place from whence the 'light' beyond the physical emanated. The hydra's weak point.

He leapt away from the hydra as it fell, spasming in death throes.

"Phe-o-nix! Phe-o-nix! Phe-o-nix!" The crowd chanted.

He turned away from them. The doors opened and the slavers poured into the arena to beat him like always.

The spectators filed away, off to various dens of iniquity and every depraved pleasure the worst minds could cook up, but a few did stay to watch. He endured the beating without sound, without reaction, and eventually they dragged him to his feet and through one of the four entrances into the arena bowl, back into the halls that would deliver him into blessed silence.

The fifteen-year-old boy sat in his cell, and he watched, and he listened, and he thought.

He entered the state that passed for sleep for Pheonix (he'd named it 'no-mind'), something he'd cultivated over the years to help the time slip by.

They roused him some time later to toss him a nutrient pill, which he swallowed. They joked as they pulled him from his cell, laughingly congenial. There was something special for him today, they said. Something very special. Ahahaha.

His brows lowered. The last time he'd heard that ...

His tension faded as they led him to the arena. The crowd was already there, waiting for him, buzzing.

The last stragglers entered the stands, bets and mind-altering substances flying. For Pheonix, it was the same, day after day. Routine in the worst sense of the word. Someone threw a cup at him, which missed by a wide margin. Laughter carried briefly over the heartbeat of the spectators. He failed to respond.

The door across from his position opened. A desolate hissing, carried with a barren chill, escaped the opening like the last breath from a dying throat. Out of the gloom came a misshapen creature, shoved into the too-bright light with the utmost reluctance. It cast black eyes burning with hatred to all sides, thin lips drawn back from long, sharpened teeth, similar to Pheonix's own. The crowd buzzed with conversation.

A nosferatu! The whispers from the crowd washed across the arena like a wave.

A rare and powerful creature indeed for tonight's entertainment.

Its pale skin, like ash, lacked life. Large eyes, ringed with blue veins and dark circles, were set deeply into the sockets of its elongated skull.

As soon as Pheonix's eyes alighted on it, the sick burning feeling filled him. He wanted to analyze why, but his body didn't give him the chance.

The crowd verbalized its shock as Pheonix rocketed across the arena floor, almost before the creature noticed him fully. It barely dodged the first rake of his demon arm and flew backwards.

Pheonix pursued. Emotionless, acting on instinct, as he always did; but this time, he was the aggressor.

This thing needed to die.

And he would end it.

Some energy inside spurred him like a ship hurtling through space, cold and unstoppable. The nosferatu desperately dodged, trumpeting in fear and rage. It lashed out when it thought it had an opening, and did manage to get Pheonix with a good few strikes, but never enough to turn the tables on constant retreat.

The crowd was restless with uncertainty. They'd never seen the passive boy go after something so hard.

The sick burning feeling was growing, and Pheonix sunk deeper into his calm. It was almost no-mind, this. Visual input, movement, muscles, calculating angles and trajectories, all in perfect instantaneous sync, his entire being as open as the yawning maw of the arena doors. The data flooded him, fueled him.

Then he slipped.

His feet had long become accustomed to shuffling through the deep sand in the dance of combat, but an unexpected slick patch sent him down, hard.

Before he could react, the nosferatu took its chance and leapt.

Half in no-mind, it was as though Pheonix could see in slow motion. Rebellion burst up from his depths.

You will not touch me.

His non-demon arm streaked for the nosferatu's chest, suddenly wreathed in cerulean fire — the cold flame of Pheonix's concentration and drive given shape.

A ghostly blade of that same flame formed in his clenched fist — which speared the nosferatu, mid-air. Instantly it burst into a crackling blue fireball, its tortured keening echoing throughout the arena floor as though amplified. The crowd themselves screeched in response, but Pheonix could only hear them dimly.

His entire self was focused on the shadow of the twisted and gaunt features in front of him, an ugly mockery of a hominin face contorted with pain.

Now be gone.

A deep *thoom* of cerulean power rocked the sand around him and the arena itself, leaving trails of glass and shuddering pieces from the arena walls. Above Pheonix's still-raised fist, ash drifted gently down in the still, dead air.

Pheonix, in the aftermath, was panting and staring upward. He couldn't move. The overwhelming amount of input had frozen him, and it was only increasing. A pressure was building in his body, his head spinning. He was buzzing, as though there were two of him fighting to separate. But soon enough, the buzzing ceased, and he fell back, limp.

The crowd was the kind of silent that spoke of analysis ... and fear.

Pheonix automatically began performing the customary checks of his mental and physical state. He was aware that something within him had changed. Things ... felt different.

Slavers poured into the ring. The crowd wasn't in any mood to celebrate, but pushers cajoled the spectators to the after-party, simultaneously ushering them out of the stands.

This time, the slavers seemed hesitant to approach Pheonix, stepping gingerly over the glass tendrils left in the sand by whatever freak power he'd unleashed.

Pheonix sat up, and they flinched back as one.

His self-analysis complete, the only thing he could find was that he felt ... great. Full of energy.

He gestured at the slavers to lead him away, and they did so without touching him, a silent escort reeking of terror.

They left him down there for days. Pheonix sank into no-mind until startled by laughter, high-pitched and chilling. He looked around, trying to pinpoint the source, and eventually realized that it was coming from above him. The laughter got louder, echoing down the hallway, accompanied by the sound of boots. Soon enough, the boots passed over his grate, dragging a body. Pheonix blinked and shook his head to dislodge the flakes of dried crap that had drifted onto his cheeks.

A neighboring grate scraped open and there was the wet thud of a body dropping into the pit next to his. The grate closed, the angry boots and mutterings of the slavers retreating into the distance.

All throughout, the laughter continued. It tapered off after a little while, and Pheonix settled back down, ready to go no-mind again.

"Hey, kid."

Pheonix jerked towards the wall separating him from the newcomer. It wasn't thin enough that he should be able to hear anything but muffled grit, but the voice wasn't hampered in any way.

He didn't answer.

"Kid!" it came again, more insistent.

"What?" It almost surprised him to hear his own voice. He'd spoken perhaps a handful of times in his entire life.

The wall shifted. He stared at it and backed up, crouching into a ready-stance.

The hard-packed dirt parted like water, yielding to the head of a man with a rictus grin on his square face. His eyes flashed like metal as he glanced up to the grate and then back at Pheonix. On alert, Pheonix took in the rest of his body as it was birthed from the wall. He was about the same height as Pheonix, who was still taller than most people, but easily twice the boy's width, with arms so thick with muscle that he couldn't hold them tightly to his sides. His neck alone was the size of Pheonix's thigh. The man was too clean; despite coming through the wall and the presumed state of the other pit, none of the grime seemed to cling to him.

Pheonix waited, taut, ready for the stranger to make the first move. The man rolled his shoulders and cracked his neck, grin still plastered on his face. He looked as unused to emotions and facial expressions as Pheonix himself was.

"I swear to the Creator, these fuckers don't know how to treat a special guest. Eh? Eh?"

Pheonix stared at him. The word 'Creator' stirred something in him that felt different — better! — than anything he'd felt before. Studying his own reaction paralyzed him. The man waited a moment longer and then frowned.

"Boy, you're about as fun as they are," he sighed dramatically. "Well, I don't care much for this place, so I guess I'll scoot my happy ass on outta here." His eyes locked on Pheonix once more, frighteningly intense. "You, boy, you're something else, you know that? ... No, you wouldn't."

Pheonix tensed again. He felt suddenly vulnerable, but not in any way he could explain.

"Well, after the treatment I've gotten today, I think I'll just have a little bit of my own fun." He leaned forward and filled Pheonix's vision. Pheonix found he couldn't move, couldn't fight back ... sudden internal pressure arose, so intense he couldn't breathe, followed by the sensation of falling backwards. That rictus grin dominated his mind; he could think of nothing else.

Then, as the blackness closed in, words floated through his brain:

I'm gonna help you out, kid ... don't know why, but I am ... remember this at the end, yeah?

FIVE
Some Things, We Don't Take

Pheonix landed hard.

Disoriented, he struggled to his feet. An unfamiliar landscape swam in and out of view.

"It's about time, boy."

His vision focused. Silhouetted by light, the speaker's features weren't immediately discernible. Pheonix looked up; something huge and blue stretched over him where the stars usually were. It was bright, everywhere, with no obvious source of light. Below was something fuzzy and green. To all sides were uneven groups of tall brown things. He took it all in at a glance and filed it away, just more data. He was not in the slavers' hands anymore, but that changed nothing. The moment to moment task of survival still loomed.

"Come now. You've made me wait, and we've got chores to do."

Pheonix focused on the speaker and got an impression of gnarled hands, thick knuckles and rough calluses, the weathered brown skin and wiry, stooped frame of someone who had known hard work for many long years. A bushy beard jutted from a face collapsed in wrinkles above a stained apron.

Pheonix stood as the last echoes of dizziness faded away. He towered over the little old man.

The old man turned, and, without quite knowing why, but perhaps purely because he'd crafted himself to be fully obedient unless the situation called for otherwise, Pheonix followed him.

It turned out that he'd fallen on the very edge of a cleared-out area surrounded by the tall, green-capped brown things.

"Those are trees," the old man said, as if reading his mind. "A lot of trees is a forest. We are in a forest. This is my home. And now, yers as well."

The old man gestured to a small building that looked to be made out of the brown part of the trees.

"This is wood," the old man said, waving a hand towards a large pile of shorter brown cylinders. With a jerk he freed a weapon from a 'wood' nearby — a long-handled thing with a broad, flat, square blade. Pheonix tensed, though the reaction proved to be unnecessary as the old man flipped the weapon to proffer the handle. Pheonix took it automatically, but simply held it in the same position he'd received it.

"This is an axe. I want you to cut this wood. Winter — that's when it gets really cold — will be here in a few months and we need to be prepared with lots of firewood, and to be usable, it has to be properly seasoned, which means dried by wind and sun. That's one of the reasons we stack it."

Pheonix, operating on intake mode, his every sense fully and eagerly open, drank in the surfeit of new information.

"You cut the logs like this," the old man said, and took a 'log' up, placed it on a larger thing embedded in the ground (it looked like the bottom of a tree, with the rest of the tree hacked off), balanced it on its cut edge, and pantomimed cutting it with the axe. He pointed to a neatly stacked pile of already-cut logs. 'Firewood,' he'd said.

Pheonix took a moment to calculate the angles and shapes, then neatly split the log in half. He then split each half into halves, which gave him four vaguely-triangular pieces from one cylindrical shape. He put them on the pile, matching the pattern of the rest of the firewood, and looked at the old man for confirmation.

"Just like that," the old man said. "Now do the rest. I'll be inside."

And then, he disappeared into the 'home.'

Some weapons have uses beyond killing, Pheonix concluded as he worked. The motion was hypnotizing, not unlike his no-mind, and he powered through the entire pile in no time.

The old man came out to find Pheonix staring at the wood, not certain what to do next.

"Come on, boy," he said. He carried a bar of something he called 'soap,' a 'brush,' and a rough 'wool towel.' "You'll need bathin'."

He'd been bathed before, though he hadn't known the word for it until the old man briefly explained. Usually, Pheonix had only been bathed at the casino before he was to be shown off to prestigious guests. And then only by being dunked repeatedly into different tubs of liquids while still in his cage. The old man took him through the forest to a big outcropping of land over which water fell (straightforwardly named a 'waterfall') into a small basin over large boulders. The water then ran down into a river that wound through the trees.

The old man handed Pheonix the soap and brush, then walked into the treeline, calling over his shoulder; "Scrub til all the grime's gone! Call me when yer done. And don't forget yer hair!"

The water was frigid, but Pheonix ignored the discomfort and did as he'd been told.

"I'm finished," Pheonix called loudly, not sure how far away the old man had gone. The old man reappeared around some trees and tossed him the towel, waiting as Pheonix dried himself off. Next from the old man's hands came a bundle of rough wadded cloth. Pheonix shook it out to find that it was clothing — which he knew of since often the other slaves wore them, though he'd never been tasked to wear them himself. Even in the arena, he'd always been naked.

With no genitals, anus, or even nipples, though, it wasn't like there was much to hide.

He deduced the configuration based on how the old man's clothes were arranged, and donned what he had been given.

"I know yer not used to 'em," said the old man as they made their way back to his home. "But here in the civilized universe, we all must put somethin' on our bodies. It's protection ... and it's polite. While our nakedness ain't nothin' to be ashamed of, also t'ain't right to force it on people who never asked to see it. That's part of consent and boundaries, which we'll talk about later."

Then they were at the old man's domicile.

Pheonix stared. *Made out of wood? Cut thin and long and squeezed together somehow to make this shape.*

"Well, come in," the old man said brusquely.

The inside was cluttered with things. The old man named them, somehow sure in the knowledge that Pheonix knew nothing.

A hearth glowed on the right side of the room across from a window with heavy woolen drapes, currently drawn to let in what little light one small window could. Flanking the door was a wooden table with two wooden chairs on one side, and a stained butcher's block on the other. The floor was bare dirt. Set in the floor to the left of the hearth, in the furthest rightmost corner of the room, was a wooden hatch. A wooden rocking chair sat a safe distance from the front of the hearth. A colorful woven rug lay in front of the hearth, the only non-brown color in the entire place. Under the window was a large chest, and behind it, against the far wall, was a bed.

"Sun's goin' down," the old man remarked, and closed the door behind Pheonix, who hadn't moved. The old man settled in the rocking chair in front of the hearth with a grunt and gestured to a large, heavy-looking black round thing set on a solid brick ledge in front of the actual fire.

"This is a cookin' pot," the old man said. "You make food in it. It's made of iron, which is a kind of ore that you dig up from the ground. We call those ores metal. Mind liftin' it, boy? My back ain't what it used to be." The old man pointed from the handle attached to the pot, to a hook positioned over the fire.

Pheonix grabbed the pot's bulbous sides, leveraging it to hang by its handle on the swinging hook next to the fire. The old man took hold of Pheonix's wrist as soon as he let go of the pot and flipped his hand over to show the burning and blistered skin on his palms.

"Next time use yer brain," the old man said, rough but kind. "This is hot. It has a handle for a reason."

The words echoed in Pheonix's mind as he watched his skin heal and the blisters smooth out. Once his hand was unmarked again, the old man released him.

Pheonix filed it away.

The old man, with lots of muttering and groaning, poked at the embers deep in the hearth with a long metal weapon.

Not weapon, Pheonix corrected himself. *Things aren't always what they seem to be.*

"Bring me some firewood," the old man said over his shoulder.

Pheonix did as he was bid, dumping an armful of wood at the old man's feet. Chuckling, the old man arranged the pile and tossed a couple of pieces into the hearth, which summoned a brief geyser of sparks. Then he took up a wooden implement, moved aside the lid of the cooking pot, and poked at its contents.

"It'll be a bit yet 'til it's done. Come, let me brush yer hair."

Pheonix knelt with his back to the old man. Deft fingers detangled, smoothed, applied oil to, then finally braided his long black hair, before tying it off with a leather strip.

"There's books in the chest over there," the old man said when he'd finished. "Bring me one that looks interestin' and I'll read it to you."

Pheonix opened the chest. There were so many 'books,' and of so many sizes and thicknesses as to fill almost every available space. He carefully removed the top layer, laying them out next to him. He wasn't sure what a 'book' was supposed to be, but he did his best to scrutinize the front of each one to see if it stirred any reaction in him, as he was told. Eventually he found a large one that he was immediately drawn to because of the complexity of the symbols on its front.

But as he reached for it, the old man said from across the room, "Not that one. You'll need it later, but yer not ready for it yet."

Dutifully, Pheonix put it aside without further thought. The next one that drew him was a thick text with a complicated, intriguing etching on the front depicting several concentric circles and other intricate shapes.

He carefully put each of the other books back into its puzzle-like configuration and closed the lid, delivering his selection to the old man.

"Ah, good choice. Come, sit."

Pheonix settled on the colorful rug. It was rough but held the warmth from the fire well. Compared to sludge filled pits, too-small cages, and cold floors dirty with the unmentionable remains of miserable sapient beings, it was the most comfortable thing that had ever touched his skin.

The old man opened the book and read from it:

"'The place in which we exist is called the metacosm. Inside the metacosm are innumerable encapsulated universes, known as verses.' Each verse is subtly different, but we will talk about that later. Each verse contains its own various domains, realms, and streams. What you experience with yer physical senses can be attributed to yer existence here on the physical plane. What sapient species refer to as 'life' generally takes place entirely on the physical plane. The physical universe is made up of lots of celestial bodies, which you will study in greater detail later. You and I, physically, right now, are on the planet known as Archaic Earth.

"I suppose makin' a brief interlude here about where we are, currently, would be appropriate. Archaic Earth has one of the highest magic quotients in the known metacosm. While the people here as a whole are initiated — meanin' that they have been brought into the fold by the Accord and are aware of the universe beyond themselves — they use higher technology sparin'ly, choosin' to focus on self-sufficiency and minimalism. This is part of Archaic Earth's overall social focus on chivalry and integrity.

"I myself have never seen much use for technology," the old man said as an aside, "but to each their own."

He went back to reading:

"'The ordered metacosm is governed by five bodies: the Universal Accord, the Rangers, the Twelve Consortium, the Chosen and their Obelisk of Time, and the elven Council.'"

The clacking of the pot lid shivering with boiling liquid interrupted the reading. The old man closed the book with a sigh and leaned over to carefully remove the lid and stir the contents of the pot.

Pheonix's brain was already so full he felt lightheaded. So much new information to process — too much! He didn't have context for most of the words in the old man's long explanation, but he extrapolated that he would gain it at some point. To distract himself from his swimming thoughts, he watched the old man preparing two bowls of the stuff in the pot. The old man handed one of the bowls to Pheonix, who stared at it. Aside from raw meat and bits of whatever he could find, he'd never eaten an actual meal. (Nutrient pills hardly qualified.)

"Watch," the old man said. He spooned up some of the stuff, put it in his mouth, and mashed it with his teeth, then swallowed. Pheonix processed, then copied the motion. It felt strange at first, but soon, the action of eating lit up parts of his brain that had atrophied from lack of stimuli.

He closed his eyes and focused tightly on the flavors and sensations. Once it was all filed away, he took another bite, and repeated. Before the bowl was empty, though, he was eating at a normal pace. There wasn't much complexity to it after the initial rush.

By the time he and the old man had finished eating, night had fully fallen. The old man heaved himself out of his seat with a grunt to close the curtains.

"We'll start the real work tomorrow," he said, finding a blanket. With the blanket over his knees, he settled back in the rocking chair and closed his eyes. "You can have the cot over there, boy. These old bones are more comfortable in front of the fire."

Pheonix did as he was told and stood, moving to the 'cot' to inspect it.

There came a gravelly sigh.

"Lay down," the old man said, then muttered about 'pups' and settled again.

Pheonix tried laying on his back. That was awkward because of his wings. He rolled to his side and closed his eyes to go no-mind. The cot, like the blanket, was rough, but by far the most pleasant thing he'd ever rested on. He found himself unconsciously tucking his knees up with the expectation of having no space — then, realizing he *could* stretch, did. The bed was long enough for his tall frame, which was odd considering the height discrepancy between himself and the old man.

But he was exhausted and now was no time to consider it.

Pheonix surfaced from no-mind abruptly, sensing a shadow standing over him. He held every muscle still but coiled with tension, ready to act if it was a threat. But his demon arm wasn't reacting, which bade him to pause and seek input on what had roused him. A soft white-blue light was glowing just beyond his closed lids and he remained unmoving until it faded. Slow, deliberate footfalls creaked the floorboards, accompanied by groaning, and then the rasp of the rocking chair.

"I know yer awake, you little scamp."

For the first time in his life, Pheonix smiled.

The old man got him out of bed before dawn.

They quietly ate the leftover stew, kept warm over the embers all night, as well as a few hunks of 'bread' the old man had 'baked' the day prior.

The old man sent him to get water from the well — which, though it wasn't explained, was fairly intuitive once Pheonix studied it. The old man stopped to watch the 'sunrise', and Pheonix copied him, realizing that the sky held data he hadn't bothered to notice on first glance.

Colors he had never seen, seemingly all spectrums at once, highlighted wispy fingers stretching across the breadth of the sky. One side, a summation of fire; the other, the dregs of night. It was a profound moment to a mind that knew only the ugliness of life and had no name for beauty.

What other things had he passed off as being insignificant because they weren't functionally relevant to that current moment? He'd have to study hard to reroute his thinking process.

After the water, they delved into the woods just as the fiery circle (the 'sun,' as the old man called it) ascended into the treeline, diluted enough to provide a warm glow that both lit and awakened the forest. The old man hurried him along, though, so Pheonix was only allowed quick glances at the various flora and fauna dwelling within. They didn't have to travel far before coming across a monster tree, a grandfather of the forest, long fallen and dried, its space in the foliage free to be vied for by the surrounding greenery. With many chunks taken out of it, it was clear the old man used this tree for firewood frequently.

"Never kill somethin' livin' if you can find somethin' dead, boy," the old man said, hefting one of the two axes he'd brought and holding it out for Pheonix to take. "That's one of the rules of real survival."

Pheonix nodded. The old man swung his axe down, biting easily into dry bark with a loud *thwock*. Despite his small, stooped frame, wiry muscles stood out in his arms and shoulders with the motion. He directed Pheonix to another of the thick branches coming off the main trunk. Pheonix duplicated the old man's actions.

Soon, they had three of the giant boughs. The old man leveraged one onto Pheonix's broad shoulders, then hefted another onto his own back.

"We'll have to come back for that one," the old man said.

Pheonix stared at it, then shook his head.

The claws of his demon arm — surprisingly inert since landing on Archaic Earth — dug deeply into the third one, and he lifted it partially off the ground, then looked at the old man expectantly. The old man huffed, smirked, and turned away.

The trek back to the cabin, short as it was, was laborious and difficult because the enormous branches caught on everything. Though there was a faint path made by the old man's back and forth to the giant fallen tree, nature continually attempted to take back the space that sapient beings made for themselves — especially if that space encroached upon or took from nature.

The old man explained this, then ended with: "I've never been able to convince her to soften that habit."

During the walk back with their firewood-to-be, the old man talked constantly, pointing at things, naming them, meandering through many subjects. Pheonix listened with rapt attention.

Upon reaching the cabin, they cut down the branches into logs, and the old man had Pheonix split the logs into firewood while he disappeared inside.

The sun was well into the sky by the time they headed back into the woods, this time carrying rough woven baskets.

"We need to replenish some of my supplies of herbs and roots. I've got another mouth to feed and body to care for now, and what I've got won't be enough," the old man explained as they went.

Their pace was slow and less direct this time, which let Pheonix become distracted by anything and everything — a caterpillar munching on a leaf, a bird hopping from one branch to the next and then taking wing, tree branches swaying in the breeze. He took in every sound, sight, and sensation he could.

The old man chattered as he wandered in a broad circle, plucking leaves and flowers out of the foliage, digging in the soil, stripping plants of berries or twisting twigs, and piling it all in his basket. Much as he had done before, he named the things he picked up and the things Pheonix looked at, filling the boy's brain with facts to pair with observation. And Pheonix drank it in. He apparently had no limit; each little thing was neatly filed away in the inexhaustible void that was his mind.

They ended up at a small brook cutting through the trees. The old man dug around in an inlet of trapped water, hushed to stillness over small round rocks.

Pheonix leaned over the quieted water. In it he saw a young man. He tilted his head; the young man did the same. He raised a hand. The young man followed his movements with an exactness that Pheonix instinctively felt was impossible to mimic.

Oh. This must be me.

He was dark-skinned, with cobalt blue eyes and pointed ears. He looked hominin enough. The major differences were in his body, not his face (aside from his pointed teeth, which were apparently a rarity among hominins, in his experience). Compared to others he'd seen, his shoulders were too broad, arms too long. He was barrel-chested, had an oddly narrow waist, his feet were more hand-shaped than the average hominin's, and the hand of his non-demon arm had talon-like fingernails. Looming behind him were the two black lumps of his deformed and tattered wings.

He looked at his reflection for as long as it took him to file away the information, then stood. He had no real interest in his appearance, after all.

When the sun was just lowering under the tops of the trees, the old man directed them back to the cabin.

Pheonix paused at the door as the old man continued into the interior. A new, pleasant smell permeated the home, emanating from a small round cob of bread. The bread they'd eaten the night previous wasn't nearly so aromatic.

"I baked it while you were cuttin' firewood this mornin'," the old man said. "I'll show you how to do it another day; for now, come here."

The old man bent down with a grunt and opened the door set into the floor. Cool air wafted from the opening. He turned, dropped his legs into the hole, and stepped down out of sight.

Pheonix took up the spot the old man had vacated and looked down. He saw a ladder, which he climbed down. By the time he'd wedged his tall bulk into the hole, the room below had been lit with a single candle. It was a simple rectangular space with only one entrance and exit, dug straight out of the earth. A slatted rectangular vent set into the ceiling in one corner provided not enough light to render the candle's presence unnecessary.

The old man gestured to and named wooden shelving units containing preserves (varying colors and textures of liquid in glass jars), brown sacks of roots and other things, a rack of tools, stasis units, and bottles of varying other liquids. Hanging from the ceiling near (but not too near) the vent were bundles of leaves, chunks of meat, and other shriveled unidentifiable things, all tied with twine.

The old man took a roll of said twine from a nearby shelf and cut off several lengths with his ever-present small knife. He showed Pheonix how to tie some of what they'd just gathered and Pheonix helped hang them from hooks jutting from a wooden beam. The old man took down some of the dried things and put them in the basket, and then they returned aboveground.

The sun was on its way down. The old man sent Pheonix out to get more water and firewood for the night. Pheonix returned to find the dried things tossed into the cooking pot. The old man paused from cutting up roots to ask Pheonix to pour some of the well-water over the stuff already inside.

With the concoction gurgling over the fire, Pheonix sat in front of the hearth and the old man in his rocking chair. Out came a new book.

"If yer to learn, you need to know language. All of 'em. We'll focus on that for tonight. So I don't have to sit here and read you everythin'."

The sun long gone and night settling its silken blanket over the forest, the old man closed the book and ladled out what he'd cooked with the rest of the day's bread. This time, the bread was accompanied by hard chunks of pungent cheese and sweet preserves scooped from a small jar.

When they'd finished their meal, the old man had Pheonix fetch his patchwork blanket.

"Bed, pup," the old man said around a yawn. "This elder needs his sleep."

Pheonix lay down on the cot as he was bid, but no-mind proved elusive. He had to process the day's events. In his memories and mind, he could recount details too minute for immediate recognition.

Upon further inspection of his memories of the day, Pheonix recalled that a variety of things had flown over the forest, in the distance, while he and the old man had worked outside. He didn't know what the flying things were — creatures and machines too far away to make sense of. While the forest *they* lived in was apparently isolated, the old man's description of Archaic Earth being a bustling place of plenty now had a bit more context.

"Nice to have the company," came the old man's gravelly voice, pulling Pheonix out of his memories.

Pheonix smiled.

The new day started much as the last.

Instead of going to look for herbs, the old man had Pheonix practice with a bow and arrows out on the pile of firewood. As with all of the weapons he had used in the arena, the boy became proficient easily.

"Come, pup. I'm low on protein," the old man said as they headed into the forest. "Today we hunt."

He warned Pheonix to be silent and they crept past the treeline. It was still very early, the remnants of night not yet chased away by the sun. The old man followed secret cues that even Pheonix couldn't pick up on, and soon they came to a parting of the trees that opened into a small field cut through by a shallow brook.

The sun, almost precisely in front of them, shone through whorls of low mist and made blinding rays arc across tall grasses glistening with dew. From the brook and silhouetted by this light, a creature looked up — almost before Pheonix noticed it directly — and straight at them.

Pheonix froze, because the old man had.

The creature was a tall, cloven-hoofed quadruped, with a powerful body and short, coarse brown fur. A long, elegant but thick neck came to a narrow head with large ears and a graceful muzzle tinged grey. Many-pointed horns curving from its skull like branches from the base of a bole. Wide-set, huge deep black eyes bored into Pheonix's soul. He couldn't have moved even if the old man had ordered him to.

The moment lasted for just that — a moment.

With a spray of drops that caught fire in the sun, the creature bounded into the haze.

Pheonix looked to the old man in confusion and was presented only his profile.

"Some things, we don't take," the old man said gruffly.

They moved on.

The old man stopped at a covered spot and they waited.

And waited.

Hours passed, though Pheonix knew nothing of boredom.

The old man, tensing, brought his attention abruptly around. Pheonix peered through the branches and caught a glimpse of a brown body. The old man silently, steadily, raised the bow, arrow already nocked.

A heartbeat, and the arrow flew with a sharp *twang*.

Birds took frightened flight from the trees at the sound that emerged from the animal's throat and echoed in the suddenly-hushed woods.

They crunched through the underbrush to come to the animal's side. It was the same species as the one seen earlier, but smaller and with less horns, and no grey around the muzzle. It lay on the ground, its front hooves dug in as though trying to raise itself, but its back legs were useless and limp. Its round sides heaved, mouth open and tongue hanging with its great panting panicked breaths. Pheonix met the same huge black eyes, but these were rimmed in white and rolling in fear. Blood poured from the wound on its back, staining the brown hide.

"Tch," said the old man, disgusted, though for what reason Pheonix couldn't fathom. The old man pulled a knife, larger than the one Pheonix had seen him using previously, and presented the handle to Pheonix. He fixed the boy with a burning stare.

"Don't let him suffer, pup," the old man said roughly.

Pheonix accepted the knife mechanically, knelt down — and stopped.

The animal stared at him, utterly helpless. Froth dripped from its open maw, propelled in great slimy ropes from hyperventilation.

Pheonix clenched his teeth. He'd killed thousands. People, creatures, beasts. It had never mattered. He'd killed them in horrible ways, ripped them apart, for the amusement of others. Why, now, did he hesitate?

Why was this different?

"Do it," the old man commanded.

Pheonix took the animal's head with his demon arm and — gently — bent it down, then jammed the knife to the hilt into the base of its skull in one decisive strike.

It twitched once, a violent full body convulsion, and fell limp.

He watched the light fade from its eyes — then a ghostly image separated from the animal. Pheonix could almost swear he was being watched for a split second, then all the strange sensations — and the image — were gone.

Shaking, Pheonix stood.

The old man said nothing. He crouched, removed the knife, rolled the creature over, and got to work gutting and partially skinning the corpse.

As shocked as Pheonix was by what he'd just experienced, a part of his mind was still hard at work noting the precise cuts, and which organs were delicately handled and which were tossed into the brush.

Finished, the old man stood and hefted the satchel of organs over his shoulder.

"Grab him, pup. Now that we spilled blood, the predators will come sniffin'. We need to move."

Still reeling, Pheonix picked up the body.

Back at the cabin, the old man finished skinning the animal, then butchered it, all the while making small verbal notations to Pheonix, who was always watching.

The old man portioned the meat up deftly with a cleaver in one hand and a hook in the other. Some pieces were destined to be hung from twine, similarly to the herbs from the previous day, some into a jar filled with pungent liquid, though the majority were for the stasis pods in the root cellar.

While tradition and technology, the old man explained, would seem on the surface to be at odds, one requiring progress and the other demanding adherence to the past, Archaic Earth managed a balance based on efficiency. Very little technology existed on Archaic Earth that wasn't for the utmost of economical purposes. So, while his house was made of wood gathered from the forest and he employed vinegar preserving and dry curing, he also had stasis pods to keep the majority of a large kill from going bad. The fact was, if one was going to eat animal protein, it was most nutritious as fresh as possible from the kill. That meant stasis. Aside from that, poor storing led to waste and the waste of something killed for consumption was tantamount to a sin. It was the responsibility of any sapient creature who chose to end a life in order to survive to do so in a humane, respectful, and efficient manner.

Whereas wood, dirt floors, fires, and manual labor were mostly as efficient as their technological counterparts, technology was superior in convenience and comfort.

And that was what set Archaic Earth apart from other places that had access to or chose to use technology in any capacity. Due to its history and the influence of its leadership, the cultures existing on Archaic Earth generally chose a technological option only for its practicality and no other reason. That wasn't to say there weren't outliers, but generally if someone wanted a fully-technological life, Archaic Earth wouldn't be the best spot for them and initiated citizens knew that.

"Archaic Earth is a place of choice," the old man finished. "That is what you need to take away from this. All sapients livin' here understand what it means to do so, and that makes us fight that much harder to survive and find meanin'."

Pheonix nodded, quiet, while his mind absorbed the new information. He could relate. His entire life had been a struggle to survive in situation after situation specifically designed to kill him.

And only by pure luck and significant privilege had he made it through any of it.

To be someone who *could* feel pain, who *could* die, and to *choose* struggle? Pheonix wasn't sure how he felt about that. It seemed odd, counterintuitive. Maybe that's why the old man had brought it up: to show Pheonix that there were many types of people out there.

"Now get to yer books while I fix supper," the old man said.

Pheonix did as he was told.

SIX
Some Things Aren't What They Appear

Many days passed, with Pheonix taking to the routine of living in the little cabin in the woods, working next to the old man as easily as though he'd done it for years. Their daily routine varied, but usually rotated between gathering materials, weapons and martial training, preparing food or supplies, spending time in the forest (either with a purpose in mind or just to take a walk), with Pheonix's nights dedicated to reading the books the old man provided. Conversation was sparse but meaningful.

Pheonix learned quickly, devouring books at an astronomical rate. A new set was always waiting at the top when he opened the trunk during his designated study time, though he hadn't discerned the mechanism by which the books were replaced.

There was much mystery about the old man, but Pheonix didn't question it. He didn't question anything. What was, simply was.

He learned about the broader universe, thousands of different species, mythology, the Accord, languages, psychology, mathematics, technology, and hundreds of other subjects.

His favorite subject, though, was the Creator: the progenitor of the universe and everything.

Something burned within him and drove him to search every tome he could find for every stray scrap of information on this entity. There wasn't overly much, as could be expected from sapients on something so beyond and above their comprehension. Only an extremely ancient scroll from the elves had any solid information on the Creator, which told the story of the genesis of the universe, the conception of the sapient species, the Firsts, and the Ascended.

Though Pheonix had no talent for magic, the old man taught him what he called 'peeking.' A 'peek' was a tiny glimpse into someone's essence. Pheonix realized he'd done it before without knowing. Seeing the hydra's life essence, feeling the fear of the slavers when he had dismembered them as a child, armor and all. It also explained what he'd seen when he'd killed the deer.

The old man admonished him to use it sparingly, as it wasn't polite. Pheonix didn't understand the context of the grin that stretched the old man's lined face, but he filed the information away nonetheless.

As time went on, Pheonix began to feel increasingly that something was wrong with him. He had hot and cold flashes, pressure in his abdomen, difficulty concentrating, difficulty maintaining no-mind, weakness, shivers.

One night, the symptoms were so overwhelming, he couldn't study. He put his head down in the book and took deep breaths to try to get control. It irked him; his body had always obeyed his commands. Now, suddenly, it refused, and took his mind with it.

It was no use. The old man said something but Pheonix couldn't hear it over the pounding in his ears. A tightening pressure in his stomach and the feeling of something rising in his throat made him bolt outside —

Just in time to vomit vile black sludge. It poured out of him until he saw stars. His body was wracked with tremors and weakness; he was barely able to hold himself up on his hands and knees.

Finally empty and on the edge of unconsciousness, he slumped forward. The old man caught him and helped him inside with strength that belied his small frame. Pheonix fell onto the cot and remembered no more.

He awoke several days later feeling disoriented, but stronger.

"Glad to see yer awake," the old man said from his bedside. He put down the book he'd been reading and fixed Pheonix with an intense stare. "Do you know what happened?"

Pheonix shook his head.

"I ain't sure'a the details but I can extrapolate some of it," the old man said. "You ain't equipped with the typical hominin way of eliminatin' waste, a physical disparity that would have killed anyone else in infancy without emergency intervention. So, there must be a significant difference in yer internal processes, which allows you to make use of a vast percentage of what you intake, moreso than others. It seems there is still — somethin' — that you can't digest, in what most hominins consume. The slavers fed you nutrient pills?"

"Yes."

"Well, they did somethin' right," the old man smirked. "We'll have to go to the Market and get some. I need some supplies from there, anyway. Lucky I have a few on hand. Here, take this."

The old man forced him to remain in the cot and read books for the rest of the day after taking the nutrient pill and plenty of water.

By the end of the day, he was restless and feeling better than he had in quite some time. He struggled to maintain no-mind when the sun lowered, and it was almost a relief when the old man roused him before the next sun rose.

He wore a satchel over one shoulder and directed Pheonix to grab a large skin of liquid.

"It's two days' walk to the Market," the old man said. "We'll need to get movin'."

They left the cabin and were in the dark overhang of the forest well before the sun touched the leaves.

Though Pheonix was well accustomed to his life with the old man at this point, and this forest was the closest thing he'd known so far to a 'home,' he still kept his head on a swivel. There were always new things to record, and this trip wasn't any different. They followed a faint, overgrown path, and finally came to a road cutting through the trees just as the sun was directly overhead. The road was huge and paved with amberrock — a clear, orange-yellow mineral ubiquitous enough on Archaic Earth that Pheonix had already seen much of it. The road's width was Pheonix's height several times over.

It was here Pheonix got his first close-up view of 'the Peoples' of Archaic Earth.

Primarily hominins (called 'smallfolk' here), hominid mixtures of various beasts (which the old man said were called 'beastfolk'), and 'modfolk' — individuals who had augmented themselves so as to look completely unique from everyone else, including each other.

Mostly, those that traveled the great road (and there were many) ignored Pheonix and the old man, so the two got moving. However, it quickly became obvious that the old man was known in these parts, because it wasn't entirely uncommon for someone to wave at him or flag him down. But he was skilled at keeping conversations short and genial, so despite these interruptions, they made good time.

As they walked, they passed off-shoot roads and the occasional building making lively business off the constant traffic, as well as permanent camps where travelers could stop and rest. A socialist affair, everyone pitched in with whatever resources they could spare as well as the physical labor of cooking, keeping the place tidy, or pulling guard duty for those who were resting.

Infractions, the old man informed him, were punished swiftly and with extreme prejudice, so major roads like this were generally as safe as they could get.

Night had long fallen by the time the old man and Pheonix stopped at a permanent camp, already occupied by a few other weary travelers. Someone passed around bread, someone else handed out dried meat and cheese. The old man shared his jar of preserves and a skin of wine. He had Pheonix gather firewood, which the boy did easily and without complaint, to replenish the stocks for the night.

Pheonix offered to pull first shift guard duty. He didn't sleep, and really only needed one or two hours of no-mind to be functional. Aside from which, it was interesting to observe the kinds of travelers who would still be on their feet at such hours. He wasn't often outside at night, and this gave him a chance to take in a whole new environment. The movement of the stars and constellations in the sky above particularly fascinated him.

After a while, he pulled out a book and read by firelight, occasionally tossing a log in to feed the flames.

Hours passed.

Someone got up and relieved him. He nodded, sat by the old man, and slipped into no-mind.

They took to the road again sometime before dawn.

That afternoon, it was clear they were approaching their final destination. Many smaller roads joined with the one on which they traveled, leading to a swelling crowd of all types of bodies. Pheonix saw more cargo-carrying vehicles as well; some simple wagons harnessed to the shoulders of beasts of burden, some zipping overhead, some apparently magically-powered autos of all shapes and sizes, some hovering just above the ground in a careful dance to avoid pedestrians.

More security was evident as well: a mix of Marshalls (armor-wearing, sword-and-gun-wielding peacekeepers) and Enforcers (uniformed but with no obvious weaponry).

In the distance, something hovered near the horizon; a giant glass-mosaic dome stretched over the Market, making it hard to see inside. Floating in the sky high above the dome was a shadow — but it was so far up there that no part of its form could be discerned even with Pheonix's sharp eyes.

The flow of bodies crushed into a slow-moving tide, and Pheonix's tension rose. He didn't like to be touched.

Ahead was a checkpoint through an opening in the dome and the reason for the backup. It took many long minutes to get to it but once they did, the Marshall Captain manning it waved them through. The old man's notoriety extended even here, it seemed.

It wasn't quite sunset yet. The old man stopped them just inside the entrance. The amberrock road continued inside as the main boulevard.

"We made good time," the old man said.

Pheonix took in the sights. Stalls of every shape, size, and color lined the road as far as he could see. In between and everywhere were people, some whorls of activity here and there gathered around folks dancing, or spouting fire, or singing, or playing instruments.

"What purpose does that serve?" Pheonix asked of the performers.

The old man looked at him out of the side of his eye.

"Not all things serve a practical purpose, pup. You and I live a life of survival; once survival is fully taken care of, what is there to pursue?"

"Knowledge," Pheonix said.

"Aside from that?"

Pheonix shook his head, indicating he didn't know, and the old man chuckled.

"You have a lot yet to learn, pup. Let's get goin' before it gets too dark."

They hadn't gone very far into the Market when someone flagged the old man down.

"Oh, Master Apothecary Jan-Üss," the old man said.

"I'm so glad I ran into you!" The Master Apothecary enthused. She was an older, bearded woman with a copious amount of mushrooms, fronds, and flowers sprouting from her personage. "You really saved my ass last time with your herbs. You're the only one I've found that can get deep in the forest — no, I know, I won't ask how you do it, trade secret, but it's remarkable nonetheless. I'm running dangerously low on leyleaf. There's been an outbreak of Stonesblood infection in some of the villages."

"That's terrible to hear. Of course I'll do what I can. I'll dispatch a bird when I've found some."

She clapped her hands together, sending a puff of spores into the air. "You have *no* idea how relieved I am to hear that. Thank you, Maester." Then she waved and was off.

"What did she call you?" Pheonix asked as they got moving.

"Maester. A title of respect given to me by the people."

Pheonix was aware that he didn't know the old man's name, but it also didn't matter to him. 'Pheonix' was a name given to him by people that attempted to kill and harm him at every opportunity, so names didn't hold much significance to him. The old man had never offered Pheonix his name, so he didn't think it important to ask.

He was just him; that's all that mattered.

It wasn't long until another person approached, and then another. This one thanking the old man for the herbs that cured her daughter's deadly blood-fever, this one saying that their crops were blight-free because of a tincture the old man provided.

"You see," the old man said as they walked, "one of the basest sapient philosophies is this: if you can do somethin', you should. I have no family of my own. I have only my — and, well, now yer — needs to think of. But I live in a place that is not well accessible to others, a place of high magic concentration. Things grow there and live there that others may well never see, some of which cure or treat dangerous ailments. And I have the ability to get them, so I do. It's just that simple."

It made sense then, why the old man had taken in a deformed teenager who had shown up out of literally nowhere and knew literally nothing. He was just that kind of person. His life, when not being spent in the solitude of survival, was in dedication to others.

If you can do something, you should, echoed in Pheonix's mind. Was that how he, Pheonix, wanted to live? His entire life thus far had been survival. What was *living*? If he had a choice, what direction would he take from this point forward? Would he stay with the old man forever, helping people?

But then what of his promise to kill the slavers?

He'd had a child's mind when he'd made that vow. While the desire remained, he now couldn't be sure it was even possible. Yes, he could spend his entire adulthood on a campaign to kill every slaver he came across. But what would that really accomplish? The slavers themselves were disposable — he knew that from a childhood spent with them. What he really needed to do to fulfill his promise was change the system that allowed trafficking and slavery to even exist.

From that perspective, it certainly seemed like the regulatory bodies — like the Rangers and the Accord — were remiss in some of their core duties.

And, as much as the thought rankled, one person couldn't change an entire system. The metacosm was huge, complex, intertwined with the lives of countless individuals and the effects their actions had on the whole. To have so much as a hope of changing things, he'd first need to unravel those knots. To even begin to do *that*, he'd have to learn the shape of the knots and which individual threads he could pull, which needed to be snapped. And he'd probably need either powerful allies or to become someone with power himself — though more likely, both, considering the scale of the task.

With the honesty of someone without ego, he knew that at that moment in time, he simply wasn't ready yet. His knowledge and physical prowess were both lacking.

Though, it didn't seem to be a hopeless goal.

He shifted his attention to the here-and-now with that thought in mind.

There was so much to see in the Market. Pheonix's eyes darted from one thing to another, the colorful and varied stalls of food, magical items, clothes, plants, and too many things to name immediately. He took a mental picture of each thing and moved on to the next. He'd have a lot to process during no-mind tonight.

"Stop, thief!" someone called.

"Oh no," the old man muttered. Pheonix followed his gaze.

The crowd in front of them parted and a body blurred past, then arced overhead. Pheonix tensed but the old man was relaxed, so he didn't act. He managed to catch a glimpse of overwhelming brown. The purported thief wore (potentially) leather clothes, a mask, had long brown hair and a scraggly beard. But those were all minor details compared to the one major thing about him: he was repeatedly leaping forward with the distance and strength far exceeding even deer — on only one leg.

Under one arm he held a very unhappily squawking chicken, which shed feathers as he fled.

Before the unfortunate shopkeeper had a chance to even come up to where Pheonix and the old man stood (which the one-legged thief was long past), a knight stepped out from the crowd. He wore extremely bulky armor — perhaps more than was practical or necessary — most of which was shiny, with the exception of the boots, which were dirty and grimy. He carried, with ease, a simply massive shield and a giant mace.

"Have no fear, I will apprehend this miscreant!" the knight shouted with perfectly knightly cadence and confidence.

The knight bull-rushed forward and everyone hastened to get out of his way — with the exception of Pheonix, who hadn't been told to move and didn't know the knight wouldn't simply go around him.

The knight crumpled like shattered glass as he hit, at a full run, the steel wall that was Pheonix.

Pheonix blinked down at the still body, and then turned to look at the old man, who was hiding his face in one hand.

"Is this part of that entertainment we saw earlier?" Pheonix asked.

People rushed to help the knight up, but he was dead unconscious. Someone called for a Healer. Several people gave

Pheonix dirty looks. The old man hastened his young charge away from the crowd and stopped in the shadow of some stalls some ways down the road.

"Pheonix," the old man started, "you know what a hero is?"

"I've read accounts of heroes, both mythical and real, as part of our lessons."

"What do you think happens when a hero gets old?"

Pheonix accessed his memory.

"In most stories, the hero dies in battle, or otherwise doesn't get old. Or, the story doesn't specify."

"In bygone days, an early death *was* the most common fate of those later dubbed 'heroes.' But, sometimes, someone given the title does manage to get old. On Archaic Earth we have a few; you just met two. The thief was Hoppy Jack, and the knight was Godfrey. In their day, they were both men of renown to be feared and respected. Jack was well-known in the Dark Sector, stealin' from the evil factions that live there and bringin' his spoils back to impoverished colonies. Godfrey was a knight of the Golden Paladin, who kept order here and anywhere else he was sent. Jack was a wild youth and stole where he pleased once he realized he had a knack for it. One day he stole from a knight, who shot him in the ass and subsequently caused him to lose one leg. It didn't stop him, though; he found a wizard who had need of deft fingers and, in exchange for his services, the wizard crafted him the Shoe of League Hop, thus gainin' him the nickname 'Hoppy Jack.' But somethin' about what happened changed Jack. He shifted the focus of his thievin' on the baddies in the Dark Sector and came to be hailed as a hero. As he got older, he became unable to leave the planet and went a little senile. Now he sometimes filches a chicken or two. We tolerate him and try to take care of him because he took care of us for so long, and that's only right.

"In Godfrey's case, he and a group of other paladins went to take on a coven of evil witches, with disastrous results. He was cursed to lose that which made him a paladin: wisdom and constitution. So he isn't very bright, and a wind can bowl him over. He can still kill a ZZZ with one blow from his mace, and his faith is unrivaled. But for his protection, we don't let him go on patrol anymore. He's a fixture around the market and has foiled many shenanigans attempts. The Golden Paladin still loves him. But we can't risk losin' him when he can, as you saw, be knocked unconscious by runnin' into someone — and isn't observant enough to go around. It's only fair that because these heroes gave their lives and livelihoods for us, now in their twilight years, we take care of them."

Pheonix nodded, unsure of what to say. What initially seemed a farce from a street performer in fact had far more depth when plumbed. Once again Pheonix was reminded that things weren't always what they appeared. He mused that it would probably be a difficult concept to grasp, given his trouble with social interactions. None of what sapients did made any sense to him, and this was no exception.

The Market changed as they traveled deeper into it, with less stalls and tents and more buildings. Signs hung outside these structures advertised the sale of technology and magical objects, rare materials and offworld supplies. The amber road eventually split in front of a huge platform. Those that stepped onto it were immediately whisked into the air and towards the floating terrace Pheonix had spotted as an airborne shadow before entering the Market.

"That is where the Golden Paladin resides, when he is on-planet," said the old man, gazing skyward.

Pheonix accessed his memory:

The Golden Paladin. A Hero, the only Paladin chosen to directly wield the Creator's power, both by his strength and his faith. With the Creator's power, he united the many disparate factions of Archaic Earth and brought them to the stars, where they met with the Rangers and were initiated. Wields also the sword known as Alpha, which causes calamity when swung. It remains in a stasis field in the heart of his Seat, and he has sworn not to remove it. The many Kingdoms of Archaic Earth rule by the Golden Paladin's tenets and remain all too aware what would happen were they to deviate. In that way, he single-handedly keeps the peace of Archaic Earth.

Pheonix followed the old man to one of the offshoot paths from the main road, this one colored blue. The path lit up underneath their feet. It felt like they'd stepped into another city. The buildings along this path were metal and plastic, sleek structures reminiscent of the technology they housed.

They entered a building whose electric sign was unreadable to Pheonix. Probably a language he hadn't learned yet.

On the shelves lining the walls inside were packs and packs of labeled metallic objects and machines. After a moment it clicked that this was their destination. These were likely nutrient pills and the supplies to make them.

The man behind the counter smiled and made what sounded like a greeting, but he spoke a language Pheonix also didn't recognize. The old man responded in kind and they conversed shortly. The shopkeeper took out from behind the counter a massive sack and the old man gestured that Pheonix take it. He heaved it over one shoulder, careful not to hit his wing, and waited for further instruction.

The two men finished their conversation, and Pheonix and the old man left. They made their way back through the busy twilit hub along the amberrock road.

SEVEN
Out Of Time

Five years later ...

Under the old man's tutelage, Pheonix grew into a formidable young man, replete with tens of thousands of books worth of knowledge on hundreds of subjects. His physical strength and basic understanding of the use of weapons was honed into the martial art of the survivalist. Their life together was one of quiet companionship; once the majority of the basics were safely seated in Pheonix's memory, the old man only had to direct him to a book or say a few words in explanation on any new subject. The forest became his home and he knew it almost as well as his teacher, so he often went into the trees by himself to gather herbs, hunt, or just enjoy and study nature. One of Pheonix's favorite places was the brook where he'd seen the deer known as the 'old man of the forest' on his very first hunt.

One evening, Pheonix was returning from a day spent in quiet meditation among nature. As he emerged from the woodline, he immediately knew something was wrong.

The door of the old man's shack was flung open, the interior dark. There was no smell of dinner from inside.

He paused short out of pure shock, taking in the long shadows of sunset and the lack of movement or light from inside.

While, to someone else, it may have been logical to assume that the old man was simply out wandering, or to worry that he had collapsed, Pheonix had cut the teeth of his youth on combat and death of the worst kind. His sense for danger was abnormally keen, so despite a lack of any obvious signs of struggle, he *knew* that there had been an attack.

He hurried across the intervening space between the treeline and the shack, slowing a few steps from the door to the pace that he knew rendered him completely silent from long years spent in wild woods. Crossing the threshold, his eyes instantly adjusted to the interior darkness.

The door closed behind him without a sound.

Confirming his intuition, three unknown figures were inside the house. Two crouched in the center of the room and one beside the window — men, swathed in black and wearing crude studded leather armor. They were murmuring quietly to each other, but the blood rushing in Pheonix's ears made the words incomprehensible.

He reached out with shaking fingers to the butchering table and gripped a hilt in each hand. He jerked the cleavers free, the slight *shing* of metal on wood a bullhorn in the quiet.

The two that hunkered together jerked towards him, hands going to their weapons. In the near-absolute darkness, they could not see him, so he immobilized one, then the other, with two precise strikes to the forehead with the flat of the cleavers. They both dropped and he turned to the third.

The assailant backed up into the wall and flailed his weapon towards the sound of Pheonix's footfalls. Pheonix knocked the clumsy strike away and buried one cleaver into the man's sword arm. It stuck. He brought the other cleaver up from the bottom. In two chops that made the man scream, Pheonix separated arm from body and viciously jerked his cleaver from it.

(Warning, gore/extreme violence.)

Systematically, he chopped each man apart, feeling both an all-consuming fury and a logical sort of detachment — the former controlled his reactions, and the latter controlled his actions. They suffered, they bled — one's stomach split open, intestines yanked out and tied around his neck, stuffed down his own throat so he gagged and choked on his own shit. They begged him for the mercy of death —— one's scalp peeled back and a cleaver tapped into the skull, shards shattering away to reveal the wetly gleaming gray matter beneath. They called out to their gods —— one's eyeballs torn out, eye sockets probed with the claws of the demon-hand until they punched through the back of the skull and into the brain. They cried and pissed themselves —— one's testicles chopped off, squeezed in his hands until they burst like over-ripe tomatoes. They babbled about things coherent and otherwise —— one's lungs and heart and liver dug out with slow, questing fingers, like the gentle exploration of a lover's body — their deepest secrets, the name of the person who had paid them to commit the act: Kavash — anything to make the pain stop ....

(Continue here.)

After a while, the screams were no more.

Suddenly the silence overtook Pheonix and he stood, covered in blood that wasn't his own from his twitching eyebrows to the curl of his toes.

He wheeled around to face what he knew would be there. The old man's desecrated body lay in the middle of the room. Multiple slashes and bruises and contortions of his old body told of many broken bones ... and of torture. Pheonix's wavering gaze focused on the trail of blood from the neck, followed it. The old man's head sat askance near the open book chest. Books were strewn about in the general mess, but one tome seemed suspiciously placed, unmarred, near the head.

He dropped to his knees … and froze.

On the severed head was an ear-to-ear grin. Unmistakable for a grimace of death, his smile portrayed serenity, the perfection of profound joy. Pheonix's thoughts erupted into a whirlwind so chaotic it was impossible to string two rational words together.

He staggered to his feet, overcome by the sudden need to get *away*, away from this den of death. He looked around wildly, feeling hunted, desperate. He snatched the book near the old man's head for no reason that he could put name to, unaware that he was still clutching the cleavers, or maybe just incapable of letting them go. He hesitated, and in that pause, the sense of *needing to get the fuck out of here* was too powerful to deny.

He thought of the old man's sword, which Pheonix had so often trained with, but it was nowhere to be found.

And he was out of time.

He rushed out of the shack, into the new night, with the hounds of his own hell at his heels.

That flight through the forest was a blur. He slammed into trees, stumbled over roots, almost eviscerating himself several times with the cleavers his hands had cramped into uselessness around. Branches slashed at him, but he didn't feel their fingers. Thorns lodged in his flesh. The forest fell to silence with the crashing bedlam of his passage, in fear or reverence of his torment.

Directionless, he ran for most of the night.

Something loomed ahead of him, but his eyes were gritty and refused to focus, and his velocity didn't let him avoid it.

He plunged through the tear without stopping, face-planted on the other side.

His head swam.

Murmuring voices circled him. He struggled to get to his feet, but his body was spent and had nothing left to give.

EIGHT
Introductions

"We've been reading some very recent fluctuations in this part of the forest. We're honored to have you for this patrol, but I doubt we'll see as much action as you normally do," an elf said.

"Trust me," Chani said, "that's a good thing."

Soft laughter.

Chanilinaicanau M'Tyoiderit Abyssterilon, Rangers Special Projects Commander, had chosen to dress for this op in elven clothing (specially tailored for her, as few willowy elves were her shape or muscle density), a tight weave made of fibers from the trees of Terelath. Elves were the ultimate vegans: they did not kill for food, and they took nothing unless it was freely given, which was made easy by the fact that they could communicate with the flora of Availeon.

Availeon's twin suns shone merrily; the air of the forest was crisp and fresh, and she thought to herself, *Creator, I missed Terelath.*

All good humor aside, there was a real, serious reason for her presence on Availeon. The fluctuations mentioned were of the type that preceded a tear, and one so close to Terelath was indeed *extremely* serious business. Thus her accompaniment: a sniper, four bowmasters, an elven sub-Captain, and two long-range recon.

And just last night, terrifying howls had emanated from the forest.

Chani walked lightly, resisting the urge to whistle. She wasn't the type to be solemn under almost any circumstance, much to the chagrin of her peers. Far too much combat had taught her that even in the worst, most hopeless situations, humor could be utilized to strengthen failing morale in soldiers that had come face-to-face with their own mortality.

She'd learned to think that whatever happened a few minutes from now was what happened a few minutes from now. Right this second, she strolled through one of the most achingly gorgeous places in the universe, and it was good.

But, as these things often went, the 'getting down to business' happened all too soon. One of the scouts signaled, and the party came to a halt. Chani could see the tear, a jagged-edged open door leading to another forest as though it were simply another room. It was night there, and she could tell immediately by the shape of the trees that it wasn't anywhere on Availeon.

Chani approached, her entourage following, then lifted a hand. She squinted.

"Something's coming."

What was one moment merely a shadow among the trees, was the next a figure belly-flopping out of the tear, raising a puff of dust as it landed. Weapons sprang into the hands of every individual standing around the tear.

And then ... nothing.

The figure lay face-first on the ground, unmoving.

"Arven," Chani barked to a nearby elf. "Demon?"

The elf paused, then shook his head. "No. I ... I don't recognize its life-spark, only that it's very young."

Chani nodded brusquely and holstered her pistols. "Get a Lady here right the fuck now."

She knelt by the form to examine it — humanoid, covered from head to toe in blood, although it was hard to tell what was underneath the simply gigantic black wings that lay over it like a heavy blanket. "Ethin, triage," she said to another elf.

A drop ship punched through the clouds and two Ranger medics dropped lightly next to the limp form. Chani watched with interest as they rolled it — him? — over. She'd guess at male, and if he corrected her once he was awake, she'd amend that. Clenched in his hands (both of which were taloned, but one was an overly large claw — the skin of that arm was red and bumpy) were cleavers, and clutched against his chest, a large book. Despite the pointed ears (which hundreds of hominin and humanoid species had), he definitely wasn't an elf.

Though, if an elf couldn't tell what his life-spark was, that didn't bode well for him being a recognized species.

The medics went to work and a Lady flickered into being beside her. Chani straightened up and faced her. The Lady nodded in greeting; she was a serene robed presence, a sapient leaky faucet seeping magic. Enrobed in her uncontainable power, the Lady floated a few centiunits off the ground.

She turned towards the tear without Chani having to say anything, a small frown creasing her features. With a single gesture from one of her elegant hands, the tear dissolved. The Lady smiled at Chani and then she, too, was gone again.

Chani approached the medics. "What's his condition?"

One of them shook their head. "He seems fine, just unconscious. No wounds, so this blood most likely isn't his."

The large red claw twitched. All three people watching the young man stopped cold, but he didn't open his eyes, didn't move ... aside from the claw, which raised the cleaver and brought it menacingly over his throat.

Chani made a snap decision and kicked the cleaver away. Still the boy didn't react. She stepped on the wrist and held the claw down while it thrashed at her.

"Creator … what the Fug is going on?" she muttered to herself, then raised her voice: "Get a shuttle. We need to take this kid to Terelath."

One of the medics tried to take the book that the boy still gripped to his chest with his normal arm. His eyes flew open and he tensed. The reactions to his movements rippled through the assembled, but the seeming lucidity passed quickly and his head lolled to one side, eyes closing again. He mumbled something incoherently.

Chani jerked her head towards the arriving shuttle. The medics levered him onto the stretcher. Chani went with them, helping them by restraining the flexing claw. When it was strapped down securely, she grasped the hand-bar inside the door. The shuttle lifted off smoothly.

She watched the ground fall away below her with stomach-dropping speed.

Even with the little craft's state-of-the-art speed, it took long minutes to fly over Terelath, the elven main city on Availeon and the current center of 'Universal Chosen' operations. Availeon was classed as an Origin or First planet, made by the Creator itself for the Firsts (according to the Firsts themselves). That and the fact that the Ascended of Nature, Spiraea, lived at its core made Availeon a place that 'real' physics didn't quite touch.

Though air traffic was strictly controlled, they did pass some crafts of varying sizes and shapes traveling to and fro. The elves didn't want the vision of their crystal sky obscured, and for good reason; even housing so many other species, Terelath was still built, run, and maintained by the elven Council, and the elves were very serious about keeping as low an impact on the planet as possible. Ranger activity was not exempt from that.

Spiraea might pitch a hell of a fit if they weren't careful, the way she'd been acting lately.

Finally, the mammoth amethyst building that was the Medical Center peeked over the horizon. The shuttle settled down in front of it and elves dressed in Healer robes hurried out. They rushed the young man inside and Chani followed.

She took a deep breath. The headache that had been forming between her eyes was washed away by the power suffusing the Medical Center, charged by the elven Healers and trapped in the largest natural amethyst formation in the known metacosm.

By the time the elves had settled the young man in his own room, open to sunlight and sparsely decorated, he was shifting around and muttering.

Several things were happening at once: one elf held a small crystal near his head, other elves stripped him of his torn and stained clothing, and a third group of elves worked on re-restraining the claw that was now attempting to strangle its owner.

They cleaned him, checked him over, then re-dressed him in a robe that barely fit his tall, lanky, oddly-shaped frame.

Chani was a lot older than she was willing to admit to anyone in an unofficial capacity; she'd been *way* the hell around, and nothing she'd ever seen quite matched this boy. It was almost like ... he was cobbled together from bits of many species.

She scowled. That stank of genetic experimentation, although she would keep that suspicion under wraps until she had proof. The Rangers did some minor genetics work, but it was extremely regulated and mostly only related to life-threatening medical issues. They had stopped doing any genetic experimentation that attempted to create a new being Ages ago.

But just because the Rangers weren't doing it didn't mean it wasn't still being done.

Uncontrolled genetic experimentation was one of those problems — like slavers and space pirates and the dark magical arts — that were a constant thorn in the Rangers' sides. Things that, if they got out of control, would bring down everything she held dear.

If he *was* a genetic experiment, there was a high chance he would have to be terminated, for the safety of all Terelath. She'd have to discreetly contact the Lady responsible for closing the tear and request the report on where it had led; taking care of the results of such an experiment was, after all, only the beginning. They would need to confront the source, which was arguably a bigger issue. The tools for genetic experimentation weren't widely available.

The boy's eyes opened, and Chani could tell that, this time, his mind was active behind them. His gaze darted, settling for a split second on everything in the room, though his expression remained terrifyingly neutral. The elves backed off; Chani came to the bedside, her arms crossed over her chest. He had not moved at all (with the exception of that claw, which was starting to really annoy her), but his eyes locked on and followed her with an unnerving intensity.

"Hello," Chani said in Ranger common, intending on prompting him to see what language he spoke. If he was initiated at all, he'd at least know what she was saying. "Can you understand me?"

"Yes," he responded in Ancient Man, according to her translator implant. This meant he was likely from — or had been through — Archaic Earth. "But I am not fluent and I won't be able to respond in kind."

"You're doing fine. You are in Accord space, on Availeon, in Terelath. Specifically, in the Medical Center."

The boy looked around and seemed to accept that.

"Would you like to receive an implant to be able to communicate with us better?" Chani offered.

He stared at her with that piercing, off-putting, dark gaze. At first impression, he seemed completely without emotion other than calculation. An AI?

He tilted his head and she got the brief sense of being vulnerable — she was being read. Chani ignored her instincts to lock up against psychic attack and left herself open. The vulnerable feeling faded and she let out a mental breath.

That was a hell of a dangerous thing you did just now, Abyss, she thought to herself shakily. To cover her consternation, she said, "My name is Chanilinaicanau M'tyoiderit Abyssterilon —"

"... Abyssterilon clan of the Rangers, a greater family, headed by Taylor and Dwayne Abyssterilon," he recited in the monotone of an encyclopedia.

"Yes. I'm a Special Projects Commander for the Rangers."

"I have read of them. I will take your implant, if it will assist me."

Chani waved forward a medical corpsman who was holding a sterile tray with the tube-like device used to inject the implants. The corpsman took up the device and pressed it behind the young man's left ear. He didn't so much as twitch.

"How is your understanding of our language now?" Chani asked in elven.

"You are speaking elven. I can understand perfectly."

"Good. Let me continue: I gave you my full name and title, but I would prefer if you called me Chani or Commander. Now, there are three other implants I could give you right now if you wish. This next one is for communication. It allows us to speak to each other directly over long distances."

"Why would I need that?" he asked, his eyes darting between the individuals popping in and out — Healers assessing his condition, people measuring and running scanning crystals and other technology over him as their individual jobs required.

"As of right now, you are the temporary responsibility of the Rangers. We found you, but we don't know your circumstances and that means we don't know how best to help you yet. There is a process to that. This will facilitate that process and allow you more freedom."

His eyes returned to her, gauging. "Fine," he said.

He was given the second implant.

"This next implant is not necessary to you at this moment; it's generally for combat personnel. It is a database for various military operations that runs on a subconscious level to allow for instantaneous adjustment to various active battle scenarios."

If he *was* the kind of genetic experiment who *did* have to be terminated, it would take time. Best to make that time as comfortable as possible. It wasn't his fault he was what he was.

"Interesting. Most of my life has been spent killing. I will accept it. It may be useful."

She was dying to ask about that blasé comment but bit her tongue as the corpsman injected him with the third implant. As she'd told him, there was a process. They weren't at the 'ask questions' step yet.

"This last one is the Accord archive; whatever declassified information we know, you will know. All you need to do is access — "

"Yes."

"I'm sorry, I must ask — why so quick to agree to that one?"

"My primary goal for the last five years has been information acquisition. A subconscious archive I can ... access ... seems considerably more efficient than the method I was using previously."

This kid was more interesting by the second. She privately hoped she could keep him around. He was given the last implant.

"Now that that's done, how do you feel?"

He looked upward, his eyes going distant. "Fine."

"Would you mind if we asked you some questions?"

"No."

Chani nodded, took a breath. "What is your name?"

"The slavers called me Pheonix. P-h-e-o-n-i-x."

Chani thought: *Fucking slavers. Great,* but said aloud: "You are male? Do you mind if we call you 'he'?"

"I was led to believe that genetically I am male. You may call me 'he' if you wish. I have no preference. I am just me."

The clawed arm was so violent by that point that its thrashing was threatening to break through the restraints. Chani sighed in irritation. "I assume you aren't doing that?"

Pheonix shook his head.

"Do you mind if I get rid of it?"

"Please," Pheonix replied calmly.

Chani gestured another person forward, who pushed a tray on which surgical implements lay.

"We will give you something for the pain — "

"I don't feel pain."

" ... What?"

"I don't feel pain, and I can't die."

A pause. Chani's brain didn't quite want to swallow that one. But she'd met enough Ascended and Ascendent beings to know that damn near anything was possible.

"Okay then," she said.

I guess we won't need the stasis field to keep him from bleeding out, either, she thought. *But how is that possible? And do I want to risk that he's lying? Why the hell would someone lie about that? What the hell **is** he?*

Pheonix, as though reading her mind — or at least intuiting the reason for her hesitation — easily tore out of the restraining strap holding his other arm, and, with a speed that even Chani almost couldn't follow, seized one of the crystal scalpels on a tray nearby. He sliced into his own flesh to separate the clawed arm from his torso.

There was a collective intake of breath and everyone froze.

His face showed neither pain nor discomfort, and Chani could sense neither in his mind. The black but oddly-iridescent blood that pooled from the wound floated near and did not run down, despite the cut being deep enough to show bone. Pheonix paused and looked up.

"Am I doing this myself?"

Chani swore under her breath, tried to keep her amusement off her face, and called for a surgeon. She didn't have to wait long. The benefits of an integrated instant transportation system. The surgeon's expression as they entered to see Pheonix's state was priceless. No matter the outcome, Chani knew she'd have a hell of a story to tell over a drink by the time this was all over.

The surgeon attached a box to Pheonix's shoulder and Chani called for a standard cybernetic arm and xeno-mechanics from HQ. By the time the surgeon finished, the xeno-mechanics had arrived, and the transition from clawed arm (which had been forcibly calmed with a stasis field) to cybernetic arm happened smoothly.

Pheonix watched the process with rapt fascination.

The surgeon, his face plastered to his box, carefully disconnected every nerve and blood vessel and muscle fiber bundle with micro-manipulators. His assistants waited at his elbow, and elven Healers worked at a physical and genetic level to ensure acceptance of the tech.

Acting in concert, the team reinforced the arm by sliding biometal plates along his ribs, spine, scapula, and collarbone which would biofuse to the bone and support the arm's function. Once the arm was attached to the surgeon's satisfaction, the xeno-mechanics took over, tuning and wiring the organic to the inorganic. Chani flexed one of her hands, remembering how the procedure had gone for her. It was not a pleasant memory, but her circumstances had been a little ... different.

Chani pulled a waiting Healer aside. "I'll be blunt — is he organic?"

The elf blinked. "Yes, Commander. Fully." He smiled nervously. "Well, with one exception, now. The genetic strands I could see were a mess, though. There are massive errors, ones I could not begin to correct."

Well, that was to be expected. Evil didn't have the resources, brains, or patience needed to create functioning genetic experiments.

If he was one, he was the most intelligent and coherent experiment she'd ever met, seen, or heard of, despite his strange shape and the arm that seemed intent on killing him. Most experiments were volatile monsters, apt to dissolving into a puddle of goo with too much stimulus or time.

She let the Healer move on and stared hard at Pheonix.

What are you? I feel nothing. I'm one of the first trained empaths the Rangers have produced, and yet — nothing! You have no emotions! I trust the Healers, there is no technology — anywhere — EVER — so advanced that it could fool a look straight into the soul, and any magic you had about you would be dispelled the moment you entered this place. Curiouser and curiouser.

The oculus opened. Chani inclined her head slightly as Commander Steele walked through. They paused and gave Chani a slight smile of congenial greeting — though everything Steele did was congenial. Light-skinned and fit, with short, neat black hair and hazel eyes, Jae Steele had been born with the proverbial silver spoon in their mouth. At one-hundred-and-eighty-six years old, they were the youngest Commander in Ranger history.

Despite their age, their career and attitude had been exemplary since moment one. Additionally, their accomplishments spoke for themselves, especially regarding interspecies relations on Terelath. They had an uncanny (almost magical) knack for solving problems.

They took up a position near Chani. She stood at almost two units tall, and Steele was shorter only by a small margin.

"Commander," Chani said by way of greeting.

"Commander Abyss, good to see you again. I think I've got it from here."

Chani snorted. "With all due respect, you couldn't drag me out of here with a raging Gygamus. This is the most interesting thing to happen to me in centuries."

Steele chuckled. They didn't seem surprised; but then, nothing surprised them. "Really? You pulled the 'with all due respect' on me?"

Chani just grinned. Everybody in any military knew 'with all due respect' basically meant 'fuck you.' Ironic in the first place, considering she outranked Steele.

"Very well then," Steele went on when she declined to respond. "Care to get me up to speed?"

"Not much to tell. Found him out of a tear, rushed him back here, he had this ... clawed arm, and it kept trying to kill him, so we removed it and I requisitioned a cybernetic replacement for the moment." She lifted her chin to indicate the xeno-mechanics. "Looks like they're finishing up, though."

She gestured that Steele should precede her and the two of them approached the bedside. Pheonix looked up with calm dark eyes. Steele opened their mouth to say something, and stopped, frowning. Steele looked almost ... petulant. Chani focused on them; they were — confused? Irritated? They felt thwarted. And a little fascinated, fearful. At what? Pheonix hadn't even moved.

The lapse was momentary. Steele smiled. "I am Commander Jae Steele of the Steele clan with the Rangers. You may call me 'Commander Steele' or 'Steele.' Once they are done configuring your new arm, we will need to ask you some questions, with the help of a machine to help us make sure you are truthful. While you were out, we copied some of your memories onto this crystal and we'll be reviewing those, as well, with you present."

Pheonix nodded.

Steele turned away. Chani hung out by the bedside, watching them surreptitiously, as they made a call. The xeno-mechanics had Pheonix move his fingers, tilt his hand this way and that, and made micro-adjustments as he did. Finally they drew back and had him pick up a cup of water that was on a stand next to him. He crushed it, spilling water everywhere. The lead xeno-mechanic placed another cup of water on the stand; this time, Pheonix picked it up with no problem.

The two mechanics looked at each other in surprise. The lead shrugged and stood, picking up his instruments.

"Seems like it's working fine. He'll ... adjust to it as he uses it more." Even he sounded confused by the ritual words. *Nobody* meshed so quickly with cybernetics.

Chani bade the xeno-mechanics farewell and thanked them. When it was only her, Steele, and Pheonix in the small room, she looked back at the boy. Pheonix studied his inorganic hand, moving each finger down the line. By focusing on him, she could catch a sense of ... interest? An echo of emotion.

So, he does have emotions, she thought, not without some triumph and relief. One mystery solved, at least.

Another assistant brought in a simple, unassuming box. The response measurement system (RMS) worked off of vocal input and had a set of dials and three lights as the only adornment: a green light for the truth, a red light for a lie, and a yellow light for indeterminate.

Pheonix sat up, his attention now on the box, as Steele set it on the bedside table. Chani pulled out the crystal with Pheonix's memories in it and stuck it into a slot in the single piece of technology in the whole minimalistic room, a terminal.

"We'll view this first." Chani said, and because she could sense his curiosity, turned to explain how it worked. "As Commander Steele said, we downloaded ten years of your memories, but we won't be sitting here for ten years. This crystal displays memories that left the biggest impact on your mind — shall we say, the abridged version of 'you.' It helps us get an idea of what we're working with."

She touched the screen to begin the display.

Memories in snippets and flashes, sometimes lasting as long as ten or fifteen minutes (but more often just images that didn't make sense out of context) raced across the screen, one after another. The casino, slavers, a shadowed figure with glowing green eyes (Chani startled when she recognized him: the Death Dealer), the hydra, Pheonix's many 'deaths,' and then a rictus-grin-wearing face — Temperjoke, Ascended of Chaos — that both Steele and Chani knew all too well.

Chani thinned her lips, and the memories rolled on: the old man, Pheonix learning how to read and write and speak in other languages, his explorations of the forest, learning to take care of himself, learning how to fight ... and then, the day of the old man's murder. That was a movie, unbroken. Chani had to look away at the brutality. Then, running ... and then, nothing.

The crystal flickered and the screen returned to its default. No one said anything.

Chani looked at Steele and could sense in them the same maelstrom of emotions she was feeling. *What the hell did we bring into our midst?*

Steele nodded just slightly, almost imperceptibly, as though responding to her thought.

Pheonix waited with the patience of a mountain, watching them.

"Well, Steele, do you want to start or should I?" Chani asked quietly.

Steele laughed. "Let's trade off."

The sparkle in their eye made Chani wonder how much they knew of her attraction to them. They were certainly amused by the double entendre, but that proved nothing.

"Alright," she said to Pheonix. "You said you can't die."

"To my knowledge, yes."

Green light.

"Do you know why?"

"No."

Green light.

"The slavers pitted you in arena fights; they raised you. From infancy?"

"Yes and no."

Green light.

"What exactly happened?"

"Your crystal only went back ten years. I am twenty-one. I remember my birth."

Green light.

"Do you remember before birth?" Steele asked, and Chani shot them a sharp look.

Pheonix met Steele's gaze evenly. "Of course not."

Green light.

Steele's brows lowered. Chani stared at them. What the hell was up with them today?

"Tell us what you remember," Chani said before Steele could pursue more useless questions.

"Being shown to a man. My father, I suppose. He was displeased. After that, I was taken away by a woman. She gave me to one group of slavers, though I was passed around between varying slaver vessels because I kept destroying them."

Chani was certain the other two would hear her neck snap as her head jerked to look at the box but couldn't stop the motion.

The green light shone as if laughing.

She pinched the bridge of her nose between forefinger and thumb and squeezed her eyes shut. Steele seemed equally speechless, because for a few moments, silence reigned.

"You," Chani started when she felt she could control her voice, "as a — a toddler — *destroyed* — *several full-sized slaver vessels?*"

"To my knowledge."

Green light.

Despite herself, she had to ask: "*How?*"

"They were unable to contain me by any method they tried, at first. Paired with my apparently-unnatural strength and inability to feel pain or die, I would escape and find things to play with. But toddlers naturally play in destructive ways until or unless taught otherwise, a life skill no one bothered to impart to me at the time. I remember opening metal panels and pulling wiring, and smashing consoles, among other things."

Green light.

"And they eventually did find a way to contain you?" Steele asked, their voice weaker than usual.

"Yes. Though I don't know by what method. It was metal of some kind, which kept me caged for another few years before I could bend the bars. At that point, I'd consciously chosen to stop trying to escape, though."

Green light.

"And — because you can't die, you survived the ships catastrophically failing in various ways," Chani confirmed, and neither she nor Steele stopped themselves from staring openly at the box.

"That is correct."

Green light.

The two Commanders shared an incredulous look.

"How did you end up on yet another slaver vessel each time?" Steele asked.

"I don't know."

Green light.

"Except for when 'the Death Dealer' interfered, which was later in your life?" Chani prompted.

"Yes."

Green light.

The Death Dealer, Chani thought. *Wonderful. Well, silver lining, this kid could be the key to finally getting his ass, Creator. If I'm right, he's literally been passed around between some of the worst, most elusive criminals in the Dark Sector. How did they let him escape? They're doing genetic manufacturing now? Or was he sold to them from some completely separate agent? If he's a product of it, how is he immortal with no magic and no technology? Did they make some kind of incredible breakthrough that even we couldn't?*

Either way, if the Death Dealer is involved and came for him **twice**, *that suggests that he's been following this kid's development, which is in itself ... I don't even know. It's pure ridiculousness no matter which way you look at it. Not to mention Temperjoke's involvement. What the actual hell is that?*

Then, with striking clarity, she thought, *This kid could be the find of the Age.*

Focus.

"There were many individuals who interfered in your life. Other than the moniker 'the Death Dealer,' had you heard names, bits of interesting information, anything that could point us to their identities?"

"No. It seemed everyone referred to each other in code."

Green light.

Chani swore internally. Well, it had been a long shot.

She considered asking if he knew the location of any of the places he'd been to, but with almost none of the Dark Sector mapped, even if he somehow knew the direct coordinates used by the slavers, it wouldn't make any difference. They couldn't get there. The frustration was choking.

The one place they might have been able to find, the 'pleasure ship,' had been destroyed, so that was no help, either.

"Okay, so here's part of it," she said. "You had many high-profile criminals and other persons of interest involved in your life somehow, inexplicably. The Death Dealer is well known to us, as is the man who teleported you out of the slavers' pits; Temperjoke, the Ascended of Chaos."

"I have read of the Ascended."

Green light.

"Why Temperjoke would appear now after so long being under the radar," Steele said as an aside to Chani, "and in this fashion ..."

Chani shrugged in bafflement. "Let's try to stay on-topic." Then, to Pheonix: "Are you a product of genetic experimentation?"

"I don't know."

Green light.

"Hmm. Do you know what you are? Are you hominin?"

Pheonix paused to consider this. "I don't know. I don't think so. My appearance seems to deviate from hominins in significant ways."

Green light.

"There weren't any others like you, at your ... father's home, or with the slavers?"

"There were no other children at my father's house, though I am led to believe by his statements that there have been more. I don't know where they might be — if he disposed of them or if they met a similar fate to mine."

Green light.

"Okay. The old man. Who was he?"

"I don't know."

Green light.

"You never got a name?" Steele pressed.

"No. One person called him Maester."

Green light.

"Well, that's a common title on Archaic Earth. We could potentially find record of him, given your general location in relation to the Market. His murder will likely get around quickly. We can trace back from there, potentially. How long were you with him?"

Pheonix's eyes rolled upward.

"Five years, two blocks."

Green light.

"The name," Steele said, slowly, "of the one who hired those men to kill the old man. Kavash. Do you know him?"

Chani felt rage dart through Pheonix, like a lightning strike, which startled her thoroughly. It was the first 'true' emotion she'd felt from him.

"I do not," Pheonix responded.

Green light.

"He was on Archaic Earth … easy enough to find." Steele said. "If nothing else we can correct that injustice. He was — "

Pheonix's reaction to the word 'injustice' was strong enough to ricochet in Chani's head.

"Can you help me to do that? *Correct* … injustice?" Pheonix asked, his voice raw.

Chani stared at him. She could sense Steele doing the same.

"Perhaps," Chani said, finally. "But it isn't entirely our choice. If you'll excuse us."

NINE
Not Another Prophecy

Chani and Steele ambled through the halls, taking their time getting to the main entrance of the Medical Center so as to give the individuals who *could* make the choice a chance to arrive. Integrated instant transportation system or no, one didn't rush the King and Queen of the elves, the Xenobiarch (head of the xeno-mechanics) and the Biarch (head of all the elven Healers on Terelath).

But one also didn't make them wait, so they weren't ambling *too* slowly.

"What do you make of him?" Chani asked Steele, her arms crossed over her chest.

"Just what you say; a puzzle. Origin unknown, species unknown ... but I don't think he's dangerous. In fact, I feel rather ... drawn to him."

Chani nodded slightly. Her own thoughts on the subject, almost word for word.

Just as they stepped into the foyer, the main oculus leading to the outside opened and four people entered.

Chani was always stunned by the King and Queen of the elves, no matter how many times she saw them. The Queen could have been carved from alabaster, her every move so graceful she gave the impression of moving through water, or being unbound by gravity. She had matching apple-red eyes and hair, the latter of which fell to her hips in lustrous waves and was held back by a simple crown of delicate, pure white leaves. Today she wore an understated robe of hunter green lined with emerald green.

The King could have been her twin, but for green eyes and shoulder-length black hair. Elves didn't generally have much or any body hair — except for the King, who sported a full, neat beard. He wore a crown and robes matching the Queen's, though his crown held a single, perfectly cut emerald set just over his forehead.

The most striking thing about the elven royalty, though, wasn't their beauty, but their air of profound sadness.

They were burdened with the weight of the elven species, who themselves bore the whole of the ordered metacosm split between them and the Rangers. If it weren't for the elves and Rangers, evil would certainly overrun everything in short order. While the Accord was technically the intra-metacosmic alliance of sorts, the Accord generally looked to the Rangers and elves for support on most things — resources, knowledge, technology ... and firepower.

The Accord legislated, and mediated, and as an organization it was damn good at that. But it was toothless to enforce any legislation without the Rangers, and the Rangers were necessarily beholden to the elves.

Chani had a great many complicated feelings about *that* bit, none of which she was particularly inclined to ruminate on while looking at two people who were her dear friends.

Aside from the expected stress of politicking, there was great sacrifice to even take rule of the elves; the Queen had once been a Lady, and the King a Bladesinger. One didn't become a leader of the elves for want of authority. The prospective leaders volunteered, and if confirmed by Yggdrasil, gave up their powers and immortality (reducing their lifespan to about two thousand). The King had returned his Lawblade to the Altar of Law, and the Queen had transferred her power to a chosen child.

The elves, in the time before Time, had had their Iyavesti (meaning forever-teacher in ancient elven) Shahharath Aaldur, who had raised them alongside Spiraea. After the Great Demon War, the Iyavesti and the elven Firsts went to sleep in the Vault of Firsts. The elves had then adopted a de facto monarchy, but for some reason most of that royalty only lived a hundred or so years after being crowned.

Oddly, that pattern had been broken with these two, who had been alive since the Fourth Age — something that likely frustrated the Council, consisting of elven Seconds (the direct children of the Firsts, who themselves were birthed directly by the Creator) and a few Thirds.

The rapid change of monarchy heads in contrast to the immortal Council had wildly swung the power balance of leadership to the Council's favor, to the point where the King and Queen were figureheads and damn near everyone knew it.

Even them, Chani suspected, gazing at the King and Queen. Probably another reason for the sadness.

Behind the King and Queen were the Xenobiarch and Biarch — two Firsts, themselves — individuals that, despite being complete opposites, were astonishingly good friends. The Xenobiarch was as flagrantly machine as possible. Undisguised cybernetics were chromed and polished, lights flashed on his body in tune with his movements, his thoughts, his impressions. It made him hard to ignore and easy to read. There were only two things left elven on the man: his brain ... and his eyes. In his words, machines 'see things weird.'

Being a First, Chani wasn't exactly sure how he'd accomplished any of that or how it functioned (Firsts were closer to demi-gods than the rest of the species they'd spawned), but she hadn't gotten a chance to ask yet. The Xenobiarch was the penultimate social butterfly, and finding time to talk to him one-on-one was as difficult as securing a seat for a concert of the latest sponsored genius to come out of Pit Stop, the manufacturing planet where creatives went to 'make it.'

The Biarch, on the other hand, was a completely natural elf. Dressed in a simple, undecorated robe, his long hair had never seen scissors and never seemed to get tangled. Chani, with her hip-length hair a rat's nest every morning, envied him for that. He piled it atop his head in an arrangement that was more function than beauty, mostly to keep it from dragging on the ground. It still managed to look nice, even so.

The oculus for the Medical Center closed behind the four elves and Chani felt a brief surge of triumph. Neither the Chosen nor any Council lackeys had tailed them to inject their unwanted opinions. That meant that they'd heard of Pheonix (there was no way they hadn't; like everyone else in the room, they had their secret eyes and ears) but had dismissed him as unimportant. *Good.* If Chani's hunch was correct — and her hunches usually were — Pheonix would prove his importance too late for them to do anything about.

Chani and Steele crossed the intervening space and both officers saluted. The King smiled and waved the gestures down.

Four of the most influential people in Terelath — and by extension, the metacosm — stood in a line in front of Chani and Steele.

"So, we're here because of this ... Pheonix, was it?" The Xenobiarch said in his brusque manner.

"Indeed, sir," Steele replied.

"Fell out of a damned tear," the Xenobiarch said, shaking his head. "Can't believe this."

Chani tried not to laugh at his characteristic bluntness. "Did you have a chance to talk to your people that worked on him?" she asked both of them.

"Ayup," was the Xenobiarch's response, and from the Biarch Chani got a "Mhm."

"Opinions?"

"His body taking to cybernetics as fast as it did is a wonderful opportunity," the Xenobiarch said. "If we can keep him around and study what makes him so synchronous, we may be able to use that knowledge to lower the rate of rejection and adjustment time."

"What if it's just something unique to him, like he has an unusual force of will or control over his body?" Steele asked.

The Xenobiarch smirked, lights flashing down his cheeks. "There's nothing we can't learn to duplicate."

"My Healers were wondering how he wasn't a puddle of goo, given the kind of genetic errors they saw," the Biarch said thoughtfully, in his quiet manner. "Aside from that, he apparently cannot die, and feels no pain. What could that mean for us, to find the alleles responsible for that? Do they exist in us as well? Could they be simply turned on? Or could we manufacture something similar?"

"Here's the real question; what do you *sense* from him?" Steele pressed.

The Queen looked up, her eyes distant; then the King did the same. The Biarch closed his eyes.

"I sense no danger from him," the Queen said in her husky voice.

"I sense … awakening," the King added cryptically.

"While I agree," the Biarch said, then sighed, "he is still an unknown. We have been fooled before."

Silence fell.

As much as the elves and Rangers, with the metacosm on their shoulders, wanted to provide a comforting competency for the role they'd had thrust upon them, infallibility was impossible.

Just after the Elysian Conflict, a mere three hundred years past, an Elysian had come to Terelath, claiming asylum. He'd been subjected to all the tests, had passed them, and was eventually put on probation. Years went by. He was a model citizen. Then, just when everyone's attention had turned elsewhere, he struck.

Chani closed her eyes, trying not to think about it. A sobering day for Terelath.

The oculus opened; six heads turned. Those heads immediately bowed to the elven Prophet.

The elves did not physically age. They were not subject to the cellular breakdown that so many other sapient/humanoid species were, which caused the process known as 'aging.' Yet this elf was hunched, his face weathered and wrinkled. He was another First, like the Xenobiarch and Biarch, but remained strangely distant from them and the few other Firsts on Availeon. Chani could never put her finger on what the deal was between them, but she wasn't nosy enough about interpersonal relationships to pursue it.

"Ah, here you all are." He smiled.

He wore an undecorated robe and leaned on a rather plain staff. The only thing spectacular about him was his age.

"You have been looking for us, Prophet?" The King prompted.

The Prophet nodded a few times in the manner of the elderly. Chani smiled to herself; she happened to know that he affected that 'elder, infirm of mind and body' thing. For what reason, though, wasn't really apparent. He never honestly answered any questions on the subject.

Or, really, on any subject.

He apparently just liked to tweak peoples' noses. Quirky old dude.

"Knock it off." Chani said. "Why'd you come all the way down here?"

The Prophet snorted. "You, missy, are no fun."

Chani stared at him with her brows raised and he grinned cheekily in response.

"Fine, fine," the Prophet said. "About this Pheonix lad. I wanted to catch you all before you made your final decision."

"Did you have something to add?" Steele asked.

"In a manner of speaking. I merely wanted to remind you of the prophecy."

"*Which* prophecy?" The Biarch asked, smiling.

The Prophet cleared his throat and stiffened his back, looking up. His manner took on that of a child asked to perform something memorized. His voice became the sing-song recitation of someone else:

"*In the waning Age, upon the disappearance of the Prime Forces, the creation of justice will be the herald to change and bring new life to the Creation.*"

Silence took up its crown and surveyed its subjects.

"I'm curious," Chani said, "as to what that gobbledygook has to do with our current situation."

The Prophet whipped around and drew himself up, fixing her with an angry, bright eye … and then deflated, laughing.

He spun around on a heel and strode away with dexterity belying his apparent age, waving his staff over his head.

"Could be no-thing, could be all-thing. Do I have to explain *every-thing* to you people?"

The oculus opened, swallowed the Prophet in light, and then closed again.

The Xenobiarch shook his head. "Crazy old kook."

"Did that help us any?" Steele asked.

The King chuckled. "Despite his … nature … I'm certain the Prophet would not involve himself if it weren't important. And, more particularly, if this boy weren't important. Perhaps we should show a little blind faith and try to forget the pain of the past."

"I agree," the Queen added softly. "We shall just have to keep an eye on him." She lowered her chin and smiled, looking at Chani. "I anticipate seeing what you make of him."

Chani pressed a hand to her chest, feigning surprise. "*Me* Whatever, Lady Queen, makes you think I will have anything to do with the matter from this point on?"

The Biarch smiled, the King put a hand over his mouth, Steele chuckled, and the Xenobiarch rolled his eyes.

"Malarkey and falsehoods," the Xenobiarch said.

Chani just grinned.

"Then, I believe we are decided?" the King said.

"What do you want us to do with him?" Steele asked.

"Teach him, train him. He asked you to help him 'correct injustice'?" The King responded, to which Steele nodded. The King gave a ghost of a smile. "Then show him how."

"Under whose authority?" Chani asked.

The King and Queen exchanged glances.

"I believe we shall take responsibility for him. He was found on our lands, and that will suffice until we have a better idea of whose jurisdiction he falls under," the King answered.

Chani bowed her head in a sign of respect and assent.

The King and Queen inclined their heads in return and turned. The Biarch crossed the room to speak with a couple of Healers that were waiting for his attention, and the Xenobiarch followed the King and Queen.

Chani turned slightly to Steele, folding her arms slowly over her chest. She took a deep breath. Steele met her gaze and lifted their brows, smiling.

She shoved their shoulder with hers. "Don't give me that look."

She spun on one heel, shaking her head. Steele chuckled behind her and fell into line as she made her way back to where Pheonix was being housed.

Time to break the good news to him. She could guess what his reaction would be.

TEN
Broken System

Pheonix stared at Chani after she'd delivered her news. "Okay."

Someone came in, handed off a bundle that Pheonix found to be clothes. Guessing what was expected of him, he got off the bed and looked at Chani and Steele.

"I am not supposed to show other people my naked body," he recited blandly.

The two Commanders about-faced. Pheonix tore open the wrapping of the bundle, which appeared to be some kind of plastic. It immediately began to degrade as it was breached, which he found interesting. Atop the cloth was a card proclaiming this to be a 'Ranger Generic Jumpsuit' with a list of numbers that he guessed were his measurements. They'd probably been taken when he was unconscious.

He shook out the cloth: it was a loose bodysuit, dark blue and soft. Beneath it were black boots of the same odd shape as his feet.

Pheonix discarded the robe he'd been dressed in when he awoke on the table and put everything from the bundle on.

"I'm done," he said.

Chani turned around and clapped her hands, looking first at Steele. "What do you suppose we do next?" she asked Steele.

"Lodging, a brief tour of the relevant parts of Terelath. We'll need to do aptitude testing." Steele looked thoughtfully at Pheonix. "Round up a group of trainers who'd be willing to take him on. I'll make some calls, see who I can rope into it, if you'll handle the tour? I'll tell them to meet you at the training field at, uh …" they glanced at their finger for some reason, "Fourteen-hundred?"

Chani nodded. "Sounds good to me. Come with me, Pheonix."

Chani left the room and Pheonix followed her. He looked to all sides, noting the abstract patterns of reflections from the sunlight through the amethyst, noting the Healers (who mostly appeared to be elves of some description) passing to and fro, and their reactions to him. Chani was easy to follow even without watching her; he could orient himself based on the click of her boots.

He was willing to trust these people because he'd 'peeked' Chani and found nothing concerning. She seemed to be exactly what she said — someone actually trying to help him.

Anyway, the old man's teachings had covered much about the Rangers and the Accord, and Pheonix had so far not found any reason to believe he wasn't exactly where they'd said he was.

And even if they *were* lying, well … he'd deal with that in good time. He also had no reason to believe that if the slavers — apparently one of the most depraved, evil, and murderous groups out there — couldn't kill him, that the Rangers and Accord and elves would fare any better even had they the desire to.

They crossed the wide space where all the halls met, opening into the courtyard, and Chani paused.

"Welcome to Terelath, home city of the elves, on the planet Availeon, system Vega. We are standing before the Medical Center."

Pheonix drank it in. White cobblestones paved the path to the Medical Center, but the feel under his feet was not unpleasant — smooth and almost soft. Artfully abstract living trees — their bark a shimmering silver, leaves the purest emerald — lined the wide, gently sloping pathway that led down into a massive thoroughfare. The city itself was so large, it disappeared into atmospheric distortion beyond the farthest distance he could see. Sapients wandered by — of all shapes and sizes, forms and types — some recognizable, some not, even with all his reading. Almost no two were alike. The Market, while it had been a bustling place of plenty, had nothing on the sheer diversity of Terelath.

As his eyes settled on each thing he didn't recognize, something in the back of his mind piped up with names and information. Probably one of the new implants. It was somewhat disorienting at first, but he wasn't averse to new information in any form.

He suffered a brief flash of understanding; this was where he was meant to be. Maybe not permanently … but here and now.

He could hear Chani as she turned, feel her gaze on him. He nodded and met her eyes. She seemed to need some kind of response. Was she waiting for him for some reason? Social interactions other than with the old man, who didn't talk much but to teach, was proving much harder than anticipated.

She jerked her head to indicate a pedestal next to the oculus entrance to the Medical Center, over which a blue crystal floated.

"Hey. 'Mere." Chani said. "This is a transportation pedestal. You touch the crystal, tell it where you want to go and how many people you will be transporting. Terelath is like a lotus flower." She held her hand out, palm up, fingers curled, in a basic representation of the shape of a lotus.

"The bottom layer of 'petals,' if you will, of the Terelath 'flower' are four in number, and support the rest of the super-structure. Aside from supports, they're used as transportation hubs. The next ring of petals above that are six in number, and those are the ones you'll be most concerned with while you are here. On each petal is a district. We're in the Elven District, which houses the elven governmental buildings, Medical Center, and one of the three lifts to the Seat of the Chosen, as well as the homes of people who work here and a few other things I won't bother naming."

He nodded.

"Next to the Elven District is the Evil District," she continued. "That's a no-go zone for our people."

He stared at her, briefly stunned into an inability to react. "Am I to believe that you *harbor* evil?"

She studied him, then sighed and cracked a grin. "You hungry? I'm starving. Haven't had a bite to eat since this morning. We'll continue this conversation over some lunch, hmm?"

"I can't eat food," he said sharply, not bothering to hide his anger. "I can only have nutrient pills."

She side-eyed him. "Well come with me anyway, then. It'll be another view of Terelath."

He thought about that, then nodded, holding himself in check as best he could.

Unbidden, he remembered a thought he'd had five years ago in the Market: how in order to truly honor his young self's vow to kill all the slavers, he'd need to dismantle or change the system that allowed them to exist. He got the sick feeling that within mere hours of being in this central place of the metacosm, he'd already seen a facet of that broken system.

For now, he put the thought aside with effort. The conclusion he'd come to then — that he didn't have the power or knowledge to change things — still stood.

Teleportation was not unlike the feeling of traveling to Archaic Earth from the arena. There was the brief sensation of weightlessness, then the world abruptly reformed around him into something else accompanied by the reassertion of gravity. He shook his head and blinked hard a few times. Chani held out a hand, presumably to help him keep his balance, but he smoothly avoided it.

"I don't like to be touched," he said. "I will be fine."

She withdrew her hand. "Noted."

They stood to one side of a dome so large he almost lost its curve in the distance. From what he could see, the outer perimeter was lined in boxy metal things, all roughly the same shape and dimensions but each with different lettering, decoration, and color. Across the floor of the dome, the boxes changed to stalls, where people cooked food. The smells were varied and complex.

And in the middle, tables. More bodies — sitting, wandering, eating, talking. A couple of the nearer occupants glanced their way, but the interest was short-lived.

"The Market District," Chani said. "Or, more specifically, the cafeteria. There's thousands of cuisines from hundreds of planets and species. You can't eat anything at all?"

"I can eat occasionally, but not for every meal."

"When was the last time you did? This would be a good learning experience."

"Long enough," he said after thinking about it.

She burrowed her way into the crowd, and he followed, to a stall across the dome-space. A tiny, wrinkle-faced man with sinewy arms hovered over a deep, curved metal pan, from which steam energetically belched. Pheonix peered past Chani's shoulder (which wasn't hard; the tall woman was still almost a foot shorter than himself) into the steam while Chani and the stall purveyor conversed.

The man threw liquid into the pan and it sizzled. Next came chopped greens, onions, garlic, mushrooms, and plenty of chilis (all of which he recognized since similar varieties existed on Archaic Earth — he wondered if this was an Earth cuisine stall), which the man sloshed around vigorously with a long-handled utensil. Then in went some unidentifiable meat, and finally, the man turned and fished a handful of noodles from a bucket behind him. A few more condiments that Pheonix couldn't begin to describe followed, and the little man made up two bowls of the stuff. He handed them to Chani, who laughed at something he was saying that Pheonix hadn't been paying attention to.

Chani balanced the bowls on her forearm (Pheonix idly wondered how she didn't burn herself: the bowls were steaming) and accepted two bottles of what appeared to be water.

They settled at a nearby table and Chani broke out what she called chopsticks. He noted how she gripped them, how she balanced her bite at the end — then copied her exactly.

The food was like nothing he had ever tasted, and he was immobilized as his brain set about separating and logging the flavors and compositions of his first bite. Meals with the old man, when he had had them, were sparse and repetitive due to the limitations of their immediate foraging area. He realized when he came back around that Chani had ceased eating; she was watching him.

"How is it?" she asked.

Pheonix thought about that. "I've never eaten anything like this."

"Well, what is your opinion? Do you like, dislike? Is it weird?" she pressed.

"It's different."

She fell silent and they ate for a little while. He didn't know what she wanted from him. Nutrition was just something to replenish his reserves so he could keep going until another resupply was needed. An endless cycle of the survival of sustenance-reliant physical bodies.

It occurred to him that he likely could stop intaking nutrients entirely, given that he was somehow immortal, but he'd been starved by the slavers on occasion and it hadn't been pleasant. Much like being in a situation where he didn't have access to the right kinds of gases for breathing, he could endure it, but his body still screamed for the thing he was lacking. It was stressful, mentally, and he wasn't eager to repeat either experience.

He finished and set the chopsticks crosswise across the bowl, then drank his entire bottle of water. Chani looked up, noodles hanging from her mouth. She slurped them, glancing between his face and empty bowl.

"So ... you've eaten with chopsticks before?"

"No."

Chani's brow wrinkled. "How — "

He gestured to the table next to them, where two bowls had been left behind with the chopsticks crosswise over the rim.

"Ah."

He waited for Chani to continue, watching her.

"Pheonix," she said. "It's rude to stare at someone."

Extended period of looking at a person = not socially acceptable. Logged.

He nodded and looked away, instead observing the individuals around them eating, moving, conversing. He tried not to let his gaze linger on any one person for too long, lest he 'stare.'

The clack of chopsticks prompted him to look back. Chani folded her hands on the table and leaned over them slightly.

"In order to explain the Evil District, you have to understand the balance. The Maester you were staying with on Archaic Earth — did he ever teach you of the balance?"

"No," Pheonix said cautiously. The word made him fidgety.

"'The balance' refers to the equilibrium of good and evil in the metacosm, an equilibrium that the Chosen work to maintain, guided by the Obelisk of Time, a Creator artifact. Every initiated species and planet and civilization across every spectrum, across all the metacosm, has a representative here in Terelath. That includes evil. But in order to ensure the safety of noncombatants, the Evil District is shut down to the outside. It has its own separate transit hub and an extremely strict set of permissions for who gets in and out. I don't go there; I'd be killed. That's just the nature of it. This is what the Creator set for us."

Something about the set of her lips, the way she pronounced the words, the subtly-hardened look around her eyes, alerted Pheonix, but he wasn't nearly familiar enough with either social interaction as a whole or Chani herself to be able to decode what the hell he was seeing.

Then his eyes unfocused involuntarily while he tried to digest the information she'd delivered.

So it wasn't just that the system was cracked enough to let people like the slavers slip through — they and their ilk were being *actively protected* as some kind of legitimate culture? Is that what he was to take from this?

What kind of cruel Creator would *deliberately* set a path of such heinous suffering to a subset of its children? Nothing he'd read about the Creator from the old man's books gave him the impression that the Creator wanted its creations to suffer; rather, he'd read of only overwhelming love. According to theologians, sapients had been modeled after the Creator in some form or fashion, though there were as many theories as to the specifics of that form or fashion as there were stars in the night sky. Pheonix was in the camp that sapiency was a scaled-down copy of the Creator's unfathomable mind — that all the calculations and emotions and processes of sapiency were gifts directly from the Creator.

And while it was true that one of the criteria for sapiency was violence for the sake of it (nonsapient and sentient beings both only attacked with clear reason), Pheonix refused to believe that the Creator itself was as needlessly callous as the kind of sapient that dominated organizations like the slavers.

It was senseless on a level that made his skin crawl. But he had no evidence, and he also didn't know this woman well enough to question the basest philosophies of a culture she clearly had a lot of contact with. He realized with distaste that silence, too, was survival.

So in the end, he merely nodded.

"So," Chani held her hand up again in that lotus shape. "The Evil District, the Elven District. Next to the Elven District on the other side is the Ranger District, where our operations command on Availeon is. Beyond that is the Merchant District — which is probably self-explanatory. Then the Industry and Market District — where we are currently, as I said. And the final petal, on the other side of the Evil District, is the Manor District, where the Council lives. There's two more layers of petals, but there's no need to go over them now. You'll learn all about that stuff during your training. Speaking of … " She stood. "Come on, it's thirteen-thirty. We'd better get over to the training grounds."

Back to the crystal they went. This time Pheonix was ready for the transportation disorientation and Chani didn't attempt to steady him.

When his vision settled, it was presented with an entirely new environment.

Surrounding them on all sides were woods that seemed to stretch on to infinity. That was unexpectedly comforting. Directly ahead of him was an open area surrounded by a low wall. This area seemed to be split up into sections. There were targets and weapon racks on the far wall. Outside the wall and to his left, there was a grassy area peppered in small white blossoms and a pond with a little waterfall. Near the pond were flat rocks, worn smooth. Beyond the rocks, closer to him, a small group of cottages, set maybe fifty feet from one another.

Behind him was the teleportation pedestal.

Chani stepped past him, smiling, and clapped her hands. "I guess we're a little early. Come on, I'll show you your quarters."

Pheonix ducked slightly to avoid the plant that hung over the door; someone two inches shorter would not have even noticed it. Chani didn't notice it, but she did notice him noticing it.

"Home sweet home," she said. "Sorry about that. Can't swing a dead cat in an elven city without hitting a plant and then getting yelled at for it."

He didn't even want to try to decode that statement.

I can stand up in here, thought Pheonix. The cottage was a one-room affair, but he was used to that. It was even smaller than the space he'd shared with the old man, with a bed, terminal, window, storage chest, bookcase, a single-person booth (which his implant identified as a 'refresher,' a device for cleaning physical bodies via the utilization of sound waves), sink/mirror, a little table with two small stools, and a metal box similar to the ones in the cafeteria but smaller.

She sat down at the little table.

"Coffee, hot, sweet." Chani reached into the open face of the metal box and pulled out a steaming mug.

"A replicator," she explained. "If you do happen to want food, this is how you can get it without leaving. It also dispenses your nutrient pills. We analyzed your biometrics when you were in the Medical Center, so it has your profile already loaded into it, though you'll need retesting occasionally. But we'll deal with that when we come to it."

He stared at the squat metal box. "How does this make food?"

"Ah," Chani said, sounding delighted. She slapped the top of it affectionately. "This baby can hold so much mycelium." At Pheonix's blank stare, she sighed. "Inside each replicator is a self-contained, self-replicating ecology of a specially-engineered mycelial mesh. It has most of the necessary base species-specific nutrients, but it's lacking in certain amino acids and molecular compounds that make up flavor and scent."

"How does that become coffee?"

"When the machine gets the input for a meal, it gathers a certain amount of the mycelium threads, mixes it with the appropriate aminos and other compounds, adds water if necessary from the external hookup, and weaves it into the desired shape with this." She pointed at the nozzle from which the coffee had poured. "It's not going to be as good as fresh, but it's good enough for someone stuck on a ship in the middle of space two systems from the nearest starbase. Or, in your case, when you just don't want to head down to the Market district."

"I see."

"Well, what do you think?" she asked after a brief silence.

"I don't know."

"It's a little overwhelming, I know. Just do your best. You'll get used to it."

A voice called from outside: "Abyss?"

"Waiting on you!" she called out the door.

"Oh, you *are* here. I thought you were off still giving the ten-cred tour."

Chani stepped out, laughing, and Pheonix followed her.

Five people stood, staggered, in front of the teleportation pedestal. Five sets of eyes settled on Pheonix. It was slightly uncomfortable.

Leftmost and a step ahead of the rest was Steele.

"Pheonix, I have some friends for you to meet," Steele said, gesturing at the group. "These will be your trainers for your time in Terelath. Prime Lady Crosinthusilas will instruct you on the lore, history, and mythology of the known universe."

Crosinthusilas was an elf floating a few inches off the ground and wearing a white robe embroidered with green and gold flowers. A jagged scar ran vertically across her throat. She had the manner and features of a bird of prey, all predatory sharp angles. Her long hair, the color of brass, was pulled back into a tight braid. Her eyes were a bright green and her skin the white of freshly fallen snow.

"It is a pleasure to meet you." She didn't open her mouth to speak; her voice was whispery and it tickled Pheonix's brain.

Steele went on: "First and Foremost Ranger Faranthalassa, Elven Master of Propriety, Servant of Matilde, Acolyte of Spiraea Lady of the Woods. He will be teaching you about metacosmic interactions, ethics, and propriety."

Faranthalassa was a tall, serious-looking and elegant male elf with medium-length, unbound and undecorated black hair and brown eyes with overly-large irises. His skin was brown, and he was splashed in dark green patches that almost looked like actual leaves and made it hard for even Pheonix, with his excellent vision, to focus on his form. He wore a chain skirt, leggings, and boots, though his chest was bare other than the harness for a simply enormous bow, elaborately crafted and decorated. Next to that was a large quiver containing only four arrows. Finally, he wore a circlet around his forehead of vines and common woodland leaves. Pheonix had noticed that all the elves wore such circlets, made of differing materials. (And, as he thought about it for a moment, the database implant in his head corrected him: they were called garlands, not circlets.)

The elf performed an elegant bow, his hand over his heart, and said; "Master Pheonix."

Pheonix was instantly drawn to his calm presence and confident movements, though some emotion hovered on his face that Pheonix couldn't place.

The next in line introduced himself before Steele could speak: "Lord Tyyrulriathula, though you can just as soon drop the 'Lord' part. I'm still in training, myself. I'll be working with you on martial matters and the like."

Several things made this Tyyrulriathula unusual: his hair was short in the back and brushed his cheeks in the front (most elves kept their hair long all around), and it was also two-toned — black with a patch of cerulean that matched his eyes to either side of his part in the front. He also had several silver piercings in each ear and a sword medallion on a thin silver chain around his neck. He wore a loose slate grey, long sleeved shirt, contrasting against medium brown skin, which was tucked into tight, dark green pants. His garland was one of iridescent crystals, silver metal, and iridescent leaves.

An elaborate Lawblade across his chest denoted him as a Bladesinger, chosen warrior of the Ascended of Law. An image of a Bladesinger flashed across Pheonix's mind's eye, probably provided by the implant, and Pheonix wondered at the difference between the sword this elf carried and the one in the database example. Did each Bladesinger have a different Lawblade?

"He may be young," Chani said as an aside to Pheonix, "and he has a hell of an attitude, but he's one of our best."

"Done, Lord?" Steele asked.

"Yeah, I think so," the young elf chirped, overly cheerful.

Pheonix decided that he liked this elf.

Steele shook their head. "And at the end is the druid Minrathous."

Minrathous was a female hominin. The shortest among them, she had brown hair pulled into a ponytail that fell to the middle of her back, dark blue eyes, and beige skin. She wore an olive-green robe and a red sash, and carried a gnarled staff inset with crystals along its length.

She smiled and inclined her chin in greeting to Pheonix. He mimicked the motion.

"With me, you'll be studying the theories of the schools of magic, and, if you show any prowess, we can teach you the actual application of such things. We'll also cover the general workings of the mind: focusing, meditation, imagination."

"Commander Steele and I," Chani spoke up, "will oversee and be given reports on your progress, and you are free to contact us should you need anything during your training." Chani dug in a pocket and pulled out a small blue crystal surrounded by a brass-colored ring. "This is a communicator crystal. Focus on the face or name of the person you want to 'call' and we will answer if we are able."

Pheonix put it in his pocket.

"Aptitude testing should be next," Chani said.

"Where should we begin?" Steeled asked.

"What are you good at?" Chani asked Pheonix.

"Killing." His blunt response seemed to make them uncomfortable, so he added, "I seem to take well to anything I try, although due to my time in the arena, my current skills seem to lean more towards combat."

"Martial it is then," Chani said. "Lord Tyyrulriathula?"

The elf nodded and broke away from the pack. Pheonix glanced at Chani; she gestured him forward. He followed the Bladesinger through a gap in the low wall and across the yard, aware that the rest of the group was lining up to watch. The elf stopped by the weapons racks Pheonix had noticed earlier and turned around.

"Pick whichever appeals most to you," Tyyrulriathula said, indicating the rack.

Pheonix's eyes ranged over the racks: bows, pikes, axes, two-handed swords, hammers, shields, daggers, even some small firearms — at least one of every type of weapon was represented. He picked up a sword, as that was the weapon he'd trained with the most with the old man. He went to step back … and stopped, feeling somehow naked.

He chose a short sword to hold in his other hand.

Yes, he thought as he stood there, considering his choices. *This feels right.*

Though his studies with the old man hadn't overtly focused on martial training with the intent of combat, and Pheonix had never had to fight for his life on Archaic Earth in the same way as he had in the arena, he still *had* done martial training. The old man had explained that *everyone* in the metacosm knew how to fight — or *should* — so he'd practiced with many weapons and forms of combat. Pheonix had found that dual-wielding — carrying a weapon in each hand — was the most comfortable for him, and he'd often practiced with the old man's sword and the type of handaxe used for chopping vegetation.

Since the specific axe he'd used was a tool, not a combat-designed weapon, it wasn't represented among the ranks in the rack. The short sword had a similar weight and balance, so he figured it'd be a decent replacement.

"I'm ready," Pheonix said, facing Tyyrulriathula.

The young elf nodded. The two squared off in the center of the ring.

Though he hadn't experienced true combat in years, it was almost as though it was set in his core, and he slipped into that mindset with ease. The weighing of the opponent, watching posture and expression, gaze and breathing — all things he did without thinking. But it was more than that; he *felt* his adversary, on some visceral level that no explanation could be put to. Time slowed as Pheonix's body prepared for the fight. But Tyyrulriathula hadn't drawn his Lawblade, so he held himself back, waiting.

He'd long ago learned that the first one to make a move was often the one to lose.

Then ... Tyyrulriathula began to sing.

An unearthly melody that transcended mere sound, it touched something in Pheonix and all around him that was beyond his comprehension, raised goosebumps along his arms and neck.

Tyyrulriathula reached for the sheath across his chest. He pulled the blade within, then released it. It floated away from his hand, and six other blades burst from it to hover nearby. These ghostly copies were not made of metal; one burned, one dripped ice crystals and mist, one was of shifting earth, one a swirling vortex of air, and two others were merely distortions of reality that Pheonix could only occasionally see when they passed in front of something solid.

In any case, the weapons had been bared. A threat was present, and that meant it was time to act.

Pheonix leaped forward and aimed a graceless chop at the elf, intending to gauge his speed and reaction times. A sword was instantly in the way. Pheonix darted to one side and swung both weapons; he was rebuffed.

He realized suddenly that here, in this situation, against this opponent, he could just *fight*. No crowd dictated his every move, no old man yelled from the sidelines about his form or footing. That was interesting. He wondered what would happen if he simply let himself be.

Pheonix shifted his attack, and surprise rippled through the song.

The sparring match was a dance, a back-and-forth of *dodge, thrust, chop, sweep*, turned back by swords that were there or weren't. Many times, Pheonix felt the kiss of flame or the whisper of ice on his skin with near misses. Frankly, he'd have preferred to have watched a Bladesinger fight first, simply because it was fascinating, but he understood why they'd put him immediately against an unknown opponent. This was all part of the test.

Tyyrulriathula remained at the center of his whirling blades like a conductor, dancing away on light feet from Pheonix's strikes while maintaining the song unbroken, his long and lean figure striking an elegant silhouette even in the midst of battle — it looked more performance than martial style.

Pheonix was clunky compared to Tyyrulriathula's Creator-given grace, and it was soon apparent to him —

— the minutiae of his lagging muscles, his inability to regain balance after a four-sword-strike that made him stumble back, his inability to break out of the defensive, the one-two of flying metal streaking for a target that wasn't there any longer —

— that he wasn't going to win.

He stopped.

Pheonix put his weapons down at his sides and stood, watching, listening, to piece together the movements and rhythm. Without the distraction of needing to physically respond, he could focus on getting a better measure of it. The cadence of the song, and the intrinsic pattern within the movements of the swords, were indicators of the mind behind them. Just as surely as a muscle twitching before a stroke, the song was the elf's tell.

The ending blow stopped a hair from Pheonix's chest and Tyyrulriathula's song cut off with an ungainly squawk. There was silence, then, just the wind.

The Lawblade hovered a moment longer, then absorbed its other blades and slid back into its sheath.

Tyyrulriathula stared at him, his face registering a mixture of surprise, suspicion, and confusion.

"What are you doing?" the elf asked.

"Watching," Pheonix answered.

Tyyrulriathula twisted to look at the other trainers, who seemed to share a moment of silent communication, then Tyyrulriathula turned back around with a grin full of child-like mischievousness.

"I guess that's it for me."

The druid — Minrathous — made her way around the wall and into the yard. She and Tyyrulriathula passed, and then she was before Pheonix. She smiled up at him, gently, and raised her hands.

The fireball exploded against his chest before he could even see its formation. He blinked and coughed, the smoke from his bodysuit (which was miraculously not shredded or burned, but now had an unsightly black mark across the chest) irritating his throat.

Minrathous stared at him, wide-eyed. He looked at her curiously, and she, too, turned to have some silent conversation with the other trainers.

Chani vaulted over the wall and came to stand next to Minrathous, her hands in the pockets of her odd blue trenchcoat.

"That was supposed to blow you back ten feet on your ass," Chani explained.

"What does that mean?" Pheonix asked.

"Most likely that you have some natural resistance to magic, which is ... interesting."

"I don't like how you say 'interesting' in this context," Pheonix remarked, testing out some sarcasm. As awkward as it felt, he had to try to adapt to the intricacies of social communication.

Chani's brows went up, then she laughed. "You'll find out why soon enough."

Before he could say that he didn't like how much she was using the phrases 'you'll learn' and 'you'll see' as well, she'd pivoted on one heel.

"Okay gang, looks like we're done here for now," Chani said, then looked back over her shoulder. "Pheonix, everything you need should already be in the cottage for you, but if you do find yourself lacking in something, have questions, or crave sapient companionship, you can either call us via your crystal or find us in the other cottages. We'll be living on-premises for the remainder of your training. Tomorrow we start at oh-four-hundred."

Pheonix nodded. Chani joined the other trainers, and they wandered off.

He looked down at the swords in his hands and decided to train by himself for a little longer, to become more comfortable with a weapon and using his new cybernetic arm. After all, it wasn't like he needed to sleep.

It suddenly hit him that, for the first time in his life, he could make his own decisions.

Fuck no-mind. There was a whole metacosm of things to learn and experience.

"Alright," Chani said and leaned forward, taking a turn to look in each trainer's eyes over the table in a previously-empty Ranger conference room. "Let's talk. What the hell is he?"

"Fun," Tyyrulriathula piped up, but shrank back at the look Chani shot him.

"A problem," Steele said, but *they* didn't shrink from Chani's displeasure.

"That's obvious," Chani said, clipped.

"The answer," Minrathous said wonderingly. She was staring at the table distantly.

"To?"

"A question I didn't know I had."

"For Fug's sake. You all are professionals — excepting you," Chani shot another dagger-glance at Tyyrulriathula.

"Take this more seriously. His early testing came back inconclusive. He's clearly a genetic experiment, but our technology didn't — couldn't — confirm it. The Chosen and Council both have been hounding me all day. I need *data*, not shenanigans. What do we classify him as? What are our informed recommendations on how to proceed? At the very least, whose jurisdiction does he fall under?"

"The Creator's."

Crosinthusilas' whispery voice shut Chani down completely and the Commander openly stared at the Prime Lady, who met her eyes guardedly. But it was Steele who was the first to verbally respond.

"What?" they asked.

"He is Justice," Crosinthusilas continued calmly. Her next word fell with the weight of a starship: "*Ascended*."

The silence that followed was thick.

"That's — impossible," Steele choked, finally. "Ascended *know* they are Ascended!"

Chani sat back, thinking hard, while the others talked around her.

"Do we know enough about Ascended to say that for certain?" Minrathous asked.

"It's never been recorded!" Steele protested. "On the rare occasion an Ascended has gotten involved somewhere, they've announced themself before even showing up!"

"What about Temperjoke?" Tyyrulriathula said.

"*Chaos* is hardly the example for Ascended behavior," Steele said with a snort.

"Even so, things change," Minrathous countered.

"To the point where an *Ascended* wouldn't know its own self? Even if it *were* true, from a purely political standpoint, we can't even *suggest* it without *irrefutable* proof, and if the boy himself can't provide it —"

"I came into being with Spiraea as sister, and Shahharath took me as lover. Do you question my recognition of those who bear the Creator's Light directly?" Crosinthusilas asked, soft and deadly. While Steele didn't fear Chani's ire, they hesitated at rousing the Prime Lady's.

"Faranthalassa?" Chani asked, watching the elf, who had been unnaturally quiet. He glanced around the table, then lifted his chin.

"I agree with the Prime Lady."

"*What?*" Steele started, but Chani put up a hand and they subsided.

"I believe you," Chani said, holding Crosinthusilas' gaze.

The Prime Lady's expression became slightly less prickly.

"But Steele has a point. Our official consensus stays at this table. The King and Queen might already know: they directly ordered myself and Steele to help him 'correct injustice.' But the Council and the Chosen *would* demand proof. And, as illustrious as you are, my Lady, I don't think opinion would suffice." Her heart was pounding as she gave Crosinthusilas a calculatedly empathetic smirk.

To Chani's relief, the elf's lips quirked up, though her gaze didn't soften.

Chani knew she needed to play this right. Just then, she felt as though the entire metacosm were watching her.

"*If* Pheonix is Ascended, *is* Justice," she said, looking from person to person to impress upon them her seriousness, "then something has happened. Farbeit for us lowly sapients to know or get involved beyond supporting him. *If* Pheonix is Ascended, he will make himself known well enough without our interference. And all we must do is protect him until he can protect himself."

After giving them a moment to let her words sink in, Chani leaned back, folding her hands across her lap, and said:

"So let's figure out how to do that."

ELEVEN
The Trainers

Pheonix had fallen into a meditation of physical activity — practicing the movements of using his two weapons — through the night, which made time pass similarly to his state of no-mind. By the time he heard someone calling his name, Availeon's twin suns were up again.

He blinked owlishly, lowered his arms, and turned towards Chani. She strode across the field, Tyyrulriathula trailing behind.

"Have you been up all night?" She asked as she came close.

"I don't sleep."

"Right, of course," she said, almost to herself, and Pheonix wondered at it. Then, to Pheonix: "Well, here's your schedule from now on. In the morning, you have martial training with Tyyrulriathula. After that, Faranthalassa and Crosinthusilas will trade off depending on their particular curriculum, and then it's meditation and magic training with Minrathous.

"Now, that's all pretty regular. Here's where your training differs for any others we handle: we'd like to be able to scan you. Now, what that entails is about an hour of standing completely still while an extremely high-powered scanner breaks you down, unit by unit — " *Unit: a Ranger form of measurement*, one of the implants they'd given him translated in Pheonix's brain " — on a molecular level. We're really curious to find out ... no offense ... what you are."

Pheonix shrugged a shoulder. "I'd like to know, as well."

"Good. After that, due to the nature of your childhood, we believe it would be best if you underwent some counseling."

Pheonix stared at her, processing. "Very well."

"After the counseling, you'll have free time. Since you don't sleep, it's pretty much whatever you want to do. Sound good?"

"Yes."

"All yours, then," Chani said to Tyyrulriathula.

"Ready?" the elf asked, beaming his infectious grin.

Pheonix rotated his shoulders, assessing his physical state, then said, "Yes."

At the end of the last battle with the Bladesinger, Pheonix had gotten the measure of him. He'd spent the hours of the night practicing against that style. So when Tyyrulriathula began to sing, and the blades came out, Pheonix did not hesitate.

The pattern in the song pounded in Pheonix's ears, dissected and flayed apart, and he reacted to it, almost before the swords could.

Shock colored the tone of the elf's song and Tyyrulriathula jumped to the defensive. Pheonix could feel, in that cold logical center of his brain detached from all things, how much faster he was after just one night of practice. And now he had the key to getting inside the Bladesinger's formidable defenses.

"Pardon," a voice said, cutting through the back-and-forth stalemate that had occupied Tyyrulriathula and

Pheonix. Simultaneously, both stepped back from one another. Pheonix lowered his weapons and Tyyrulriathula resheathed his Lawblade.

Faranthalassa stood at the edge of the ring. "Lord Tyyrulriathula, Master Pheonix, I apologize for the interruption. It is time for Master Pheonix's lessons with me, and I request his presence."

They'd fought for hours, judging by the positions of the suns, and now it was time to move on to more intellectual pursuits.

Tyyrulriathula turned to Pheonix. His grin threatened to split his face as he shook his messy bangs from his eyes.

"Tomorrow, then. I look forward to it."

"As do I," Pheonix said, and attempted a little smile.

He seemed to do it right, for he received a wink and an elven salute.

"Have fun," Tyyrulriathula said cheerily, then turned on his heel, inclined his head to the patiently-waiting Faranthalassa, and left the practice ring.

Much later that evening, the setting suns found Pheonix reclining on his cot, book in hand — one of many now scattered around his tiny cottage. The books were all home studies assigned from his classes with Minrathous, Crosinthusilas, and Faranthalassa. To be encircled by knowledge felt right.

A knock sounded.

"Come in," Pheonix called, then set down his book as the door opened. Chani entered, and Pheonix swung his long legs off the side of the cot to sit up.

"Good evening, Commander."

"Wow," she said, washing a brief glance over the interior of his room littered with books. "This just from today?"

"Yes."

"You won't read it all, will you?"

"No. Maybe half. But I am only required to read a chapter each from three."

Chani squinted one eye at him in an unknown expression. Confusion? Suspicion, perhaps. "You're kidding," she said.

"Did that come across as a joke?" Pheonix asked in honest confusion.

"Never mind." She cleared her throat and her demeanor changed slightly in a way Pheonix couldn't identify. "So, how was your first day?"

"It went well."

"How did you get on with the trainers?"

"Faranthalassa was knowledgeable, but boring," Pheonix stated. "If you could, please let him know that I don't need to have the same thing repeated to me over and over. He wouldn't listen to me on the matter; in fact, he became somewhat incensed when I tried to correct him. Everyone else was quite pleasant, and I find myself very much looking forward to sparring again with Lord Tyyrulriathula." He thought about it a moment, then added, "I like him."

Chani laughed heartily.

"What?" Pheonix asked.

Chani's eyes sparkled as she regarded him. "Calling the elven Master of Propriety 'repetitive' to his face is perhaps the funniest thing I've ever heard. And almost everybody likes Tyyrulriathula, at least to his face."

"'To his face'?" Pheonix echoed.

"Hmm ... let me give you a piece of advice, Pheonix. Don't just take everything in and file it away like a computer. Apply your knowledge. Look past the surface of things, learn to read people. It will help you get through this easier, and is a large part of being an effective — and more importantly, alive — fighter."

Pheonix let this sink in and, as it settled into his brain, knew it to be very important. The old man had given similar advice.

He nodded.

Chani smiled genuinely. "I think you'll do just fine," she said warmly. "And I'll make sure to talk to Faranthalassa. I know exactly what you mean — he tends to use many examples regarding the same thing. He thinks it bolsters the point. Anything else?"

"The counselor deemed I have no adverse psychological effects from my childhood," Pheonix said.

Chani tilted her head and looked at him oddly, then seemed to accept this. "Alright, well, if that's the case, more time for other things. I'll be off, then. Let me know if you need anything; I'll be in my quarters. All the cottages look the same, but mine is special. It has my name on it." Chani grinned, and Pheonix determined that she must have made a joke and nodded.

Chani waited, then sighed. "Good night, Pheonix."

Tyyrulriathula stumbled back, his swords interweaving in front of him to form a wall while he recovered his footing.

Slowly, Pheonix had been honing his natural ability to see beyond the physical (the 'peeking' taught to him by the old man, though he didn't call it that in his own head).

The glowing pools within the hearts of living beings, he'd found from his books, were called 'life-sparks," and though his books named the phenomenon, they couldn't give him much more than that. The only information he'd managed to gather thus far was that they seemed to change in shape and color slightly depending on the species of their owner, and were somehow tied to a person's life. While it had been an inborn ability he'd subconsciously used since he was a child, he couldn't control it, and that irked him. So he'd been working on being able to passively see them even while otherwise occupied, like in combat.

Outside a sapient body, the lights and shapes he saw were simply concentrations of power. In other words, a weak spot.

Pheonix hammered at one of the glowing spots in the shield made of swords. The swords scattered, wheeling uncontrollably.

Tyyrulriathula dodged with preternatural grace while his swords came at Pheonix from different angles, attempting to catch him off-guard, but a quick dash forward left them behind.

A moment later, Pheonix's swords hovered, rock-steady, at Tyyrulriathula's throat, the flesh trembling with the elf's racing breath.

Tyyrulriathula stepped back, his arms up. His other swords dissipated like startled birds into shards of light and his Lawblade returned to its sheath. His cerulean eyes sparkled with laughter. "Damn, you got me again."

Pheonix straightened and sheathed his swords. "You fought well."

"Not well enough, apparently."

"No," a deep, quiet voice said from behind. Pheonix turned. "You fought exceptionally. However, Master Pheonix is like nothing we've ever seen."

Another elf had apparently been watching them spar. Like Tyyrulriathula, he wore a garland of crystals, and he also wore the garb of a Bladesinger. He was quite short, with skin almost the color of charcoal, and long, shiny, straight black hair. His features were sharp, his eyes so dark they barely reflected light. Across his chest was not one Lawblade sheath, but two. He had the feel of ... a subdued whirlwind, like a tornado viewed through glass.

Pheonix immediately knew this man was one to command respect.

"Prime War-Bladesinger Zasfioretaeula," Tyyrulriathula said.

Pheonix accessed: *Elven society prizes dispassion, a veiling of emotions, under the impression that it encourages an open mind and peace. Bladesingers infected by the chaos of battle threaten what is termed a Bladestorm, where the force of the emotions all elves repress mix with their natural magic to conjure thousands of blades. While an uncontrolled Bladestorm from an unprepared Bladesinger is capable of massive power, it will attack anything in a given area, including, ultimately, the one that spawned it; thus, Bladestorms are always fatal to their originator. However, Bladesingers caught before they fully manifest a Bladestorm become War-Bladesingers, and are taught how to harness the Bladestorm in battle.*

War-Bladesingers were venerated and feared in elven society for being able to take on an army.

Alone.

"Thank you for coming," Tyyrulriathula continued. "Was that demonstration sufficient?"

Zasfioretaeula stopped close enough for polite conversation, but far enough away to be comfortable. He crossed his arms over his chest, looked Pheonix up and down. "Yes," the War-Bladesinger said in an even tone. "I will take him on as student. But not against me. Master Pheonix, how quickly did you learn Lord Tyyrulriathula?"

"By our second sparring match."

Zasfioretaeula nodded. "Multi-enemy training, against other species, other styles, other techniques, other weapons — this would benefit Master Pheonix the most at this point. I'm afraid battling me by myself would be a waste of our time, although I will certainly pit him against the Bladestorm when I feel he is ready."

Tyyrulriathula's mouth hung open. Finally he laughed and put up his hands, palms out defensively. "Alright, you two have at it."

"We start tomorrow. This will take your martial training time," Zasfioretaeula said. "I suggest you get some rest."

"What is the point of propriety?"

Faranthalassa looked up with an unabashedly startled expression at Pheonix's bold, and out-of-nowhere, question. His gaze went blank for a moment.

"Well, I — propriety is the ... the *rules,* for how elves interact both with each other, and with non-elves."

"Then what is a Master of Propriety? Why do the elves need that?"

"The Master of Propriety is a ... cultural weathervane, if you will. Let me put it this way: we elves are — tied together. We are one. In a very real way. What affects one of us will eventually and inevitably affect others. *This* is why things like Bladestorms and mana-storms are so dangerous. High emotions are an infection among all sapients, but this effect is compounded among elves. We must always be vigilant to act with the utmost of propriety to avoid mass outbreak."

"Shouldn't it just be taught? Or is that what you do? What is your actual job?"

"No, I don't generally teach. You are an exception. I am present at many Council meetings, I help negotiate, I oversee charged situations. The elves' emotions as a whole or in an enclosed area affect my own, allowing me to recognize and quickly respond to agitation."

Pheonix was momentarily stunned.

"That sounds unnecessarily cruel," he said finally.

Faranthalassa blinked. "As Master of Propriety, I feel it is my duty to tell you that what you just said was very rude."

"I cannot lie, Faranthalassa. It goes against everything I stand for. If that means I am, on occasion, 'rude,' then I will accept the consequences. I understand that you are here to teach me how to interact with other sapients in the metacosm and that this is vital information, but I'm swiftly coming to the conclusion that I will be unable to act in any manner that is consistent with the expectations of 'propriety.' Why don't you teach individual elves to control their own emotions? Elves being emotionally tied to one another by nature may be the Creator's design, but the onus for protection against mass infection should be on the society to teach individuals to appropriately respond to their own emotions. Shackling *an individual* to every elf's uncontrolled emotions *is* cruel, and I stand by that."

"I — well, individual elves — our children are — the, the renewal tree ..." Faranthalassa floundered, then fell into an uneasy silence. He cleared his throat. "Culture and tradition are often difficult to explain to outsiders. The only thing you need concern yourself with is the *balance* between directness and politeness. You tend to be too direct, and blaming it on an inability to lie won't get you very far. You don't have to be painfully blunt to avoid lying. Best you keep that in mind, Master Pheonix."

"Concentrate, Master Pheonix," Minrathous murmured; quietly, so as not to distract him.

Pheonix stared at the patch of grass between his outstretched hands, willing it to flame, envisioning the colors, imagining that he could feel the heat. With his mental construct in place, he reached for the Thread of Fire within the Weave ... and, frustratingly, didn't know what he was looking for or how to find it.

The same as the last dozen attempts over several weeks.

An unimpressive wisp of smoke spiraled up from a single blade of grass, swiftly vanishing into the light breeze. He sat back, dropped his hands.

Minrathous sighed heavily. "Stand, Master Pheonix," she said. "I shall be honest with you; you have very little, if any, talent for the spellcasting arts. But," she held up one small hand, index finger extended, "that does not mean you should abandon magical studies completely. Understanding magical theory and application will aid you immensely in forming a solid defense against mages and those enemies who will use the Weave even in hand-to-hand combat. You are a warrior; you know your own strength, but don't let the opposite of your strength be a weakness."

Pheonix nodded, seeing the wisdom in her words and filing them away.

He knew he had no talent for magic. There was no lack of concentration and certainly no lack of study — but he couldn't see or sense the Weave. Which was an oddly specific deficit for him to have, he rather thought.

Though ultimately, he didn't care; he considered magic cheap. He respected Minrathous and the other Weave-users he'd met who obviously used it correctly and for the right reasons, but he'd also read far too many historical accounts of evil mages.

Hell, half of Archaic Earth's history was evil mages.

No temptation would ever be so great for him to turn to using any skill or power for evil. But then, once he made a decision, it was set in stone; it seemed others were not so invariable. One of the things he apparently didn't understand about sapient minds, he supposed.

"Why does your voice not come from your mouth?"

Crosinthusilas looked up from the thick tome open before her and speared Pheonix with an intense look. Perhaps she meant to be disapproving, but the expression softened and she placed her hands carefully on the pages.

Pheonix had learned much in his time on Terelath so far, and some of that knowledge included information from others — students, colleagues, even complete strangers — about his trainers. The Prime Lady was known by many nicknames: the spectre of Terelath; Shahharath's rabid dog; the Thorns of Ice; and yet others. She was a harsh mistress, unyielding in her personality and beliefs, as sharp as the predator she resembled, and remorseless when challenged. But there was a side to her that not many saw, and she'd developed somewhat of an affinity for Pheonix — the boy with the endless lust for knowledge and the perfect memory that defied all logic.

His love for history and lore was almost as great as hers; and so, they had a sort of accord. Neither of them were in any way predisposed to affection, as warriors in their own rights; but they were alike, and that bred familiarity.

That was why, Pheonix thought, the incredibly impertinent (but completely innocent) question hadn't gotten him something far worse than a look.

"I suppose," she said slowly, "that is a historical account of a sort, and would not be too far outside of our current studies to relate. I will begin with things you likely know. I am a First."

Pheonix accessed: *Firsts: the first individual sapients, brought into existence directly by the Creator. In many cases, these Firsts went on to procreate and are on record as the primary progenitors of certain species, like the elves and hominins.*

"I am also the first Lady. What this means is that, in the before-times, I was the first to pluck the Threads of the Weave in the way that Ladies do. I discovered the sounds they made, how they reverberated through Creation, and passed that knowledge down to other elves who were interested. We became Ladies — which, though sex studies is not my forté, I will remind you was originally a physiology-neutral term. I am not a woman nor a man nor anything in between: I am a First. I identify as a woman because I *like* women."

A brief smirk crossed her lips. "It was only after the garlands that the elves delineated into anything resembling the physical sexes of lesser species, and that 'Lady' was restricted to elves with female physiology. But that is irrelevant to the topic at hand.

"We elves weren't originally pacifist by choice, but only because there was no need otherwise. However, the balance was already well-established before the demons ever showed their ugly maws in the Creator's Light. It taught us that we should accept any difference that we came across with open arms; that coexistence was the ultimate expression of the Creator's love. So when the demons burst from their hellish void demanding fealty, the Seconds were content to allow them to subjugate us, so long as we did not have to violate what they saw as the Creator's will — the balance — by killing them.

"Most of the Firsts saw the demon invasion as a rally to change — that how we had always been was not a law set in stone, but growth tailored to our environment. I, especially, was horrified by these ... things, these demons. They warped Creation, tangled the Weave, left burning holes wherever they went. So the Firsts gave the battle call, and we fought, and we paid the ultimate price. That was the Great Demon War."

She steepled her long fingers, leaned forward, fixed her eyes on him intently. Her ghostly voice lowered.

Pheonix stiffened; his entire being focused on her at that moment. Something screamed in him: *This is important! Listen!*

"The demons were not right. They didn't feel like us, or like the Ascended, or even like the angels; their Song was discordant. No matter what shape the Firsts took, no matter what shape our children took, we could always communicate and sense within each other the spark the Creator had given us. But not these things. They felt only of hunger, and burning, and hate. Why would the Creator make something to hurt its children? And not just hurt *us*, but *Creation itself*? Nothing that came before was like that, and, *I* think," she drew herself up proudly, a challenge in her eyes, "they are not of the Creator."

Pheonix was riveted. She had just given him something of massive import — it frustrated him that he couldn't place why, though. But it was filed away, this thing that seemed crucial with no context.

He'd been collecting a lot of those.

"Here," Crosinthusilas said, "if you wish to learn more of the Great Demon War, this will be of *some* use." Her gently stressed *some* was also important, but in that same unplaceable way.

She waved a hand and a book dropped into it, which she held out. He took it from her and cracked it open.

Corroborating the Prime Lady's anecdote, the book recounted the story of the demons rending portals from the place that came, later, to be termed 'the Nether,' and demanding the elves allow themselves to be enslaved. But that was where the book's narrative veered off: it told that the elves had immediately recognized the threat and fought valiantly.

The disparity between the Crosinthusilas' story and the official one made Pheonix's neck prickle. He couldn't identify the reaction, so he filed that away, too. He read on, becoming more confused as he went.

The demons had almost achieved a quick victory. After incurring heavy losses and being pushed back almost to the city that would become Terelath, the elves formed a nigh-impenetrable defense line, but that was all. Nothing they did could kill the demons.

It wasn't until the Rangers (then known as the Planetary Rangers), fresh from their own war on their homeworld of Techno-Earth, had dropped into the fight — bringing lasers, ballistics, plasma, and kinetics — that the elves had managed to catch their breath. Even then, it had not been an assured victory. It had taken a sacrifice of unequaled proportions to end the War — that of the elves' True Immortality.

Elves were initially perfect — one step below the Ascended, indestructible by blade, disease, time, or magic. The only way an elf could cease to exist was if they were to release themself into the life-stream — or, as they found during the war, if they were infected by Nether-flame.

Nether-flame, the demons' substance. Only two things were known about Nether-flame: that it had not existed before the demons poured out of their portals, and that it acted somewhat like fire in that it was ever-hungry and ever-spreading.

To save the universe from the demons, the elves relinquished their True Immortality. They were still immortals, in a sense — they had extended lifespans. But now they could be cut down by blades or destroyed by magic. The energy that was released by the elves' sacrifice pushed the demons back into their tears and sealed them away.

Even such an immense sacrifice could not destroy the demons utterly, however.

"It was during the Great Demon War," Crosinthusilas said suddenly in the quiet of Pheonix's reading, "that it happened. I was engaged in battle with Vulgoth, Lord of the Demons, and he stabbed me through the throat with a Nether-blade. I killed him, though, by reversing my power through the contact. He took it all, and disintegrated. I would have died, but the Rangers purged the poison. They had figured out how to negate a Nether-flame infection. But it did irreparable damage to my voice, and now I speak through magic." She allowed herself a rare, small smile. "Thus, my words do not originate from my mouth."

TWELVE
Imbalance

Pheonix looked up and set his book down at the knock on his cottage door. A glance at his clock — 0045? Who would visit so late?

He opened the door and stepped back, letting Tyyrulriathula in.

"Lord Tyyrulriathula," he said formally by way of greeting.

Tyyrulriathula scrunched up his face, turned in the tiny cottage, and punched a few buttons on the replicator.

"You don't have to be so formal."

"Faranthalassa says — "

Tyyrulriathula turned, rolling his eyes. He held two mugs of frothy brown something in his hands. "Franny has drunk a bit too deeply of the Iyavistis."

Pheonix's database implant supplied: *Iyavistis, the knowledge 'well' of the elven people. Accessible to anyone with elven genetics, it is an information repository contained in the vast mind of the Iyavesti herself, Shahharath Aaldur — and the primary reason why her title, Iyavesti, translates to 'forever-teacher.' Even asleep in the Vault of the Firsts, she continues to teach whichever of her peoples seek her knowledge.*

'Drunk too deeply of the Iyavistis' is a Terelathian elf colloquial saying meaning taking things too literally or seriously.

"Being polite is one thing," Tyyrulriathula was saying while Pheonix accessed, "but propriety doesn't have much of a place among friends."

"I wouldn't know. I have never had a friend before."

Tyyrulriathula plunked the two glasses on the tiny round table in front of the replicator and sat across from Pheonix on one of the two stools. "Well, then I guess since you've surpassed me in martial training already, I'll have to teach you about friendship."

"Is that even something that can be taught? I was under the impression that friendship was one of the more subtle forms of sapient interaction."

"Not literally, not in a classroom setting. And it is, but it's also forgiving and flexible. A friend can be as distant as someone you see once every few years, but you enjoy their company, to someone who is as close to you as a sibling. See? You're already learning." Chuckling, he grabbed one of the mugs and took a deep drink, then pointed at the mug he'd placed across from Pheonix. "Try some, it's beer."

Pheonix took it and obediently drank — and drank, and drank, until Tyyrulriathula said, "Hey, not all at once!"

Pheonix put it down. His fingers were tingling, but other than that, the alcohol had no effect. "But it's good," he protested.

"Of course it is," Tyyrulriathula laughed. "It's dwarven. Crafting beer is a part of their religion, after all."

"I don't think I can get drunk," Pheonix mused after another sip, savoring the flavor.

"That's unfortunate. You've never tried before now?"

"No inclination to do so."

Tyyrulriathula studied Pheonix. The expression on his face, insofar as Pheonix could tell, was somewhere between curious and thoughtful.

"What happened to you?" the elf asked. "How did you end up here? I mean, we had the brief as trainers, but I'd rather hear it from you."

So Pheonix told him — about his birth, infancy with the slavers, his time on Archaic Earth.

"You must have really loved him. The old man," Tyyrulriathula said quietly.

"I don't think I can love. The old man was kind to me; he shaped me from the animal I was into a semi-functioning individual, and taught me about the metacosm. His death was a terrible injustice," he said. Then, sharply, "... one that I have yet to correct. But I will."

"How can you be so sure you can't love? You enjoyed being around him, you miss him, you want vengeance for his death. That sounds like love to me."

Pheonix shook his head slowly, analyzing himself. "You're wrong. I don't 'miss' him. I fully accept that he is dead. I have done some studying on grief and it's often characterized by 'wishing' for more time, or that things hadn't happened the way they did, or some other reaction tied into a desire to change things that can't be changed, which is likely rooted in an emotional response. I don't feel any of those things: neither the emotional response, nor the desire to change things that are in the past or otherwise inherently immutable.

As for 'enjoying' being around him — he taught me many things, and I enjoy learning. He was murdered, so I want vengeance. Not for him, but for the act itself. There would be no difference to me had I found a stranger in that cabin instead of him. At the core of me, I feel nothing."

"Ever?"

"Well," Pheonix amended, "in certain extreme situations, I do feel *something*, as in the case with the old man's murder. I was angry and I still am. Things that people say and do sometimes make me angry, as well."

"Is that it? Anger?"

Pheonix thought long and hard on that. "It is the strongest. There are others: contentment, curiosity, surprise, confusion. But they are subdued. I seem to be most affected by anger and related emotions. Intellectual process seems to dominate what little emotional process there is in me. There are times I can shut down even anger. Though, is useful to me, so I don't often turn it off."

"Sadness?"

Pheonix shook his head.

"Even seeing the old man dead on the floor in front of you?" Tyyrulriathula pressed.

"No. I was confused. But not sad or scared or other things that people ascribe to experiencing the death of someone they spent time with."

Tyyrulriathula hid behind his beer, his eyes downcast. The sounds of the night took over — animals and insects outside, wind through the trees, Tyyrulriathula's sedate breathing. Pheonix respected that his companion must be lost in thought, and so didn't impose.

"The elves must be like you," Tyyrulriathula said finally. "Most elves, that is. I'm not like them. I live in my emotions, from moment to moment ... it's as though, in me, someone turned off the suppression switch." He smiled ruefully. "I'm not sure how many of my people know the whole truth, but I can imagine what the response would be, were they to find out. I'm already not very popular."

"Chani mentioned as much, but I don't understand why," Pheonix said. "You are very friendly."

Tyyrulriathula half-smiled, but the expression was not a happy one. Even Pheonix could tell that. "'Friendly,' yes. It's hard to be openly cruel to someone who smiles all the time." He almost seemed to be talking to himself. He'd been staring into his drink, but looked up as he said: "Pheonix, do you know how old I am?"

Pheonix shook his head.

"I am seventy-three years old," Tyyrulriathula said. "I received my Lawblade seven months ago, and instead of the expected four blades, I was given six. I'm not even considered a true adult in my own society — and I already hold a seat on the Council as befitting my station as a Lord. I was given at the outset, by our patron deity, more blades than half the other Bladesingers have to this day, millennia or even Ages after receiving their Lawblade."

Tyyrulriathula paused, his voice lowered. "They bow to it because Law is infallible, and the Lawblades are incapable of being influenced, but they talk. They aren't sure that I can handle the responsibility, that I can make informed decisions with no life experience — a legitimate concern; I'll give them that. And I stay out of their politics as much as I reasonably can. Though, admittedly, that's more for my own benefit than theirs. When they force me, I work my ass off to make sure they find no flaws in my judgment.

"If they were to find out about my heightened emotions, they wouldn't hesitate to send me to become a War-Bladesinger, regardless of my capabilities ... which would be fine with me, honestly. But the idea of letting myself be shuffled off as a problem to be disappeared bothers me on a level I can't quite comprehend. I feel beholden to tweak their noses; what good is a Council that only hears itself?"

Tyyrulriathula's brows furrowed; he was irritated. This was the first time Pheonix had ever seen him without a ready smile. Pheonix respected Tyyrulriathula; he was a strong fighter for being so young, much like Pheonix himself, and he had a personality that wasn't repugnant. For something to get on the nerves of the easygoing Bladesinger, it must be serious.

"To be honest, I don't get this fascination with being emotionally constipated," Tyyrulriathula went on bitterly. "Why *must* we suppress? The Firsts weren't like this, and look at the things they accomplished! Shouldn't the War-Bladesingers themselves be a hint, a clue that we're going down the wrong path? It happens more and more, and not every Bladestorm is caught before it manifests. A senseless waste of life, because my people can't admit that we need to change.

"So what if it worked in the past? If there was a reason for it then, it's gone now, and it's becoming a detriment. Don't tell anyone I said this, but it all comes down to the balance. We think we need to be neutral in everything we do to respect the balance."

Tyyrulriathula took in a deep breath, held it, and let it out. His shoulders slumped as though the rush of anger had taken a physical toll on him.

Pheonix was paralyzed. Tyyrulriathula's words echoed in his brain, waking that same *something*, that same sense of *importance* that he'd felt only a few times before: when he'd first heard of the Creator, when he'd talked to Chani about justice, and when Crosinthusilas taught him of the Great Demon War.

"I hate the balance," Pheonix said with a venom that left Tyyrulriathula staring.

After a very long pause, the young elf shook his head. "Pheonix, I have a request."

"What is it?"

"Don't say that in front of anyone else. You took a chance telling me that's how you feel, but bring it up to others and you could end up charged with treason. At the least, you'll be ostracized, which might affect your training."

"That doesn't concern me," Pheonix replied evenly. "'Place the laws of God above the laws of Men,' — that's from *human* scripture. Even the most self-absorbed sapients in the universe know it. The balance is wrong. I can't die and I don't feel pain; what is the worst they can do to me? Even the slavers couldn't break me. I doubt my honesty will land me in much worse trouble here."

"That doesn't make your case much better; you sound egotistical."

"That's an interpretation of my words. The perception of others is not my responsibility. Facts and opinion cannot be held as equals, lest the communication within a group seeking to form a consensus on how to progress forward sink into zealotry and petty arguing. Opinion holds weight in the mind that carries it, but it is not objective and can't be taken as such."

"How do you *know*?" Tyyrulriathula asked softly, after a pause. "About the balance, I mean."

"I don't *know* … yet. But meeting evil in the middle can only create more evil, because the evil I know so well has no desire for anything less than total domination. I can't honor your request. It goes against my very being to be untruthful." He hesitated, thinking. "I need to do more research. But the shape I'm beginning to see … if the balance is why the Rangers can't move against the slavers, why the elves are stagnating, why the Iyavesti and other Firsts are sleeping … it can't be what the Creator wants. Lady Crosinthusilas said as much: why would the Creator want its children to suffer?"

Tyyrulriathula's eyes widened at that. He gripped his mug with tense fingers, though the drink itself was long forgotten. "The *Prime Lady* said that?"

"Her exact words, in fact. She told me of the Great Demon War from the perspective of one who had been there. It was her belief that the demons are not of the Creator."

"Not of the Creator ... then *how*?" Tyyrulriathula breathed.

"I don't know, and neither did she. But that is the shape of things. You must feel it, too."

Tyyrulriathula froze. "Yes," he finally admitted in a whisper, almost as though the words were forced out of him — as though he were listening to himself speak. "The balance is wrong."

Pheonix dipped his chin meaningfully, then raised his glass to let the warm beer, pleasantly bitter and complex, slide down his throat. He finished it while Tyyrulriathula struggled with himself, and set the mug down with a barely-audible *choonk*.

Finally Tyyrulriathula raised his own mug and downed half of it. When he placed it on the table, it seemed to have steadied his rattled nerves, because a slight smile played around his lips.

"Thank you," he said to Pheonix.

"For what?"

"For listening," Tyyrulriathula said at last. "And for talking." His lips twisted, but it was still a smile. "But most of all for saying what I never had the courage to."

"How could you?" Pheonix asked. "You live in a society where to voice such things is blasphemy. It's only self-preservation to suppress a thought that goes outside the norm in such a society; it makes one dangerous, a threat to the stability of the whole. The other Bladesingers certainly seem to want you to 'know your place.'"

"Where are you getting all this?" Tyyrulriathula's tone was incredulous.

"I spent most of my life as a silent observer. The slavers thought I was intellectually deficient, so they didn't bother to hide much around me. Then, with the old man, I read every day on a variety of subjects, and my studies have continued here. I've learned that sapients are predictable, to a point, if you can recognize the patterns common to sapient thought. Though I don't understand emotion, I can see those patterns, which manifest as action and reaction. And, from my research and other data points, I can intuit likely motivations. That's it."

"That's an awfully ... scientific way to look at what is generally thought of as a not-scientific subject."

"I have no other way *to* look at it. I'm twenty-one with few emotions; I'm unlikely to spontaneously develop them now. And according to the professionals, I'm not suffering from a treatable mental illness that would cause it. So, I can conclude that this is just how I am. But emotions are a fact of sapient life, and I have to figure out how to interact with them in a way I can understand. Especially if I am to pursue justice as my life's work. I must understand what 'justice' *is*, both metaphorically and realistically. The very last damn thing I will let happen around me or because of me is more of the shit I saw as a kid. Anything standing in the way of that is a threat. I just need to learn how to deal with that threat effectively, regardless of its face, but without hurting more innocents. Why do you think I'm here?"

Tyyrulriathula studied him for a long, long time, with an expression that was utterly unreadable to Pheonix. (Privately, Pheonix was aware of the irony.)

"You know what, Pheonix?" Tyyrulriathula raised his glass, not letting Pheonix respond. "You're going to do something great someday. And I'll be right here by your side when you do."

Pheonix had begun retiring to his cottage when the suns set, after Commander Steele professed their disapproval that Pheonix would frequently stay up all night in the martial training ring. Apparently, they preferred he be in his living space after dark. Pheonix didn't understand, but didn't care either way. So, nighttime became his dedicated study time.

The terminal in his cottage gave him access to the Terelath library, one of the largest in the universe. While he could read any number of books digitally, the library offered a service to deliver books, and he preferred that. Something about holding the physical artifact gave him an insight that was impossible to glean through a terminal screen; the feel and smell of the pages told him almost as much as the words themselves, though if pressed, he couldn't explain how. He'd learned all of the most prevalent languages, as well as many dialects from lesser-known species — quite a few that were ancient or dead, and some evil — so there was almost nothing he couldn't read.

The woman caught him just as he was about to enter his cottage.

She was quite short, dressed in semi-sheer, cream-and-pink robes clasped at her throat with a single, gold ornament.

"Good evening, my lady, is there something I can assist you with?" he asked, using lines from the script he'd long memorized from Faranthalassa's lessons.

"Xuri. It is a pleasure to finally meet you, Master Pheonix," her voice was low and calm. "I have heard so much. Perhaps we can speak further inside?"

Pheonix silently opened the door to his cottage, letting her precede him.

The interior was too small for more than one person, and so he settled himself on his cot while she accessed the terminal.

"I am here at the behest of Commander Abyssterilon," she said over her shoulder, "to begin your sexual education training."

Ah, Pheonix thought. *I was wondering when this would happen.*

In his ongoing efforts to read every book in the Terelath library and all the material available on the Ranger informational extra-net, he'd naturally gravitated towards things concerning his training. Sexual education was one of the things covered in depth by the Rangers as a part of every soldier's basic instruction.

So this must be a sensimite.

He studied her. She was the general hominin shape and had a purple glyph on her forehead. Similar glyphs flashed on the palms of her hands as she used the terminal. But considering how many cultures, religions, and societies used forms of permanent marking as expression and to delineate between subgroups (the Rangers included, with facial clan markings), and given the proliferation of magical enhancements, her subtle glyphs wouldn't have made her stand out in a crowd. Among sensimites, there was a religion that thought enlightenment was only attained through the perfection of the act of intercourse. Because of the depth of their knowledge on the subject, it was sensimites who were chosen to teach Ranger sexual education.

Rangers instituted this as mandatory after learning from their past mistakes — Techno-Earth's early society had rotted to such a degree that sexual abuse and harmful deviancies were abundant. Thus, when John Abyssterilon and Damien Rivios spearheaded the Rangers, they were determined to form a society free from the problems plaguing their people.

Pheonix analyzed his opinions on the subject while Xuri pulled up images and texts, but there wasn't much to analyze.

Aside from the most obvious and egregious problem (a lack of genitals), he also had no libido and seemingly no capability of either love or sexual attraction. While enslaved, he'd had plenty of opportunities; it wasn't uncommon for pushy wealthy people to come to his pit frothing in sexual lust after seeing him in the arena. He'd always turned them down. The prospect of touching someone else (since that was all he could do) in that way didn't interest him — even if they offered to buy him, take him out of the arena and into a cushy life as their personal attendant. Even if they were considered attractive by hominin standards. None of that had ever swayed him, not even for a moment.

Before his time in the arena, he'd of course seen the enslaved taking comfort in one another, but had always associated that more with desperation than any attachment to the act itself. It certainly wasn't love. And he'd been too young for any of his fellow enslaved people to proposition; despite what a lot of people seemed to think, violence among the oppressed against one another in those sorts of dire straits happened very rarely. He'd only witnessed it being attempted a few times — and had even stopped it once as a child, beholden to the auto-protection of the demon claw.

So he could objectively judge an individual based on their species' idea of attractiveness, but all of that was just rote memorization. He had no attachment to the information.

Ultimately, he himself had no preferences.

"Has the Commander instructed you on exactly how this is supposed to work, given my physical peculiarities?" he asked.

"There is much education to be had before the physical training, Master Pheonix," she said, smiling. "And while you may not be able to engage sexually in the expected fashion, there are other ways. And you will be able to make that decision at the appropriate time. If you decide that information is enough, we need not engage physically in any manner."

She turned, still smiling.

"Let's begin."

For the next several weeks, Xuri visited him at night. They had in-depth and intelligent discussions — on what was acceptable and what wasn't among the initiated general public, sexual anatomy, the reproductive organs and gestation cycles of the various species a humanoid was able to engage with (and also the sexual norms and taboos of each related culture), pleasure centers for various physical anatomical structures, sexual safety and warnings regarding sexual activity with the uninitiated, gender identities and sexuality, and finally, instruction on techniques. While all of this was a fascinating view into a heretofore unknown aspect of sapient interaction, for Pheonix personally, it indeed only did serve to cement that he had no interest in such things himself, and so he decided to forgo the physical instruction.

One night with Xuri, Pheonix asked, "Why would anyone choose a mate that wasn't healthy? Why *isn't* health the foremost defining factor for that decision matrix?"

Xuri let out a slow breath and crossed her legs. "It's true that the urge to mate and procreate is an instinct lodged essentially in the proliferation of the species. One would assume, then, that the most likely mates to be chosen would be the ones most likely to survive. But that doesn't always equate to 'health,' even in non-sapient or non-sentient creatures. And there have to be more considerations than just health! For genetic diversity's sake. There's a lot of variability in choosing a mate; just like anything, the ability to take in information and make a choice — free will — is one of the things that separates sapiency from other structures of thought."

She smiled gently. "So there are too many correct answers to that question to really discuss it as a generalization. However, among sapients, many intellectual processes, governed by many subconscious factors, go into choosing a mate, even when one doesn't intend on procreating or even engaging in sexual activity with said mate. You would have to weigh the positive and negative aspects of any decision; sharing your life with other sapients is no exception."

"Beauty, what defines a desirable mate — these are less biological and more cultural and social. There *is* a biological factor, pheromones and such, for those species that have pheromones or a similar mechanism, but it's often outweighed by the psychological process in a sapient mind.

"When you consider that, at least for the vast majority of species in the universe, aging and dying is a given, choosing a mate based on health in any capacity is a short-term consideration at best. Everyone, at some point, becomes sick. Everyone, in some way, is flawed. And life is unknown. On a philosophical level, we can almost leave health entirely out of the equation, because we have a multitude of ways to compensate. What is far more important to the sensation-greedy and isolation-fearing sapient mind is companionship. Love."

"So the key factor is wanting to be around them?"

Xuri laughed softly. "Essentially. *Choosing* to be with someone who hurts you is self-destructive. Companionship is one of the ultimate learning experiences, one of the best ways to enrich oneself. And that person or persons with whom you feel a deep kinship, the relationships that may form, may not be in any way a societal norm. There's an old saying: 'Follow your heart.' Do what makes *you* happy, as long as that thing doesn't harm yourself or anyone else, and anyone else involved is enthusiastically consenting and capable of doing so. As long as those rules are met, the universe is limitless."

"Is that why sensimites consider sex the ultimate act of worship?"

"Well, that's a little off-topic, but you're not wrong. We are deeply empathic. We ... *feel* life and emotions, in a way that I, at least, can't explain to other species. It's a part of our biology. It would be like trying to ask an Akeela to describe the composition of a smell or a hominin to describe a color. The best you'd get is something subjective. A description of how that smell or color makes that individual *feel*. It's just something unique to us. Unless you can experience it, you can't understand it, and verbal language is exceedingly inadequate for *those* kinds of things.

"The more intense the emotions and sensation, the more we can resonate with the universe. It's a kind of — meditation for us. One of motion instead of stillness, connection instead of solitude, and engagement instead of separation and introspection. Our goal isn't to understand ourselves, it's to understand the universe — but through that, we can begin to understand ourselves, as well. Intercourse acts to facilitate *that*."

"I don't think I'm capable of any of this," Pheonix said after a long moment in thought.

"You may not be. You are so unique, and none of us yet knows what you are — least of all you. And there's nothing wrong with that — with being the you that you are, regardless of whether or not there are words to describe you. But, the prime takeaway is that the principles are mirrored elsewhere. Most decision-making matrices have the same, or at least a similar, root."

"So it's not just about sex," Pheonix said.

"No, not at all, because many sapients choose not to have sex or relationships in any form, and that's entirely valid. Choosing how to engage, or procreate, or share your life with others — or whether to do so at all — it's all a part of figuring out who you are, what your values are … and then staying faithful to that person, representing that person to the universe. Live your truth, whatever it may be."

"This is a lot more complicated than I gave it credit for," Pheonix said.

Xuri laughed. "There's a lot of philosophy that goes into sex; isn't that wild?"

THIRTEEN
Ugly Truth

"Pheonix!"

Pheonix lowered the sword he was practicing with and followed the sound of the voice: Chani. She looked exasperated; it was an emotion he'd quickly learned to recognize in her.

"Am I to believe it's been six months and you haven't left these grounds *once?* Listen," she said, rubbing one temple with three fingers. "Learning isn't all about sequestering yourself with books and weapons. Get in the refresher, put on some nice clothes, go to the market — or the woods, or go get something to eat — but just get out."

Pheonix returned the sword to its place on the rack, contemplating the Commander's words as he watched her return to her cottage. Of course, like nearly everything she said, it was a good point — perhaps he had been neglectful. Part of his training was supposed to be full integration into initiated society, wasn't it?

And, as she'd just reminded him, again, there was only so much one could learn from books.

Well, he *could* go get something to eat. It had been long enough since his last real meal. And he'd probably been accumulating a decent amount of training bounty on his chit in the months he'd spent in hermitude.

He took a brief turn in the refresher — not so much because he needed to but because he'd been ordered to and that was just how his mind worked. Aside from his head and eyebrows he was hairless — including facial hair — didn't sweat, and judging from his time with the slavers, bacterial or fungal colonies probably didn't find his skin a particularly pleasant place to live, as he hadn't ever gotten infections or some of the other maladies associated with living in squalor.

He dressed in his training uniform with his chit in his breast pocket and approached the teleportation crystal. He stared down at it, working over the memorized map of Terelath to come to a decision about where he wanted to go.

Chani had made several suggestions, which he mulled over. A walk in the woods wouldn't really give him any new data, so he discarded that immediately. The market was a tempting idea; species from all over came to the Terelath markets. It would give him data on the people, economy, resources ... and, yes, he could get something to eat there. That would fulfill all of the requirements from her request, and some of the goals he'd made that languished in the back of his mind for the 'right time.'

He supposed that time was now.

While it wasn't his first time in a crowd by a long shot, it was the most interesting crowd he'd seen so far. Growing up on the slavers' ships, he had mostly been around interchangeable armored individuals, some humanoids/hominins, and few others. Though the slaves had come from all over, he hadn't seen many since he was a child, except those he'd faced in the arena. The casino ship had only catered to a certain clientele, so his experiences with people there were limited.

Even the Market and roads of Archaic Earth, though he'd only been there a few times, were repetitive. Archaic Earth was a niche world, and didn't attract the kind of sheer variety of offworld visitors that the effective seat of the metacosm — Terelath — apparently did.

For the sake of gathering data, he struck up conversations with shopkeepers, listened to their stories, and eavesdropped on people that passed him.

It wasn't long before he began to notice the *wrongness*.

While the conversations he participated in (or overheard) were mostly banal when it came to the non-elves, the same couldn't be said for the Availeon natives.

Curious about the disparity, he focused on the elves. Nearly every one of them spoke in hushed voices, shared furtive glances, moved with an air of anxiety.

Pheonix overheard one pair as they walked past:
"— It got my neighbor's house yesterday."
"Are you planning on moving?"
"To where?"

Another group:
"The Council's verdict was that he submit again in six months or challenge."
"No ... a duel? In this day?"
"Yeah, they've been happening behind the scenes. Hadn't you wondered where Felianeffin has been? He challenged, lost, and they took his garland..."
Murmurs of horror.

Another pair:
"I can't get her to wake up. Oh, Spiraea, what am I going to do?"
"They say if you bring a wilted to the edge of the wilds, an ent will come and take them to the maze."

"I can't give her up, I love her too much. I just need to figure out how to find some mana ... I guess I'll have to go *there* ..."

Confused and concerned, Pheonix worked his way to a teleportation crystal pylon, but hesitated. He was agitated now, and didn't think he could concentrate on his studies.

What the hell was this data? By all accounts, Terelath was the jewel of the Accord — or, it was supposed to be. How could its people be suffering this much? The elves he'd spoken to directly were guarded and tired, and those he'd overheard were anxious, terrified, and had even given up hope entirely.

There was a disconnect between what he thought he knew and what he was witnessing. A disconnect he'd seen mirrored elsewhere — the difference between Crosinthusilas' account of the Great Demon War and the 'official history.' How Tyyrulriathula had warned him off of speaking ill of the balance. Even Faranthalassa's reaction to Pheonix criticizing the position of the Master of Propriety.

He needed more context — context that wasn't tainted.

Who could he rely on to tell the truth? Who wasn't beholden to the system?

"So you've seen it," Crosinthusilas said.
"What am I seeing?" Pheonix asked.
"The signs and symptoms of a dying culture."
"How is that possible? This is the center of the metacosm."
"Where did you hear that?"
"My original teacher, an old man who found me in the woods of Archaic Earth and took me in. He had a lot of old books."

"*Old* books ... yes, it was true that for a time, long ago, Terelath could be called the center of the metacosm in some of the things that matter: social thought, magical technology and theory, communication, faith. That time is long past."

"I don't understand. Why are the Chosen here, then? Why do the elves stand on equal footing with the Accord? Why does the primary Ranger HQ orbit this planet?"

"Why, indeed." Seeing Pheonix's brows lower in confusion and irritation, the Prime Lady sighed. "Have you not wondered where the other Firsts are?"

Though he was mentally thrown off-balance by her sudden apparent change of subject, he said, "There isn't much information on Firsts. The sense I get from history books is that there weren't many."

"Oh, we were plenty. Of every shape and ability. But now ..."

She gestured expansively at the ground.

"Dead?" he asked.

"No, not dead. Sleeping. Awaiting their time — *her* time."

"Whose?"

"The Great Demon War changed us," she continued, ignoring his question. "There was ... discord. It was as though the war had infected us, and once there were no more demons to kill, we turned on each other. We had to make a hard choice. Most of the Firsts went to ground, with myself and a few others remaining to keep our species from perishing entirely."

"Perishing from what?" Pheonix pushed, more and more frustrated with her cryptic answers. "How was it *that* dire a situation and nothing I've ever read has spoken of it?"

Crosinthusilas turned to meet his gaze, her eyes intense. "*You're not ready.* You still have so much to learn. But ... if you are truly certain you must walk this path, then right now you need to read, listen, and learn, as much as you dare. Our ugly truth will become clear in time."

Pheonix did exactly as Crosinthusilas suggested. Her phrasing of 'as much as you dare' alerted him; he felt her words were a warning to cover his ass. Over the next few weeks, he carefully interspersed brief and seemingly (from an outside perspective) benign visits to public spaces. Occasionally on these outings, he caught signs of being watched — someone, always different, always in his peripheral vision. These trackers either underestimated him or were simply not very good, as he was always able to pick them out from the crowd. Spending years alone in the woods had honed Pheonix's instincts for when he was being hunted.

Tyyrulriathula's warning about the balance was always present in Pheonix's mind. Pheonix slowly came to realize that a lot of what he was seeing was tied into the ideal of the balance. The entire concept was so nonsensical to him that he was struggling — *logic* said that if you gave self-professed evil a place at the table, it would hoard all the food and leave none for anyone else. Since he was supposed to be learning about the metacosm anyway, researching the balance would be not outside his current plan of study. He needed to know where the concept of the balance had come from, why it was adopted, what its specific benefits were purported to be.

To its origins and adoption, there wasn't much in elven literature or the Ranger archives his implant gave him access to. The official story was one sentence: that the elves as a whole had decided to adopt the balance after the Great Demon War. Even if Crosinthusilas hadn't outright told him that the balance had existed *prior* to the Great Demon War, that official statement still sounded an awful lot like 'it happened because we fought back' to Pheonix, who had heard that sentiment many times in the slave pens.

Ostensibly, if one *accepted* evil, one could *control* it.

As though evil were simply an unruly sibling that just needed some love and understanding to come around.

Pheonix could already dismiss that as bunk. The Firsts (who, Crosinthusilas had hinted, had done most of the fighting) had been so incensed by *something* (*Can't imagine what*, Pheonix had thought sarcastically) that they'd gone to ground just after the War, abandoning their children. It didn't take a genius to put the pieces together.

Yet, puzzlingly, the elven Firsts on record were only ten in number — not nearly enough to spawn a species. They were:

Crosinthusinlas, Prime Lady; Zasfioretaeula, Prime War-Bladesinger; Pitantherinthalassa, Prime Bladesinger; Cyvaliengarullan, the Prime War-Lady; the Biarch; the Xenobiarch; the Arborer; Fqisabargarrullan, Commander of the Elven Host; Ruémilanthrasia, Spiraea's Prophet and Prime Ranger; and Andural, Bladesinger-Smith.

Of the others that Crosinthusilas had assured him existed, no mention.

Also strange was that nine held a position of power in Terelath, with the tenth, Andural, declared dead. If both living and dead Firsts were acknowledged, then what of the ones who had gone to ground? Being unlisted made them effectively *scrubbed from history.* But why? Had going to ground been so insulting, to deserve such a fate as to be intentionally forgotten?

That had led him to research the current elven political hierarchy.

Supposedly sharing decision-making duties were the main Council (made up mostly of the Seconds, a few Thirds, the Prime War-Lady and Prime Bladesinger, various other few elves of note, and headed by two Second brothers: Aolenthalassa and Aunrielthalassa), and the King and Queen of the elves.

The first red flag was that there were two separate Councils — the Council and the 'Greater Council,' on which all Bladesingers and Ladies held a seat.

But the Greater Council hadn't been called in Ages.

The second red flag was that information on the Council was neither easy to obtain nor decode. Terelath had no laws on transparency, and the Council seemed to have no interest in providing either laws or transparency. And while it chafed, Pheonix knew he had to be careful in prodding questions about an apparently abusive authority. While he did have options, he ended up discarding them in favor of prudence.

Besides, learning what the average elf had access to told him all he needed to know.

And based on that, he wasn't exactly sure *what* the Council did, simply because despite the vague official descriptions of being one of the legislative bodies of Terelath, he had no actual *proof* of them doing any legislating.

The next red flag was what he had managed to dig up: that while the outer edges of the Council seemed to rotate with fair frequency, its core — specifically the two brothers (Aolenthalassa and Aunrielthalassa), the Prime War-Lady, and Prime Bladesinger — had remained in their positions since the inception of the Council.

The other Council members were elected, so why not those four?

The fourth red flag was that every previous King and Queen from the First to Fourth Ages died about a hundred years after taking the crown. The official explanation of those deaths was that taking the crown meant taking the weight of the elven people, and that, mixed with the required relinquishing of both power and immortality to assume office, it had been 'too much.'

Those Kings and Queens hadn't been ascribed to any major legislative changes in the entirety of the time the position had been extant. They mostly backed what the Rangers would call 'area beautification' — a new grove here, a new sculpture there.

However, buried in Ranger media archives, Pheonix found traces of rebellion within the current monarchy, who had been around inexplicably since the Fourth Age. Now in the Sixth Age, that was around two hundred thousand years. The elven media and official reporting on the subject said that 'a golden age' was responsible for their longevity.

Though, they'd tipped their hand. Multiple obtuse reports released to the elves by the Council had dubbed them 'the recalcitrant King and Queen.'

As Crosinthusilas had said … discord.

Information from the Ranger archives was turning out to be more informative than anything put out by the elves (big surprise, given the pattern emerging). While searching for anything to do with Terelath, Availeon, or elves, he found a recent warning from Ranger HQ to Rangers of the elven species not to return to Availeon until further notice.

Elves had been disappearing at an alarming rate within Terelath.

He'd gotten a lot of data during his outings that could have been associated with disappearances — between overheard conversations and the things let slip in friendly conversation — but the Council had suspiciously not made a single announcement on it.

Following the rabbit hole of the disappearances, he found a Fifth Age report detailing an attachment of Rangers, including elves, being taken by Bladesingers in Terelath. Strangely, the elves among the group had escaped. A familiar name popped up.

Chani (then a Sergeant) had taken immediate action and landed an occupation force in Terelath — which was literally exactly what it sounded like, a force massive in size and scope, usually used at the beginning of a war — and demanded the soldiers' return.

It had almost been open war.

The only thing that had prevented further escalation was that the contingent of Bladesingers who had showed up to confront Chani's force hadn't drawn their weapons. After a tense standoff, the Council called for the release of the captured squad.

The person writing the report could only assume that an Ascended — probably Law — had interfered, though they had no explanation as to why the incident had even happened in the first place.

That had given Pheonix one important piece of information — that Chani was likely to be trusted, insofar as that she had a long history of not glossing over injustice in favor of politics — and a lot of questions. Why would Bladesingers be involved in abduction? If there had been any inquiries made or answers found, there hadn't been anything written on it that Pheonix had access to.

That was something he found himself butting his head up against over and over. Access.

He knew he wasn't entitled to anything — if anything, the elves and Rangers had been exceedingly kind to him by taking him in and training him. He wasn't unaware that they had done it purely for their own benefit — to figure out if he was worthy of further use — but he was content with that. He was under no illusion that his continued presence on Terelath wasn't contingent entirely on being useful to *someone*, though who and for what purpose wasn't entirely clear.

Of course, he was developing his suspicions.

Ultimately it didn't matter, though. He would take what he could from the situation and address any changes in said situation as they arose. It wasn't as though people hadn't been out to use him his entire life: he was on even footing here. And he got something out of it — knowledge, which was arguably priceless.

But that did mean they kept him at a careful distance, and he was himself careful to respect that distance so as to not show his hand before he was ready. Unfortunately, a side effect of that distance was said lack of access, which, while expected, was nonetheless a frustrating roadblock. One that he was determined to scale.

The solution he eventually came to was that he could offer to join the Rangers once his training in Terelath was complete, and from there, hopefully he could work his way to a position where he had the access he needed. As much as it rankled to put aside all the wrongs he was seeing, at the very least, it seemed to be no more than your run-of-the-mill power-hungry status-quo-humpers. Many governments in the books he'd read seemed to have those, so he was depressingly familiar with their shape.

There wasn't any information that led him to believe that people were *dying*.

As long as there were no deaths, he could afford to be *somewhat* patient. Death was the one thing he couldn't forgive. Injuries could be Healed, there were incredibly advanced procedures for recovery from trauma, but death was final.

Besides: he still had the biggest question of all to answer.

Even if he found clear evidence of evil within the elven hierarchy, what the hell could *he* do about it? He was nobody. And becoming 'somebody' wasn't as easy as it was often made out to be.

Pheonix continued with his research and outings — alongside his normal training — over the next few months.

The pattern he'd begun to see was crystallizing.

He'd always had an instinctual recognition for *suffering*. Though no one had ever sat him down to explain the difference between 'good' and 'bad' things, acts that caused suffering were easily categorized as 'bad.'

Perhaps one of the ways he managed to relate to other sapients was that, despite having few emotions, he had *empathy*. Empathy and a recognition of suffering had informed Pheonix's early definition of 'evil' as people who did 'bad' things with the express purpose of causing suffering.

But that had turned out to be a limited definition and hadn't served him very well outside the slavers' pens.

That exact evil obviously existed here; they had a whole Creator-damned *district* to themselves. Despite the fact that they actively harmed metacosmic citizens, the leadership tolerated them — hell, even welcomed them.

Why?

The only answer he could come up with was that said leadership was a more subtle form of evil.

The balance required tolerance of evil, and professed that 'everyone is/does a little evil, so why should we discriminate against those who identify fully as evil?' — which was simply incorrect; not only incorrect, but impossible. While what constituted a 'good' person was wildly subjective, Pheonix was coming to believe that 'good' was simply the default. It meant 'not evil.'

By that logic, good and evil did not and could not coexist.

Sapients *often* made sometimes egregious errors in judgment, poor choices, acted on emotion or incomplete data or out of simple jackassery. And while, subjectively, those were 'bad' things that frequently had devastating consequences, they weren't *evil*.

There were key differences.

Evil was continuous, proud of itself/its actions, arrogant, cowardly, untethered to truth (which was itself treated as malleable in spite of any contradictory proof), and didn't suffer regret.

And most of all, evil was entitled. It felt that it *deserved* the things it took, and would scapegoat the people it destroyed. It served its own needs above anything else, and made excuses for its behavior without any attempt at introspection or growth. Oftentimes, if threatened, it would double down or escalate.

And because evil was just as capable of finding or manipulating allies as it was at finding victims and exploiting or creating loopholes in systems, it seemed to be frustratingly ubiquitous.

And evil wearing a kind smile was still evil.

It didn't matter if the slaver master treated his pet bird to special food and a gilded cage and pillows and fancy toys. As soon as that bird ceased fulfilling the needs of the slaver master, it would be discarded — or worse. The slaver master doing something that appeared good without broader context didn't erase the fact that he was a *master of slavers.*

Intent, mindset, and context were all things Pheonix had to thoroughly consider.

But here was the kicker taking shape in his mind throughout this process: subtle evil made way for blatant evil. They were always in alliance, working toward the same goal — more often than not, by way of sheer apathy. All it took was negligence and self-centeredness to ignore it because it didn't affect them personally.

And, by all evidence, the elves had been under the rule of this subtle evil for Ages … and it had spilled over to corrupt the entire metacosm.

Ugly truth indeed.

On one of his scheduled public outing days about a year into his stay in Terelath, Pheonix decided to hit another spot on his list: the Temple of the Ascended. While the Library was able to ship its books to him, he wasn't afforded such luxury with religious artifacts; and besides, to physically walk the halls of one of the holiest places in the metacosm held too much appeal.

He set the Temple as his destination, which was, surprisingly, not within the main Terelath 'flower.'

He arrived inside a massive grown stone building, in a garden — though with the proliferation of foliage in Terelath, with structures made out of living plants, the line between garden and building was sometimes blurry. A straight path through the garden stretched just ahead of him, leading to the four large shrines at the far end. To either side of them, like wings, were annexes of the same wooden construction one was likely to encounter all around Terelath; sung from the earth and carefully tended, nature provided a living structure for the elves, and so existed in harmony with them.

The Temple's interior was relatively sparing of decoration on the approach to the shrines but for one exception: the bells.

Bells of all shapes and sizes were set into alcoves along the walls and hung from the ceiling, in such profusion that there was nary a space without them.

Pheonix took to the path and peculiarly, the bells began to ring in his wake.

An elf standing before the statue of Spiraea turned and Pheonix was surprised to see it was Faranthalassa. The elven Ranger stared at Pheonix with wide eyes, which flicked from Pheonix to the bells and back again. His offering, an intricate sculpture crafted out of leaves, was crushed in a white-knuckled grip.

"Master Faranthalassa," Pheonix said loudly, to be heard over the bells. "Is something wrong?"

"The bells," Faranthalassa managed, pointing a shaking finger.

"Yes, they are very loud."

"No, you don't ... I — I must go."

Faranthalassa swept past him, and Pheonix blinked.

He wondered what could put the Master of Propriety so out of sorts. Well, whatever it was, he was bound to hear about it sooner or later. He turned his attention to the shrines: raised statues of the four main Ascended worshiped in Terelath, with enough space for offerings around their feet.

From left to right was Law (a stern elven man wearing plate armor, protector of the Bladesingers and worshiped by many elves), Spiraea Lady of the Wood (Ascended of Nature, patroness of the elves and protector of Availeon, a smiling elven woman wearing robes), Lazarus of Justice (a hominin wearing plate armor and wielding two daggers), and Life (Ascended of life and patroness of the Healing arts, an elven woman wearing the garb of a paladin).

By the time people began pouring in, Pheonix had already disappeared down one of the corridors leading to the scroll and artifact rooms.

"Commander, we have a problem! It's happened!"

Chani looked up as a panicked Faranthalassa burst into her office. The fact that the Master of Propriety hadn't bowed, hadn't greeted her, hadn't even knocked, immediately alarmed her.

"What's up?" she asked, outwardly calm.

"The bells — that boy has rung them!" Faranthalassa shook his head, then corrected himself: "*Justice* has rung the bells! Are we prepared? We are not prepared!"

Chani's mind instantly kicked into overdrive. *Were* they sufficiently prepared?

While Pheonix was expanding his perceptions, Chani had been watching. She wasn't privy to the kid's judgments

— he was frustratingly private and hadn't written his observations down, either via physical medium or on the terminal (which made her wonder at the capabilities of his mind), so she wasn't sure what conclusions he had come to.

But if the bells in the Temple of the Ascended — those meant only to ring when an Ascended entered the building — had recognized him, then something within him had certainly awakened.

Which meant they were out of time.

They'd have to act before the Council did. They had been on shaky ground with Pheonix on Terelath this past year, as it stood. The bureaucratic solution they'd come up with to keep the Council off his back was for the King and Queen to 'gift' Pheonix to the Rangers — as in, he was Ranger property. And then the elven royalty had loaned out that training area and those trainers for him as a 'sign of goodwill to the continued cooperation of the Rangers and elves.'

The Council had grumbled but couldn't fight their own bullshit language.

It had been a temporary measure, and everyone involved — Council included — knew it. They were starting to pressure the Rangers about when the kid's time on Terelath would be complete.

From Chani's observations, she'd guessed that he was pursuing some deeply-engrossing line of thought, and her intuition was that if he was ripped from Terelath — where he appeared to be gaining some important data — it would throw him off.

So she'd pulled every trick in the book (even calling in a couple of favors) to stonewall the Council and their dogs.

Even that had a limit, though. Recently, rumblings had reached Chani through unofficial channels that the Council was tired of hosting him and were considering just ordering him to leave.

Maybe this was for the best.

The kid had been training under some of the most powerful and dangerous individuals in the known metacosm — in not just combat, but also thought and tactic — and he had come in already a deadly weapon in his own right. With Chani's under-the-table political support keeping them off his ass, what could they really do to him?

Moreso: if the Creator was ready to claim him, who was she to have an opinion?

Maybe it would be enough ... and they had no choice but to find out.

She clicked a button for a vid-screen set off to one side of her desk. Within a moment, the dignified face of Zeta, one of the three ruling Chosen assigned to Ranger HQ, appeared on the screen. Without preamble, she explained the situation to him.

"Take him to the Obelisk," he said crisply. "It will know what he is or isn't."

"You sure?" Chani asked, alarmed. Zeta nodded slowly, and Chani's lips tightened. The screen went dead.

"Well, you heard him," Chani said to Faranthalassa with a heavy sigh. "Go find the kid, bring him here. I'll meet you with a transport."

She sat back as Faranthalassa performed a graceful, if shaky, bow and left. She prayed that, whether they were right or wrong about him, the Obelisk wouldn't be his death knell.

"Creator help us," she muttered into the empty room.

"No, you've got it all wrong, Steele, this'un would *easily* go for a hundred bars on the black market!"

Steele held their laughter and peered at the chunk of ore proffered by the eager dwarven merchant. Two gnomes — one in a normal gnomish floating mech and the other wearing an unusual ground-based exo-suit — pretended to look over the merchant's items nearby, but were unsubtly instead listening to the loud argument.

Steele nodded their head slowly. "I see, I see," they said agreeably, not needing their ability to look into sapients to feel the triumphant flush rise in the dwarf's face. Dwarves had stone skin and lava blood, so 'feel' was not a euphemism. "I suppose it would, considering that whomever bought it would likely not have the discerning eye to notice this — "

One manicured finger traced a line, barely noticeable, following a natural curve in the ore's jagged surface. It shone a subtly different color than the rest of the ore, and that spoke of impurities.

The dwarf blustered, the gnomes tittered, and Steele straightened, smiling.

"Bah!" The dwarf harrumphed. "Any dwarf worth his mithril could smelt that out in no time flat, and you go ahead and tell me that isn't so!"

"But what if it isn't bought by a dwarf?" said a gravelly voice behind Steele.

Steele turned and met the eyes of a sneering orc. Time slowed.

Four orc Berserkers, some wielding weapons in each of their four hands, fanned out in a semicircle to trap Steele and the others against the stall. Only loosely humanoid in physical form and far from it in spirit, orcs were twisted by any definition. Their skin was greyish-purple, pulled tight against wiry muscles and covered in purple pustules and grey crystallized chitin. They had no hair, and the purple gunk in the pustules ran through their veins, leaking out of every orifice. These four didn't have much chitin, yet — which meant that they were still young.

"That just means you're *scamming* people, doesn't it, dirt-sucker?" the orc in front grated around sharpened teeth.

Another orc who carried two weapons thrust his grinning maw into the face of the gnomes. The one in the floating mech dodged, but the exo-suit couldn't move quickly enough, and its owner was snatched up by the throat.

Steele turned, put themself in between the dwarf and the other orcs, and lifted their hands, palms out. In the corner of their eye, the gnome thrashed and scrabbled at the huge hand around his neck, his mech's legs kicking futilely in the air.

No one but the orcs were armed — weapons of any kind were forbidden in the common areas of Terelath, unless for recognized religious reasons and with the appropriate permits — regulations which these gentlemen apparently cared nothing about. Aside from that, evil were supposed to be confined to their own quarter, where they had their own merchants.

There was only one reason orcs would be here, and it sure wasn't shopping or sightseeing. The fact that they'd gotten past the guards reeked of interference. Steele gritted their teeth.

But, weaponless as they were, they had few options. They had to do what they were best at: talking. Stall the orcs until the Grey Mages sensed the disturbance.

"Come now," Steele said at their most persuasive, "he's an honorable merchant. Perhaps my eyes were deceiving me. Let's — "

They edged towards the gnome, and the lead orc lifted his arms, his eyes aflame with manic glee —

— a blur swept through them. The orcs didn't even have time to react to the threat, let alone defend themselves. Arms and legs and pieces of instantly-stinking orc meat flew in all directions (one hitting Steele squarely in the chest), and foul-smelling black blood gushed, mixed with the purple 'pustulence' from orc boils, and the gnomes screamed, and the dwarf bellowed in rage and fright —

Steele blinked. And there was Pheonix, cradling the choking, seizing gnome in arms that were slick with orc blood and viscera. His eyes were burning cerulean, almost glowing, and Steele recoiled to meet them.

Justice, their mind whispered in horror and awe.

"Commander Steele, are you injured?" the youth asked flatly.

Steele looked down at themself, absently noted the smear of black blood across their uniform, and looked back at Pheonix. Steele shook their head, without words.

Pheonix turned and was gone again, carrying the gnome.

Steele found that they could breathe easier once released from the choking pressure Pheonix had been exuding. The stench of rotted orc meat and the carnage around them — the splashes of black blood mixed with purple pustulence, which carved deep scars into the ground nearly on contact — hit Steele all at once and they reeled anew.

Why Pheonix? How had he known? It was ludicrous to think it had just been a coincidence.

It must be the power of Justice, something in their mind whispered and they shuddered in response.

That was the only explanation. Pheonix had shown up and dealt with the problem before even the Grey Mages — Terelath's magically-automated defense system.

As if thinking of the Grey Mages had summoned them, the air rippled before Steele and three figures in nondescript grey robes appeared. They had no identifying marks, not even a shape of biological sex or species or idiosyncrasy distinguished one from another, and only silver eyes could be seen in the depths of the hoods.

One of them looked around. "There ... *was* an altercation here," it said.

Steele nodded, trying to dredge up their professionalism from the ditch Pheonix had dumped it in.

"Commander Steele?" another prompted.

"Ah, yes," Steele answered, then cleared their throat. "There w — ah, it was taken care of."

"Clearly," the last Grey Mage replied dryly. Then they were gone.

Taking a moment to put themself together, Steele turned to make sure the dwarf and the other gnome were unharmed, and then hurried from the scene. They turned a corner and whipped out their communication crystal.

"We have a problem," they said into it as soon as Chani's face appeared in the crystal's facets.

"That's funny," Chani responded. "You're the second person to tell me that today."

"What?" Steele asked sharply.

"Pheonix rang the bells."

Steele's hand tightened around the crystal. "And?" they pressed.

"I sent Faranthalassa to bring him up to the Chosen. Zeta's orders. What did he do now?"

"I'll tell you about it later." They flashed a grin, though it was strained.

"Over a beer?" Chani asked. "You look like you could use one. Hell, I guess I could, too. Today has already been rough and I get the feeling it will only get worse."

"Amen to that."

"Do you know where he is?" Chani asked.

"Yes, he's heading to the Medical Center with an injured gnome."

"A what?" Chani said, alarmed. "What happened?"

"Later. I've got to contact Faranthalassa and get him over there before Pheonix wanders off again."

*With that speed, he doesn't even **need** teleportation,* Steele thought, awed and chilled by the thought. *What in Jesus-Man's name did we bring into our midst?*

Chani made a noise of indignation. "Fine, but you owe me."

Steele smiled, genuinely this time. "Sure. Penny's, nineteen-hundred?"

"Works for me."

The communicator crystal went dead.

Steele closed their eyes, gathering up the last of their composure. Then they opened them again and rang Faranth-lassa.

FOURTEEN
First Of Many

Pheonix raged silently.

None of the Healers at the Medical Center would look him in the eye as they rushed the injured gnome into an intensive care room, not even to see if any of the blood that soaked him was his own.

He flashed back to the shack, looking down at the corpses of the men who had murdered the closest thing he'd ever had to a father. The urge to go back to the crime scene and grind the bodies of those orcs into mush was so strong he twitched, but the need to make sure the gnome would pull through was even stronger.

Why is this feeling so intense?

Any other emotion he could rise above. But this one, this need for justice, was all-consuming.

Pheonix had spent the better part of his life ending other lives, but that didn't mean he sought it out, now that it wasn't tied into his own survival. And the deaths at his hands were mostly monsters or evil who'd been careless enough to get caught scheming. The times when an opponent in the arena had come at him crying or screaming in fright or desperation, he had dodged until it was exhausted. If it had only cowered on the other end of the floor, he would sit, motionless, until the slavers removed both of them. Thus, the slavers had learned quickly to only put him against truly aggressive creatures — things that liked to kill. The crowd needed its bloodshed and Pheonix wouldn't oblige unless it was something he could condone ending.

It wasn't like they could torture Pheonix into submission or kill him for his insubordination.

The odd thing was that, even exercising as much autonomy as he'd had in the situation (only granted by his immortality, demon arm, and freakish strength) to minimize his personal involvement with the continued abuse of innocents, Pheonix didn't consider *himself* innocent.

After all, they'd all been subject to the depraved whims of the slavers, who had absolute control and demanded complete obeisance. And when one didn't have agency in a situation, one could hardly be held to blame for the actions taken to survive.

But Pheonix *had* some agency, and had chosen not to exercise it. He had chosen to learn, and watch, and prepare for the time when he could better fight back. A time that had never come. He'd been rescued, unlike any of the others — and his actions had left all those people to die.

In the inextricably intertwined dichotomy of life and death — fight to survive, kill to live — it mattered not if it was a predator taking down prey so as not to starve, or a slave killing another slave at the behest of someone who would end them if they didn't — the nucleus was the same.

Everything on the physical plane was connected: everything in existence was both harmful and beneficial without ever being aware of either effect. At its core, the concept was neutral and balanced. By its very nature, existence was struggle.

But.

Add sapiency into the mix, and things got complicated, *fast*. A society — a grouping of sapients — required maintenance. Maintenance predicated conflict. Accord had to be established for a society to progress, or even survive, and accord among sapients was rarely established without argument. Conflict wasn't evil, though it certainly could be frustrating.

If the true name of 'peace' was conflict avoidance —

— when even living was conflict —

— then allowing evil to do whatever it wanted just to keep from having to fight it —

— was *wrong*.

The Chosen and Council used 'the balance' to justify evil's presence because, according to them, if they brought evil into the fold, they could *control* it.

But evil was inherently uncontrollable.

And what had he *just* promised himself? As long as no one died, he could wait. But if he hadn't been at that specific market, on that specific day, at that specific time …

And how many times had it happened just this way when he wasn't there? He couldn't even find that out, because the Powers That Be routinely buried that kind of information. He'd learned that well enough during his research on the elven Council.

He realized he'd been doing it again — waiting on the sides, relying on his privilege, gathering information, while the vulnerable were trampled underneath.

He felt like he'd betrayed himself. He'd been wrong; there was no time.

*And no one but him seemed to care one fucking whit to even **try** to stop it.*

That was what fed his rage.

The metal oculus connecting the hallway to the treatment room opened behind him. He didn't need to turn to know that it was Faranthalassa.

Pheonix heard the elf approach him. Faranthalassa seemed to be out of breath, but he hesitated before coming into Pheonix's line of view.

"Is this your precious balance?" The words ripped out of Pheonix's mouth. He could *feel* Faranthalassa flinch. The anger in Pheonix was something alive, a beast he had thrown down the reins for. "Is this what you protect? Is this what you elves and the Rangers stand for? What the Accord was formed for? To allow evil to roam free, to give it the right to do … *this*?" He whipped a hand out and Faranthalassa recoiled as though Pheonix were aiming to strike him — but Pheonix was pointing at the gnome surrounded by medical personnel who were doing a good job pretending that they weren't hearing the exchange.

"If that's so, then put me on the first ship out of here. I won't stand for this."

"Master Pheonix," Faranthalassa said after a long silence. He waited until Pheonix turned to look at him before speaking again. To his credit, the Master of Propriety didn't look away, but his voice was thick. "I request that you accompany me. To speak to the Chosen."

The Chosen. Yes, he would take this up with them.

Pheonix glanced back at the Healers.

"He will live," one of them said.

Assured of that, Pheonix brushed past Faranthalasaa and out the oculus.

Pheonix and Faranthalassa used the teleportation crystal to go to the military district, where a transport — a boxy vehicle that hovered silently a few inches off the ground — waited.

Pheonix squished his large frame inside next to Chani, while Faranthalassa took the spot next to Steele. The door closed.

Chani looked him up and down, clearly noting the blood, but said nothing.

Pheonix had no intention of changing out of his stained clothing. He was going to speak to the Chosen, the representatives of the Obelisk — a supposed Creator artifact. So, let them see what their laws had allowed. Let them be confronted with the very real consequences of their precious 'balance.'

Let them all bear witness.

"Well," Chani said, after clearing her throat. "As you know, we're taking you up to speak with the Chosen. We … we just need answers."

"Yes, we do," Pheonix said, his voice still tight with rage.

Chani looked at him, silent.

One of the many walls Pheonix had run into in his research is that not many citizens were ever allowed to (or needed to) speak with the Chosen, so he had no idea of what to expect. But he fully intended on holding them accountable, by whatever means necessary.

Faranthalassa, Steele, and even Chani were nervous and unsettled, though. Their mannerisms screamed it. That was … interesting.

The Chosen and Obelisk were wreathed in much mystery to the 'average' citizen (a fact that irked Pheonix for many reasons). Maybe the same was true for those in power.

Unsurprisingly, that thought didn't soothe his rage.

The transport took their group to the Ranger compound, a sprawling place that was almost threatening in its sterility, like a war camp. The signature Ranger dome-roofed buildings were neatly spaced across its breadth. At the very far end of the compound, there was a circular, metal lift, and it was onto this that the transport drove.

As the lift rose smoothly and the world dropped away below them, Pheonix was finally able to get control of his anger. He looked out the window. Even viewing it from (he would guess) several hundred feet in the air, Terelath stretched into atmospheric distortion.

"Commander Steele and I won't be accompanying you into the actual Seat of the Chosen," Chani said as the lift began to slow. "You will be going with Faranthalassa. Just remember his training on propriety and you will be fine."

Pheonix barely held back a derisive snort.

Sending Faranthalassa out as a sacrifice again, were they? As if propriety would help either of them against a foe that refused to be known.

The transport entered a tunnel that plunged its occupants into complete darkness, though Pheonix's eyes adjusted instantly.

After a few long moments, the transport turned completely around and stopped. The doors opened, and Pheonix climbed out, followed closely by Faranthalassa, Chani, and Steele. Pheonix found himself just inside the entrance tunnel to a giant amphitheater. Filling the seats were people and creatures of all types, no two alike — the representatives of every species and planet in the entirety of the initiated metacosm. Pheonix noted the resemblance to the arena of his childhood, but had no attachment to the information.

Dominating the middle of the floor was the Obelisk. Matte black and unimpressive aside from its sheer size, the Obelisk was shaped like a roughly-worked crystal: hexagonal, pointed, many times taller than it was wide. Facing the entrance, in the center of the circle-shaped room, was a table. At that table sat the twelve Availeon Chosen, each individual connected to the crystal by a thin line of green energy.

There was no fanfare. The Chosen didn't sit on thrones or wear crowns. Their clothes weren't even necessarily better than what Pheonix himself had been issued. No decorations lined the sides of the coliseum (though there were flat rectangles that Pheonix thought looked like vid-screens). In the stands themselves, each representative had their own visual marker to announce their allegiance.

And yet, something about the line of Chosen — and the Obelisk, itself — radiated such an intense sense of superiority that Pheonix had to battle a resurgence of his rage. He wasn't sure how much longer he could hold it back.

In front of him were those responsible for the political grandstanding and blustering that had resulted in all the shit he saw as a kid, and continued to be responsible for the current suffering metacosm-wide.

Chani and Steele remained by the transport. Faranthalassa gestured Pheonix forward, and Pheonix gritted his teeth and complied.

"Pheonix," the Chosen said as one before he could even attempt to speak. "Touch the Obelisk."

There was an intake of breath from behind him: Faranthalassa.

An outright denial jumped to Pheonix's tongue and he barely swallowed it back. Ordering him around before so much as a greeting? What the fuck was the point of propriety if only one group was beholden to it? *The insolence.*

He felt that he was becoming unhinged.

Fine. This harbinger of 'the balance' and all its vultures wants to taste my essence? **Let it.**

Every gaze pierced him as he approached the Obelisk.

The sheer pressure of the attention of the representatives, the Chosen, and indeed the Obelisk, weighed on him as surely as shackles, but with sheer will, he forced his limbs to move.

Doubt crept in through the persistent rage. He didn't know anything about this thing — didn't know what touching it might mean. For all he knew, this was an execution. If that were the case, he wouldn't go down quietly, but wasn't sure how to fight an enemy so unknown.

It seemed like the inexorable tide of history had swept him up, and his feet kept moving, steps echoing in the timbre of silence that only a crowd of very quiet people could produce.

His thoughts ricocheted and fragmented into splinters he couldn't make sense of in the time it took him to reach the table of the Chosen.

In the shadow of the Obelisk, he looked up. It loomed, a black that sucked in all light and returned nothing. Up close, it was malicious in a way he couldn't rationalize.

Uncontrolled fury and unfamiliar terror screamed through his system, frying everything in its path, leaving only one thing behind:

DON'T

TOUCH

IT

It was too late.

He came within arm's reach of the Obelisk —

lifted a hand —

And the world dissolved. Sight, sound, smell, sensation, shut down instantly as his mind flipped into pure survival mode against the onslaught. He hadn't ever experienced it himself, but he'd seen it in others enough to instinctively recognize it.

Pain.

Although, perhaps calling it pain would be equating a supernova to a candle. What the Obelisk subjected him to left pain far behind. It was tearing him apart, and he could feel it questing for his core.

Yet before it reached said core, it was checked. A brief internal struggle ensued, with Pheonix helpless but to watch. The Obelisk finally withdrew, thwarted, but did not leave him unchanged.

He felt hands on him. His vision returned. He'd slumped over onto his knees at some point during the white-out and Faranthalassa was supporting him. It was like all the beatings by slavers that Pheonix hadn't felt at the time had caught up with him at that one moment.

Anger flared hot, and he decked Faranthalassa.

Pheonix stood, wavering, over the stunned elf.

"*Why didn't you fucking warn me?*" Pheonix screamed.

Then Chani and Steele were running across the bowl, and his fury bled away. He was more exhausted than he'd ever been, and he sagged into Chani's arms. The world swam and he couldn't make sense of any input. There was movement, then darkness.

Chani, Steele and Faranthalassa loaded the massive bulk of the unconscious Pheonix into the back of the transport. No one had tried to stop them from taking him: only that same dead silence had followed them. Similarly, none of Pheonix's trainers seemed willing to defy that silence as the transport brought them back into the black tunnel with the lift at the other end.

Chani clenched her hands in an attempt to calm the shaking.

The Obelisk *spoke.*

THIS ONE IS THE FIRST OF MANY WHO SHALL APPEAR.

The 'voice' howled in her mind which, like the booming of a too-close hundred-caliber, had left her ears ringing and head pounding.

HE WILL TAKE UP THE SWORD OF JUSTICE IN THE CREATOR'S NAME. BESIDES THIS, YOU KNOW THE TIME — THAT THE HOUR HAS COME FOR YOU TO WAKE FROM SLEEP. FOR SALVATION IS NEARER TO US NOW THAN WHEN WE FIRST BELIEVED.

Take up the sword of Justice ... the first of many ... wake from sleep ... Chani reeled.

The boy really was Ascended — and didn't know it.

She could feel the other two trainers in a similar state. Emotions hung thick like congealed blood on that long, dark ride back to the teleportation crystal. Faranthalassa cradled his jaw, his face swollen from Pheonix's hit; the elf looked like Spiraea had manifested before him and demanded sapient sacrifice. Steele was troubled, their eyes downcast.

Pheonix stirred and slowly sat up. Perhaps to someone who hadn't spent as much time around him, he would have seemed no worse for his ordeal. But Chani was able to read him pretty well, and could pick out the mannerisms unnatural to his norm. The way he slumped in his seat, supporting himself with his elbows locked, his head forward, long dark hair messily spilling over one shoulder — the day's events had taken a toll on him.

"What happened?" he asked no one in particular, voice rough.

Chani thought reflexively:

The Obelisk enrobed you in sickly green power and lifted you off the ground and multiple people threw up seeing it and thinking about it again now is making my bile rise but you weren't screaming you were tense in every muscle and fighting it wearing the most hideous expression I've ever seen on a hominin face and I've seen people get ripped apart and eaten alive...

"The Obelisk ... examined you," Steele replied, but they sounded unsure. A diplomatic answer. Of course Steele had one at hand. Chani wasn't sure she could speak yet.

"It *hurt*," Pheonix growled.

"We didn't know," Faranthalassa said, apologetically. "It has never done anything like that before, in all our history. The Obelisk has never ... "

Even he couldn't say it:

Spoken. The Obelisk *spoke.*

"Do you want to know — " Chani began.

Pheonix's eyes flashed angrily as he glanced at her. "Fuck that thing," he snapped. "I don't care."

There was a long, heavy silence.

"Maybe it's time for that beer," Chani said.

Aolenthalassa sighed impatiently and adjusted his robe. Next to him, his brother Aunrielthalassa waited with a snarl while a servant put his shoes on for him. The siblings shared a glance to confirm that the other was ready. Another servant opened the door to their personal quarters, and they descended one of the many staircases in their great mansion — indeed, the largest and grandest private residence in Terelath.

The brothers had made sure of that.

Only the best for the dual heads of the elven Council.

Though it was, at times, an annoyance to cross the length of their home in any reasonable amount of time, under normal circumstances they wouldn't be tasked to do so. But these weren't normal circumstances.

They'd been roused — rudely — from their rightful rest by some very upsetting news: that the Obelisk had screeched about some child and 'justice' or some nonsense. So, the brothers had sent a message to the Chosen to await their presence with the expectation of a full report.

Oh, they'd been briefed about the child by their information agents. Some mutant creature who'd fallen through a tear. But things like that happened every day in Terelath, and so it hadn't made much of a ripple. Let the Rangers handle it; it was their job to protect Terelath. After all, being guard dogs was the only thing those puffed-up rejects were even somewhat proficient at.

The brothers didn't know why the Chosen had allowed such ridiculousness to cause a stir, but they were about to find out.

They shuffled through the courtyard lined with impeccably curated rare plants and into their private shuttle on the other side. Aolenthalassa, the elder of the two, allowed his lip to curl. He was in a particularly foul mood. Exhausted, and annoyed having to don his full regalia to be seen by the Chosen, he lowered himself gratefully into his shuttle seat. Crossing that courtyard was getting harder and harder…

After the brothers' personal Bladesinger bodyguards took their seats, the shuttle smoothly lifted off. It sailed over the mansion's massive gate, which didn't open and, in fact, couldn't. The only way in or out of the brothers' compound was by shuttle. Small shuttle. Which none were allowed to own. For the preservation of Availeon's beautiful open skies, of course.

Aolenthalassa watched out the window idly, the city streets miniaturizing in moments as the shuttle gained height and arced around toward the Seat of the Chosen. But the view soon bored him, and he was developing a headache. He pressed a nondescript panel in the interior wall of the shuttle, and a cup holding mana pearls popped out.

He took a handful and crunched them noisily all at once, some of the tension easing out of his shoulders as the rush of life energy filled him. His headache dissipated, but only slightly. He ate a few more to pass the time. He'd likely need the energy to summon the righteous anger required to put the Chosen in their places. He brushed pearl shards off of his robe, fallen from his messy eating. The brothers were due another mana infusion; the pearls were barely helping these days. He grimaced at the thought. Mana infusions hurt, and no attempt to manage the pain dulled it at all.

He and Aunrielthalassa didn't talk on the long shuttle ride. While they didn't speak 'telepathically,' as so many of these blasphemous implanted freaks had taken to doing, they didn't need to. They were of one mind.

The sudden darkness (offset by crystalline light from the interior of the shuttle that offered an unobtrusive glow in low-light conditions) warned Aolenthalassa that they were approaching the Seat of the Chosen. He straightened and stoked the anger he felt at being bothered. Next to him, Aunrielthalassa also shifted.

The shuttle stopped; the door slid silently open, and each brother's personal Bladesinger duo flanked them as they stepped out and took to the path up to the Obelisk.

Aolenthalassa didn't particularly like the thing — it unsettled him, though he would never admit it openly — but it was necessary to keep control, so he tolerated its presence.

He liked to imagine that the Obelisk, if it could think, regarded him much the same way.

The Chosen stood in a similarly unsettling single line in front of the massive black crystal. He drew himself up and let his power surround him in a bubble to remind them *all* who they were dealing with.

The first son of a First.

"Now that you've disturbed our peace," Aolenthalassa called when he was close enough, his voice supported by his magic to ring across the space. Even that was hard enough. Privately, he knew he'd pay for the unnecessary show of power, but felt it must be done. "You may as well make your report."

The lead Chosen's lip curled ever-so-slightly.

As one, the line of Chosen said: "Abyss's latest pet project rang the bells. Our master saw fit to see the creature personally, and during the examination, something happened. The Obelisk, mm, spoke. Claimed the boy to be Justice."

Rang the bells and *Justice* echoed in Aolenthalassa's mind, but he managed to choke down the shock.

"And?" Aunrielthalassa spoke up from beside him. "You did what about it?"

"We were ... incapacitated by the incident ... until very recently. The creature and its caretakers left with it."

Aolenthalassa covered his face with a hand. "You incompetent slugs. Left us to clean up your mess again, I see."

The screens placed strategically around the space flickered to life. Aolenthalassa initially ignored them, intent on berating the Chosen further, until the elven King's voice rang out.

He slowly wheeled to face the nearest screen.

"We rejoice," the King was saying, "that at long last, Justice is among us."

"We are overjoyed to announce," the Queen said, "the full cooperation and support of ourselves and the Council with Lord Justice — "

He didn't want to hear any more, and whipped around on his heel to stride away, Aunrielthalassa at his side.

"Those rats," Aolenthalassa snarled when they were back in their shuttle.

"They moved fast," Aunrielthalassa mused.

"And they'll regret it," Aolenthalassa said.

The King and Queen of the elves slowly made their way from where they'd made the announcement, conveniently (and purposefully) only a leisurely walk to where they'd inevitably be called next.

They were already walking by the time the messenger got to them, demanding they meet the brothers in the conference room.

The Terelath Nexus was the precise center of the Terelath 'flower,' and at the center of the Nexus was a nondescript circular building. The Seconds called it, unimaginatively, 'the conference room.'

Though, they supposed, the name was warranted. When Andural had crafted Terelath, for some reason he'd created this building with it, though the purpose for its design was unknown to anyone who wasn't Andural. Genius that the Bladesinger-Smith was, his designs were often more practical than not — very function over form — so the place was oddly out of character.

It was made of the same white metal he'd made all of the superstructure of Terelath out of, whose composition was still a mystery. It had no windows. Its interior walls were a faceted white stone. It was sterile and austere, and had only one major feature: a massive table dominating its center, with chairs surrounding.

Thus, because it looked like a room made for meetings, it was used as one.

Aolenthalassa and Aunrielthalassa had hurried to the conference room, but it still took them some time. As many mana pearls as they shoveled into their greedy maws, no amount of mana could stop what was happening to them — what they'd done to themselves.

Species with Weave-strands in their genetic makeup may have enjoyed more power and longer lifespans, but their composition wasn't without its downsides. One of which was that if they didn't have a steady and stable supply of Weave or one of its byproducts, they would decay.

The brothers had made their own addition to the conference room: two grown living-wood chairs at the 'head' of the table, higher than the other chairs — chairs in which the brothers found the King and Queen to be sitting as they burst in.

The echoes of their mother (who the King and Queen hadn't known, but knew *of*) were still there: the dark hair, now thinning. The pale skin, now dotted with disease marks that makeup couldn't entirely hide. Their garlands were an ostentatious rainbow of crystals, dull and chipped, their metal frameworks tinged with patina that daily-replaced flowers couldn't entirely hide. The layers of colorful robes, medals, and ornamentation only served to highlight their frail forms.

"*Just who do you think you are, claiming authority to speak for the Council?*" the elder, Aolenthalassa, roared.

"Well?" his mousy brother, Aunrielthalassa, snapped from slightly behind him.

"Just how many times have you tried to have us killed?" the Queen asked softly.

The brothers physically recoiled in shock.

"And always, we have survived," the King added smoothly.

"After all these long Ages, we have found ourselves immune to your machinations," the Queen said, her husky voice carrying the edge of obsidian under silk. "Unlike those that came before us."

With each sentence, the brothers' faces tightened further with horror, until naught remained but taut death masks.

"Terelath is dying," the King said. "And so are you."

"The Iyavesti comes."

"And we have chosen a side."

Pheonix's shuttle arrived at its destination a short time after leaving the Seat of the Chosen. Faranthalassa stayed in the transport and the others disembarked.

Pheonix's head was still wreathed in pain as he took in the details of the bar by rote: a small building, dark-shingled, with a narrow entranceway over which glowed a large, neon-lighted sign: 'Penny's.' Chani preceded him and held the door open for him to enter. The inside was cluttered with stuff and people and tables, but he was still too pissed off and distracted to bother cataloging it all. His mind was working overtime to process what he had experienced. Between that and the fact that he apparently could now experience pain, he wasn't sure how he was still conscious.

What he did notice was the small, slender hominin behind the bar. They wore a vest made of some kind of white fur, black hair styled in a bowl cut, and had delicate features. And behind them, the walls all around were decorated with bottles set into lighted shelves. No two alike, it seemed. Across the bar top were the unmistakable nozzles that spoke of beer on tap.

The delicate individual looked up from the drink they were fixing. Their face brightened as they saw Pheonix's group. With practiced motions, they flipped a precise amount of something from another bottle into the glass, then slid it to a patron sitting at the bar. They clapped small hands together, squealing with delight, and rushed forward. Chani stepped around Pheonix, smiling wearily, and took the offered hug.

"*Dar*ling, it's been so long," the person said. "And you look simply awful! Bad day?"

Chani grunted assent. She heaved herself onto a stool and slumped over the bar, weight on her elbows. Steele sat next to her, a little more stiffly. Pheonix stood where he was until Chani gestured him over. He sat on her other side, trying to keep his wings tight to his back to keep anyone from brushing them in the tight space.

The bartender reached for a mug and, while filling it from a tap, turned to Steele.

"And Commander Steele, you know your stunning face always just *makes* my day."

Steele smiled in response.

"Who is your friend?" They tipped their head in Pheonix's direction, handing the mug to Chani.

"Penny, this is Pheonix. Pheonix, Penny," Chani said over the mug. She nodded toward the bartender — Penny. "They run this place."

Penny smiled sweetly and came close enough to offer their hand to Pheonix. Pheonix stared at it, various reactions to a proffered hand depending on society and cultural expectations flashing through his mind, though he couldn't settle on one without asking questions or making assumptions. And in his current state, he just didn't care to do either.

"Nice to meet you," Pheonix said instead, to which Penny lowered their hand and cackled.

"No touching?" Penny asked (though by their tone, they didn't seem to be offended).

"I wasn't sure how I was supposed to perform."

"Perform?" Penny glanced at Chani, an eyebrow cocked.

Chani chuckled. "Don't tease him. He's had a rough day."

"Alright, alright."

Penny swiftly pivoted to talking at Chani while they bustled around to fix a drink for Steele (something clear in a flute). After placing the flute in front of Steele, they said to Pheonix, "Are you thirsty, love?"

"Yes," Chani said before Pheonix could open his mouth. "Just have a drink with us and unwind."

That amounted to an order.

"You know what you want, or would you like the master to find something for you?" Penny asked.

"Trust the master," Chani said, again before Pheonix could respond. "They always know what you want, even when you don't."

Pheonix shrugged this time. He wasn't about to try to make sense of all those bottles. Liquor hadn't made it into his studies yet.

Penny stood back and put a hand to their chin, scrutinizing Pheonix. Finally they nodded and turned around. They opened a small metal box that looked somewhat like a safe, and withdrew a beautiful, multi-petaled flower. On each gently curved, pale pink petal rested a small amount of shimmering liquid, and cupped in the center was a slightly larger amount, in which three blue fronds waved of their own accord.

Penny set it down very carefully in front of Pheonix so as not to disturb the liquid.

"Really, Penny?" Chani asked as Pheonix picked up the flower.

"Mm-hmm," said Penny. "Just watch."

Pheonix sipped from one of the petals and was almost immobilized by the rush of information. The ongoing attempt to process the violation he had suffered from the Obelisk suddenly took a secondary role to the more immediate concern of sorting out the subtle, intertwining flavors on his tongue.

Relief surged through him and he closed his eyes to shut out the world and enjoy the simple pleasure of tasting.

"Wow," Chani said. He could hear her only distantly.

"The master does it again," Steele chuckled.

"Was there *ever* any doubt?" Penny asked, coyly confident.

"I wanted to offer my apologies," Pheonix said after he'd calmed down.

"Hmm?" Chani asked. Now on her second mug of dwarven beer, she seemed to be relaxing, as well.

"For my behavior," he said, then paused, examining himself. "The Obelisk was … unpleasant."

Chani barked a sardonic laugh. "Unpleasant? Kid, it was more than unpleasant to *watch*. I'll have nightmares. To experience it must have been … I don't even fucking know. The only person you probably need to apologize to isn't here, anyway. You made a mess of his face."

Pheonix nodded. He did need to track Faranthalassa down.

"What happens now?" Pheonix asked.

"We need to figure out where to go from here," Steele said. "Give us time to talk about it. Tomorrow we'll let you know. Until then, just stay in the training grounds."

Pheonix nodded, then cracked a little grin. "And just think, you told me to 'get out more.'"

Chani snorted. "Don't get smart with me. I don't believe in coincidences."

FIFTEEN
Ultimatum

That night, Pheonix was subjected to another new and unpleasant emotion.

After all of the day's activity, his cottage seemed tiny and too quiet. Even with books littered about in stacks almost as tall as he was, books he would normally lose himself in, he couldn't focus on them. He felt alone, caged.

They were wrong — the Obelisk hadn't just examined him. It had changed something in him. He could feel it.

But what, and why? These were questions he couldn't allow to remain unanswered.

Research was becoming his way to make sense of an increasingly nonsensical world. So he dove back in, starting with the bells at the Temple of the Ascended. That was when the trouble had started. The bells supposedly only rang when an Ascended entered the Temple, but it stood to reason that they *may* respond to anything the mechanism couldn't readily recognize.

No information existed on Ascended construction. Besides, even the elves couldn't tell him what he was — not until the results of the molecular scan were compiled.

He moved on to researching the Obelisk, and as he did, the sense of wrongness throughout Terelath and regarding the balance, solidified and came into focus.

The Obelisk was tied to the Chosen, who were tied to the balance. Was his pain a punishment for his hatred of it? Not just pain, but violation, digging into his very core, disseminating his essence with all the tact and care of a grenade. The malicious intent he had sensed from it — had it been to determine if he was a threat?

The image of the mangled gnome from the market flashed in front of his mind's eye and his rage flared again. Whether or not the Obelisk had been actively trying to kill him earlier, or if it had been simply examining him without regard for his wellbeing (and what its motivations were for doing so) — was all ultimately irrelevant. What it had subjected him to was no less than an attack. Furthermore, it was the harbinger and enforcer of the balance. That alone made it an enemy.

Any comfort the strange liquor served up by Penny may have offered was long gone by the time Pheonix came to a decision.

He stepped out into the dark, quiet night and crossed the cropped grass clearing to Chani's cottage. There was no light inside, and no answer came when he knocked. Something knotted up within him.

He pulled out his communication crystal and focused on her image. After too long, her face flickered in the facets of the crystal.

She smiled, but it was strained. "What's up, kid?"

"I need to talk to you."

The smile disappeared as though she'd sensed his urgency. Relief flooded him when she didn't question it. "I've been in meetings all night. I'll come by."

"Thank you," Pheonix said, and meant it.

Her image faded.

He paced the two steps back and forth in his tiny cottage. The room lightened with the suns easing over the horizon, and finally a knock announced Chani's presence.

He stopped in the doorway.

Chani, Steele, Faranthalassa, Tyyrulriathula, Minrathous, and Crosinthusilas stood in a ragged line before his cottage, framed by the sunrise. Somehow, he wasn't surprised to see them though he had only called Chani.

Pheonix called to the group of them; "Do any of you have an answer for me yet?"

"To what question?" Faranthalassa asked.

Pheonix speared him with a look. "You should remember specifically, *Master of Propriety.*"

"What question is that?" Chani asked Faranthalassa.

"Master Pheonix asked if we … if we intentionally protect evil."

Tyyrulriathula drew in a sharp breath.

"This is about that gnome?" Steele said. "No system is perfect, Pheonix — "

"Don't give me that political bullshit," Pheonix snapped. "Systems are only as 'perfect' as their greatest flaw, and I'd call living hand-in-hand with those who only desire personal power and absolute control *damned* flawed. A social structure's survival necessitates that those with power take care of those without. You are all failing that. It is already crashing down.

"How many of you have walked among the elven people recently? Have you heard of the disappearances, how they are living in fear, or how the Council controls them, breath and blood? Why is one of the highest Weave-born species eating mana pearls to survive, *on their home planet*? Tell me, Commander, is there a numerical value for how many flaws must be present before something becomes so far from perfect it must burn? Or is that measured only in pain?"

Pheonix barrelled on, not letting the shocked Steele respond. "And you all claim to be a part of the system that leads the rest of the metacosm? Yes, that makes sense, based on what I've seen here. Every disgusting thing I saw in my childhood — the things that they attempted to do to me, the things I saw them do to others — all predictable ripples from this seat of corruption. What would the Creator think?"

"The balance — " Minrathous attempted to interrupt.

"*The balance?*" Pheonix spat, his wings unintentionally flaring out with the force of his conviction. His unholy rage rose like a thunderstorm. "*Did the Creator tell you to uphold the balance, or did you tell yourself in its voice?* The balance is *fractured*. It respects only status quo and power. Status quo is a stagnation that directly benefits those actively seeking ways to take advantage of a system. If you're not progressing, you're falling behind, and you've all ignored the evidence and buried it because you couldn't face that you were *complicit*. You comforted yourself with the thought, 'I'm just one person, what can I do?' and kept marching. I'm giving you the chance to step away. We need to change before it truly is too late."

Abject silence and stunned faces were all that met the end of his impassioned speech.

Caught up in his righteous fury, Pheonix didn't care what happened to him. If they chose to cast him out, then he would go with the satisfaction of knowing that he'd made the right decision.

After a long, charged moment, there was finally movement.

Tyyrulriathula, hesitantly at first and then with growing confidence, crossed the intervening distance and stood beside Pheonix. He put a hand on Pheonix's shoulder and faced his colleagues.

"Pheonix is right." He paused as if to say more, then shook his head. "Never have I been more sure of anything."

Crosinthusilas floated to stand on Pheonix's other side, her sharp jaw held high. She, too, rested a hand on his shoulder.

"You know where I stand — where I have always stood," she said, each word lashing out with the force of a whip strike.

Chani's face was a storm. When Pheonix's heated gaze lit upon her, the storm broke and she laughed, crossing the space between them with long strides.

She murmured to Pheonix as she came up next to him, "You have no idea how long I've waited for someone to say what you've just said. Well done, kid." And then stood next to Crosinthusilas.

Minrathous silently took her place by Chani. Tears poured down her cheeks, though she neither looked up nor spoke. She clutched her staff with white-knuckled, shaking hands. Chani wrapped an arm over her shoulder, pulling the druid to her side. Minrathous buried her face in Chani's coat.

Only Steele and Faranthalassa remained silhouetted by the rising suns.

Faranthalassa looked tortured, his face taut with emotion, eyes wide.

Pheonix held out his hand. "Come, servant of Spiraea. Do not torment your beloved Lady any further by suffering evil's malignant presence in her heart."

The tears veiling Faranthalassa's eyes spilled, and he came to Pheonix's side. When he turned to face Steele, he held himself proudly.

Steele sighed. "You all do realize some might consider this treason, don't you?"

Pheonix spread his wings behind the line of souls who, beside him and within him and throughout him, resonated.

At that moment, they rivaled the suns.

"Let them." His voice took on an odd tone and ring, carrying further than it should, echoing where it shouldn't. "Let them come for me and their own darkness will swallow them in the pursuit. As long as innocents are afforded no justice, so this I swear: evil will be made to answer for its crimes."

Something shifted on Steele's face. It was so subtle Pheonix may not have caught it, were he not in a hyper-aware state.

Steele nodded. "I see." Then they clapped their hands together and grinned broadly. The dissonance of their expression seemed so ephemeral that it almost could have been Pheonix's imagination — but Pheonix knew better. He filed it away. "In that case, let's sit down and figure out how we're going to do this, eh?"

There was a collective return to normal breathing, the choking tension bleeding away. It was surviving a battle — the feel of remaining standing after the enemy had been defeated. Not cheering triumph, but a bittersweet entwining of relief and surveying the battlefield to see what has been lost.

Chani and Tyyrulriathula comforted Minrathous. Faranthalassa collapsed on the ground in prayer, his fingers buried in the grass. Crosinthusilas hovered near Pheonix.

"You do know what you have done?" The Prime Lady asked quietly.

Pheonix set his jaw. "I am doing what is necessary. Terelath, Availeon, the Rangers, and even the Accord *will* be brought down by this if it continues. And if I fail, I will take whatever punishment is deemed appropriate."

"Rebellions are ugly," Crosinthusilas said. "Take it from one who has been in the trenches. Innocents are *always* claimed by them. That is inevitable; it is history. You may thrust yourself on the sword, but there's no telling who that sword will seek after it has drunk your blood."

Pheonix turned burning eyes on her. "Innocents are already being lost even as we speak. Taking action will result in losses, but the losses will be greater if we do nothing. The innocent are still people; let them be given *choice*, instead of conditioned to tread one path through fear and forced ignorance. Those that have yearned to fight can choose to do so with full agency. Those that can't, we will protect. Those are my terms."

Crosinthusilas studied him carefully as he spoke, a look dangerously akin to pain flashing across her face. Finally, she said, "Then I advise caution. You are idealistic, and that is necessary for change; but do not let your idealism carry you away."

Pheonix lowered his wings and took a breath. "I appreciate your counsel. And I hope I can rely on you to continue to provide your wisdom. It will be invaluable."

Crosinthusilas smiled, the slightest tugging of the corners of her lips. But it faded quickly. "One more word of advice for the moment; you want to protect innocents. Who decides innocence? You?"

The violet-eyed woman from the slave ship, now long-dead, flashed in Pheonix's mind's eye. "I have seen the face of innocence," he said, "and it dissolved in front of me at the hands of an evil man, who still walks unpunished. To any person who has been in that situation, the divide is clear. I think you know that better than most."

Crosinthusilas's lips twitched once more, and Pheonix continued:

"Morality *comes* from the trenches, not from sitting in safety and philosophizing about things that don't affect you personally. That is also why it is not just me. As I value you, I value each one of the others gathered here. But we must also go to all sapients — especially the enslaved, the dregs, the sick, the colonists and rim-worlders — and give them space, and shut down the voices of those who would try to silence them. How can we call ourselves agents of justice if we listen only to our own thoughts, or those of people who live just like us?"

Crosinthusilas bowed her head and moved to the side to make way for Chani and Tyyrulriathula. Minrathous, now pacified, excused herself and quickly exited the training grounds. Faranthalassa had not moved. Steele hung back, watching.

Tyyrulriathula's whole being was still tense; he overflowed with emotion so visceral even Pheonix could taste it. Chani moved with the fluid economy of a predator, her unease transcribed into a forced calm, leaving her muscles loose and ready.

Chani slung an arm over Tyyrulriathula's shoulder. At the touch, some of her calm seemed to transfer to him.

"Uh — well, I need a beer. Anyone else?" Tyyrulriathula said, just slightly too loudly.

"Normally I'd agree, but we have a lot of work to do," Chani said. There was an edge to her voice.

"Where do we even start?" came Faranthalassa's voice from beyond them. He looked lost.

"Spiraea not communicative, huh?" Tyyrulriathula asked sympathetically.

Faranthalassa ignored him.

"I may have an answer for that," Chani said, "but I'll need time. And we'll need to start small and stay quiet. We can't go around overthrowing things just yet, as impatient as we are. Revolutions only happen quickly if there's significant bloodshed — and bloodshed begets bloodshed."

"We need to shift the system, not overthrow it," Pheonix said.

"That's plan A, anyway. For now, I think we stay in a holding pattern. We have the advantage of having a reason to meet frequently. Keep your eyes and ears open. Find the cracks, and report to me before you do anything rash."

She met Pheonix's eyes with a piercing focus. "You. Learn." She tightened her grip around the young elf's neck, yanking him down. "You, behave. And finish *your* training." While he squawked and fought her, she looked at Crosinthusilas with a lopsided smirk. "I don't need to tell you shit." The Prime Lady answered with a wolfish, cold smile of her own. Chani let Tyyrulriathula go and looked back at Faranthalassa. "You. Pray. Find your answers in Spiraea."

"What will *you* do?" Tyyrulriathula asked, rubbing his neck.

Chani gave a rictus of a grin. "What I do best. I'll see you guys tomorrow. Let's go, Steele."

She pivoted on one heel and left the training grounds with Steele in tow.

Tyyrulriathula shook his head, watching her leave. "She's scary when she gets like that."

"Have you seen her like this before?" Pheonix asked.

"Not personally," Tyyrulriathula said. "But we've all heard the stories. You should check out her file, if you end up with the security clearance. Though, the way things are going, I can't imagine you won't." He took a breath and let it out. "I've got a lot of thinking to do."

"We will resume tomorrow," Crosinthusilas said. "Rest, if you can."

Pheonix bowed his head as she and Tyyrulriathula left, leaving only Faranthalassa.

The elven Ranger stood, straightened his shoulders, and looked off after the others into the shifting distance of the training area boundary.

"I will do as the Commander says. I must commune with Spiraea. Ultimately her wishes are the directives under which I live my life — if she objects to this, I cannot go any further in good faith."

"Do what you must," said Pheonix.

Faranthalassa met his eyes solemnly. "You … everything I've held as truth is called into question now. And I don't know whether to thank you or berate you." He sighed. "If nothing else, I respect your commitment and will. I only hope Spiraea will answer me."

"Best of luck," Pheonix said.

"And to you."

"Oh, and Faranthalassa," Pheonix called.

Faranthalassa turned, looked over his shoulder, haloed in the newly-birthed sunlight.

"I'm sorry," Pheonix said. "For hitting you."

Faranthalassa smiled. "I would have hit me, too."

Pheonix bit back an argument, Faranthalassa's resignation to being a receptacle for the emotions of those around him threatening to stoke his barely-sated rage. Instead, he let the elf leave the training ground.

Then, Pheonix was alone.

He stared out at the sunrise, taking in the opalescence cascading through the clouds. The silence hit him, but it wasn't grating. He had a plan. *They* had a plan.

For the first time in his life, he had a purpose.

SIXTEEN
Spiraea's Choice

His mind in turmoil, Faranthalassa immediately left for his favorite spot to pray on Availeon, deep in the forest, far from the outskirts of Terelath and well beyond any sapient influence on nature's zero state. Terelath was a nature-focused place, but not a *natural* place. It still stank of sapient interference. It rather had to be, though, given that it was host to so many. Not every species was as willing or capable of living as deliberately in-tune with *all* faces of Nature — not just the palatable ones or those more easily-controlled — as elves did.

And not all elves are willing to live as wild as we should, Faranthalassa thought bitterly.

The thought sparked the panic he had struggled with since the meeting.

Should elves live wild? What was right? Who made that decision?

Everything he thought he knew was teetering on the edge of a black hole of the unknown. Since childhood, Faranthalassa had known his place. Or so he had thought.

He settled down in a hollow of one of the largest non-sapient trees in the deep woods of this part of Availeon. While they were demonstrably non-sapient, Faranthalassa still felt that the trees were sentient; the earth and plants were all alive. Just because he couldn't converse with them in the traditional manner didn't mean they were silent. The familiar thought comforted him, and he closed his eyes to let the sounds of nature fill his mind.

The everpresent whisper of wind, fluidly sailing through and around the flora, left audible shivers from the greenery in its wake. Shifting light and shadow danced across his body, trails of alternating cool and warm. He felt the rough bark behind him, the cool prickly grass under him. The smell of plants and ground were carried on the air itself, that perpetual traveler to unknown places.

And he sensed the fauna all around: birds, insects, the occasional larger creature.

It was a symphony of both random and predictable, a concert for all the senses.

For Faranthalassa, this was meditation. This was prayer.

In time, the light and sound changed.

Faranthalassa opened his eyes.

"Yes? What?" Matilde barked.

She was an extremely tall mixture of ent and elf, skin cobbled and striated, with leaves and ferns coiling in and out of the long green vines that were her hair. But unlike the ents she resembled, to whom 'urgency' was a concept that simply didn't exist, 'patience' was similarly a concept foreign to Matilde. She was the demigod who oversaw all of Availeon. Therefore, in order to get to Spiraea, he had to go through Matilde first.

"What is the balance?" Faranthalassa asked, unfazed by Matilde's terseness.

"Seriously? You called me here for that philosophical feces? I'm a working-class demigod. I have an entire ecosystem on a First planet to maintain and no one to help."

"Do you not have an answer, or do you not have the time to explain it?" Faranthalassa pressed.

She speared him with an angry look. "Go ask Spiraea that, mortal. It's not my job."

And she was gone.

"Thank you," Faranthalassa said plaintively to the empty air.

Spiraea's mood being what it was these days, she didn't tend to manifest for anyone who wasn't serious. And that meant going directly to her temple.

In the deepest, wildest part of Availeon.

Faranthalassa let out a long sigh and stood.

It wasn't safe for solo elves even of his caliber to make the trek, but he'd have to take the chance. He didn't have time to gather a party, and he couldn't offer an explanation as to why he needed to speak to Spiraea urgently, which wasn't fair to anyone who would be risking themselves to come with him. If Spiraea disapproved of his supporting Pheonix, he needed to know immediately.

He'd have to ground-walk, an ability taught only to elven Rangers wherein the individual dissolved into the earth and traveled through it as an ephemeral being. The different subspecies of elves had similar abilities — Faranthalassa, being a forest elf, could tree-walk if he wanted. But given the distance he had to travel and the time in which he had to do it, ground-walking would be more efficient. The earth offered its own energy and nutrients, meaning he could go longer without sustenance or rest.

Elves themselves were not made entirely of physical elements the way other species were, which made things like element-walking possible.

Availeon was beyond huge. It was eighty percent water, and what aboveground land it did have was still larger than most planets in sheer square units. Said land was arranged into three continents, with the largest being Spiraea's Realm (where Terelath had been built). Spiraea's domain — the entrance to her actual temple — was smack dab in the middle of a far-reaching forested area that stretched across most of the continent of Spiraea's Realm.

Faranthalassa couldn't conceive of trying to travel to Spiraea's doorstep in any way other than element-walking. Elves were fast, and had great stamina, but it would take him weeks of running and jumping through the trees to get there on foot — months, if he had to walk.

He didn't have that time.

And so, he initiated the ground-walk and headed for Spiraea's domain.

The wilderness changed around him, gradually. It became harder to ground-walk as, several days later, he approached Spiraea's inner domain.

Finally, he was forced out entirely. He emerged on his guard, knife in hand. Time to go it on foot.

There were things here that could and would kill an elf, not even counting his mistress. He could only hope she was in good humor and would tolerate his passing, and that he'd get lucky and only run into things he could deal with.

He pushed deeper into the forest, climbed over exposed roots and tumbles of boulders, slid down gravel-covered hills, crawled through thickets of thorns that tore at him to leave burning welts, circumvented wide gorges filled with dragonsteeth rocks and rapid whitewater, and carefully picked a path through a festering, fetid swamp with skeletal branches woven thick overhead through sometimes neck-deep muck, where he hoped his next step wouldn't dunk him completely under.

The awareness of Spiraea's presence — her gaze — was heavy on him.

He didn't even know where he was going, exactly.

This was the first time he'd gone to see Spiraea; while he'd heard many stories of elves who had made the trek, there hadn't been any for Ages, and none solo for even longer, as her capricious whim and strict requirements made it more and more difficult to see her. He didn't have much to go on.

So only his intuition led him, step by step. Through the pain, exhaustion, and self-doubt. Through a wilderness that was suddenly not only inhospitable but not speaking any language he understood.

It was a humbling meditation in suffering.

Despite it all, he wasn't afraid. If anything, the harder Nature pressed on him, the more exhilarated he became. It almost felt as though the trials were stripping him bare, peeling back the layers he'd folded over his wild core to become the ever-elegant and reserved Master of Propriety.

If I am to die here, then so be it, he thought feverishly. *If this is how my Lady wants my life to end, then so be it. I give my soul to you.*

Bright light blinded him, and he stumbled forward —

— no longer held back; nor cold, exhausted, wet, or in pain.

He straightened and looked around wonderingly.

The brightest and most beautiful of nature spread before him in a landscape of dreams. In the distance, snow-capped mountains wreathed in rolling prismatic clouds stood against a cobalt sky splashed in paintings made of galaxies. Hills of waving green-and-yellow grass and spotted in colorful flowers surrounded a deep, silent lake fed by a wide river.

He stood at the crest of the hills with the proud, tall forest stretching out behind him. At his feet and all around, bunches of flowers in every color and shape waved their greetings in the slight breeze that smelled of water and faraway places.

Beyond the mountains, violent squalls raged, lightning arcing across the sky. On the edge of where the mountains met the forest, a fire seethed, ever-hungry, devouring grass and tree and flower alike but never quite seeming to advance.

He took a deep breath and blinked tears from his eyes.

In that blink, *she* arrived.

Clothed in pure white armor of spiderwebs and lily petals, an aureole of summer storms wreathing her head, through which hair the shifting colors of sunset floated, Spiraea looked down her nose at him.

Faranthalassa dropped to his knees and bowed his head.

"My Lady …" he said tremulously.

"'*I give my soul to you*'," she mocked in a voice like the baying of wolves on a cold night. "Do you love me so?"

Startled, he looked up. "Of course, my Lady! I meant every word!"

She watched him silently for a moment, seemingly torn between bemusement and irritation. "Why did you come?"

"My dearest Lady, this humble servant has a question, if you would so —"

"Dispense with your 'propriety' nonsense. Your heart is as clear water to me. Attempting to ply the Ascended with shaped sinewaves is an insult."

"I — I must know … what is the balance?"

"Which?" she asked coolly and quickly. "The Creator's balance or the other?"

His heart stopped for a breath, cold pouring through his veins and leaving numbness behind. This was a worse sensation than all of what her domain had thrown at him. He struggled to inhale.

"There are … two?" he finally managed.

"You must be referring to the false one."

Faranthalassa wanted to vomit. He opened his mouth, but no words came out — but also, thankfully, no vomit.

Spiraea's lips quirked in a partial smile; it seemed bemusement had finally won over irritation. "You lights are so dense — but funny. You use language as I use the winds, but you take the current and turn it to stone."

When Faranthalassa blinked at her, uncomprehending, she sighed and said, "Who offered the idea of the balance? What was their aim? Your answer lies in the veiled past."

She knelt down to put her face close. The essence of Nature enveloped his senses. He was instantly once again a child bounding through the forests — free of 'propriety', the constant low-grade worries that had plagued him dissipating like fog in the morning sun. The pain of longing for those days lanced through him.

"Which do you intend to follow, little elf?" Her orange eyes wandered over him like she was assessing him for market.

He got the distinct sense that saying anything remotely close to 'your will' would be a mistake. This was a direct call for him to think for himself.

And the thought didn't scare him. In fact, it was as though her presence buoyed him, awakening something within him. The last dregs of his anxiety at conversing with an Ascended sloughed away, and he looked up at her with fire.

There was only one answer. There had only ever been one.

"The Creator," he said, firmly.

Her smile widened, eyes slitted. "You are the first in a long time — and most interesting by far — to make it to me. So I ask again — do you love me?"

Her way of double-speaking made his brain do flips to attempt to comprehend. She was terrifying up close, but somehow also exuded the kind of sexuality that would make even a well-seasoned individual blush (which Faranthalassa was not; he was, in fact, very under-seasoned.)

He loved his Lady, of course — but she was asking if he was *in love* with her. He wasn't sure how to respond; wasn't sure he knew what the kind of love she spoke of even was.

His parents had passed from mana-sickness before he'd even emerged from the renewal tree, and so upon his 'birth,' he essentially became a ward of the state, with the King and Queen responsible for his education and wellbeing. As he grew, he had learned he had a connection with nature even deeper than most other elves. That was why he had taken on the rigorous training of an elven Ranger, why he had given himself to Spiraea.

Adventure, exploration, climbing the highest tree, diving under cold clear water until his lungs were fit to burst, hiding in a bush to watch the creatures go by — all were his daily routine, his solace, his reason for living. Then he was offered the position of Master of Propriety. There was good reason for it — being the last of the forest elves, he was uniquely suited to a position of finding common ground between other elves. Even the stuffiest elf would find it difficult to argue with the final son of an entire subspecies. And he was certainly humbled by the opportunity to serve all of elvenkind — and all of sapientkind.

So he had taken the opportunity.

But he'd always missed what she represented. Wildness.

Pheonix was exactly right.

Faranthalassa had known about the wild woods encroaching on more and more of developed Terelath, because there weren't enough left with the power to influence Nature. The food shortages. The mana pearls.

Hell, he even knew about the maze. But that was too painful to face even now.

And most importantly, Faranthalassa knew that the Council and Chosen were facilitating it all.

The representatives of evil cultures and organizations sat on high with their self-important smirks, driving long-winded sessions about the ethics of slavery versus destroying an important market — when *of course* the answer was to free the taken and punish the takers, because sapients weren't products.

They keep to their own and we keep to ours, said the elven Council regarding evil.

Except that wasn't how it worked.

Those orcs in the market hadn't been the first to 'escape' and cause havoc and wouldn't be the last. If anything,

Pheonix would probably be facing a harsher punishment for interfering than the orcs would have even had they killed that poor gnome.

Evil constantly took what wasn't theirs and 'the balance' allowed them to hide behind bureaucratic stonewalling and semantic filibustering.

A representative would say to the Chosen: "You need to get control of your slavers in this region; they're preying on this protected colony planet."

And the Chosen and other representatives would respond: "Preying is a very harsh word, Councilor."

And just like that, the bait was taken and an issue of sapient rights and sapient lives would be whittled down to a discussion about which terms should be used in session — which would never be resolved, so when the attacks happened again, so did the argument over words.

And evil did it because they knew they could. They knew that by taking legislative time to argue over bullshit, nothing would ever change, nothing would ever get done. The system would forever be skewed (and, over time, become more and more skewed) in their favor.

Faranthalassa, in his naïveté, had sensed the problem but could never put it into words. Not until Pheonix had blown into his life with his sharp, unyielding questions and that dark, piercing gaze which coaxed the truth from everyone it lit upon. Yes, Faranthalassa had known something was wrong, but when that wrongness was the very backbone of one's society, what was there to do? He had only been able to work with what he was given, and worse —

His real love had always been nature. The confines of sapients and social interactions fraught with subtext and fabricated truths — it made him edgy and stressed. It made him not *him*.

But he'd taken the opportunity to maybe change things, make it a little better, shoving into a locked box his wildness and bafflement at the intricacies of the statecraft jungle. He wanted to do it — he'd done it — for his people. But now that Pheonix had dissected the lies, why invalidate his essence for hollow efforts inside a system that would have never yielded in the first place?

Pheonix — no, *Justice* — had given him a chance to make change, without continuing to uphold the abuses.

And here, against all odds, was wildness calling him back. Asking him to choose.

Something wanton took flight in his chest.

"I was in love with you before I ever saw your face or knew your name," he blurted, a husky confession that was equal parts intoxicating and embarrassing.

She chuckled warmly — the sound sent shivers through him — and stood. "You will find me a most interesting mate, but neither you nor I are ready as we are. I will come to you when the seasons change. Make sure you prepare yourself for me."

"Yes, my Lady."

"You have your answer. As for what to do about it: I have a request of you as my future mate. Prove your love to me. There is a blight on my beloved Availeon. Some red mage has created himself a spot — untouchable even for me — in the outskirts of my forest. The Meta-Rangers know of it. Ask them. And eradicate it."

"Yes, my Lady."

Her thorny face melted into a smile. "I like how *you* say that. Here, my love. A gift," she ran her fingers over his garland. "But you will have to wait until you return home to see it. I am not overly inclined to being affectionate in my current phase. Now, go. We both have much work ahead of us."

She raised a long-fingered hand and blew. Whipping winds enveloped him, catapulted him backwards: the world shot by in a disorienting blur. He stumbled and landed hard on his ass but was too dizzy to stand immediately. When the world solidified, he realized he was in the Grove of the Ascended, the garden that grew all around the Temple of the Ascended. Through the branches he could see the bulk of the main Temple. It was night, and everything was cool and quiet but he could still feel her presence; he reached up to touch his garland. A slow stream burbled nearby. He knelt by it and caught the glimmer of his own reflection.

Pure golden leaves had replaced the garland he'd previously worn.

I never asked her what the Creator's balance entailed, Faranthalassa realized suddenly. *Shit.*

Then, on its heels and with some embarrassment, *I suppose I'll ... be able to ask her later.*

Well, it's time for a name change.

"Come in," Chani called. She took a sip from a large mug of black coffee and peered over its rim at her visitor.

Faranthalassa entered and gave an elegant and confident bow.

Chani's brows raised.

The change about him was immediately visible (both with eyes and senses). Aside from the obvious garland of golden leaves (which, from elven legend, signified him as having been chosen as the consort of an Ascended), he was more emotionally open than she'd ever sensed from him before, despite him being quite tense in that moment.

He'd disappeared for almost a week directly after the meeting with Pheonix. While she knew that Faranthalassa — as one of the premier elven Rangers in the universe — could handle himself, the length of his absence and the circumstances surrounding it had her prepping a Research Operations team on the down low to go find him. But now, it was obvious where he had been.

"Faranthalassa," she said in greeting.

He shook his head. "It is Faran. I have been accepted by my Lady, so I can dispense of the unnecessary trappings of elven culture."

Elven name suffixes — thalassa, thula, and the like — denoted the individual's location, affiliation, and subspecies, though the direct translation of such was rather obtuse to outsiders like Chani.

Rather purposefully, Chani thought. *The Firsts hadn't had such naming conventions.*

"Alrighty then, Faran. Spiraea answered, I take it?"

Faran averted his gaze. "Master Pheonix — no, Lord Justice — is right. About everything. The Chosen's balance is a false one."

Chani closed her eyes, emotions tangling within her like a nest of snakes. She trusted Pheonix, had seen the evidence of it herself, but there was still a part of her that doubted — no, hoped. Hoped the situation was salvageable, that by shifting her resources or her approach, with powerful allies and an Ascended on her side, she could avoid a complete reconstruction.

But confirmation that the entire system was *broken* from an Ascended — it didn't get more serious than that.

Of course, she thought bitterly. *It's never that simple.*

"Then I suppose we can go forward with light hearts," she said, flashing Faran a pained look paired with a rueful smile.

"As long as you remember, 'violence begets violence.'" Faran warned, quoting Chani from the day Pheonix called them all to action.

Chani snorted. "I'm only violent when I absolutely have to be. No, the very point of all this is to save the lives of those crushed under the grinding wheel of bureaucracy. I've seen entirely too much of it. Evil is hard enough to deal with without inviting it in for fucking tea."

"I never knew you felt that way," Faran said.

"Speaking it would be akin to treason from someone in my position, as Steele said," Chani sighed. "So I did my best to work within the confines of my role, to do what I could."

Faran grimaced. "As did I." He hesitated. "Do you think Lord Justice was right? That we were … complicit?"

"Listen, philosophy isn't my thing. I don't bother to analyze *why* I do things, I just do them as I feel I must. I saw a problem, I did the best I could to maneuver without losing the power facilitating maneuvering. By doing so, did I become complicit? Probably. But what other choice did I have? If I had attacked the system head-on, it would have crushed me. If I had chosen to turn a blind eye, I would have been the worst kind of coward. Either way, falling to depressive self-flagellation at this juncture isn't going to accomplish anything. Neither is trying to assuage our guilt. Right now, action is the only thing that matters."

"My Lady said something similar."

"Was that *all* she said?"

"She posed me a query: who first brought up the balance?"

A tense silence greeted the question.

Chani finally said, sounding irked: "I … can't seem to remember."

"I can't either," Faran said quietly, clearly disturbed.

"Huh," said Chani after a long pause. Her voice was oddly sharp. "You'd think that would be something taught in every classroom, Ranger and elf. I'll have to look into that. Anything else?"

"She gave me a task: to remove the red mage in the forests of Availeon."

"Ah, him," Chani said, swiftly moving to the new topic. "Here, I'll send you what we've got." She accessed her wristcomm to transfer the relevant documents to his implants. "Done. The gist of it is that about thirty days ago, a red mage built himself a tower outside Terelath, and put some kind of barrier o' death around the location. We have visuals but nothing can survive going past the barrier — not even tech — so there's very little intel of substance. You can read what we've tried and the little we have gleaned through outside scanning, though.

"And of course, said bureaucracy being what it is, I'm having a hell of a time even requisitioning for further intel. The higher-ups want to leave it alone. He's way out there, supposedly not hurting anyone. They don't think it's worth throwing resources at."

Faran made a face. "If the barrier is that sophisticated, where do we even start?"

"That's what I was thinking, at first," Chani said. "But I might have an edge on it now. Now that we've seen what *he* can do."

Faran blinked, then comprehension dawned. "Lord Justice?"

"Yes. But, as a side note, I think we should keep calling him Pheonix. He doesn't want to know; hell, it seems like he's fulfilling his role without knowing. So let's respect his wishes. Anyway, he's Ascended ... somehow. Let's train him up and throw him at it."

She sighed and tapped an index finger on her desk. "See, the whole damn thing feels familiar, but I can't pinpoint how. I just have this hunch Pheonix is what we need. But he'll need some help once he gets inside. Mind taking that mission on? Having a seasoned fighter with him would be useful."

"Against a red mage? Yes, I think that would be workable. I will have to join his combat training until the mission to ensure we can work effectively together."

"Good. Every single representative we host from across the metacosm was watching the day the Obelisk spoke to him. We'd be careless not to think they've put it together and are planning something already. It was quiet while you were gone, but I don't trust that. I don't think they'll act on him directly here in Terelath — too many eyes — but one of our prime objectives from here on out has to be to make sure the kid can defend himself against anything they might throw at him once he *leaves*."

"You're still certain he will leave?" Faran asked.

"He'll have to. There're too many variables. If nothing else, because this is the seat of the metacosm — and, with the influence of the balancing reigning, also the seat of evil. But they have bureaucracy on their side, too. We can only hope it takes time, and that they're scared — or at least fighting amongst themselves about who gets to claim the bragging rights of ending him." She rolled her eyes.

"Understood."

"Coordinate with Tyyrulriathula and keep me updated?"

Faran nodded, bowed again, and left.

Chani looked at the door as it closed, but she wasn't seeing it. Her mind was a million miles away on a million different subjects. Sometimes it was hard to keep them all straight, even with implants and cybernetic support.

Sometimes she fleetingly questioned what it would be like to have a normal lifespan, a normal life.

But as she always did when such questions occurred, Chani shook it off.

Too much to do to die.

She stood and went to the open center of the room. Out of fold-space, she pulled a personal subspace displacement device: a tool developed by the Mahji in conjunction with the gnomes. She was one of the few to own one.

Teleporting in and out of places without following the threads of the Weave was not safe for general use. At least, not yet.

Next, she pulled out the key, a multi-faceted orb. She shifted its facets along complicated inner mechanisms until it showed the long-memorized coordinates to a place she visited often. Once the last coordinate clicked in place, the orb pulsed in her hands once, and activated.

The closest kin to the sensation of subspace travel was sliding left. Physical reality melted and reformed instantaneously — one place literally becoming another in a way that made her brain hurt to witness — which left some residual dizziness, but not the same kind as magical teleportation. She unconsciously braced for the increased gravity and tuned out the rush of minds and their emotions.

She'd appeared at one end of a completely spherical room, the walls of which were paneled in concentrated clusters of discs made from iridescent crystal and the purple metallic threads of imperium. A catwalk stretched from nothing (there was only one way in or out of this room and Chani had it, no physical door) to the very heart of the sphere, which contained — another sphere.

Made of some kind of liquid housed in an anti-grav field, it was probably twenty times the size of its only occupant and filled with a miniature underwaterscape, all of which shone with an internal gentle blue light — the only light in the place except for the ephemeral sparks that occasionally drifted from the imperium.

"Undine," Chani said. "It's time."

Inside the blue sphere, an aquatic elf slept. They were blue-skinned, long-limbed, painfully thin, with long-clawed hands. Their body was entirely wrapped in multiple layers: black mesh, blue mesh, then finally numerous hot-pink straps. Pink hair longer than their entire body flowed all around them, gently tugged by the internal current.

Aquatic elves, while in the water, often took on a finned lower half. Undine's fins were many layered, tattered, and iridescent.

Commander, a voice whispered within Chani's head and from all angles like the echoes in a vast cave. *You know my terms.*

Chani sighed gustily and waved her arms. They'd had this conversation far too many times.

"Look, it's not that I don't want to — it's that I don't have the authority. I've *tried*."

Crossroads, the voice insisted.

"Undine," Chani admonished.

No response.

Chani sighed again. "Here's the thing. You know about the kid. If things work out, *trust me*, we will be able to deal with Crossroads sooner rather than later."

Still no response.

"Not good enough, huh? Fine. I uh, I probably have some operators I can throw at it. At least until the thing with the kid pans out."

Who?

Chani thinned her lips. "The girls, the old man, annnd … Sabot?"

*Sabot's **team**.*

"Ugh, fine," Chani said. "You drive a hard bargain."

What about the other children?

"Not ready. Though I don't doubt they will end up on Crossroads eventually. Hell, we've had a couple come in through doors, you know that. Any news on the Professor?"

He's changed locations, and I haven't found him again, yet.

"Think it's the same place he was before?"

Probably. He's too arrogant to even dream that I exist, or that we know about him. But Abyss, he's begun taking people.

"Fuck," Chani said and scrubbed a hand down her face. "Right. I appreciate the tip."

SEVENTEEN
Firsts

After Pheonix's impassioned demand for change, things mostly went back to normal. He continued his martial training with Zasfioretaeula and Tyyrulriathula, then crammed at night.

His training was certainly ramping up, not that he was complaining. He'd taken it relatively easy (for him, anyway), and a period of higher activity was neither good nor bad. It just was. And he'd take it in stride.

If nothing else, it would help keep his mind off of the Obelisk, and everything else. People were acting differently around him; they'd slip up and start to call him a different name, and then catch themselves. They showed Pheonix the kind of respect he'd previously only seen them give to Crosinthusilas or Chani.

He'd also been all but ordered not to leave the training grounds at all. He had an inkling of why, but didn't consider it important, so he wasn't going to bother pursuing that puzzle.

The puzzle he *was* having trouble with: his new 'ability' to feel pain.

The increased training did cause pain, which he wasn't especially pleased about. He'd seen pain affect others when they'd overworked their bodies — the old man, the slaves — so he was familiar with it in concept, but he'd never had to personally deal with it.

It wasn't that the pain was particularly difficult to handle, physically. He adapted quickly to the muscle soreness after a workout or the twinges when he'd stretched his malformed wings too far. He found he could rise above mild pain with no trouble, and middling pain with little issue. He wasn't going to seek extreme pain as a test — too much risk — but with those two data points, he was relatively confident he could at least endure it.

However, the mental effects were more prominent. His hatred for the Obelisk had deepened — that the accursed object masquerading as something of the Creator's had violated him, and left him changed.

As Pheonix entered the training space one day, he found Zasfioretaeula standing at its center, with an uneasy Tyyrulriathula off to the side.

"Come, Master Pheonix," Zasfioretaeula said. "Today, you face the Bladestorm."

Zasfioretaeula waited in the center of a complex seal that felt like power. Pheonix rolled his shoulders and nodded.

The Prime War-Bladesinger started to hum.

It was a tuneless little song, somehow lonely in its singularity. At the same moment, Zasfioretaeula's two Lawblades slid from their sheaths, and from them, the blades of the Bladesong.

Then, the Bladestorm began.

Pheonix had, even to his hyperfast mind and reflexes, literally no time to react. The blades were suddenly there in the air — his brain sent urgent *move!* commands to his muscles, but interrupting that was the pain of an ethereal sword spearing his thigh.

He parried a blade, but three more stuck into his bicep. As he shifted his leg back, four sprouted from it. He tried to jump away, but his leg was useless from the blades that he hadn't even seen. The pain was staggering.

He ceased to resist.

The blades hit him all at once, from all different angles, and he went slack.

As Pheonix fell, time seemed to slow. He could see them now, darting like intangible silverfish in and out of existence — multiplanar, multiphasic weapons spawned by the anger and fear of a magical species that crammed all its emotions into its boots.

The blades themselves made the melody, rupturing air, trailing Weave, sparking light — a melody into which Zasfioretaeula's humming fit perfectly.

The blades rocketed towards Pheonix — but dissipated before contact. Pheonix hit the dirt and stared up into the white-blue sky — thinking, processing.

Zasfioretaeula filled his vision. "Master Pheonix. Why did you stop?"

Tyyrulriathula closed his eyes as the Bladestorm began. He tensed every muscle in his body to keep from running away or screaming or … something. He didn't have a name for what he was feeling and balked at seeking the answer. The intensity of it took the breath out of his lungs. It was like nothing he'd ever experienced, in the worst way possible.

Just when Tyyrulriathula had begun to consider death preferable to enduring one more second, and as if in response to his very desperation, the whirlwind that was the Bladestorm died. Tyyrulriathula opened his eyes to find Pheonix on the ground, a bloody mess. Tyyrulriathula's heart jumped, fearing him dead for a moment.

Sounds seemed to come from too far away and his vision felt like it was lagging just barely perceptibly behind the movement of his eyes.

He blinked, confused by the afterimages in his vision. His brain struggled to make sense of the conversation between Zasfioretaeula and Pheonix.

"I had to analyze it," Pheonix said.

Buzzing. That's what it was. The Bladestorm had left behind a low buzzing in his ears and brain and teeth. His stomach knotted.

"You can analyze it after it's not killed you," Zasfioretaeula responded drily.

Am I vibrating? Tyyrulriathula thought, lifting a hand slightly — it was steady. *What the hell is going on?*

But there was definitely something crawling under his skin. The sensation continued to amplify, and he gritted his teeth against it, for all the good it did. His body was coming apart and he was helpless to stop it. Rage bubbled up — *stop it* — terror swirling under it — *MAKE IT STOP* — his vision wavered —

"Tyyrulriathula."

Zasfioretaeula's curt tone cut through the noise of his mind unraveling.

He met the Prime War-Bladesinger's stern eyes and realized he was breathing too hard. His heart pounded a sickly rhythm around which his anger wrapped spiked chains, dragging him back into the pit —

"Demonstrate the dagger dance," Zasfioretaeula instructed.

The order brooked no hesitation. Keeping his gaze down, Tyyrulriathula took a step toward the weapon racks. His feet hitting the ground, his pulse, his breathing — all yearned to join that bloody cadence struggling to rise.

He battered it down, grabbing the ceremonial daggers too hard. Like a nest of writhing eels, the knot of emotion wriggled through his grasp no matter how hard he pressed down. And it was winning.

He stopped in the center of the ring, brought up the steps in his mind, and focused on them. The dagger dance required a lot of concentration and he was short on that. But it was also buried in his muscle memory, and he leaned on that to kickstart the motions.

The dagger dance: staccato bursts deliberately without rhythm, performed completely silently while staring at the ground. Even the fingers of his rage couldn't find a hold in this highly controlled, regimented 'dance.'

The movements were not a comfort — because, in his current mindset, likely nothing could be — but the mixture of familiarity and lack of tempo at least quieted the maelstrom building within him.

After the final step, Tyyrulriathula straightened, numb.

As his cuts sealed, Pheonix stood, leaving only an iridescent dark stain in the dirt.

He watched Tyyrulriathula perform, aware that Zasfioretaeula was staring intently at the young elf throughout the whole 'dance.' The dance itself was odd enough to make Pheonix wonder why it was labeled so. Such an activity usually involved rhythm, melody, flow. Something. This seemed hellbound to avoid anything that might traditionally qualify for the moniker.

"Now go meditate in the Garden of Peace," Zasfioretaeula said to Tyyrulriathula when he had finished.

The young elf left without a word.

Pheonix was nowhere near versed enough in sapient interactions to understand this exchange.

Zasfioretaeula turned to Pheonix once it was just the two of them. "Tyyrulriathula is the youngest elf ever to be chosen by a Lawblade and is one of the most promising Bladesingers I've ever seen. But he has several flaws. He flouts our conventions, openly acting in a way unbefitting of a Lord." Zasfioretaeula gave a tight, sardonic smile.

Pheonix wondered if the Prime War-Bladesinger believed those words.

"However," Zasfioretaeula continued, "his attitude is the least of his problems. Of more concern is that he has not experienced true combat, and thus has never been blooded. We do not know how he will react to the frenzy and uncertainty of true battle. By his personality alone, there have been whispers of suspicion that he may become a War-Bladesinger. But we have no proof. He will face combat eventually and we will know — but, by then, it may be too late.

"We are bound, many voices calling for handling him in different ways. And now, his association with you adds new depth to the problem. All this to say he was here as no coincidence. Were he to have lost himself today when confronted with a true Bladestorm, the seal we stand on would have stopped it. I could have restrained him. While that did not happen, his reaction proves that he is closer than we thought — thus, why I had him perform the dagger dance. It is taught to Bladesingers early on in their training, and acts as a way to condition the body and mind, repeated exhaustively until one can perform it in one's sleep. But, and we do not tell our recruits this, it is also a way to disconnect from the Song when it becomes discordant, before the maelstrom begins."

Pheonix digested this. "But if elves prize dispassion, why is his reaction abnormal? Wouldn't overwhelming emotion take its toll on any elf? Things suppressed don't disappear."

"My people would like to believe they do. Bladesingers are connected to the blades. All of us." Zasfioretaeula stroked the ornate sheaths on his chest. "The Lawblades are of one source, one heart. If one wielder falls to the storm, those around him will, as well. His emotions running too hot are a danger to not just himself."

Pheonix remembered Faranthalassa abruptly and barely kept the scowl off his face. "My question remains. Why is his *reaction* concerning?"

Zasfioretaeula shook his head slowly. "An unblooded Bladesinger, one with low threat of losing control, would be frightened by a Bladestorm, not angered by it. The Bladestorm is a stark reminder of our fragility and mortality, the mistakes of the past — things many elves choose to ignore."

"More suppression."

The reticent smile made another appearance. "Especially in someone so young, so sheltered, so *different* ..." Zasfioretaeula paused, and both the pause and the subtle stress on 'different' made it seem that the Prime War-Bladesinger was trying to get across something beyond his actual words, though Pheonix was hard-pressed to figure out what the hell that was. "His fury is the key to my concern. Anger — not fear — speaks of emotions already running high."

"Understood," Pheonix said. "Is there anything I can do?"

"Watch him. If he threatens to lose control, neutralize him. Interrupt his flow of consciousness. The Bladestorm starts in the mind, remember that."

"And if he manifests it?"

Zasfioretaeula sighed. "Pray you can stop *his* Bladestorm."

"So, train, then."

Zasfioretaeula inclined his head.

Pheonix's next goal came sharply into the forefront:

Learn how to combat a Bladestorm.

Pheonix had three goals in the coming weeks: learn to combat a Bladestorm, prepare to siege the red mage's tower as requested by Spiraea (which Chani had given a brief on), and finish the training set out for him when he'd first arrived in Terelath.

To those ends, his personal plan hadn't changed much. Cram at night, push during the day. Speed, strength, and skill. He'd always had enough brute strength to overpower anything in his way. Even as a child, when his strength was still developing, his immortality and inability to feel pain made up for the lack. Endurance always ran out before strength. And now needing both, he had no idea what his absolute upper limits were, so a large part of his current objective was to find those limits and surpass them. Pain quickly faded into the distance as his body adjusted both to its existence and to the intense training.

However, as Faranthalassa — now Faran — returned, his trainers descended upon him in full force — all of them, with the addition of the Xenobiarch to assist him in understanding and utilizing his cybernetic arm.

In preparation for taking on the red mage's tower, his curriculum now was geared towards battling mages, red mages (which through their utilization of blood magic, had to be handled differently than the average mage), familiarizing himself with firearms, and generalized adaptability. Realistically, they didn't know what awaited beyond the red mage's barrier.

Realistically, they didn't even know for sure the barrier itself wouldn't kill him.

Pheonix understood that risk, the same way he understood any other thing that might be his end. It wasn't as though he hadn't faced death since before he could walk. It didn't inspire fear, or hesitation.

It just was.

But, he'd still do his damndest to prevent it.

He spent quite a large chunk of his time with Minrathous and Crosinthusilas, studying advanced magics and how to counter them. He still had categorically zero magical talent, and even sensing magic was difficult for him, which made that part particularly onerous. They didn't know exactly who this mage was, but they knew who he wasn't, and that was an amateur; so the magi did not hold back during their sessions.

When he wasn't training or reading, he was in tactics and intel meetings with Chani and a rotating cadre of others. Chani had gone through the exhaustive list of the most infamous red and blood mages, narrowed it down by arrogance (those willing to take bold risks), wealth (a five-story tower with some kind of ridiculous barrier doesn't happen overnight, and required resources unattainable to a pauper mage), and power — both political and magical.

Simply getting to Availeon on a ship designated as allied with evil was hard enough. Plonking a base right under the patron Ascended's nose required a massive sense of entitlement and political connections, not to mention the resources, both outside Availeon … and within.

All that led Chani to one clan: the Reshes — a longstanding family of red and blood mages going back Ages. They were the kind of evil that accounted for several whole percentages of all atrocities committed both within Accord space and outside of it.

It was another damning nail in the coffin of widespread corruption, not only in Terelath but also beyond it. The major questions now were how far it went, and who was involved. But Chani had made it clear *that* part of the investigation wasn't something Pheonix was going to be involved in.

At least, not yet.

Now, which particular individual Resh had holed up in the tower was still up in the air, but the Reshes were the family that controlled most of the Dark Sector, so they easily fit all of Chani's criteria. Because their headquarters were somewhere deep in the Dark Sector, sniffing out their whereabouts just for this would be impossible — hell, that's what the Rangers had been trying to do for a long time. Chani didn't have the resources for that, not within the confines of the current system. But with some educated guesswork, they could tailor some of their preparations. Better than going in blind.

Martial education from Faran showed Pheonix a completely new side of the elven Ranger. In combat, Faran was a deadly predator — cold, unflappable, and keen-eyed, with a nasty habit of predicting Pheonix's moves. Pheonix wondered how much of Faran's strength was due to his new status as consort of Spiraea. Though the Master of Propriety hadn't explained to Pheonix exactly what had transpired during his time away from Terelath, the garland of golden leaves said enough.

Tyyrulriathula had changed, as well. His cheery edge had been blunted, and he was more prone to inexplicable fits of anger, which subsided as quickly as they came on (and of which he seemed to have no memory).

All that made taking on both Tyyrulriathula and Faran at the same time, as they often had him do, extra challenging.

Though, with how unrestrained his trainers were being now, he grew exponentially in a short period of time. So he wasn't complaining. At least when it came to his own self, given that he didn't value himself other than as a tool, Pheonix was very much of the mindset that 'the ends justify the means.'

He didn't actively question why they were pushing him so hard, because introspection of that sort wasn't useful toward his goals ... though perhaps some part of him subconsciously gathered data and put it to the hypothesis forming somewhere deep within his decision matrix.

"Be ready," Crosinthusilas said.

Pheonix inclined his head; one corner of Crosinthusilas' mouth lifted.

Sheer power unfolded from her — layers of it so thick, he could hardly see her. It wasn't magic, which he still couldn't sense, but something more ancient.

Utilizing magic was difficult. One needed both a strong connection to the Weave and enough will to control it — and those were only the requirements to use the most basic of spells. There were many other factors that determined the ease with which one was able to shape the Weave — and how powerful the result would be.

Crosinthusilas, a First (and the Prime Lady, besides), was far above even the highest tier of magic-user — because she didn't cast magic. Magic was a consequence, the end result of the mental and metaphysical calculations used to reach into the Weave. What Crosinthusilas did was manipulate Weave directly. Ladies, in essence, were founts of Weave, and Crosinthusilas a geyser.

However, Pheonix had only a fraction of a second to analyze the sight.

Just as with Zasfioretaeula over a month prior, he went to move — even with his speed far beyond where it had been then — and found himself stabbed, bound, paralyzed, pinned, and crushed.

The power subsided, the many layers she'd conjured in that one second fading from existence as though they'd never been, and Pheonix slowly got to his feet with a short laugh.

"Bested the rest," he said, brushing himself off, "but still can't best the best. You and Zasfioretaeula both still soundly kick my ass."

"We are Firsts," said a voice from behind him. The Prime War-Bladesinger came up to them, bowing slightly to Crosinthusilas, who nodded her head at him. "That is why you cannot."

"I don't understand," Pheonix said.

"You know what Firsts are," said Crosinthusilas. "But you don't understand why we are. Each one of us is crafted individually by the Creator. We are pure Creation. In my case, you know that I can access the Weave without having to go through the parts of Creation that dilute it, keeping it separate from the physical plane."

"And I Bladestorm without the need for heightened emotions," Zasfioretaeula said.

"We have been here since the beginning," Crosinthusilas said bitterly, "and yet, we are forbidden from acting."

Zasfioretaeula jerked a hand at her and she shot him a scathing look, raising her chin stubbornly. The Prime War-Bladesinger sighed in resignation. Pheonix simply watched the exchange, confused.

"Suffice to say, despite our great power, it is as Crosinth says," Zasfioretaeula said bitterly. "We are chained. You will learn of the nature of our chains in due time. To our children, life does not have the same meaning as it did — does — to us. The Creation becomes a background hum to petty concerns. We were meant to live in its full symphony and splendor. All of us." Zasfioretaeula started to turn, and glanced back over his shoulder at Pheonix. "Creator help you remember that."

EIGHTEEN
Moron Mages Manufacture Moronic Messes

"We feel you are as ready as you ever will be," Chani said.

The seven of them (Pheonix, Chani, Tyyrulriathula, Faran, Zasfioretaeula, Crosinthusilas, and Minrathous), gathered for a final meeting before the op against the red mage commenced.

"Or," Chani added with a lopsided smile, "as ready as we can make you in a reasonable amount of time."

"We'll not send you in unprepared, though," Crosinthusilas said.

"Check this out," Chani said with a wink — and touched a small box on her shoulder. Her hand disappeared, and she — somehow, in a way that made Pheonix's brain hurt to witness — pulled out one large bundle, then another.

"Fold-space collar," Chani said, proffering the first bundle.

"What is it?" Pheonix asked, the question twofold.

"Fold-space collars are a quantum storage device tied to one's life energy. And as for the present, well … you'll have to open it."

Pheonix, under the watchful gaze of the others, did as he was told. Inside the first bundle was a familiar suit of elven ground trooper armor: a set of plate mail. The next bundle contained two weapons — small swords. About two feet long and eight inches wide, they were bluntly rectangular with serrations on the short end where the point of most swords would be. Quite thick in the middle, they tapered out to double-blades, with the top edge slightly hooked upwards.

They were undecorated, plain, serviceable weapons, weighted to his hand; and warm, which spoke of magic.

"A combat-ready set has to be much more carefully manufactured than the hastily-modded set you've been training in," Chani explained of the armor. "But until we can get you into an Armory to choose what you *actually* want to wear, at least you'll be fighting in something familiar."

"And we modified the cleavers you came here with," Tyyrulriathula said of the short swords, a touch of pride in his voice. "I helped. I may be a Bladesinger, but my true passion is smithing."

"They feel good," Pheonix said. "Thank you."

Tyyrulriathula grinned.

"Oh, one last thing," Chani said, and held out a small firearm. Pheonix nodded and tucked it away.

"Here's the plan," Chani went on. "You go in alone. Faran is strictly an observer unless shit hits the fan. Your priority objective is to take down the shield. We aren't sure exactly what it is or where it is, but similar instances have been seen on slaver vessels, so we're assuming as of now that we're looking at tek. Take it out, then wait for Faran to meet up with you. I want to make sure you understand: that shield has killed and disabled every single thing we've thrown at it. This is extremely dangerous — we don't even know that it won't kill *you*."

"My immortality."

Chani inclined her head. "That is what we are banking on. But don't put yourself in unnecessary danger. I know I often advise you to downplay your instincts, but this is the time to use them to their fullest. If something feels off, get the fuck out of there. We always have other avenues, albeit progressively less palatable as we go down the list. Still, you're more important."

He didn't see the value in his own life, but didn't want to waste time arguing, so instead he said, "Roger."

"Good. Furthermore, we don't know what's in there. But we do have a pretty good idea of *who* is in there, and that leads us to what *may* be in there. Given that the shield — by your input and our own intel — seems to be a form of slaver tech, you're likely to find more slaver tech inside. Thankfully, you're more than prepared for that," Chani grinned lopsidedly, but only for a moment.

"Relief forces will be on the perimeter and on Faran's tail to secure after you," she continued. "Whoever's up there will try to port out as soon as he realizes he's got no other choice. But since he didn't come in through a portal, he'll have to set one up and get through Availeon's magic barrier, our portal interception tech, and one pissed off Ascended.

"Your next priority is him; but Pheonix — and pay close attention to this — slow is smooth and smooth is fast. What I mean by that is don't just rush up the stairs. Take targets of opportunity and grab intel where you can."

"Roger."

Chani turned away to talk to a Ranger soldier next to her and Crosinthusilas came to stand next to Pheonix.

"Master Pheonix, I must warn you," she said, her magical whispering for his ear only. "This tower — it is not like what a mage would construct. It feels wrong. I cannot give you more than that, but if Commander Abyss' mother hen clucking didn't convince you to be careful, I impress it upon you again. However, as she said, the lord of this place is undoubtedly a mage of some type. Remember spellskin, and its weakness."

Pheonix accessed: Spellskin, bottom-tier protective magic that forms dampening layers around the target. Its weakness is that, depending on the caster, it can only absorb a certain number of 'hits' before the energy that sustains it dissipates.

"Thank you," Pheonix said.

Preparations began immediately following the briefing.

Pheonix changed into the new equipment he'd been given, and he and Faran were taken by drop ship to a small clearing quite a ways outside Terelath. Faran took point, leading the much larger Pheonix as silently as possible through the underbrush. The small hairs on the back of Pheonix's neck stood on end as they approached the woodline: it became clear in short order that it was an unnatural one.

And there, beyond where the trees ended: a red, hazy dome inside which was a ring of dirt and the mage's tower. The decaying bodies of creatures that had unwittingly passed through the haze decorated its perimeter.

Faran hesitated, taking a sharp breath of horror and pain.

Pheonix straightened and strode forward, just aware of Faran's hissed warning.

"I know what this is," Pheonix said over his shoulder. "It won't harm me."

The slavers kept their live product in cages, but not of metal or mineral. All slaves quickly learned to fear it: the shield of death. Though Pheonix didn't know how it was constructed or how it functioned, he'd seen it in use plenty of times before — enough for immediate recognition.

But Pheonix had never seen one so big.

He could feel that Faran was silently unsettled behind him, but Chani had put Pheonix in command, and Faran was staying quiet in respect of that fact.

Pheonix approached the red haze —

— and passed through it uneventfully.

As he began to cross the dirt space between the woodline and the tower, there was motion in his periphery faster than he could respond — he was mid-reach for his firearm and one of the new swords when it hit him. As he fired on the glowing eyeball (*mage eyes: magical constructs often used in the same manner as mines or caltrops, meant to immediately dispatch intruders or ground troops via disintegration beam*), part of his mind questioned why the disintegration beam hadn't affected him. Was it his natural resistance to magic?

Another spell hit him. He turned to dispatch the next mage eye, but it was gone. The field stood empty.

Threats confirmed.

The rest of the walk up to the tower was devoid of further conflict, however, which allowed him to get a good look at what he was dealing with.

The tower had a familiar look, too, just as the shield of death had. Slaver mages had a tendency to make vessels and structures tied into their life force — he assumed on the principle of 'If I'm going down, I'm taking you with me.' This one was five floors of ugly, shaped like a dumbbell sitting on its side, replete with an observation window on the top floor.

He circled the tower, on high alert, in search of an entrance. He found one — a shoddy wooden door labeled 'slaves' in thirty languages. He kept going. Another door, slightly nicer, labeled similarly: 'servants.' Then an average door: 'deliveries.' Then finally, a filigreed door: 'visitors.'

He backtracked to the slave door. It would likely lead him closest to where he needed to go. It's not like the mage would run, manage, or maintain any of his own machinery, nor suffer having it within sight. Pheonix kicked the door and it swung open with no resistance. People scattered with hushed yelps of fear.

The room that opened up in front of him was dark, dingy, and mostly bare, long and oblong and stretching out to his left with a wall immediately to his right. He was less concerned about the slaves right now — there was no way their master didn't know he was coming — than he was with the machinery in front of him.

A metallic egg, covered in panels with all manner of controls, was set at Pheonix's eye level into a rectangular base sprouting red tubes on either side. One such tube followed the wall to his left and the other disappeared into the wall to his right. The metallic egg balanced a crystal sphere containing swirling mist on its top. Light arced within the egg, barely seen behind the control panels.

This was it: the power console for external security systems. He'd destroyed enough of them on various slaver ships during his childhood to recognize it readily.

He sheathed his sword and holstered his pistol. The stupid egg had handles on either side, which he grasped and pulled. It put up little resistance and came off in his hands in a shower of sparks and groaning metal. The light inside died, though the mist inside the crystal ball remained. He cast the egg aside with a deafening clatter.

Pheonix called in over comms that he'd destroyed the security console, cautioned them about the mage eyes, then headed in the direction the slaves had run. At the far end of the long room was an elevator and a walled off section lined with open doorways that had likely been blocked by barriers before Pheonix had destroyed the control console.

He poked his head into one such doorway and met the terrified faces of slaves huddled in the corner. Something twisted in him; it had been a long time since he'd seen that look in someone's eyes. But anyone who had seen it could never forget it, and it cut straight to his core.

"I'm here to kill your Master," he said in the slave language, trying to control his voice. They didn't need to be more scared than they already were. "Rangers are outside.

Stay here, stay quiet; they will come for you. You're free and safe."

Without waiting for a response, he made his way back and stopped at the only other door in this space, halfway between the slave pens and the control console. He shoved the door open, swords again at the ready.

The room beyond was some bullshit opulent foyer meant to intimidate visitors.

Did this mage even get visitors? If so, how? He was clearly intending on this tower acting as a personal door into Availeon, which Pheonix was not about to tolerate. Pheonix swept the room and found nothing of interest except a large staircase.

By that time, Faran had caught up to him, and they ascended the stairs together to the next level. Near the top, Pheonix gestured to Faran to hang back. Once he was relatively sure, from the safety of the hallway, that the room was clear of any overt threats, he sidled into the doorway, senses on high alert. He didn't have any way of knowing what lay ahead, so there was no way to prepare. Best just to get it over with and move forward with whatever momentum they may be riding on.

Without ceremony, he rounded the corner —

— into an empty room.

A circular space fully encompassing the diameter of the tower, it was devoid of all furnishings and, apparently, defenses. However, when dealing with mages, this meant nothing. He'd made it through the mage eyes and the field of death, but that, too, meant nothing. There were things deadlier still.

While Chani's plan had openly relied on Pheonix's immortality and natural magic resistance, there was one other component that they'd likely taken into account: Pheonix didn't fear death.

The thought of facing deadly things didn't give him pause, but it also didn't inspire recklessness (both of which got people killed). He was neutral to danger no matter where he was: standing in enemy territory or otherwise.

Very few warriors could manage that — or so he'd been told. Like many things relating to how other sapients experienced reality, he didn't really get it.

Once Pheonix was certain there was absolutely nothing to this room, he gestured Faran forward.

The elven Ranger entered, eyes darting — and abruptly froze.

Pheonix followed his gaze; the walls.

Though he'd taken note of the strange swirling decorations, they hadn't meant anything to him. While obliquely familiar, further scrutiny of the designs didn't reveal any secrets. They were somewhat like screens of data on top of one another behind broken panes of glass, shattered across lines he felt he should recognize, always moving. Between the motion, the formation, and the lines, any readability was lost.

"What …" Faran finally said, his voice thick. "What …? It can't be … oh, Spiraea, how …"

Pheonix saw the breakdown coming in Faran's white-knuckled grip on his bow and the sputtering words. Swiftly making a decision, he grabbed the elf by his upper arm and dragged him away from his stupor and into the next ascending staircase.

Pinning Faran against the wall with one forearm, he grabbed the elf's face with the other hand and forced his chin straight. Faran struggled, trying to stare back into the room, then dazedly met Pheonix's eyes. His breathing was ragged and shallow, body taut.

"Whatever it is, we don't have time," Pheonix said roughly. "And I'm sorry. But we will come back if we can. I swear it."

Faran stared blankly, then, body part by body part, regained control. Pheonix loosened his grip and cautiously stepped back. Faran straightened and nodded. His hands still grasped his bow tightly but were steady once more. Pheonix dipped his chin and turned to look up the stairs, again taking hold of the weapons he'd put away to deal with Faran.

This next level had a door. Pheonix tested it; locked.

Irritated, he sheathed his weapons yet again and put his fist through the door with a booming *crack.* Then, taking hold of the hole he'd created, he ripped the door from its hinges. He braced it against his shoulder, using it as cover, and peered past it.

This room was far more decorated than the previous. Lining its walls was all kinds of machinery — both magical and non-magical. The mixing of magic and technology, called magitek or simply 'tek', was extremely difficult and dangerous, thus highly regulated. The Rangers were the biggest users of tek, though some mages were known for it. Interspersed among the machinery were huge spheres of unknown function.

"Wait," Faran whispered, peering past Pheonix. "Traps. Let me handle it. Lean to one side, please."

Pheonix pressed himself against the wall while still gripping the door to keep it steady. Faran lifted his bow, aiming through the hole Pheonix had made in it. Pheonix held himself still as Faran drew, nocked no arrow, and smoothly loosed. A spike of cold nothingness shot past Pheonix's cheek, raising the hairs on his neck.

Chaos erupted in the next room. Several things hit the door before the ruckus died down.

"I believe it should be safe," Faran said with quiet certainty.

"You think?"

Faran shot him a look but Pheonix was already setting the door aside, taking up his weapons again.

Nothing happened as they entered, but Pheonix trusted Faran's expert eye and aim and hadn't expected further resistance.

Now inside, Pheonix got a better look at the spheres. They were big enough to hold the average hominin and probably magical in nature. Inside most of them were what could only be corpses based on their level of mutilation and lack of life-spark. In the center of the room was a larger sphere holding a small person curled in a fetal position, surrounded by a cloud of dust. He wore several layers of singed robes and his round face was crowned by a poof of dusty, unruly hair of indeterminate color. A staff floated next to him in the bubble.

Unlike the other spheres, the thick cables that hooked to it were active — and, curiously, on fire.

Pheonix confirmed the person was alive by peeking at his life-spark, which was like staring into the heart of a volcano. It made him wince.

"It's an oodl," Faran said, referring to a species with varied genetic roots who were generally looked down upon by genetic 'purists.' "And still alive. Smells like fire." His nose wrinkled slightly. Elves tended to not be huge fans of fire. "I recommend leaving this one for the crew; they will have advanced analytical instrumentation."

Pheonix digested his words but couldn't walk away. Something nagged at him.

"No," Pheonix said. "I'm going to release him."

"What?" Faran responded, surprised. "Why?"

"I feel I must."

Faran fell silent, but Pheonix could feel his disapproval.

Pheonix thrust one of his swords at the sphere — which burst with a dainty *pop!*

The person crumpled to the ground. The staff bonked him on the head and clattered to the ground. He sat up with the rustling of robes, shedding dust clouds, and rubbed his head.

He opened one large eye, then the other, and stared up at Pheonix. "Oh. You're finally here."

The statement put both Pheonix and Faran off-guard.

"Excuse me?" Faran said, incredulous.

"My Lord, Schieta, told me to wait for you. He said, 'Wait for Pheonix.' My name is Theodric. I tried to take out the booty butt at the top and he cheated and caught me. Is he dead yet?"

Pheonix accessed: *Schieta, one of the Elemental Lords, the literal embodiment of all things fire.*

Pheonix had no time to ponder why an Elemental Lord would know his name, nor why he would tell this ... person to wait for him, nor how he had even gotten inside the shield of death to begin with. Theodric seemed to be waiting impatiently for an answer.

"No," Pheonix said belatedly to Theodric's question.

Theodric grabbed his staff and leaped to his feet, giving off more dust. "Can I come with you to kill the booty butt?"

"Why?" Pheonix asked, bewildered.

"Because Schieta sent me here to come with you," Theodric repeated impatiently. "C'mon, he's trying to open a portal. We gotta get him!"

As bizarre as the whole interaction was, Theodric was right on one count; they didn't have time for delays.

"Fine," Pheonix said, ignoring Faran's hushed protest. "As long as you don't get in my way."

Theodric jumped up and down, shedding dust that, no matter how much drifted off, seemed to be ever-renewing.

"Yay! You ready, Barnie?"

The staff sparked, which apparently annoyed Theodric. He shook it vigorously and scolded 'Barnie' until it stopped. Pheonix and Faran exchanged a glance.

"On your head be it," Faran said as an aside to Pheonix.

Theodric bounced, bringing their attention round. "Oh, get ready! Here they come!"

An earthquake of sound and vibration preceded the huge metal bodies that emerged from the gloom of the next ascending staircase. Pheonix recognized them from his reading: metal golems. These ones were vaguely humanoid, stocky, and with no neck to speak of. Two were at the forefront, with at least two behind.

After some quick thinking, he exchanged a sword for a firearm just as a wall of fire sprang up at the doorway to the staircase. The first two golems barreled through it — their metal plates swiftly turning an angry, glowing red, which spoke of the strength of Theodric's fire. Pheonix was impressed. Ice exploded at their feet — assumedly Faran's contribution — which rapidly supercooled the metal. The next steps the golems took had them toppling forward, broken off at the legs, their metal turned as brittle as glass. The sound was deafening when they hit the floor and shattered to pieces.

Then the next two were coming through. The one to Pheonix's right charged at Theodric, preventing him from channeling another wall attack. Pheonix stiffened, but Theodric seemed capable of handling himself. He bounced out of the range of its sweeping arm with surprising agility.

Pheonix had his own troubles. As the remaining golem came at him, with little space to maneuver, he acted without thinking and fired his pistol into its 'head.' Trailing sparks, it fell and didn't move.

The first golem crashed down a moment later, a smoking hole in its side courtesy of one of Faran's acid arrows. Theodric, just out of reach, slammed a fireball into its head and melted the top quarter of its metal body. It ceased to move.

"It's not over," warned Faran.

As soon as Pheonix caught the barest glimpse of their next opponents, he took the fore in a silent indicator that he'd handle it. War-Bots rattled down the stairs — robots with a round head, one little red eye, a blocky body, four arms, a shock taser on one set of appendages, and vibro-blades on the other.

Pheonix dispatched them with ease as they piled into the room, hampered by the corpses of the golems, with a neat shot in each eye.

At the looks of shocked incomprehension from both Faran and Theodric, Pheonix said: "When the slavers realized I wouldn't fight innocents, if they didn't have monsters for me to kill, they put me up against these things. The weak point has always been that eye, so I'd rip the vibro blades off them and spear them through it. Why bother with that though, when you have a gun?" Pheonix looked at Faran. "I suppose this has gone beyond a solo op, at this point."

"Well beyond," Faran agreed grimly.

The trio climbed past the mess and up the stairs.

A bizarre crescent-moon-shaped room spread out to their left, obviously a barracks for soldiers Pheonix's little group had seen neither hide nor hair of. The reason for that was instantly clear: signs of a hasty retreat; open trunks, bedding strewn about, furniture knocked over.

Pheonix, Faran, and Theodric carefully wove their way through the detritus. As they rounded the curve, dead portals came into view — the pylons and superstructure for outdated crystalline portal technology. A set of double doors waited at the other end of the crescent. In front of the doors were two cowering and trembling figures in elite slavers' garb. Pheonix took a step — and light arced over his shoulder. The figures dropped, motionless. Pheonix turned to look at Faran.

"Stasis arrows," the elven Ranger explained. "They'll last at least until we are done with the master. Hold another moment."

Pheonix nodded. Faran drew back and rapid-fired three arrows, one on top of the other, into the black corner of the wall. Surprisingly, a creature fell limp out of the darkness. It was a drakkan (Pheonix recognized it from his reading), but something was terribly wrong with it. Its scaled hide was dotted in patches of crystallized green, with more green oozing out from under the thick collar bolted to its neck.

The elf shook his head and pushed on the double doors wedged in the corner. He looked back at the drakkan, his eyes sad. "They have been injected with drugs which shut down their consciousness and leave them open to suggestion. They're lucky we got to them without violence. The more of their natural ichor that they lose, the harder it is to save them. Come. The master awaits."

The final staircase was sandwiched in between the two crescent-shaped halves of the barracks. Sword in one hand and pistol in the other, Pheonix took the lead.

The circular sanctum had a high ceiling and wide, open windows that flooded it with light. Its floor plan was an exercise in the same type of pointless extravagance seen elsewhere in this misbegotten place.

The man of the hour himself, back to the door, was fiddling with the interface on a crystal/tek pylon set in front of an elaborate golden portal frame inset with jewels, all of which sat on a raised dais. He was a hominin with an ashen ochre skin tone, wearing a lush red robe and bedecked with as much jewelry and tek as he could possibly physically wear. He muttered angrily and stabbed at the interface, which beeped indolently at him.

"NOPE!" yelled Theodric and lifted his staff. A wall of flame roared to life, engulfing the portal frame and its pylon. The man squealed in surprise and turned around.

"Do we *have* to do this aga — " he stopped mid-sentence.

"Zu'Resh," Faran spat.

Pheonix had the measure of Zu'Resh instantly. The subtle rainbow shimmer clinging to the mage's frippery told Pheonix all he needed to know — just as Crosinthusilas had warned: spellskin. Essentially, layers of magical shields.

Zu'Resh threw a massive fireball. Theodric leapt and thrust his staff into the air — which drank the fire down to the last ember, to the tune of Theodric's manic giggling.

The red mage thrust out his other arm.

Pheonix swiftly curved his wings out to cover his companions, nullifying the chain lightning arcing towards them. He snapped his wings back, dissipating the resulting smoke, and strode forward.

Zu'Resh's eyes widened and his face tightened with fear as the angry Pheonix advanced on him.

The mage wore a wrist-comm, and flailed around trying to access it while simultaneously throwing spells at Pheonix, jewelry clanking and tangling. Phantom weapons materialized and sped towards Pheonix, only to be deflected easily.

"I'll find something that affects you!" Zu'Resh shrieked. Pheonix, now within range, reached into a pocket of his armor. Zu'Resh, in arrogance or panic, didn't bother to cover himself and caught the cloud of sand right in the face. Coughing and spluttering, he stumbled back, the telltale shimmer of his magical shields gone with the grains of sand.

Pheonix ascended the dais.

Zu'Resh, eyes tightly shut against the sand, raised the arm with the wrist-comm, and Pheonix shot his hand off.

Now face to face with Pheonix, Zu'Resh could only whimper. He didn't even see the blade come up and tear into his abdomen. Pheonix twisted his blade and pushed it harder into Zu'Resh's ribcage, through bone and sinew, ripping internal organs to jelly.

Zu'Resh's body dissolved into burning particles that streamed over Pheonix's shoulder, leaving nothing but a smear on his sword.

Pheonix blinked and turned.

"Oh, sorry," Theodric said, the last of the particles still swirling around the tip of his staff. "My Lord wanted that one. He is to be used as fuel."

Faran let out a surprised laugh, then covered his mouth, his cheeks lighting up in embarrassment.

"Okay." Pheonix said in a monotone, because a response seemed to be needed. He turned to Faran. "What now?"

"My Lady says it is time to leave," the elf responded.

Outside, they met a giant dryad Faran called Matilde.

Taller than the tower itself, she was a creature of thick mossy tree roots, twisted vines, blooming flowers, and rough bark. Once the cleanup crew had gone through and retrieved the stasis'd elite slavers, the drakkan, and any intel they were interested in, she gripped both sides of the tower with hands as massive as thousand-year-old trees and rent its top eagerly off. Pheonix, Faran, and Theodric waited at the edge of the death zone — which was already sprouting grass as Spiraea's essence flooded back into it — and watched Matilde demolish the tower to rubble with fierce glee.

With her work done, Matilde shrank in size, enough to be eye-level with Pheonix.

"Lord Justice," she said, and Faran stiffened in response. She pointed. "There is something there for you."

Pheonix followed her finger: surrounded in debris but carefully exposed was a small, innocuous bump of grass. Pheonix approached it. An entirely unmarked stone pedestal rose from the ground when he got near.

The hafts of two weapons stuck out of the stone. Figuring what was expected of him, he gripped them and pulled. The stone gave no resistance, and Pheonix studied the swords once they were in his hands.

These hilts fit him more than any other weapon he'd wielded. The blades were identical, curved and long, with a portion of the edge serrated. They flared to life, accompanied by the sudden appearance of a red glow on the blade in his left hand — Malol, something told him — and a crackling blue lightning on the right — Bedaestael.

He had no sheaths that would fit them, but the knowledge came into his mind that he could merely mime putting them away and they would remain where he placed them.

"Malol and Bedaestael," Faran breathed. "So it is true, then."

"What are they?" Pheonix asked.

Faran hesitated as if considering his words. "Well, they are special weapons. If they allowed you to pull them, it means they have chosen you."

"They rejected Lazarus," Matilde said bluntly. Faran shushed her and she gave him a scathing look.

"Come," Faran said, keeping Pheonix from questioning what the hell had just happened. "We must return to Terelath. We have much to report."

NINETEEN
Becoming, and Bargains

The transport raced over Terelath. Theodric talked about everything and nothing during the ride, though both Pheonix and Faran remained silent. Theodric seemed unbothered by the lack of reciprocity.

During the flight, Pheonix was deep in thought.

Chosen by the special weapons, Malol and Bedaestael, Pheonix repeated in his head.

Information on 'Malol' and 'Bedaestael' wasn't hard to find in the archives he could access via his implants. They were the swords of Justice, entombed to await Justice's return. Lazarus had been the Ascended of Justice from the beginning of the metacosm to the Second Age, where he'd been ambushed and killed by Bast, the evil God of Murder.

Pheonix scowled.

Truthfully, he'd recognized the names of the swords immediately, as they'd been in one of the books he'd read during his time on Archaic Earth with the old man.

Malol and Bedaestael had been forged by the Bladesinger-Smith Andural and presented as a gift to Lazarus, but the swords had rejected him and put *themselves* in the ground to await the 'true Justice.'

Once again, here was a situation where the 'official' story seemed to differ significantly from evidence.

Matilde, demigod of Spiraea, had called Pheonix 'Lord Justice' and said that the swords had 'rejected Lazarus.'

Lord Justice, Pheonix mused mentally as he stared out the transport window. *Am I really to believe that means what I think it means?*

As the transport carrying Pheonix and the others came to the city proper and its main thoroughfare, something caught Pheonix's attention. Colorful spheres, likely magic, drifted into the sky all around them. Below, the varied denizens of Terelath lined the streets, dancing, laughing, or enjoying food and drink.

Pheonix looked at Faran in irritated confusion.

"They're celebrating the death of Zu'Resh. The Chosen have drones," Faran explained. "Everywhere. I can only imagine we were being tailed. There will likely be some political … fallout. And the people celebrate because Zu'Resh was a Red Mage Master of infamy. In a very literal sense, he has a lot of blood on his hands. Any decent person would be glad to see such evil punished." Faran looked out the window with a wan smile. "It's nice to see that we still have this many decent people in Terelath."

They flew over mile after mile of celebrants, seemingly involving the entirety of Terelath. Pheonix noticed them passively. He was drained and thought only of getting to his quiet cottage and going no-mind.

They touched down in the training area and the door hissed open. Pheonix ducked his head to exit, and immediately had the wind knocked out of him by Chani sweeping him into a tight hug. Only a quick assessment of the situation stopped his hands from going for his swords. Behind her were the rest of his trainers.

Chani put him at arms' length, her exultant grin threatening to split her face in two.

"You're back! You did it!" She released him and stepped back. "Not that I ever thought you wouldn't ... but still! You *did* it!"

The other trainers came close to offer their congratulations as well.

"I only did what you asked of me," Pheonix said, uncomprehending.

"Oh shut up and take your praise with grace," Chani said and slapped his back. Her eyes lit on Faran, just emerging from the transport, and the happy edge to her smile soured. "F aran?"

Faran looked haunted. "Zu'Resh was plotting the life-stream of Availeon — correctly, I might add — and he had quite a lot of it done."

"Is that what was on the walls?" Pheonix asked, making quick connections.

Faran nodded.

"What does that mean?"

"Mapping a life-stream in itself isn't necessarily a bad thing," Minrathous said. "Many scholars have done it in the past. But it's *this* life-stream and *who* he is."

"Knowing the points of intersection of a life-stream means that one can potentially tap into it," Crosinthusilas said. "Which would be the only reason a blood mage would be interested in it. And taking from the life-stream around Availeon would reduce the available life here — which would start killing people."

Tyyrulriathula stiffened. No one seemed to notice but Pheonix.

"It's worse than that," Faran said. "From what I could tell, he was attempting to find the Source."

There was a confused silence, quickly broken by dark and deep laughter.

Crosinthusilas turned and floated a little ways from the others, her shoulders still shaking with laughter, keeping her back to them.

"Care to share with the class?" Chani called.

Crosinthusilas shook her head. "My apologies for my outburst. I am not at liberty to explain why I found that amusing — but, my little brother," she looked at Faran, her eyes creased with a grin, "do not fret. Moronic mages will only find moronic answers."

Faran blinked at her in slightly-hurt puzzlement, and Chani waved her hands as if to dispel the atmosphere.

"Enough," Chani said. "He's dead, and his immediate research is destroyed. Whatever he managed to get out, if anything — well, we'll deal with that when the time comes. For the moment, we will have to trust a First that it's likely he didn't gain anything of import. Moving on," she looked at Pheonix. "Malol and Bedaestael accepted you, I see?"

Pheonix gestured at the swords that hovered near him. "These? Yes, I suppose."

"Frankly, you're done here," Chani continued, looking at his trainers. "As far as I'm concerned, he needs to go to Ranger HQ. Yes?"

Pheonix himself held up a hand. "*I'm* actually not ready to go yet. I'd like to stay for a bit longer to finish out my training. Is that going to be a problem?"

"I agree that I have more to teach him," Crosinthusilas said.

"Well, alrighty then. You're welcome to go at your own pace. Just let me know when you're ready to head to Ranger HQ — I think you'll find it quite the enlightening experience, so don't put it off *too* long," Chani said. Then she turned her attention to Theodric and knelt so as not to tower over him.

"Now," she said, amused, "what are we to do with you?"

Theodric reached out to place a hand on Pheonix's bracer.

"My Lord has commanded me to stay with Justice," he said firmly, holding Chani's gaze. Chani glanced at Pheonix, her eyebrows raised.

"Well ... you heard Justice, he needs to stay here for a little while longer," Chani said. "And you won't be safe or welcome here in Terelath."

"I know that." Theodric's voice held a wealth of experience with being unwelcome.

"Hmm ... Pheonix is coming to HQ after this, though the timeline would be up to him. Have you ever been?"

Theodric blinked at her. "To Ranger HQ? Why would I?"

"Well, you being a GDC puts you squarely in our protection jurisdiction, and being a Kaehin deis Ohd won't be a problem with our null fields. While Pheonix is finishing up here, we can get you registered with the Accord and all that, so you can be ready to talk with Pheonix about your Lord's orders."

Theodric looked down, blinking again. His eyes seemed wet. "I ... thank you."

Pheonix accessed:

GDC: short for Genetically Diversified Collective. The Ranger term for the 'species' also known more colloquially as 'oodl(s).' Also known as the slur 'dregs.' GDCs are individuals with multiple specific genetic ancestries.

Chosen of Schieta: the Kaehin deis Ohd, translating to 'fanatical priest of fire.' Kaehin deis Ohd has no place among mages and their hoards of artifacts and spell-books, despite using elemental fire, because they have a tendency to wantonly set things on fire as 'fuel for Schieta.'

"Alright!" Chani clapped her hands and raised her voice to make sure everyone assembled was paying attention. "Everybody: go get some rest. You earned it."

While it was true he needed rest, there was one more thing Pheonix wanted to do.

He sought out Crosinthusilas, but couldn't find her. After some back-and-forth with various people, he was told to check the Vault of the Firsts.

Pheonix consulted his mental map and found his way there. Another place outside the 'flower' of Terelath. Interesting.

As Pheonix arrived, he saw no 'vault' — nor, indeed, any building at all. There was only an archway of vines at the mouth of a ramp leading underground.

Crosinthusilas, dramatically shadowed by the fading sunlight, sat on the archway, some dozen or so feet above ground. Pheonix bowed; she quirked a humorless smile.

"Lady Crosinthusilas," he called up to her.

"Lord Justice," she said.

There it was again. That name.

"Do you mind if I ask you a question?" Pheonix asked.

Rather than speaking, she leapt off the archway and drifted down into the hole. The darkness swallowed her and, after a moment of confused hesitation, Pheonix took to the ramp and followed.

At the bottom of the ramp was a blockade — a tightly interwoven wall of foliage that reeked of power even to Pheonix's blunted magical senses. Crosinthusilas floated toward it and buried a hand among the leaves — which shook and trembled and swirled out, revealing a black doorway.

Into the doorway they went, Crosinthusilas floating blithely despite the complete lack of light in the narrow hallway beyond. Pheonix didn't have an issue seeing in complete darkness, but he hadn't been aware that elves like Crosinthusilas had night vision of any sort. Perhaps another perk of being a First.

Eventually the hallway opened to a large rectangular room with stone walls and a metal floor. Lining the walls on both sides were machines and thick cables, though that was of less immediate interest than the hundreds of metal caskets stacked vertically throughout the length of the space. The caskets were generally person-sized and windowless. Some had ancient words written on them, long-dried flowers or little trinkets at their bases.

Crosinthusilas touched some lettering on one of the caskets. A tight, angry smile pulled at her lips.

"*We will never forget you,*" she said mockingly as she moved on with something that had the spit of an invective. "This family does not even remember that there is a First down here."

"This is the Vault?" Pheonix asked.

Crosinthusilas' answer was to gesture around her. "You see? It is not dead," she said, apparently referring to the dim flashes of cerulean light sparking occasionally from the machinery. "That is how we know you are Lord Justice. It never responded to Lazarus."

There, again, associating me with Justice, Pheonix thought, but didn't question her. Crosinthusilas seemed to be in the grip of some powerful emotions, and he guessed if he followed her long enough, he would get some form of explanation.

She clearly had something to show him.

On the opposite end of the rectangular room from where they'd entered was another doorway. This led to a large dome-shaped cave — not quite a cavern, but not a small place — with rock walls and flooring. Lining its walls were thousands more caskets, though its floor was empty … save one object.

A metal dais, on which a singular casket rested. It was covered in thick ice and oozing clouds of condensate. The air palpably cooled as they approached it.

Deep sorrow creased Crosinthusilas's face. She ran her fingers across the ice with great familiarity and tenderness.

"The Vault. Where the Firsts chose to lay down and sleep instead of confronting their obstinate children. And my love, with them. But I am commanded to weather these Ages. Alone." Crosinthusilas turned to Pheonix, her eyes ablaze. "Waiting for you to come and show my people their error.

"But you, my savior, who I agonized through these Ages for — are not who I expected. You are so young, and you know nothing. That is why I chose to train you. So you would not be bound to their lies. Commander Abyss is exceptionally cunning, but she is at times overly cautious, and much of her plans rest on her ability to play at bureaucracy. I am bound by no such shackles. Do you see now? What is expected of you? No," her tight smile made another appearance, "I suppose all of this is still very confusing." Her face softened. "What was your question?"

Pheonix was stunned and unable to respond. Data whirled in his mind — her raw emotion was so unlike what he'd experienced of her up to this point. And he had no way to ease her mind at all.

"I forgot."

"That's not likely."

"Well, I tried. I'm sorry. I'm not good with emotion."

Crosinthusilas slowly turned back to the casket, pressing a hand to it. "I do not require comfort; not from you. I should not have brought you here. My burden is not yours."

"It seems as though it is. If the Firsts wait for Justice, then ... I will become the Justice they need. For you, and your love ... and us all. *I swear it.*"

His conviction echoed, bouncing between receptacles for the waiting shells of elves who were forced to make sacrifice after sacrifice. First to save the metacosm, then to let their children destroy themselves — along with everything else — for false belief.

He understood their position. After suffering so much loss, the last thing the Firsts wanted was to war with their own progeny.

Perhaps, here, was where it all started to go wrong.

Though he could only see her profile, he thought he caught a genuine smile.

"What is your question?" she asked again.

"Why did you laugh when Faran said Zu'Resh sought the Source?"

Crosinthusilas snorted. "The Source is the Creator."

Spiraea startled from the half-sleeping state she spent her time in, awash in sensory input and pain.

Someone was using a simulacrum in Terelath.

Though she wasn't the Ascended of the Weave and wasn't overly intimate with its Threads, she knew enough. A simulacrum was incredibly advanced illusion magic, but not elven in origin or practice. Elven illusion was innate, and thus didn't tangle the Weave in as ugly a way as did the 'School of Illusion' (as non-elven mages called it). Because simulacrum were channeled, they also acted as a window to anything with enough power to 'peek.'

Which, for Spiraea, wouldn't be a problem.

These simulacrums' source was somewhere in the Dark Sector — which fully roused her interest.

She traced the end point to the Council chambers. She hovered over the squat octagonal building (one of the few crafted not by Andural but by the Seconds), disgusted, but peeled back the layers nonetheless.

Inside was another amphitheater-style setup: a flat central area taking up about half of the internal space with multitudes of benches radiating from that point, angled upward on steps. The steps followed the walls, with the entrance and the opposite end across from it being the two exceptions. A dinky podium sat in the exact center of the floor, which faced two uncomfortable and plain chairs. Behind those chairs, in the hollow left by a lack of stairs, were two more chairs, these raised and decorated. Four balconies ringed the perimeter, well above the stairs and benches.

The balconies were for the 'noble' elven families. The benches were for the Councilors — two Firsts (the Prime War-Lady and Prime Bladesinger) and the remaining Seconds, with a few Thirds of wealth and status. The podium was for the entertainment of the day; usually some poor sap caught in the schemes of the very elves that sat in the benches around them and in the balconies above. The two chairs on the level of the podium were for the King and Queen, who, ostensibly, the poor sap would be addressing.

In reality, anyone at the podium would be addressing the brothers pulling the strings behind the Council, who sat on their 'thrones' behind the King and Queen.

Spiraea thought the brothers must consider themselves terribly clever for their 'subtle' use of interior design to reinforce hierarchy. Like most evil men, they held themselves in higher esteem than anyone else did.

At the moment, though, the room was empty but for Aolenthalassa and Aunrielthalassa — sitting among the Councilors' benches — and the simulacrums.

The simulacrums made their way across the floor towards the elven brothers. They were in the shape of hominin men wearing a particular type of ochre-stained robe that made her want to strike them down where they stood.

She railed that she wasn't allowed, but admonished herself to be patient.

The simulacrums of the two remaining Resh brothers, Tha'Resh and Ka'Resh, stopped in front of the elven brothers. Aolenthalassa and Aunrielthalassa stood. Dressed in their full finery, they clearly, by their arrogant postures, felt their home advantage.

"So," Aolenthalassa, the mouthy one, drawled. "You demand a meeting and don't even show up in person? So little trust."

"Trust is earned," one of the ochre-robed simulacrums said.

"Yes, how trite of you to speak of trust," the other spat. "Why oh why should we extend anything, let alone *trust*, to contract-breakers? It was you who allowed the Rangers to start sniffing around, which led to Zu'Resh's death at the hands of that *wretched* abomination."

"All his research was lost *and* the Rangers walked off with the evidence," the first added.

"We claim no responsibility for your brother being sloppy and getting himself caught," Aolenthalassa sneered.

The angrier simulacrum shot out its hand, with the other following a half-second behind, and both elves stiffened, jerking.

"We will do you this one favor," the first simulacrum gritted. "Since we know that mana is at a premium on this dump of a planet, and how *weak you are* because of it, we will provide you with some."

"But consider this a gift in name only," the other said. "Tell the Secretary-General to make the abomination go to Krasynth II. Use the agent of metal if need be. We will have the false God's head as retribution, or we will have yours."

"Your choice."

The simulacrums snapped their hands back and the elven brothers slumped in tandem with grunts of pain. Smoke roiled from under their collars, and they could do nothing more than glare weakly.

"We will take that as an affirmative," the first simulacrum said, straightening its robe-sleeves.

"We *trust* … you will hold up your end of *this* bargain," said the other.

And both disappeared, each leaving behind a small pile of glass.

Spiraea followed the threads of magic as they disengaged from their catalyst, the glass, and were pulled back to their source. She pinpointed the location within the Dark Sector, and committed it firmly to memory.

Two startled faces plopped quickly into her awareness, then faded.

Let them see; soon it would not matter.

She sunk back into her miasma to wait.

TWENTY
To Ranger HQ!

Over the next few months, Pheonix completed the remaining tasks on his personal list, ensured he had everything he needed from Terelath, and finally gave Chani the go-ahead that he was ready to move on.

So it was a crisp morning about a year and a half after belly-flopping into Terelath that Pheonix, Chani, and Steele made their way to the transportation hub. He'd never been there before, and found it to be unpleasantly packed.

The crowd ahead parted to let someone through. Pheonix angled to move past and found a body blocking his.

A wrinkled, dark skinned man floated cross-legged at waist height to Pheonix. He wore a series of colorful robes, one on top of the other, although one shoulder remained bare. A loop of emerald-colored beads hung down from his neck to pool in his lap, where his hands — long-fingered, ancient — rested. Red tattoos, an extremely old form of Mahji script, covered every exposed inch of skin.

Pheonix met knowing eyes buried deep in mountainous furry brows, and noted the smile that blossomed on his angular face.

"Well hello, Justice. It's been a while, hasn't it?"

"Mulahajad — " Chani warned.

"I'd prefer if you all would stop dancing around the subject," Pheonix interrupted, drawing surprised looks from

Steele and Chani. "I know what I am, or what I'm supposed to be, or what you all think I am, but I am still Pheonix. That being said, do you have any business with *Pheonix*?"

A long silence followed, during which Pheonix accessed:

Mulahajad, a high Mahji and First.

Mahji, one of the very few innately magical hominin species and one of the first species crafted by the hand of the Creator. The magic in them runs exceptionally hot and exceptionally strong. Nomadic in nature, it is not uncommon to find Mahji from one family line spread across the metacosm

Mahji have a naturally long lifespan and will live for thousands of years barring incident; though between struggling to control their magic from infancy and the grisly death awaiting failure, many Mahji do not live to see the upper reaches of that long life.

"I confess I do not," the floating man — Mulahajad — said smoothly. "But it is ultimately immaterial whether you call yourself Pheonix or Justice or Bob the Farting Dog. I was told to deliver something to *you*."

Pheonix, by no means pacified, asked, "By whom?"

"The Metatron."

Pheonix blinked. Of all the names he could have given, that was not one Pheonix expected. It almost seemed like a joke, but Mulahajad was not smiling.

"What could the Voice of the Creator possibly have for me?"

"Something Lazarus was keeping for you."

"Lazarus — the previous Ascended of Justice?"

"Just the same."

Pheonix sighed, then said, "Fine. Deliver, then."

He held out one hand for Pheonix to take, and Pheonix did.

A deluge of knowledge, images, sensory input — memories — hit Pheonix like a transport. He couldn't breathe, paralyzed by the rush. And yet, unlike what the Obelisk had done to him, this didn't hurt. It was just confusing and unpleasant.

Pheonix came back to himself with a sharp intake of breath. He stared down at Mulahajad, unconsciously attempting to make sense of the memories — which brought a stabbing pain in his temples. So he blocked them out, burying them deeply in his subconscious to let them sort themselves out. Fuck that shit.

A beatific smile beamed up at him. "When it all makes sense again, come visit me."

With that, Mulahajad made his way around Pheonix, not giving him a chance to respond, and was swallowed by the crowd.

"What was that all about?" Pheonix asked Chani.

She sighed gustily. "How should I know? You'll probably find out in time. Let's just get going."

A teleportation crystal brought the three to the Ranger District transport hub, the docking station for all ships and shuttles, in-atmospheric and space-faring.

Pheonix would board a shuttle that would take him to Ranger HQ, his personal effects already on their way. Steele took the lead here, and they passed craft after craft, of too many designs and origins to count in such a short time.

Steele stopped at one, a medium-sized thing vaguely shaped like a giant beetle, and turned to Pheonix. Chani came up to stand next to them. Steele held out their hand; Pheonix took it, and the Commander grasped his forearm firmly.

"Master Pheonix … your presence here has turned us inside out, and for that I thank you." Steele's blue eyes were alight. "But this isn't good-bye, not by a long shot. Abyss and I will be on our way up in the next several hours. I wish you a quick and smooth in-processing."

Steele released him.

Chani took Steele's place, grinning. "Don't cause too much trouble till I get there, huh? See you on the other side, kid."

Pheonix nodded and stepped inside the shuttle. There were rows of front-facing seats placed next to thick windows, some already filled. Pheonix, at random, chose an empty one in the section meant to accommodate large bodies such as his.

It was a reminder of how an individual of his stature, in the wider metacosm, wasn't that uncommon ... although, perhaps among hominins, it was.

The remaining seats quickly filled. After a briefing regarding the destination, time in transit, and emergency protocol, the shuttle hummed to life. Pheonix watched out a nearby window as they rose above the transportation hub, maneuvered and hovered in place. Then, with stomach-dropping speed, Terelath — and eventually Availeon — shrank beneath them.

He turned his attention to their destination. Though Availeon still loomed large in the side window, they quickly approached the metallic sphere that was Ranger HQ. There was significant space traffic; millions of ships swarmed like satellites. The shuttle Pheonix rode dove into the melee smoothly, heading for a large open port.

They docked and Pheonix waited his turn to disembark. A female hominin, uniform proclaiming her a Sergeant, caught his eye in the narrow hallway lined with people outside the shuttle.

"Pheonix, I presume?" she called as he got close.

"Yes, Sergeant."

Pheonix thought back to his studies on Ranger ranks. Sergeant was a middling officer rank. The highest rank in the Rangers was the Commanding-General, though this leadership position itself still took instruction from the three Chosen assigned to the Rangers, the Elders. Unlike the elves who were a monarchy of sorts, the Rangers' function and structure was essentially an independent military.

"I am Sergeant Oriana Beowulf. I will be assisting you with in-processing today, if you'll come with me."

Pheonix accessed while he followed her down the unnecessarily long hallway: *Beowulf, one of the bottom-tier, lesser clans associated with the Rivios great clan. The three great clans are Abyssterilon, Rivios, and Akamatsu, named for John Abyssterilon and Damien Rivios, the two pioneering Firsts who ended the Unification war and assisted the elves in beating back the demons during the Great Demon War, then went on to found the Rangers. Latecomer Akamatsu was given great clan status well after the formation of the Rangers for Ryu Akamatsu's contribution of the fold-space engine, which allowed for instantaneous interspace travel.*

A machine waited at the end of the hallway: an arch of metal with two large turrets aimed threateningly down the hall. Two armed guards stood beyond, accompanied by a bored-looking Captain with a datapad. Sergeant Beowulf preceded Pheonix, stopping just under the metal archway. A screen flashed before her at eye-level, data scrolling at a rapid pace. Finally the screen cleared and a green light proclaimed her to be Man before the whole holographic rig disappeared entirely. She took her place next to the Captain and gestured Pheonix forward.

Pheonix stepped under the archway. The screen appeared, information rolling by — then an alarm blared. Red lights flooded the area, and the turrets trained on him with ominous clicks. Pheonix stood still, waiting to see what would happen, but he couldn't help the instinctual fight response pumping his blood faster. The two guards perked up, looking to the Captain for orders.

The Captain scrutinized Pheonix from over his datapad, but before he could so much as open his mouth, Sergeant Beowulf called out: "Sir, this is Pheonix from Terelath; you should have the report from his liaison regarding his … unusual genetic construction."

After a moment of flicking through his datapad, the Captain nodded. "Yes, here it is." He waved an arm. "Come on through, son."

The red lights turned off, the turrets relaxed, and the soldiers looked disappointed.

Pheonix fell into line behind Sergeant Beowulf once more, and she led him towards a long, tiled thoroughfare thronged with people. Just like in Terelath, he had a hard time picking out two of the same species in the expansive crowds moving through the docking area.

He and Sergeant Beowulf passed row after row of the same door-machine-guard combination, all leading to crafts of all shapes and sizes attached to the moon-sized HQ like parasites. Waiting areas with holo-screens broadcasting local news were spaced out between each doorway.

They passed through a concession area and Pheonix took in a deep breath of the varied smells of cooking food. Shops hawking souvenirs, necessities, snacks, entertainment, and all sorts of other things were interspersed with the food stalls and peculiar Ranger vending machines he'd seen in places around Terelath.

"We'll have to take a shuttle; if we tried to walk the length of the docking zone, we'd be lucky to get your in-processing done this week," Sergeant Beowulf said over her shoulder, then directed him with a curt wave of her hand to pass out of the main thoroughfare and into a side-passageway. Pheonix glanced up at the sign marking this as a shuttle portway.

The shuttles were large, bullet-shaped, and splashed with the Rangers' crest: a black set of sharply-curved wings arcing up, with their bases meeting at a blood-red cord tied into a knot. Cradled in the U-space between the wings were three small, white, four-pointed stars and one larger yellow four-pointed star.

Pheonix accessed:

The black wings of the Rangers: taken directly from the Unification War of what was now Techno-Earth, John Abyssterilon and Damien Rivios's home. In the war, the symbol of the Race of Man was a blue bird, and the humans' a red bird. The black wings were meant to show the coming-together of different factions and species for the greater good. The red knot was a reminder that their unity was forged in blood. The three small white stars represent the great clans, with the larger yellow star representing the Creator.

Despite the number of people milling about, the wait wasn't terrible. The shuttles moved at blink-speed, and dozens of bodies poured into each compartment, to be whisked away and replaced with another in a split-second. Loading the shuttle to its capacity took a few minutes, but that was the longest part of the whole operation and most people seemed well used to the process.

Pheonix and Sergeant Beowulf were soon boarding. Seats lined the inside, but the Sergeant gestured Pheonix to stand near the door, saying in an undertone that they'd be getting off in a couple stops and it was easier not to have to fight from the back. Pheonix saw what she meant — these compartments got pretty packed.

He accessed once again:

Instant transportation systems such as are utilized in Terelath are incompatible with many Ranger ships due to the integrated null-shield technology that became standard operating procedure (S.O.P.) after the Third Galactic War. Null shields are designed to create an area where, within, no extrasensory abilities or magic may be used, although they can be tuned to both prevent entry/exit into/out of the effective range of the field and to neutralize compounds of many compositions within the field itself. This became especially useful during the Elysian conflict. Elysian, much like the demons, were able to move freely through space and wrench open portals (or in their case, tears) at will.

The shuttle sped off so fast that everything outside the windows was a blur, but he didn't feel it. Motion dampers or some such thing, he supposed, but didn't care enough at that moment to access the engineering archives directly. He people-watched and let his mind drift as several stops — and far more than several bodies — came and went. He had wedged himself into a corner near the front of the shuttle to avoid being touched, but couldn't quell the spike of irritation as he was, inevitably, brushed by bags and limbs squeezing past.

He was quite grateful when Sergeant Beowulf indicated that the next stop was their destination.

A sign hung over the hallway he was about to enter: 'Processing.' Sergeant Beowulf took him to a sterile, nondescript room with a desk that had a chair on either side of it, and a wall of terminals. She indicated that Pheonix should sit in the chair nearest the door, while she went around to the other side of the desk and sat. She rummaged around, then brought up a stack of datapads.

"Welcome to the Processing department," she said. "Here, we enlighten new recruits as to what we expect of them here in the Rangers, get their accounts set up and all their affairs in order so they can go straight into training. I've been briefed that you can read and retain like a computer? Must be nice," she said drily and placed the stack of datapads in front of him. "Let me know when you're done."

It took Pheonix all of twelve minutes to get through what took most recruits several hours. His required conduct, what he could expect in the next few days, an outline of the most basic of training schedules (meaning those courses that all Ranger inductees, regardless of future job status, were required to take and pass), facilities location and function, out-of-bounds zones, bounty and credit accrual, and non-disclosure agreements were only some of the giant stack of datapads he skimmed and marked with his thumb.

Beowulf fed the completed datapads into the terminal one at a time. The computer flashed her an error message. She scowled at it, brought up the holo-keyboard, and typed for a few moments. The error message persisted.

"Hmm. Well. I've called your liaisons to come meet us here. The computer's telling me I can't enter your information."

She stood and gestured him over to one of the other terminals, which was a simple holo-screen and a circular hole set into the metallic front, about an inch in diameter.

"Put your thumb in here. We'll get a sample of your DNA to set up your bounty account while we wait for your liaisons to arrive," she told him.

Pheonix did as he was asked. The screen flickered and changed, text scrolling across it at a rapid rate. It seemed to be nonsense, even to Pheonix. A message popped up: "Encrypted data, please contact your in-processor."

"What?! I *am* the in-processor!" Sergeant Beowulf shoved in front of him; Pheonix made room to avoid touching her.

The holo-keyboard appeared and she typed on it furiously. The computer gave a chipper little beep and pulsated another few error messages in quick sequence.

"I don't fucking believe this; the AI is still denying me access! *I am the in-processor!* What — I don't —"

Chani and Steele arrived at just that moment.

Sergeant Beowulf stepped back and pointed angrily at the terminal. Chani and Steele exchanged a look, then Steele took over. They typed a few words, waited for the response, and then clapped their hands together.

"Looks like this is absolutely correct. The AI is recommending we bypass this part of the in-processing because an account already exists. The issue was that the in-processee outranks the in-processor."

Three pairs of eyes settled on Pheonix. Though he was used to such inspection, he didn't like it.

"That — that makes no sense," spluttered Sergeant Beowulf, finding her voice. "It can't — it's got to be an error."

Chani peered at the terminal. "No, Sergeant, everything seems to be in order. He's even got an outstanding balance of one billion and one bounty."

The silence that fell after this statement could have knocked out a charging rhino.

"Well," continued Chani cheerfully, "that'll make getting your equipment *much* easier."

Sergeant Beowulf stared for a moment, then threw up her hands. "You know what? He's your problem now."

"And with that, shall we?" Steele waved an arm in an 'after you' gesture, and Pheonix preceded them out the door.

"We had a feeling this might happen," Steele continued outside. "Lazarus spent time here and that account is his. We weren't sure if the account would register as belonging to you or not, with you both being tied to Justice, so we figured we'd put you through in-processing and get it sorted out."

"Why didn't you just come with me?" Pheonix asked.

"We had a prior engagement," Chani said shortly, and Pheonix didn't understand but dropped it.

"Anyway," Steele continued, "because it will take a couple hours to get your quarters and equipment processed, we'll take you down to the ranges. Normally we stick new recruits in with their classes at this point and give them over to their drill sergeants, but you're somewhat of a special case and will be training separately. I doubt you want to slow your learning down to the pace of most other sapients."

"No, that would be annoying," Pheonix agreed in a bland voice.

Chani chuckled; Steele grinned.

They came to another shuttle, this one dead empty (at which Pheonix felt a glimmer of relief).

"The ranges are only used at very specific times and we're in between classes right now, so we'll have it all to ourselves," Steele explained.

"Since you show such an affinity towards weapons, we figured having the chance to play with some firearms beyond the kinetic pistol you used on Terelath would be a good introduction to Ranger learning," Chani added.

The shuttle glided to a stop; they disembarked.

"You'll be glossing over the majority of the very earliest of Ranger training meant to instill discipline, obedience, teamwork, and physical strength. We know you have all of those things. You will be learning our hand-to-hand techniques and other Ranger-specific combat and tactics. We've tailored your studies so that most of the memorization — regulations, S.O.P., history, and the like — will be done on teacher off-time and through terminal. How does all that sound so far?" Steele asked.

"Fine," Pheonix said.

"While your training compared to the average cadet will be accelerated," Steele continued, "you will also be given subjects they don't take. We will continue working on your social interaction and will set aside a time for you to finish the scanning of your genetic structure. Luckily, the facilities here are more advanced than those in Terelath, so we can complete it all in one session. Granted, that session will be several hours long. You'll be notified of the time and date of that appointment."

"Wasn't I already scanned?" Pheonix asked.

"By the elves, sure. But that's for their records. We don't have access to that." Steele's face was carefully neutral. Pheonix was beginning to pick up the subtleties in expression and tone, and this kind of neutrality tended to hide emotion. He knew communications between the elves and Rangers were broken behind the scenes, but wondered at the extent of it.

Chani and Steele led the way into the range proper — really just a huge warehouse with lanes and targets set up at the opposite end. Rather than head directly to a lane, they stopped at a control panel on one wall with a large hinged door below it. Chani pressed a few buttons on the panel.

"How about pistols first, since you already are pretty familiar with them."

The hinged door opened and a rack emerged, on which were several small firearms.

Chani pointed to the leftmost weapon, then continued down the line towards the right: "Ballistics and kinetics you'll recognize. Then there's plasma, laser, and energy."

Pheonix's eyes ranged across the assembled weapons. The ballistic pistol looked like an explosive-powder-based revolver he'd seen pictures of in a hominin history book, with a spare frame and round cartridge. The kinetic pistol resembled a sleeker version of the ballistics one, with a blocky, angular form and slide magazine. The plasma pistol was long-barreled, with a bulky chamber above the grip. Four electrodes sat in a cross-formation in front of the end of the barrel. The laser was sleek and elegant, smaller than the rest, with a tiny, thin barrel. The energy pistol was short, large, and squat, the barrel wide enough to load an apple.

Firearms came a lot less naturally to him than other weapons, he was soon to learn, even with his brief training with the kinetic pistol. He tried all five pistols and, while he did manage to hit the target with each by the end of the session, he was hardly an expert marksman.

Perversely, he found himself enjoying the challenge of something he didn't immediately take to. It caught his focus, fired up a determination to conquer that he'd rarely felt before.

The energy firearm was excessively difficult because he couldn't see his shot, plasma required a charging time, and so one twitch or miscalculation would cause it to hit off-mark (which he thought terribly inefficient), and the laser was a sustained beam that became increasingly hard to aim with distance.

He was just taking another go at the plasma pistol, as that was the one he was the least comfortable with, when he heard Chani greet someone behind him.

"Hey, Dick. Was wondering when you'd get your lazy ass down here. I'm sick of doing your job."

Pheonix turned to see who she was talking to — a stocky figure of a person in bulky (clearly Ranger-made) armor, made bulkier by layers of harness and exo-suit parts here and there. He was shorter than Chani, but not by much, and his entire body was covered — not so much as an inch of skin showed. Painted across the faceplate of his helmet was a grinning skull.

"Do I look concerned, Commander?" 'Dick' replied, his deep voice flat, and somehow not muffled by his helmet.

"Kinda hard to tell under all that shit you got on."

He snapped to attention as he came to her side.

"Whatcha got?" Chani said.

The soldier settled into the 'at ease' position, legs spread shoulder-width and arms bent, hands interlocked behind his back.

"Sole survivor reporting. Ambush. Enemy eliminated; forty confirmed dead. Dark elf assassins. If I may speak freely, ma'am?" He waited for Chani to assent, though she gave him a Look for some reason, before continuing, "Quit sending me with these rookies. Recruits don't need to be on this kind of mission yet."

"Fuck me, who gave you recruits? I didn't authorize that." Chani's voice was tense enough that, despite the relatively cool words, it gave off the impression she was much more upset than she was showing.

"It was just recon," Steele said.

"Doesn't matter; that zone isn't cleared for training. Was it you, Steele?"

Before Steele could answer, the soldier responded: "Negative. Colonel Yung, ma'am. The Colonel sent the order down two hours before hit time. I argued, with all due respect, but he firmly informed me that this mission would be a 'piece of cake' and that I didn't need a fully-functioning squad."

Chani swore in dwarven. "Should have guessed. I'll deal with it." She sighed, seemed to gather herself, then, said to Pheonix: "C'mere, kid."

Pheonix set the plasma pistol down and joined them.

"This is Sabot. He'll be your Sergeant-trainer for the duration of your time here. He will personally handle your introduction into Ranger ops, since Steele and I unfortunately have other responsibilities. Speaking of, Steele, it's probably time we report and let these two get acquainted."

TWENTY-ONE
Cheshire Al

Sabot, with other Sergeant-trainers filling in when he wasn't available, started Pheonix immediately on the very basics: battle-speak, squad and solo tactical movement, continued weapons training, Ranger hand-to-hand combat, outfitting him with his own uniform and training him on its functions, etc. Most of his actual learning came from downloading manuals into his brain via the Ranger Archive, which he now had access to, but he still had to put the information to use to show that he could apply it.

Pheonix was also directed to go to the Med-Lab to finish his full genetic mapping and biology scan. The genetics department was just as interested in him as he was in himself. He was also eager to learn about the Med-Lab. This was a whole new universe to him; while he'd been exposed to some tech on board the slave ships, it's not as though anyone was teaching him about what he was seeing.

And there had been very little obvious tech on Terelath. It was as though the elves preferred to hide (and barely tolerate) its presence, whereas tech was a way of life for the Rangers. One way wasn't inherently 'better' than the other; to each culture their own. But Pheonix was fascinated by the difference.

Months passed. Most of Pheonix's time was spent in the simulator for combat training or on the range, when he wasn't in his quarters downloading and processing from the Archive.

One night, he was reading a book and resting in his cot when the gentle chime of a terminal call cut through his concentration.

Ah, I'd been wondering when this would happen, he thought, mildly amused.

"Yes Austraelus?" he said aloud. She hadn't needed the terminal — she could talk to anyone on HQ directly via their implants — but she was likely trying to be polite by not introducing herself in his head. He appreciated it.

Phoenix accessed: *Austraelus, organotek shipboard AI for the Ranger HQ stationed in orbit around Availeon.*

"Oh, please, call me Astra. All my friends do."

Why am I a friend already? What an odd person, Pheonix thought with a grin, but said: "If you wish."

"It's nice to finally speak to you," she said. She had a pleasant voice. "I've heard so much."

"Likewise."

"I wish to request a meeting, *in person*." The phrasing piqued Pheonix's curiosity. "Do you have time?"

She knows I'm just reading, yet she's still asking, he mused.

This kind of 'intrusion' didn't bother him. As the AI for the ship, she knew everything that went on, by necessity. It was difficult to embarrass him, and he didn't do anything in private he wouldn't do in public. Even if he did, what did an AI care for the private actions of organics?

"I do."

"Can I send the directions to your implants?"

"If you like."

"Prepare yourself," she said, and he braced mentally for the internal data transfer.

The directions came to the forefront of his mind with the gentleness of natural recall, but he was surprised to learn she meant it *literally* when she'd said 'in person.' Judging by the complexity of the instructions she'd transferred, he was likely going to be heading to her core: the place where her physical computing body was stored.

Of course they wouldn't want just anyone walking up to the core of the AI. Still, why trust him with this knowledge? And alone? He briefly considered asking Chani but rejected the idea. She was always telling him to go off and do his own thing, and this seemed a harmless way to follow her advice.

"If you find yourself lost, simply say my name. I look forward to meeting you, face to face."

Pheonix smiled at the joke.

The way to the core was convoluted, as he'd predicted, and there were many security stops along the way. Each group of guards waved him through without so much as a pause. He got the sneaking suspicion he was already *known* around HQ.

A nondescript hallway led to a less-than-nondescript bulkhead door that his instincts told him was loaded with well-hidden ways to dispatch any intruders. The beauty of Ranger over-engineering.

The bulkhead door to his final destination opened before he could touch it, and he entered an octagonal room. In the center was a floor-to-ceiling tank made of a clear hard paneling, also octagonal. Inside the 'tank' was about a foot of blue gel. Blue light poured from somewhere, possibly the gel itself.

And there, in front of him, with its face and hands pressed against the paneling, was an androgynous ethereal blue form who looked simply enthused to see him, as far as he could tell from her expression.

The door closed and the form leapt away from the paneling and danced around in the tank above the gel, sometimes rising well over it, sometimes only enough that the tips of its toes barely touched its glowing surface. The light in the room seemed to pulse. The form ceased its cavorting and floated downward, coming *through* the paneling and stopping at eye-level to Pheonix. She was much smaller than he was; though, if this truly was the HQ AI's projection, she could likely take whatever form she pleased.

Pheonix gave a short but respectful bow. "Miss Astra."

Astra clapped her hands together and grinned. Her 'teeth' were a solid white-blue bar, which was also the color of the sclera of her just-slightly-too-large eyes. It made her look like a fae — something definitely not quite real.

"Master Pheonix. Or, Lord Justice?"

"I prefer Pheonix."

She chuckled. "How are you finding your time on my ship so far?"

My ship. The possessive was subtle, but there. Not aggression; pride.

"Well. There is much to do and learn. I am comfortable."

"You have been the subject of much talk since you arrived — since they found you on Terelath. Some of it filtered up here. So many eyes following your progress."

"They must not have much better to do."

Astra laughed. It almost buzzed, like he could hear without hearing a melody within. Her voice had the same quality, but less so. It set his senses on edge, and not in an altogether unpleasant way.

"Honestly, those engaged in flapping their yaps — probably not." She spun away, drifting through the clear paneling and back again, drawing slight ripples through the gel — or perhaps the ripples drew the projection. "The metacosm is always changing, for those who choose to see it. You're not as much of an anomaly as they might want you to think."

She stopped, facing away from him, and bent backwards bonelessly to look at him upside-down.

He nodded. She hadn't been the only person to say something to this effect to him: and he was also beginning to notice it in the pattern of his collected data. "I think you may be right."

The grin returned. She righted herself and floated over to him, holding her hands out.

"I won't take too much of your time," she said. "The main reason I needed to see you in person was this: *If you need anything, I encourage you to call my name.*"

Her eyes bore intently into his. In this place where none could go, none could listen, she had a message. It was not lost on him.

"I appreciate that," he said.

Her intense look faded into amusement. "And do come see me again. I get precious few visitors, and even less that I actually like."

"Thank you," Pheonix said with another bow, and took his leave.

TWENTY-TWO
Uncertainty

Chani consulted the datapad in her hands as the elevator took her and Steele to the Commanding-General's office.

Reports on the holo-screen of the datapad flashed by in tune to her thoughts, and she scowled.

This didn't make sense. The timeline was off. Was Astra having an issue? She'd have to check in with the AI when she had a chance.

She put the datapad away at the elevator's announcement of arrival. The doors opened to the austere, impressively large office decorated in the Rangers' distinctive crest and smooth lines of metal. As they entered, the Commanding-General looked up.

Chani always had to stifle the urge to ruffle the fluffy white ears that lifted in greeting; his muzzle parted to briefly show sharp white fangs and a hint of a long pink tongue. She'd seen him flop it out of his mouth in a toothy grin once or twice, but since this was strictly business, he was unlikely to betray any expressions of familiarity.

An Akeela from the icy planet Borea, one of four orbiting the supermassive star Pol Centauri in tandem, the Commanding-General was known as just that — his rank. A verbal classification for him would be Pol Centauri Borea North Forest Grey, which was just an amalgamation of the system, planet, geographic location, and clan he belonged to. He was known as his rank because his species kept their personal names personal.

In order to verbalize his personal name properly without hyper delicate sensory organs, she'd likely have to recite his pheromone chemical composition, anyway; and who had time for that?

The Commanding-General stood just under two units (shorter than both herself and Steele), with a thick neck and relatively narrow shoulders dipping into a broad barrel chest. Even with his white-furred body covered in the crisp Ranger uniform befitting his rank, the skeletal and muscular structure beneath the cloth bore very little resemblance to a hominin. He stood easily on digitigrade legs: his wide, balanced stance mixed with the obvious weaponry in his mouth and his cold blue eyes made for an imposing presence … even with the fluffy ears.

The subtle and subconscious intimidation Akeela projected was relevant to his rank; one of his many jobs was to handle the political day-to-day operations of the Rangers, both internal (between clans, for example) and external (delegations from other species and militaries).

"Commander," his simulated voice, pumped from a translating device on his chest, said. It gathered body language, pheromone, vocal, and other minor bits of data that made up the Akeela method of communication and translated it into speech. It amused her every time she saw him, only for the fact that it was well known that Akeela thought verbal communication was terribly primitive; some of them disdained using the device.

"Commanding-General, thank you for meeting with me," Chani replied.

Steele also exchanged greetings with the Commanding-General, and all three sat.

"Tell me," the Commanding-General said, leaning forward, "about the fire bird."

He, of course, meant Pheonix. The Akeela manner of speech was a little odd, but the Commanding-General was more used to verbalizing than others of his species and generally managed a seamless conversation. Proper nouns were still difficult for a species that identified others by their scent and markings, though.

"What about him?" Steele asked.

"Future plans?"

"We aren't sure," Chani said.

"Explain."

Chani took a mental breath. *Here we go. Time to set the stage. Pheonix, I hope you never find out how much trouble I'm going through to keep you under the radar.*

"He's Ascended," Chani began, "*supposedly*. He's fully immortal, we've seen that. But that's the only similarity he shares with Ascended that we know of. Other than, perhaps, his exponential learning and fearsome strength — but if we're judging by that, I could offer you several hundred Ascended. He's still very much a physical being; he can't jump, slide, teleport, or open a tear; he is still subject to a null field, he's still susceptible to exhaustion, he can't … do that disappearing immaterial thing that Ascended do, whatever that is. And none of the others have shown up to acknowledge him in any way. Temperjoke interfered before we even found him, but I don't trust anything he does, and Spiraea refuses to comment even when asked directly by her consort."

"How is that a problem?" the Commanding-General asked.

Chani twisted her lips. "Doesn't that seem *suspicious*? The Ascended predate even the elven Firsts, like Crosinthusilas who was directly involved in his training — who, might I add, trounced him thoroughly on many an occasion. How? Why would a new Ascended show up *now*, Ages later, and so …" she waved her hands to emphasize her point, "... half baked?

"My professional suggestion is to avoid getting him involved in Ranger affairs. He's not ours. He wasn't the elves' either. He's ... nobody's but his own ... and the Creator's, I guess. But we aren't hearing dick from *that* angle lately, and Pheonix doesn't seem to, either. Don't even get me started on that. We can train him — carefully — but we must let him pursue his own devices while onboard, and let him go as soon as is feasible. To be clear: he is only our recruit in *name only*. If we use him on one of our ops, it'll stir up a political hornet's nest. It may look like we're trying to claim him, and Creator forbid we attract the ire of the Chosen. I can hear 'but the balance' already. It was bad enough after the Obelisk debacle. I barely got him here."

"If I may, Commanders," Steele interjected, and waited for the go-ahead. Steele was well below the other two in rank. The only reason they were in that room, allowed in that conversation, was their involvement in Pheonix's training. "Why *can't* we use him? The Chosen may object, but it's easy enough to counter 'but the balance' with 'but protocol' if that's how they want to play it. Besides, he's *Ascended*. Whatever decision he makes is his alone. We lowly mortals can hardly be accused of influencing that."

"You have an idea?" The Commanding-General asked.

Steele leaned forward with their elbows on their knees, clasping their hands in front of their chin. They directed a keen look at first the Commanding-General, then Chani.

"Krasynth II," they said finally.

Chani stood up so fast her chair slid backwards.

"No. No, no. That's literally the *exact opposite* of what I *just* said. What, let's just invite the Chosen to dinner and announce that we're inducting Ascended into the ranks? They're bristling enough that we're even training him."

"It's a big enough action that he'd be essentially lost in the crowd, but he'd still be seeing combat as it happens for us. Even if he doesn't stay with us — which, again, we can't force Ascended to do anything — having that firsthand experience will be valuable to him."

"Look, I'm not saying that we can't send him on *a* mission, but why *that* one?" Chani protested.

"We shouldn't miss the opportunity. Having an Ascended on the field might finally turn the tide for us. We need those deutronium mines. For Jesus-Man's sake, Abyss, putting aside the Ascended thing, the kid can't die, we've witnessed that ourselves. And Sabot will be there. That's more than most trainees get."

"But what if we're *wrong*?" Chani insisted. "We've seen that Ascended can die, or disappear. They're not infallible. What if we're misinterpreting the evidence? The universe is full of weird shit — I should know."

"How is this any different than sending him against Zu'R esh?" Steele asked.

"That was a request from Spiraea herself. Kinda transcends political bullshit or resource wars. Krasynth II will be extremely public. If something goes wrong, that will also be extremely public. We have to be certain."

"Elders?" The Commanding-General suggested, referring to the three Chosen who were at the top of the Ranger hierarchy.

Chani sighed deeply and sat down again, running her hands down her face. This wasn't going her way at all, but it'd look suspicious if she put up much more of a fight. Hopefully the Elders wouldn't agree to it.

"That's probably the only way forward," she finally said. "We could sit here and argue until Gygamas shit deutronium. Ultimately, it comes down to what the Elders think — and him. I'm not about to force him to do anything."

"We couldn't very well force an Ascended *to* do anything," Steele repeated, pressing the point.

Chani thinned her lips but kept her thoughts to herself. *I have a feeling that if **I** asked him, he would. But let's not tell* *them that. I will likely need whatever favor I have curried with Pheonix under the table.*

She felt a familiar pang of guilt for a moment when she thought about how she used people, but it receded quickly. She always gave someone the option to say no; there were a million ways to get something done, and harming someone to do it always led to more problems down the road, aside from being ethically wrong. She had so many irons in the fire at any one time, though, that it was instinctual to read someone, both emotionally and via their file, and see how they could be moved into place so that a mutually beneficial relationship could form.

Being a prude about manipulation was not how one shifted an abusive system.

If she was coldly frank about it, the Rangers likely wouldn't function without her. They counted on her 'people skills.' And certainly Pheonix's little rebellion would be dead in the water without them. The kid had precisely zero concept of the kind of political and social maneuvering necessary for long-term revolution to stick.

Sometimes a less-than-perfect deal was necessary in order to be afforded the opportunity to discard that deal later, when a better option came along. Not every entity that stood in bureaucracy's shadow was evil, and not every evil was a result of bureaucracy. Sometimes people were just assholes, and contrary, and selfish, and ignorant, and there wasn't much to be done about it, officially or unofficially. Pheonix didn't seem to realize that yet.

He was smart, though, despite his social puerility. He'd get it, in time. Chani just had to protect him until he could maneuver at least as well as she could — or he'd gained enough power for it not to matter.

She put aside those thoughts for another time.

"If the Elders green-light it," she said, "send him all — and I do mean *all*, classified or not — the intel we have, and we'll leave it up to him."

Though Pheonix's quarters were easily three or four times the size of his cottage on Terelath, he'd managed to fill most of the empty space with books.

Other than the books, his room was a spartan affair, consisting only of a cot, table, chair, replicator, terminal, and refresher. A locked chest at the bottom of his bed contained his only possessions: the book taken from the old man's shack at the time of his death and his journals. The book from the old man's house remained unread. Somehow, it didn't seem right to open it just yet; and despite his time with the elves, Pheonix was still very much a creature of instinct.

Under normal circumstances, he'd be housed with other trainees in the barracks; but as an Ascended, it was protocol that he be separated from the general public while on-ship.

He'd been given access to the Ranger archives to continue his self-training during downtime and had used it to requisition the books and reports.

He had a puzzle to solve.

A puzzle that revolved around his birth, his childhood, all the strangeness that made up his early life, and the old man's murder.

He didn't necessarily care about his biological origins; he was much more interested in the many and varied injustices that those around him had perpetrated. He'd done some research in Terelath, but not nearly as much as he'd have liked to. He had more access and many more resources on Ranger HQ, so this was his opportunity to make some real progress.

He could live with everyone around him thinking he was Ascended if it gave him the resources he needed to move forward with his investigation. At this point, he didn't have the time nor inclination to question it.

The old man had lived on Archaic Earth; this he knew. And Pheonix had ended up on Availeon via what was (by all appearances) a natural tear. He also knew at this point that it was Temperjoke, the Ascended of Chaos, who had removed him from the arena ship. But that knowledge did nothing for him. It wasn't as though anyone knew how to contact that particular Ascended, and Pheonix wasn't certain if he wanted that conversation. Judging by Temperjoke's reputation, it was unlikely he'd be any help.

The arena ship's location was one of the things he still needed to figure out, but he had other ways of acquiring that information without attempting to contact Temperjoke, as hard a slog as it would be.

The man in black, known as the Death Dealer, was the biggest variable. Because Pheonix had gotten from point A to point B to point C via some pretty unusual circumstances, his trail would likely go cold many times. But if he played his cards right, he could skip a few steps and go straight to the source: his birthplace.

The biggest issue, bar none, was that even if he did secure the names or locations of all the slavers and evil people involved in his early life, the Dark Sector was mostly unmapped, so coordinates wouldn't do him much good without context. And quite frankly, he wasn't quite sure yet how to get around that problem. However, by pursuing the movements of known slaver groups in the areas in question, he theorized that he may be able to create his own map. With enough information and his mathematical mind, he was reasonably certain he could trace a path back to his origins — and bring Justice to every evil bastard along the way.

He had no strong emotions on it one way or another in regards to *himself* or things that were done to him — the father that abandoned him and sold him into slavery didn't matter. It wasn't about Pheonix himself, partially because it hadn't affected him. They hadn't managed to do anything to him at all, despite attempting every depraved trick in the book. He wasn't suffering from trauma. He'd been ridiculously privileged, given the situation.

But his lack of emotion regarding his own past broke down when he thought about the people he'd coexisted with in those pits.

He wasn't the first by far — neither of his father's experiments nor of those who were enslaved — and with every day that passed, more innocents would be claimed. People who *were* affected by trauma would become mentally or physically damaged — or destroyed — by the actions of the egotistical few.

He flashed back to the narrow corridors of the slave ship, alarm lights coloring everything a fitting shade of blood red, watching that enslaved woman dissolve when the Death Dealer shot her. Never given a chance. She hadn't even seen it coming. She wasn't even in the way — she was just nearby. Pheonix gritted his teeth, battling down the rage.

No, it's not about me, he thought forcefully.

The door chime rang. It wasn't necessary; Chani's footfalls were heavy, clearly audible even with Ranger sound dampening tech.

"Enter," he called to engage the voice activation system.

The oculus opened and Chani stepped in.

"Yo," she said, and offered him the datapad she was carrying. "We've got a mission we'd like you to consider participating in. Here's what we know; if you're up for it, I'll notify parties involved and you'll receive orders via the correct channels, yada yada."

Yes, Pheonix thought, *this is protocol. But usually trainees aren't given intel or asked their opinion. Though, my training has deviated from protocol quite a bit, so, I suppose this shouldn't surprise me.*

"Okay," he said.

Chani threw him a jaunty salute and left.

He skimmed the intel.

> Krasynth II: a desolate, deutronium-rich asteroid discovered by the Applegate family, who were granted mining and property rights by the Accord.
>
> Deutronium: one of the rarest and most important minerals in the known metacosm. A dense, superhard material, difficult to work with. A cooperative of dwarves and Rangers had devised a way to deal with the temperamental ore, turning it into a damn near indestructible compound used in energy weaponry, some power armor, shipboard armor and shipboard weaponry, many superstructures for spacefaring vehicles, and more. It wouldn't be an exaggeration to say that the current power wielded by the Rangers, and by extension the Accord, was due at least in part to deutronium.
>
> The Applegate family had been running operations uneventfully for five years prior to an attack by dark elves approximately three days ago. Initial thinking by Accord officials was that the attack was a small-time raid — until red mages arrived. The Accord sent a Battle-Guard of Vindicators (tek-knights), but they were wiped out. The Applegate family was also slaughtered, and the enemy fully took over the working deutronium mines.

An operational summary and ... that was it? It was awfully dry. Pheonix had spent, at that point, hundreds of hours poring over PARs and AARs (Prior-Action and After-Action Reviews), and this PAR was skin and bones compared to the average report, especially considering the magnitude of the problem. It was missing force delineation and general intel on combined makeup of forces. It also had no specific intel at all on what had happened to the Applegates, and none regarding on-ground conditions.

He considered calling Chani and asking her if she'd actually *read* this PAR, but discarded the idea after coming to the conclusion that it might be considered rude. Chani was too careful not to have read the report.

There seemed to be something going on that Pheonix couldn't grasp, but there was a lot of Ranger-Accord-enemy interplay he didn't quite understand yet. The gap between absorbing book knowledge and the application of said knowledge came to mind here.

Maybe this mission could help him start to understand that.

He sent Chani an affirmative and got back to his work.

Sabot found him several hours later elbow-deep in flowcharts and overlays. Something to pass the time until someone came to pick him up.

"Hey — ah, I see you're ready," the Sergeant-trainer said.

Pheonix was indeed already dressed in his full combat gear with Malol and Bedaestael hovering nearby, his short swords on his chest, and his kinetic pistols in underarm holsters.

"Let's go, then," Sabot said.

In short order, the two boarded a shuttle with a group of heavily armed soldiers. Out of the tiny windows, Pheonix watched the spherical metal bulk of Ranger HQ recede — shrinking rapidly with the vastness of space as its background. Behind it, immeasurably larger, twin red giant suns silhouetted Availeon.

Now seeing the other side of Ranger HQ, it became apparent that another level, or shell, of the multi-layered moon-like frame was in construction. The fact that he could see it from so far away spoke of its breadth.

The shuttle came into view within a few minutes of their destination — a giant starfish-like structure with a pulsating light emanating from its central body.

"This your first jump, boy?" Sabot asked.

"Yes, Sergeant."

"That's a jump-ship, though the name is unfitting. It is a living being, a species, who works with the Rangers to transport us using its own specific method of space travel. You'll learn about them at some point. Jumping will suck. Get ready."

"Yes, Sergeant."

Pheonix considered the creature as they approached it — pinkish-purple, with a rough texture and multitudes of little round metallic protrusions along its many arms. The shuttle aligned with one of these protrusions, and their purpose became clear: they were docks.

There was a long wait, during which Pheonix observed the creature from up close. It was baffling to consider how such a huge species could exist in space, let alone somehow figure out space travel, let *alone* somehow integrate with tech and share that ability.

Something new to add to his ever-growing list of research topics. If he truly was Ascended and truly immortal, not just unkillable, he'd be learning until the universe ended.

The thought wasn't unpleasant.

A light flashed along the upper railing along the inside of the shuttle. Pheonix felt an odd sense of anticipation ripple through the very air, followed by a tightening. Then the entire universe collapsed in on him. It was like being squished down into the size of a molecule. He felt the other soldiers in the shuttle, Sabot, the shuttle itself, even the jump-ship. They pressed in so tightly that Pheonix, not being one to like contact, instantly panicked. He tried to scream, tried to move — but he was locked into inaction by the sheer weight of everything.

Then it was over. He took in a deep breath and fought the irrational urge to lash out. Coming out of the red haze, he saw that Sabot's head was turned towards him, though the helmeted man quickly looked away.

The shuttle parted from the jump-ship and traveled for a scant few minutes before coming into view of another ship. Vaguely shaped like a jellyfish, it had a broad, flat, circular body with one side gently curved upward, like a cabochon. A cabochon bristling with weaponry. A translucent dome extended beyond it. From beneath its flat bottom, long tendrils uncountable hung, all different lengths, flexible and relaxed.

This was a Battle Cruiser. The third largest of Ranger space vessels, Battle Cruisers were the workhorse of the Ranger combat forces and most commonly sent to everything from small engagements to rescue missions.

They disembarked into the Battle Cruiser's docking bay and Pheonix followed Sabot as he wound his way through a crowd of other Rangers (and other not-Rangers) to a large cargo bay, where most of them seemed to be gathering. He waited in silence, watching. The not-Rangers were an assortment of species wearing an assortment of uniforms, none of which he was familiar with.

If nothing else, this excursion would provide him with a wealth of observational information.

The cargo bay had its freight piled up at one end of the cavernous rectangular room, but at the other end was a raised platform, and lining the walls were holes with signs above them. Pheonix extrapolated that these were for the air-cushioned quick-transport system found all over Ranger ships called 'J-tubes.'

Before long, the bay was packed, and someone (clearly an officer) mounted the platform. The mutterings of conversation stopped instantly and those assembled snapped to attention. Pheonix stood awkwardly, not sure if he should follow suit, as no one had laid out the expectations for him at this point. He didn't have a rank and he wasn't a cadet, so he had no data for how to proceed.

Luckily no one noticed, but his lack of data seemed like a bit of an oversight before a live op.

Something sick settled in his stomach.

"At ease," the officer said, her voice sharp and clear despite the large space. "For those of you who are not my own Bloody Commandos, I'd like to welcome you to the NC-Chevalier, the finest Battle Cruiser under Ranger command. Specifically, that is because she is captained by myself, Anders Rivios. As you all know, as of seventy-eight true-hours ago, a dark elven force crossed the neutral cordon into our space and assaulted the mine on Krasynth II, with many civilian casualties. Our objective is to establish a beachhead on Krasynth II. As these are dark elves, be prepared for magic. I suggest you all visit the armory for a null-belt if you don't already have one. Enemy force strength is unknown. Keep your eyes on the body to your left and to your right and let's give 'em hell."

A raucous, deafening cheer broke out.

"Flight deck, boots on the ground in five," Sabot said to Pheonix once the din had died down. "If you need anything, best have it."

Pheonix watched Sabot work his way through the dispersing bodies and slide into the tube labeled 'Flight Deck.'

Unsure of what else to do — his armor came with a null-belt, so he figured he was as prepared as they were going to let him be — Pheonix followed.

TWENTY-THREE
Krasynth II

The flight deck was a huge open space, even bigger than the cargo bay, and dominated by vehicles. Psyker and TKer pairs loaded into their mechs at the far end from where Pheonix emerged from his tube, as they needed the most space to operate. On one side were the larger ship-to-ground combat drop ships, known as 'rhinos,' and on the other, the one-person, vaguely teardrop-shaped drop pods. Activity swirled around him as these vehicles fired off and individual soldiers bustled to and fro. The pace was dizzying, and yet strangely organized, the pattern becoming evident in Pheonix's hyper-analytical mind the more he took in. He was strangely impressed.

By the time he found Sabot, he hadn't seen a single other trainee or anyone who didn't look fully-fledged and hardened. Those among the other soldiers (at least, the few who had bothered to meet his eyes) did so guardedly and with ... v enom?

The sense of unease he'd felt earlier persisted.

He didn't have any more time to consider it as Sabot caught his eye and waved him into the drop ship. The hatch sealed behind them and the Sergeant-trainer tossed a harness at Pheonix. He put it on, after discerning its configuration based on how it was arranged on one of the others in the small, near-lightless space.

"Gravitic line," Sabot explained of the harness. "Uses a combination of antigrav tech and thrusters to slow descent. Sit here." He motioned to the only empty seat along the two long benches following the rhino's walls. Sabot himself walked to the other end of the small space, near a door, and looped one hand around a handhold hanging from the low ceiling and turned to his squad.

"Devil Dogs, meet my trainee, Pheonix. Pheonix, Devil Dogs." Pointing at each one in turn, Sabot introduced them: "Skunk-ass, Remus, Romulus, Artemis, Aries, Thunder, Lightning, Aurora, and Delora."

The 'Devil Dogs' were a variety of species with a variety of armor. Pheonix took it all in as data, his implant droning at him about rank, symbol, and species information; but he was a little too on-edge to pay it much attention. After some brief murmured greetings, the 'Devil Dogs' fell silent, leaving the anti-air assault on the exterior shields of the rhino as the dominant sound. It wasn't a tense silence so much as it was anticipation. Surprisingly, the palpable energy of the soldiers around him awoke something similar in Pheonix. He studied the sensation while the rhino rattled onward, ignoring the occasional large explosion just feet away.

"Krasynth II has a shit atmosphere," Sabot said after a few minutes. "So if your physiology requires oxygen, slap a cup over your breathing orifice," he said, then faced Pheonix. "You got one, boy?"

"No."

Sabot pulled out of his fold-space a clear device shaped like a half-circle with a series of metallic vents on the belly of the curve. Pheonix accepted the proffered device and pressed it over his nose and mouth; it sealed. He knew he didn't need to breathe for at least short periods of time, but if he was going to be fighting, he wanted to be as comfortable as possible. The less distractions, the better.

A red light lit the interior without warning.

With a hiss and the pop of decompression, the doors on either side near the far end of the benches lifted and slid to one side, letting in a fierce wind that drowned out everything else, internal or external. At the same moment, Aurora and Delora turned to opposite doors and carefully maneuvered their way through and out in their bulky exo-armor. Pheonix couldn't see what waited outside; the black sky was only illuminated briefly by artillery.

Sabot stood, moved to the open spot between the two benches.

"Stand, check," he yelled to be heard over the wind.

Pheonix stood as the others did. There was a general patting-down of weapons and armor — bodies adjusting, stretching, popping joints, settling weaponry into position, and tuning mechanisms within the armor.

A shot of adrenaline poured into Pheonix's bloodstream.

Sabot checked his squad. "Stand by."

The red light turned green.

"Go," said Sabot, and dropped casually out the door.

One by one, the others jumped, then it was Pheonix's turn.

He swung his foot onto open air and dropped like a stone, stomach in his throat, whizzing past artillery detonations and rounds at breakneck speed.

About halfway to the ground, the thrusters on his harness engaged, and Pheonix felt a field press in around him at the same time, slowing his descent.

Below him stretched a rocky wasteland in line with the little he knew about Krasynth II: a barren asteroid (albeit nearly planet-sized), little more than a mineral dump hurtling aimlessly through space. Unfortunately, one of the minerals in high concentration in said rock was deutronium, the hardest known substance in the universe. Though its less-than-hospitable landscape made it a place the Rangers would much rather have left alone, the deutronium was too necessary a resource.

The system's star was unbalanced, which cast everything in a red/purple hue, and while the fireworks of weaponry and magic went on below him, the combatants themselves were mere shadows until he got closer to the ground. Dozens of the one-person crafts he recognized as drop ships for forward infantry formed a jagged line, which the Rangers were utilizing as cover.

Outside the perimeter (and unfazed by the attention focused on them) were red, single-pilot mech suits shaped somewhat like gorillas — Maulers. The upper half of the mech suits arched forward into long arms whose 'hands' touched the ground, providing a quadruped shape. Inside the arms, back, and shoulders of these shock-troop suits were some dozens of ranged weapons, from mini-rocket launchers to chain guns.

The enemy had set up a perimeter around a mine entrance and were using the buildings as cover, though it was apparent that they'd set up their own structures as well. One such was a flower-shaped, metallic platform with 'petals' that were sunken troughs, each big enough to hold the average humanoid. In fact, that's what they were built for; as Pheonix watched, a dark elf bullied a struggling, emaciated figure wearing a thick collar around their neck into the last empty trough and sealed them in. A red wizard stood at the epicenter of the device on a dais.

Two things happened at the exact same moment: Pheonix hit the ground, and the people in the troughs were killed. Blades underneath the platform slashed across their throats, and the blood from the dying captives flowed down catchments to pool at the feet of the red wizard. He gesticulated with his stave, drawing the blood into himself. Judging by the copper-red aura multiplied many times in the distance, this foul machine and its evil operator were not the only ones of their kind present.

"*CODE ORANGE!*" he heard Sabot bellow.

The knowledge inserted itself into Pheonix's mind. *Code Orange: Ranger Battle-speak for 'Careful, measured shots; slaves on the field.'*

Pheonix lost himself behind a sickening rage.

The violet-eyed woman's face as it disintegrated ... the gnome choked half to death ... those innocents out on that battlefield, tortured and murdered to be used beyond death by a sick fuck for his own gain...

THIS AGAIN.

The feeling burned into his mind so deeply he could almost see it.

It was his last coherent thought.

He dimly heard Sabot yelling something behind him as he vaulted unheeding over the perimeter created by the drop pods, but his brain was beyond the ability to comprehend language. He tore past the Maulers and was well into the wide stretch of rocky nothingness between the Rangers' beachhead and the enemy force before he took his first hit.

A shield of unknown origin flickered to life around him and deflected many of the subsequent attacks — but a lone figure was too tempting a target, and in short order he was pummeled to his knees.

He struggled to stand, the shield holding. Rounds that didn't hit him seemed to take something from him as they were deflected. Magic swirled in such profusion that it became a thick fog, spells layering upon spells, but his gaze was locked unwavering on the red wizard. The red wizard smirked and lifted his stave. Bloody magic power gathered into him and Pheonix found himself on his knees again, winded.

He ground his teeth in helpless fury and drew one of his kinetic pistols. The red wizard prepared for another attack, but Pheonix was just too damned far away to even leap at the bastard. He knew, somehow, that his shield was dangerously weakened, and there was just *too much* — too much distance, too much firepower pressing on him. He probably wouldn't make it back. But he'd be damned to all the hells in all the religions if he let that vile bastard get away.

He aimed the pistol in pure desperation as the red wizard cast his second spell. That was the tipping point; his shield could hold no longer. The barrage drove Pheonix into the ground, several inches beneath the surface.

Pheonix opened his eyes.

He felt a different shield arching over him. He could lift his head, but aside from that and his organic arm, nothing else seemed capable of motion. His body was in pieces, his mechanical arm reduced to shards of metal. Blood pooled against his many gaping wounds, not escaping but not where it should be, and the unnatural configuration made him light-headed.

Pheonix craned his neck up with sheer will. The wizard had crumpled to the ground, grasping at the brand new hole in his body, a present from Pheonix. A surge of vicious elation cut through the haze that was rapidly creeping over him. Someone skidded to a stop behind him and he felt a lurch as arms slid under him to yank him up.

One of the portals used by the dark elves was situated near the sacrificial platform. Pheonix shot it too, destroying the link.

He would have kept it up had he not then been pulled into the relative safety of the Ranger perimeter.

It was that moment that the floodgates of pain and the sheer amount of damage done to his body hit him, and he passed out.

TWENTY-FOUR
It's All Gone To Shit

Chani took a deep breath to settle her jangled nerves outside the conference room.

She'd gotten a brief from Sabot before being called to this emergency meeting, but some details were still unclear. All she knew was that Pheonix had had a breakdown and run out in the middle of the fucking firefight. He'd been flattened and was, last she'd heard, still unconscious in the ICU.

Sabot had been very succinct in his opinion on the intel and put no blame on Pheonix, though. Apparently the situation on-ground was *very* different from what they'd been led to expect.

She stepped forward and the oculus opened.

Most of the major players had already arrived. At the far end of the room, in the position of officiator, stood Zeta. For him to be here meant that a house cleaning would probably be the result of this meeting.

Good, thought Chani savagely.

Around the table were some faces she recognized and some she didn't. Included were all of Pheonix's trainers, presumably in case they were needed to speak on his behalf. Her stomach flipped in knots at the thought of having to defend the boy from serious punishment. If it came down to it, she'd do it, but it would suck. She silently greeted each with a nod in turn: Tyyrulriathula, Crosinthusilas, Faran, Minrathous,

Zasfioretaeula. At least they had some big names here — herself included. Chani was hardly modest about her position in, and the influence she had on, the Rangers.

The only notable absence was Steele, which was highly fucking suspicious.

Also known to her around the table were the captain of the Chevalier, Anders Rivios, and the Commanding-General.

Some others she didn't recognize very readily, but her memory implant matched faces to jobs: the stationboard Healer-master along with people from the Analysis Department, Conscience Crew, Strategic Commission, and Strategic Command.

She sat and Zeta looked over the assembled.

"It appears we are all here. I wish to waste no time on niceties. We have completely lost the beachhead at Krasynth II. The red wizards have electrified the atmosphere with blood magic. Communication with the surface is scrambled and teleportation impossible. In addition, the break in our assault led to fighters and cruisers taking up residence in orbit."

Chani internally winced. It was much worse than she'd expected.

Zeta looked at the officer from Strategic Command expectantly, who said, "Intel is light due to the aforementioned communication issues. We don't know why the front shifted after the trainee went down."

'Trainee,' Chani mentally scoffed. *Not even being subtle.*

Zeta then addressed the Commanding-General. "What is the current sit-rep?"

The Akeela deferred to Sabot, who stood before speaking.

"The LZ was correctly taken and held by drop pods. When Master Pheonix broke rank, the real estate became hot and the position overrun. My team, along with sixteen other teams, remain on-surface. However, most of the survivors are trapped in the FOB."

Zeta looked at the Analysis Department officer. "Details are still incoming as the situation develops."

Unexpectedly, Anders Rivios slammed her fist into the table. "Don't bullshit up a 'developing situation'; we all know what happened down there. As soon as that trainee was injured, the red wizards went fucking insane. The entire front is lost and now we've had to withdraw to Krasynth III! There are hundreds of vessels in orbit now! Let's not pussy-foot around it, people … we're *fucked*."

Zeta frowned mildly at her and turned to Chani. "Speaking of, what is the condition of our Lord?"

"Well, let's cover the positives. He did manage to kill a blood magic user —"

"One," scoffed Anders, "out of how many on the field?"

Chani narrowed her eyes at the Captain. If the woman saw the warning, she didn't give any sign.

"And," Chani continued, "he also destroyed a portal. As for his condition …" she trailed off and looked at the Healer-master.

"He's alive, though only *just*," said the Healer-master. "I can't tell you through what provenance; my experience with Ascended is limited. We managed to stabilize him and he … ah … put himself back together. He remains in a deep sleep, though there is still significant brain activity. It appears the only permanent damage will be to his cybernetic arm, which was completely destroyed."

Zeta glanced at the officer from Strategic Commission, who said, "We don't have anything to add at this time." Though he did glance at Anders with a furrowed brow.

Zeta pinched the bridge of his nose between thumb and forefinger. "Very well. You four, dismissed. Keep me apprised."

The Healer-master and the officers from the Analysis Department, Strategic Commission and Command filed out.

Zeta turned his back on the room as the door closed. A crystal projection system lit the wall he was facing with several frames of moving images.

"Our Lord's armor cam, Sergeant Sabot's armor cam, and the orbital cam," he said and pointed to each.

Pheonix's armor cam was just that — the events recorded from his perspective by the camera in his uniform. Sabot's armor cam was the same, from his own perspective. The orbital cam gave a bird's eye view of the battlefield — though it had been narrowed down and enhanced to focus only on the events in question.

All three frames played simultaneously, showing from three angles Pheonix vaulting over the drop pods as Sabot yelled for him to come back.

They watched as Pheonix weathered the kind of damage that would drop a tank, and somehow struggled on. Sabot shouted orders, directing his team and everyone around him to concentrate on covering fire and TK support for the kid, and calling for medevac. Pheonix took his shot and crumpled under the weight of the next attack, and briefly the other soldiers on the line froze. After the dust cleared and it became apparent that he was still alive, Sabot (with no regard for his own safety) jumped over a nearby drop pod and sprinted to Pheonix's location. While dragging him back, the videos showed in clear synchronization the young man firing his pistol, destroying the portal, being removed to safety, and passing out.

Zeta turned around slowly. The vids played on an endless loop behind him.

Chani stood and pointed at the dais where the orbital cam clearly showed the slaves' deaths. It was exactly after the slaughter of innocents that Pheonix went berserk.

"*This* — this right here! *Slaves!* Why wasn't this in the intel?" She rounded on Rivios, her eyes ablaze.

Rivios looked taken aback for a mere moment, then countered Chani's fury with her own. Her chest puffed out. "Intel was sufficient for the op — "

"*Not with the Ascended of Justice on the field*," Chani roared. "Everyone was given his file! Everyone was apprised of his history with slavers! So I ask again, why were we *not informed*?"

Rivios was stunned into silence. Her eyes flicked from face to face and, finding none friendly, her cheeks suffused with blood and she stood, slamming her hands on the table with enough force to make it shake. "You're trying to blame this on *me*?"

The Commanding-General half raised from his seat. "Captain …" he warned.

"No, you put this idiot trainee in the most important mission of my career, and then try to send me down in flames when it all goes tits-up? I don't think so! Fleet intel was fine! What does it matter if there are fucking slaves or not? If the kid belonged on the damned battlefield, he would have been able to deal with it!"

"AT EASE!" the Commanding-General bellowed.

Startled, Anders snapped board-straight and shoved her hands behind her back. It was a reflex bred into every soldier that whenever 'at ease' or 'attention' was shouted with a certain tone of voice, the body would obey before the mind had time to object.

"Your rank does not afford you the right to speak in such a manner to Commander Abyss," the Commanding-General growled at Rivios, his hackles partially raised.

"Now," Chani said, her voice soft but deadly, "what in the Creator's giant glowing testicles made you think that this op was all about *you*? Preliminary estimation was that a single Battle-Cruiser could have handled the situation on

Krasynth II by itself, which is why we sent you alone. Worst case scenario, you'd have been able to at least hold out until other vessels arrived, likely with few losses. But your *primary responsibility* was confirming what we did already know, and sending back further intel so we could be sure that we had the right forces allocated for the task. You had more than enough resources and time to fully scope the situation. And yet what intel *you ordered* your crew to send back was less than a quarter of what it should have been; you deliberately didn't tell us the full enemy force composition, about the portals and supplies, and the fact that they'd *landed a ship*. All of that pointed to a much bigger problem than it initially appeared to be. You wanted to make it seem like a much easier operation than it actually was. Why would you put yourself and your crew in such danger? There could only be one answer. You knew we were considering sending Pheonix to Krasynth II, and if we'd been aware of the true size and composition of the enemy forces, we'd have pulled him. *You wanted him on-ground.*"

Chani's gaze bored into Anders'.

The other woman seemed unable to break the contact. Chani's unanswered question of *why did you go to such lengths to get him there?* hung in the air palpably.

"Conversations with Colonel Yung." Chani continued with the force of a strike: the name made Anders flinch. "Logs from your own ship. Testimony from your crew. You aren't clever enough to hide from your shipboard AI, Rivios; it was listening to and recording it all."

Rivios' face went from brick red to snow white as all blood drained from it. Chani pinned her with a look that said, *Did you think we'd come at you without proof? This is your chance to defend yourself. Give me a name, tell me you were coerced or threatened, please.*

"I can't believe this shit!" Rivios shouted, though she looked like she was about to faint. Chani mentally sighed.

"This is a set-up! You're all his chain of command; you should be taking responsibility for this, not foisting it on me!"

"Do you really think the *Ascended of Justice* has a chain of command here in our little family?" Chani asked, too calmly.

"*More like God of BULLSHIT! Just because John Abyssterilon's granddaughter has a pet project brat doesn't make him special!*" Rivios raged.

A deathly quiet fell.

"Too far," the Commanding-General said.

"I'm relieving you of command effective immediately," Zeta said. "Regardless of the adaptive capabilities of the Rangers, your conduct is inexcusable. Return to your quarters to await sentencing."

Rivios, with an incoherent noise of fury, pushed back from the table with such force that her chair tumbled over backwards and clattered to the floor. She stomped out of the meeting room.

Chani let out a long breath and sat, taking a moment to allow her adrenaline to dissipate. She was trembling with fury. What a fucking mess. Not only had Rivios put every single life on that op in danger, but the Rangers had known something was off beforehand. Chani *had* read the reports, and questioned them (and she hadn't been the only one to do so), but the dissenting voices had been ignored. And with so little time before deployment, Chani hadn't had the opportunity to really interfere. So she'd had to let it play out, and hope that this time they'd get enough evidence to justify Anders Rivios' removal from her position. It wasn't easy to cut out a link in the chain of command. Power protected its own, and the Rangers were not exempt from that.

This hadn't been her first offense, though it was her most egregious. And thanks to Steele, Pheonix had gotten literally caught in the crossfire. Chani gritted her teeth against a familiar sick surge of helplessness and anger.

This is why she'd fought Steele on sending Pheonix to a live op so early. If it'd been up to her, he wouldn't been involved in any Ranger operations at all, but for some incomprehensible fucking reason the Elders had agreed to it.

Her innate paranoia was singing. Just how many needed to be held accountable aside from Anders? Steele, for pushing it? Zeta and the Elders, for greenlighting it? The Obelisk? Had it interfered, hoping the battle would kill or incapacitate Pheonix? Chani herself, for not fighting it harder? Some bureaucratic middleman like the Conscience Crew?

All of them were culpable.

"If I may speak freely …" Sabot said into the charged silence.

"Go ahead," Chani sighed.

"She has a point."

"Explain," the Commanding-General said.

"Sir. While I'm not downplaying her utter failure to maintain proper decorum or shirking her duty, were this a normal situation, a lack of slave intel *could* have been adapted to on the ground."

The Commanding-General, without a word, left. The expression curling his long snout boded ill for Steele, whom he was undoubtedly going to see.

"Sabot, get prepped," Chani said. "You're going back to Krasynth II. Get on a drop ship ASAP and don't forget that special package I told you about earlier. You'll need it. Dismissed."

Sabot, while by no means pacified, saluted, turned on his heel, and left.

"It seems to me," Zeta said, "that the inclusion of our Lord was premature." He arched a brow. "So, rectify it."

Why are you acting like you aren't involved? Chani massaged her temples, willing the chaos in her head to order.

"Any other business?" asked Zeta.

The representative from the Conscience Crew stood. "I shall report to the Chosen," he said, and left.

Chani resisted the urge to make a face. *Report to the Availeon Chosen, you mean. For what reason? There's a perfectly capable Chosen officiating, you lackey,* she thought scathingly.

"Are there any recommendations for punishment of our Lord?" Zeta asked.

"For what? Doing his job?" Chani replied, exhausted. "I need a drink."

"Meeting adjourned," Zeta said.

The others filed out one by one, but by some inner sense Chani hung back until it was just her and the Elder in the room.

"How long do you think the FOB can hold position?" Zeta asked Chani.

"A while, if not indefinitely, depending on supplies." Chani sighed. "It's not like we didn't expect something like this to happen."

"You've got a week."

Chani groaned internally. *Prickly bastard.*

"Roger," Chani said instead.

"One more thing," Zeta said before Chani could leave. "We just received word that the Accord Secretary-General is dead."

Chani froze, calculations spinning in her head. "Cause?" she asked carefully.

"Poison. Godslayer."

"I see. Thank you for informing me."

Zeta's gaze burned a hole in the back of her head as she left the meeting room. As soon as the oculus closed behind her, she took off at a dead run.

A lot of people would want her attention, very shortly.

Commander Steele was in a state.

As the Vanguard Representative to the Accord — basically, both a Ranger and an Accord officer — they had access to the typical Ranger officer cybernetic info-feeds regarding crime, events, schedules, and submitted requests for investigation, mediation, and the like. But, they also had access to the Accord info-feeds, which mostly related to their job as Vanguard Commander, since the Vanguard were supposed to be the first to be deployed when an incident happened — situations on rim-worlds or colonies, warnings about enemy movement, escort requests for important resources, etc. Both of these also had separate classified channels.

Approximately an hour prior, both of the Accord feeds had gone dead.

Steele had immediately attempted to directly contact people they knew within the Accord, but even communication lines to the Accord were down. It was like the Accord itself had shut down.

And yet, the news wasn't covering it, and nothing came through the Ranger feeds — which meant it was highly serious and being internally contained. Steele had no idea why no one else seemed to be freaking out. Steele sure as fuck was.

No Accord feeds meant no information on what was happening.. For someone like Steele, who needed to have multiplicative sources of data to maneuver in their very difficult position, it was like being suddenly rendered blind. Worse, they had no idea *why*, so they couldn't even plan for a response or reaction. Until everything came back up, Steele could only act as a Ranger officer and nothing more.

They wondered why they had been so insistent on including Pheonix in the Krasynth II operation. It had just seemed right at the time; but in hindsight, they should've listened to Chani. The intel had been insufficient, and Steele should have known that after reading it.

Of all the thoughts ricocheting around in their mind, the most terrifying one was: *I should have noticed it; why didn't I notice it?*

In a very real way, losing Krasynth II *was* Steele's fault. The Commanding-General's curt and cold handling of the subject had done nothing whatsoever to settle the anxiety roiling in Steele's stomach.

But they'd promised to have a drink with Chani, and since the Commander seemed to know more than she ought to about damn near everything, if Steele suddenly backed out now, it'd look suspicious. Putting on their strongest poker face, they pushed open the door to the bar and stepped in. Chani was sitting at the bar, already tonsil-deep into her third shot, judging by the glasses lined up before her. Probably hard dwarven liquor.

She signaled the bartender for a fourth as Steele slid onto the stool next to her. She knocked it back and rasped a whorl of steam.

"You get your stomach upgraded along with your arms? That shit'll burn a hole in you," Steele chuckled, struggling to hide the edge that had been in their voice since they got the news.

She shot them a venomous look out of the corner of her eye but didn't order another. "Just needed enough to take the edge off," she grunted.

"I hear you."

"You getting anything?"

"I'd love to, but I fear I'm gonna need my full wits until this shitstorm has blown over." Chani probably had no idea of the weight of that statement.

Chani barked a laugh. "Ol' Ironfur get to you yet?"

Steele pulled a face. "'We'll discuss it later'," they said in a fair imitation of the Commanding-General's husky growl. They hoped they had enough control over their voice that it came across playful. "I already have enough enemies. I guess it was inevitable I'd fuck up this badly: I'm the one that insisted we send Pheonix to Krasynth II. I just hope it doesn't mean the end of my career."

"Eh, you'll be fine," Chani said, reaching up to roughly pat their shoulder. "Your record was sterling up until now. Everybody fucks up, like you said. And, all's well that ends well?"

"I guess you're right."

They looked up and met her colorless, augmented eyes with aperture pupils, reflecting the deep mahogany hues of the bartop and the navy blue of their uniform. They felt the shift happen a split second before her expression changed. She hovered just a little too close, her hand remained on their shoulder. Her breath, still spicy from the liquor, swept across their mouth and chin.

They felt a grin tugging at their lips, and she responded, too quickly to be coincidence. A little furrowing of her brow; suspicion, a flash of irritation tempered by humor.

"You little shit," she murmured. "You're reading me."

"So?"

Some part of her instantly shut down, inaccessible to them. That was startling, but they kept it off of their face. She wanted to play games, hm?

"So, you know," she said, trailing off. The attraction plain in her voice and body posture well and truly distracted them, for the moment.

"Oh, yes. I know."

As tuned-in as they were just then, her every shift played out like a miasma of colors across their mind's eye. Their 'tuning in' wasn't mind reading, per se, nor was it anything they could control or even put a name to. The mind was not a focused, single-objective thing: thoughts, emotions, memories, sensations, and a million other processes happened all at once, intertwined and unfinished. Without context, mind reading was little more than palm reading — taking a surface attribute and assigning it meaning.

Very few people even knew they could do it. One more, now. They'd have to be careful. They'd never planned on letting her get this close.

The layers of Chani's mind seethed with many things — embarrassment that her attraction to them had been outed, the political and scientific implications of their ability, a painful awareness of their physical proximity, amusement, annoyance, and questions … so many questions.

Then she smiled.

The expression was so utterly lascivious that Steele lost their train of thought.

"I won't tell if you don't," she said.

"Deal," they agreed, and by unspoken agreement the two of them retreated into their own personal physical and mental bubbles once more (not without some regret in both parties). Being political entities made them cautious of overt displays. The Rangers were more casual about that sort of thing than most societies, but in their respective positions, it was probably better to avoid going public unless it became serious. And at the moment, Chani only had one thing on her mind.

"I'd better go visit the Med-Bay," she said, standing. "Hopefully the kid will wake up soon and we can get this show on the road. Ah, Steele … "

"Jae."

"Jae …?" The unspoken question blazed across her mind in streaks of lust and fire.

"Yes. After this whole Krasynth debacle we'll need the stress relief, so hell yes."

She flashed them a crooked grin. "I look forward to it."

TWENTY-FIVE
Preparation

This is a nightmare.
It's so dark.
Creator, I can't see.
Why can't I see?
Something is there, I can feel it just beyond my sight.
No. No, no, no.
This silence — why? Can you hear me?
He is there, damn him back to the Abyss. Damn him, damn him.
"COME OUT! BAST! YOU COWARD!"
Oh — light !
— wait — that's not ... no.
NO. NOT THAT.
— Creator! — IT BURNS — CAN YOU HEAR ME? — CREATOR! SAVE ME!!

Pheonix opened his eyes, the ephemeral screams ringing in his ears fading with the reintegration of external senses.

Before any other mental processes began, he scanned his environment, having no immediate memory of where he was or what had happened, save for a vague lingering sense of danger.

He was in a large cream-and-blue-colored room, all soft curves, the walls covered with unidentifiable machines and simplistic devices, many containing or made out of various crystals. Clad only in loose shorts, he was lying on a bed of crystal that was somehow molded to his body, making it surprisingly comfortable.

With no immediate threats seen, he dismissed the alarmed feeling and turned his attention to his sore body.

Oh, my arm is gone.

Anger surged suddenly as memory returned.

Slaves. Sacrifice. More balance bullshit.

The oculus opened and a nurse entered — an elven woman wearing the pale yellow of a shipboard Healer.

"Oh, you're awake," she said, smiling, then turned to access a console. "You can come in now, Commander."

The nurse checked him over as Chani entered, then left Pheonix and Chani alone.

"So," Chani said, "the Medical Ward ICU is a no-observation zone; I will be speaking plainly. Under normal circumstances, recruits are sent blind on a real, low-threat mission after several months or years of training. It depends on the individual's level of readiness. It's meant to show them the unpredictability of real combat and instill an ability to think on their feet." She took a breath. "However, you're not a recruit. You're not a Ranger. You're Ascended."

"So why the fuck was I expected to adhere to half-assed protocol that doesn't even apply to me, on a mission that didn't even have proper intel?"

Chani winced slightly. "I don't know. I'm trying to figure it out, I swear to you. I fought it — but somewhere in the chain, it got overridden and pushed through before I could stop it. All I could do at that point was try to keep you safe, which is why I sent you with Sabot and his crew. But they managed to fuck us anyway."

Pheonix stared at Chani hard for a moment. She met his gaze, unwavering as always.

"This is why you came to me," he said, and it wasn't a question, "and agreed to my rebellion. It isn't just Terelath or the elves or the Chosen. The whole fucking universe is rotten. Entirely."

Chani dropped her eyes and nodded. Pheonix worked his jaw, then sighed and forced the tension to run out of his body.

"I understand," he said finally. "It was only because of Sergeant Sabot that I survived at all, so I will treat this as data and we can move on. But I'm not blaming you."

"The student is rapidly surpassing the teacher," she chuckled, though her exhaustion was evident. "However, this teacher still has a couple of tricks up her sleeve. You did make one mistake: you can't rage out every time you see something that pisses you off. There's a lot of bullshit in this universe, Pheonix. You can't control bullshit, but you have to learn to control what you do in response to it."

The console next to her beeped and a nurse's voice came through.

"Master Tinkerer Arkiolett asked to be informed when Master Pheonix awakened and he is here now. Can I let him in?"

Chani glanced at Pheonix; he shrugged as best he could with one shoulder.

"Sure," said Chani.

A gnome wearing a three-foot-tall exo-suit (who was, himself, hardly a foot and a half tall) strode through the oculus. A large case floated behind him. When the gnome saw Pheonix, his droopy face broke into a huge grin.

"I'm glad to see you made a full recovery," said Pheonix.

Gnome laughter sounded a little like wind chimes — a high-pitched tinkling, not unpleasant. "Shouldn't I be saying that to you? I'm sorry we never made a proper introduction. Arkiolett, tinkerer. I know it's late, but thank you for saving me from those orcs."

"Anyone able to do so would have," Pheonix said mildly.

"Yeah, you'd think," Arkiolett said so casually that it was jarring. "Anyway, I'm here to bring you something." He opened the case to reveal a sleek black cybernetic arm. "My latest invention. The RX365 full combat model, made especially for you with deutronium filaments and plating."

"Arkiolett contacted me after the incident to ask who had saved him," Chani interjected. "I gave him your measurements after he expressed interest in replacing your arm. He's a damn fine tinkerer, one of the best on the market for augments. He's the one who made most of *my* augs, so I trust his work."

"Oh hush," Arkiolett said and looked embarrassed. "Undeserved compliments aside, she's right about the other stuff. I actually started the arm as a project to distract me while I was recovering. When I heard about what happened on Krasynth II, I rushed over. I'm here on HQ most of the time anyway since this is where my primary shop is located. I'd only happened to be in Terelath that day on vacation. *Of course* I'd almost get killed trying to take a break, right? Anyhoo, you interested?"

Pheonix glanced at Chani.

"You won't regret it. Arkiolett's a hell of a talent, and you know I don't say that lightly."

"Well, then, I gratefully accept. Thank you," Pheonix said.

Arkiolett laughed. "Don't thank me yet. Because it's so much more advanced, we need to implant more plating along your side and shoulder — reinforce your natural frame. The power of this arm moving would crumple you if we didn't. And since you were here recovering already, I figured we'd just do it now. The surgery will be a little more complex than the one you underwent for your previous arm, but if I understand you at all, you'll probably find it fascinating."

A surgery team filed in.

Arkiolett had been correct; Pheonix did find it interesting. As last time, a targeted stasis field and Healer had to work in conjunction with the surgery team to overcome his naturally accelerated rate of healing. He was given a local anesthetic and they cut him open. Fighting his body's attempts to quickly heal at every step, they implanted the plating and replaced his shoulder. The Healer closed him up and the next several hours were spent with specialized xeno-mechanics syncing the nerves to his system and fine-tuning.

Arkiolett sat back, wiped his brow, and watched Pheonix twirl a pencil between the fingers of his new hand.

"How does it feel?" he asked proudly.

"Incredible," Pheonix said. "Should I thank you now?"

"Of course! And you're welcome! I'd better head out, but you should definitely come down to my shop when you get the chance."

Pheonix smiled, and they bid their goodbyes. Chani, who'd left during the surgery, reappeared and tossed a couple of nutrient pills at him. He downed them with some water.

"Arm looks good," Chani commented. "How are you?"

Pheonix thought for a moment, then decided perhaps it would be better not to tell Chani about his dream. "Fine."

"Good. Then get dressed. We start now."

Chani caught herself nodding off as the oculus opened.

"He still at it?" Steele asked.

"Yup."

"How long is it now?"

Chani rubbed her eyes to clear them. "Time in simu," she said to the computer. "Ah, seventy hours. I've been here for … eighteen? Crosinthusilas and Tyyrulriathula were here for about twenty-four each."

"Jesus-Man's balls," Steele muttered. "Get outta here. I'm relieving you."

Chani didn't protest. She offered her seat and slumped out of the simulation monitoring room.

Steele took her place. "Open camera one," they said to the computer. It brought up an in-simulator view of Pheonix. The young man was wearing his standard Ranger gear and wielding Malol and Bedaestael against enemies that only he could see.

Look at him. He's not even tired, Steele thought, awed. *We've flagged pulling twenty-four-hour-shifts, just watching him. Is this the strength of an Ascended?*

They had him on all the normal modifiers; average hominin strength, average hominin speed. No surprises. The thought was to purely test his endurance. At this rate, he'd short out the simulator before even breaking a sweat.

"Put the kid in a choke point and he could take on an army," came a voice from behind him.

Chani meandered back up to the console, looking more put together than when she left and sipping a mug of coffee, judging by the smell.

"That was fast," Steele commented. "Take a stim?"

She glanced at him sharply over the ridge of the cup, brows raised. "Mm-hmm."

"So, Crosinthusilas and Tyyrulriathula were here before you."

"Mm-hmm."

"And by that you mean Crosinthusilas and Tyyrulriathula were here *with* you."

"Why Jae, I'm insulted. Whatever makes you think I've been here for three days?"

A derisive snort was Steele's only response.

"Besides," she continued, "I took a turn in the refresher, changed my clothes, brushed my hair, ate a snack, made coffee, *and* took a stim. Seems you lost track of time, Commander."

"It's easy to do here," they said, sighing.

"I hear that."

"That shit's not good for you, you know."

"Pretty sure my body can handle a few days of being here and not sleeping."

"What about your mind? Can't have our Special Projects division going leaderless while you get over a mental breakdown."

"I'm per-fect-ly fine," she said in a stilted voice, affecting an exaggerated twitch. Then, in her usual tone: "I'll just take it easy after this for a couple days. Chill."

Steele shrugged and turned back to the console, indicating that they were dropping the subject.

"He's hypnotic," they said.

"Yeah. Seems like either he or the program is caught in a loop, though, he does those same motions so often I wonder if he's just fighting in his sleep."

"He likely is," said another voice. Mulahajad approached the console next to Steele, clicking his tongue in admonishment. "Three days and we're only this far? No, no, this won't do. The boy is too polite. Commanders, you should really break him of that."

"Firstly: hello, Mulahajad," said Chani. "Secondly: what?"

The High Mahji declined to answer, his long fingers already crawling across the console. Too late did it register what he was doing.

"No, don't — " Steele hastened to say, but the VI's voice interrupted them:

"New parameters: 1,500% plus standard."

Red lights flashed across the display and the camera showed brief surprise register on Pheonix's face as he stumbled, movements becoming frantic. Chani and Steele watched in tense anticipation, ready to shut it down in a heartbeat if it overwhelmed him. He kept up. Each successive minute he slowed and became more clumsy, but he visibly pushed himself to continue. After thirty minutes, his eyes rolled up and he fell, with no attempt to catch himself, onto his face.

"Stop simulation!" Chani and Steele yelled at the same time.

The lights came up and Chani waited impatiently for the heavy oculus to open.

"See? Much better," Mulahajad said, sounding pleased.

Pheonix was already waking up as Chani supported him into a sitting position.

"That was fun," he said. It was hard to tell if he was being serious or sarcastic (and his emotions were still too subtle to read with any consistency). Knowing Pheonix, it was a little of both.

"What happened?" he asked as Chani helped him out of the simulation chamber.

"Mulahajad turned up the difficulty," Steel said flatly.

Pheonix glanced behind them and Mulahajad waved.

"Ah," Pheonix said.

"Look," Chani said after Pheonix had had some water and a nutrient pill, "if it's too easy you need to say something. Talk to us. Got it?"

Pheonix nodded.

"Good. Go get some rest. We'll come get you in a little while," Chani said.

She waited until Pheonix was gone, and turned to Steele. "Did you catch any of what he did in there?"

"Not a damn thing."

"Three days and we've still got no data we can interpret," she sighed. "Come on."

"How did you even get the override codes, Mulahajad?" Steele asked as the three of them crossed the simulation floor, heading to a large booth on the other side.

"Lazarus' memories, my dear Commander. I may have given them up, but I have not forgotten."

"Naughty. You aren't supposed to peek," admonished Chani. Mulahajad grinned and shrugged.

Chani knocked gently on the booth door and waited. It swung open and the three entered the sanctuary of the simulation floor operator.

Her chitinous, shiny black bulk, studded liberally with tiny, sharp hairs, filled the space. Eight spindly legs kept her in graceful equilibrium, despite the massiveness of her abdomen. A much smaller, brown spider waved one leg in greeting from her back.

The hourglass-shaped red mark on the underside of the large spider's abdomen, while advertising her venom's toxicity, was hardly the most obviously frightening thing about her. Cybernetics ran down her legs and metal armor was grafted to her abdomen and cephalothorax in places. Each of her legs were wrapped in blades, and her elongated fangs were sheathed in metal, as well.

There was really only enough space for one person to stand beside the door and address her, so the three humanoid bodies had to press together quite closely. She towered over them, almost twenty feet tall, and even wider if she spread out. Luckily, a slightly curled posture was her preferred position.

"Greetings, Great Mother Ouna," Chani said. "You know my friends. We come with a question about the session that just finished, if you have a moment?"

A series of clicks, grinds and chitters was the Great Mother's response.

"Of course. I always have time for questions," her translation device's chosen voice, an elderly female, followed.

"We are but lowly mortals and can't make heads or tails of what happened. Could you enlighten us?"

Her mouthparts moved in a cyclical motion — it translated as a laugh.

"You are nearly as old as I, you snotty mammal," said the Great Mother, whose name, insofar as spiders had names, was unpronounceable by most hominin oral cavities — something akin to 'tka-ghh-kka-k-ghgh-ouna-tkk.' Thus, she was called Ouna, with Great Mother being an honorific.

"Despite your sass," Ouna continued, "I will oblige. The young one completed the simulation twice at the accelerated speed set for him before it overwhelmed him. He was working on the Battle of Arcturus, which you may remember Lazarus himself engaged in and could complete at ten times the speed this one was given. As for what caused him to fall, it was merely his inexperience. Give him time, and he could surpass Lazarus."

Chani thanked her (spiders were not prone to small talk), and they made their way back to the upper control room.

"You're going with him, so get in there," Chani said to Steele.

"Roger," Steele said, sounding miserable. "My gear's already packed."

Chani paced, working her hands in an uncharacteristically restless manner.

"We've got four more days. We're way behind schedule, so we'll have to accelerate his training from this point on if we have any hope of him being prepared."

"Shit, there's an op in the works already?"

"Of course. Whatever big talk the balance-crats may throw around, the bottom line is: we need that rock and we're taking it back."

Despite the intensity of his recent exertions, Pheonix felt fine by the time he reached his barracks room. Once there, he found that his most recent order of books from the Archive was waiting for him. In looking through them, trying to decide which one to read first, he found one he didn't recognize

— a plain, brown journal. Written on the back cover, very small, was one word: 'Lazarus.'

"I took the liberty to order that one for you, Master Pheonix," said Astra from the walls. "Based on your search parameters, it seemed something you may enjoy."

"How so?"

"You were doing targeted research on the Great War, but it seemed your scope was lacking slightly."

"I see. Well, then, I thank you."

"You are very welcome. Good reading, Master Pheonix."

"Good-bye, Astra."

Pheonix opened the journal. On the first page was a beautiful female elf sketched with such realistic grace that it stirred even Pheonix. At the bottom was a simple scrawl in the same handwriting as the name on the back: 'Life.'

The next few pages contained lists of kills, the locations of treasures and key-codes to accessing them (which reminded him of something kept by a pirate) — then, a narrative:

> *These things normally have a beginning, so I'll start with mine.*
>
> *My first memory is of waking, enrobed in love and surrounded by others of my kind. Before us was the Creator. I saw the Creator's face, but there are no words in any language I know to describe it. I wish I could.*
>
> *I am Lazarus of the second Creation, tied to Justice.*
>
> *I am staying with the Rangers, a hominin-based military organization with whom I feel great kinship. The elves, while a very advanced people, have their Nature and Life — they are not my people. These Rangers are my people.*

Pheonix found himself staring at the words without reading them, awash in an off-putting sense of deja vu.

A knock interrupted his thought process. He let Chani in.

"You're going back to Krasynth II in four days," she said without preamble. "But you need some better shit. C'mon, let's go to the Armory."

Pheonix blinked and put the journal down. "Okay."

Chani led him at breakneck speed through the hallways of the barracks and hustled him into one of the many J-tubes scattered around Ranger HQ, to a tram, then down several more hallways that anyone without a photographic memory and perfect retention would be utterly lost in. Their final stop was a nondescript door at the end of a nondescript inlet, at what was little more than a dead end of the tram-track. There was a machine next to the door. It quite reminded him of the path to Astra's core in that way, and — he was beginning to suspect — likely for much the same reasons.

Pheonix, having taken in everything there was to see here, which wasn't much, turned to watch Chani. The Commander, with one bare foot in the machine and both hands pressed on the panel, was reciting a poem. Even he had to appreciate the ridiculousness.

"Commander, please say your password," prompted a familiar pleasant female voice from nowhere.

"My genoise has too much gelatin for my left foot, four-oh-seven-three bananarama fishsicle."

She bent down to tug her boot back on, but the door remained closed.

"Commander," said the voice again, "it's time to change your password. Don't forget it needs to be seven-hundred characters, with exactly forty-point-three capital letters, two hundred vowels, four-hundred-and-seventy-seven consonants, twenty-three pictographs, a DNA sample from four separate sources, the Wand of Power from Dark Wizard Zarkaroth — "

"You don't need to show off for Pheonix, Astra," Chani said sarcastically.

" ... Yes, Commander."

The door unsealed.

Chani paused just inside it and Pheonix followed her lead.

"Welcome to the Armory," she said.

The Armory took up the entire third ring from the center of the planetoid-like Ranger station. It stretched to either side, above and before him so far that his vision played tricks on him. Parts of the floor just seemed to drop off or meet the ceiling in a surreal way.

He and Chani started, by her direction, through even rows of stasis-tubes that he could just barely see over, each containing an object. Some of the objects looked like typical weapons, but there were some whose form simply made no sense to him.

"Weapons deemed too dangerous to play with others on the playground," Chani said of them as she and Pheonix passed through.

Above him and all around, set high up on the smooth metallic walls, huge robotic arms worked at an incredible speed assembling weaponry, which they then deposited into the network of tubes that surrounded them.

A warehouse of immense scale rose in front of them.

"And this ... this is *my* playground," Chani said proudly as they entered.

The interior was a jumble of tables and unidentifiable machines, boxes and crates of parts, individuals in lab coats running to and fro and completely ignoring their Commander.

"What, I don't even get a 'hello'?" Chani asked forlornly of no one.

One of the lab coats approached, this one wrapped around a malnourished-looking young man wearing obvious cybernetic eye enhancements that made the orbs look twice their size.

"Commander, I was just about to call you," he rushed. "I'm afraid your dying star machine is, well, dying."

"*What?*" Chani exclaimed. "Oh for Fug's sake! 'Scuse me, Pheonix."

Chani scurried off and, with nothing else to do, Pheonix followed. He caught bits and pieces of her heated mutterings that drifted behind her: "Creator-damned goblin-brained thing ... don't you dare do this to me. Not after six months."

She stopped in front of a quantum entanglement machine (or so his databank implant told him) that held a very small, very bright sphere of light — apparently a dying star.

And Chani was kicking it.

The star inside fluctuated wildly, and the machine itself seemed to be non-working, though Pheonix wasn't entirely sure what it was supposed to look like while operating properly.

"Is that a star? I don't think that manner of mechanical engineering is part of the standard operating procedures," he said.

"It is," she said between kicks, "and it's *my* damn invention; I can do what I want to it."

After one particularly vicious kick, the light coming from the star settled into a steady glow and various panels and tubes lit up. Chani stood back with her hands on her hips and glared at the thing as one would a particularly errant child.

"I knew that fuggin' fuse was loose, but I don't have time to fix it now. Magnus, get Cintunne and Treca off whatever bullshit they're wasting time on and deal with it, could you?"

"Yes, Commander."

"Pheonix, come with me," Chani said and led him into a room at the back of the warehouse. "Let's get you ready for *this* bullshit, huh?"

She turned around.

Spanning the entire back wall of the warehouse were dozens of lit tables with various gear strewn across them.

"This is the best of the best," Chani explained. "The Rangers — and I, specifically — are not in the habit of making the same mistake twice, so you'll be heading back into the fray with an arsenal at the ready." With one hand, she gestured to the items on the table she was leaning on. "This is what I'm forcing you to take, based on my professional recommendations as not only a veteran of much combat myself, but also having analyzed your style and proclivities."

The table contained: a matched set of revolver-style hand cannons, a thin torc of silver metal, a wooden case containing a rainbow of crystals, a belt buckle (sans belt), two brass-colored bracelets, and a foam-lined case containing a pair of gauntlets.

The gauntlets were made of a thin black material, and across the top of the fingers and back of the hand was armor plating which arced forward at the tips of the fingers to mimic Pheonix's natural talons. He could easily eviscerate someone with them — which was a comfortable part of his combat repertoire thanks to his childhood — so he appreciated the design element. Thin lines of neon purple ran across the sides of the fingers, something he recognized from the specialized rec-suit Chani wore everywhere. One of his implants told him it was imperium wiring, though he couldn't tell what specific purpose it served in these designs.

The final thing on the table was a weapon just shorter than the famed Ranger long sniper rifle that had clearly been modified to accommodate Pheonix's overly-long arms. A marriage of shotgun and machine gun with the sturdy frame of a grenade launcher, it had a cylindrical canister for a magazine filled with long tubes. Each tube held a round, bigger than two of Pheonix's fingers put together.

Chani went down the line: "Kinetic hand cannons. Seventy-five caliber. The rounds that come out of *these* will blow holes in just about anything. Remember this, you cannot take out your target if your target is behind a sea of meat shields, and most of the fuckers you will really want to kill like to use minions. This is more efficient than chopping forty guys to bits with swords at close-range or trying to take them out one at a time with small arms."

"Understood."

Delicately and reverently, she picked up the torc: "This — this baby is one of my prized projects. Personal fold-space. I know you've seen it before, but now's the time to give you some details. Supported by your personal energy, your life-force, the fold-space generator creates a field localized to your person. That field doesn't exist here — it's tied to a place between our reality and someplace else. So, as long as you have enough energy, you can store any number of items there. You being Ascended, your fold-space is probably infinite. Only you can access your fold-space, and anything within is impervious to harm or decay, like a quantum stasis field. It's really quite genius."

"If you do say so yourself."

Chani shot him an admonishing look. "That's right."

"Could I put something living in it?"

Chani's eyes went blank for a moment, as though she'd never considered the possibility.

"I ... don't know," she finally said. "I would certainly not suggest the average user try to. How an Ascended would utilize it ... well, you'd have to figure that out for yourself. My opinion? Don't put anyone in there that you wouldn't be willing to lose, or whose mind you need intact, just on the off-chance it does have negative effects."

"Note taken," Pheonix said, though he couldn't hide the amusement in his voice.

Chani sighed. "You worry me sometimes," she said in a comically strained tone, deliberately placing the fold-space torc back on the table.

Swiftly moving on, she tapped the bracelets with a forefinger next: "These work on the same principle, but on a much lower spectrum. As you can probably imagine, we can't go handing out fold-space to every recruit that wanders in — most of them either just don't have the energy reserves or would be stupid enough to put a whole damn house in there and wonder why they wake up in the hospital. This is what they get instead — strictly for ammo. Tip your wrists down when you're red, a machine in the device will open the cylinder, extract the brass, and reload fresh rounds faster than you can blink. And yes, before you say it, I know *you* with your ridiculous speed could probably reload faster, but physics would work against you. Aside from that, you don't want to be manually reloading in the middle of a firefight for a variety of reasons. Just let it do its thing and don't worry about it."

"Very well."

Chani pointed to the wooden box: "Spell-crystals. Did you come across these while in Terelath? Did Minrathous show them to you?"

"Yes, we trained with them after it became apparent that my magic skills are null. Spells bonded to brittle crystals with size, shape, and color indicating the magic within. The spell fires when you shatter the crystal."

"Right. You may not have magic, you may not like magic, but the fact of the matter is that it is an effective and necessary tool in many battles. You never know when you may need it."

She moved on to the belt buckle: "Shield generator. Can be tuned to accept or reject any number and combination of substances and forces. You're lucky — your natural resistance to magic means you won't have to turn that part of it on.

Makes your skin prickle. This'll replace the one you currently have, and it's more robust."

She ran her fingers across one of the gauntlets and smiled: "These are gifts from me. I give them to all my Sergeants, modded for each individual and their particular combat style. Within these is circuitry that connects the weapons to the brain — kind of like a self-contained redundant nervous system. It also prevents excess lactic acid buildup in the muscles, allowing for more endurance and strength, feeds nutrients into tired muscles through the porous fingers, and makes micro-adjustments to aim with ranged weaponry and melee strikes. These in particular will help to maintain your new cyber-arm, and — " she flicked her fingers across a metal panel on the back of the hand. "When it's attached, make this motion across this panel right here and you'll get a biometric readout. It's got some other fancy features like a compass, a TT clock, communication systems and whatnot. Oh, and — "

She slipped one on and grimaced. "Ugh. Made for you, not me."

A snap of her fingers brought a bright orb of light over her head. Another snap and it was gone.

"In case you need light," she said, putting the gauntlet back in its place.

She tapped the giant gun: "You will be a solo operative against overwhelming odds, likely more often than not. Therefore, you need at least one large-munitions weapon. This is what I'm suggesting you take: the 2-0 caliber."

"What is it?"

Chani uncharacteristically hesitated. "Well … it's a cursed weapon."

Pheonix stared at her for a heartbeat. "And you're suggesting I take a cursed weapon … why?"

"Because you're Ascended, and it won't affect you."

"You know this for certain?"

"Yes, another Ascended handled the 2-0 without issue. Spiraea, who called it gross. Anyone else who makes contact with it for longer than a few seconds will activate the curse and it will drive them into a frenzy of firing the weapon until they have nothing else to use as ammo."

Pheonix considered this. "Well, it'd be useful if the enemy ever manages to disarm me. What exactly is its function?"

"It's kinda like a railgun. Fires high explosive rounds at high velocity. There are slugs for it, which, if you end up taking a shine to it, you could requisition after this is all over."

Pheonix doubted he would, but didn't say so aloud, so Chani moved on.

"Okay. Your armor is your own choice, *clearly* what you've got now won't hold up to the kind of use you'd be putting it to. Take a look, and if you find anything else you have questions on or would like to add to your repertoire, just let me know."

Pheonix paced between the tables, occasionally asking Chani questions and picking up things that looked useful.

His final pile included a metal box that contained a tent and other outdoor survival supplies, some rations, a localized null-field generator, and a 'classic' kit — mundane tools integral to hominin survival. Other weaponry he found cumbersome or not useful; he wasn't about to keep something on his person on the off chance he may need it in a random situation. He was confident in his ability to be resourceful enough to find a way out if that occurred.

As for armor …

A set built much like the elven plate armor he'd previously worn drew his attention immediately. While ancient hominin plate armor was bulky, loud, and difficult to deal with, elven plate was impeccably crafted down to the micron thanks to elven magic and resonance with minerals. It was designed to shift in perfect sync with the dancelike battle style of elven warriors and sit close to the body. This suit was rather plain in its ornamentation, but that worked for Pheonix. The spikes and curly-cues and gems on some armor was disgusting in its inefficiency.

"Oh, good eye, kid," Chani said. "That's a Legionnaire suit. If you're going to take that, you'll want the Ranger-made armor that goes underneath it. It acts as a conduit between you and the suit to increase response time, better than just relying on kinetic force alone. That it? You're good?"

"I am."

"Then get your shit packed. You've got a date with the simulator, full-gear. Any questions, you make damn sure to let me know."

"Roger, Commander."

TWENTY-SIX
Krasynth II, Redux

Chani was into her second beer when she felt a hand on her shoulder. Steele sat at the bar and ordered tea. The bartender served it to them in an antique teacup and they smiled.

"How's it going?" Steele asked.

"Pretty well," Chani said, rubbing her eyes. "Time?"

Steele checked their finger.

"Six hours til hit time. How was the kid?"

"Sleeping — or, what passes for sleep with him, anyway. Ordered him to rest up and do something other than training until it's time to go."

"How'd he take to the chair?"

"Oh, Creator. He was fine, but you won't believe what I caught Astra doing."

"Hm?" Steele asked around a sip of tea.

"So, we were checking his capacity and I notice the light just goes green. No limit info, no warnings, nothing. Just fuggin' blinks green and starts going. So I ask Astra what's going on, where's his limit info, and the cheeky little bugger tells me that he's Ascended and his mind is infinite. She says he could take the whole Archive and not have a 'burp of a nightmare.' So I ask what she's doing. She says she's downloading the Archive."

Steele laughed into their cup. "Are you kidding? How long did that take?"

"Don't know. I had to leave him there — fuggin' emergency meeting number eight-thousand and twelve. By the time I got out of it, he was back in the simulator. Could have been one hour, could have been many hours — which is still wild to think about."

"Well, it should help speed things along."

"How are you holding up?" Chani asked.

Steele grimaced. "Sore, but I'll be fine physically. The embarrassment of being kicked out of the simulator by a kid for being too slow will sting for years, though."

Chani snorted.

"That 'kid' is Ascended, just you remember. It's been how long since you ran a mission?"

"Twenty years. I'm not so far from it that I don't remember, though I apparently need to up my PT. Honestly, kinda looking forward to it. Of course, I have never been the action-junkie you were in your heyday."

"Way to make me feel old. They had to force me to take Commander, did you know that?"

"You skipped ship to avoid the board, right?"

"I'm sure a lot of the story that gets around is embellished, but, yes, I did actually skip ship. Yelling 'Fug paperwork' the whole way. Shoulda seen ol' Flintface. The privates wanted to roast marshmallows on him. Still got my way though, didn't get stuck behind a desk or forced to organize dog-and-pony shows for dignitaries and officers."

"Hey, I resemble that remark."

"Oh, don't mind me … you'll be Fleet Commander before long. Just not my bag, you know? I like interacting with the joes."

Steele checked their finger.

"Nervous?" Chani asked wryly. Steele made a face.

"Keeping tabs. Don't want to get so distracted that I miss the boat." They arched a brow at Chani.

"Oh, cute. Save it for the port-side girls."

"Hey, now," Steele protested. "You're *at least* red-light district. You know, one of those boudoir mamas who'll smother you with their — "

"Keep it up, I'll smother you with something, but you won't like it."

Steele laughed and Chani cracked a smile.

Who am I kidding, I'm nervous, Chani thought.

It wasn't as though she hadn't gone against regulations before. Hell, that was practically her M.O. And this time they'd drilled Pheonix into the ground, he was carrying half the armory and Steele would be with him. If it failed again, it wasn't for lack of preparation, but her political reputation would take a hell of a hit in a time when she really needed it to be as solid as possible.

This would be the real test — for all of them.

A familiar hold; not the Chevalier, but a sister ship. Its captain, Frendel, stood nearby a Ranger fighter on its launch rail while Pheonix and Steele talked. The repetition was becoming annoying, but Pheonix could understand their position.

Steele had Pheonix check his equipment, then said, "We'll be handling the manipulator arms for the first part of the operation. That objective complete, we cut down into the atmosphere and the fighter will shit us out over the FOB in very specific locations, where we go our separate ways. My objective is to clear the FOB. You know yours. When we land, we most likely won't see much of each other."

"Sounds efficient."

"Only coming from you is that a compliment," Steele said with tired exasperation, then addressed Captain Frendel: "Confirm that the fleet will be following on n+6?"

"Affirmative."

"Then I think we're ready to embark. Pheonix?"

"Ready."

Steele and Pheonix climbed into the fighter, a silver-and-blue craft just large enough for the two of them and their payload. While normally a sleek, birdlike design, this one was modified specifically for this sort of application; tucked under the fuselage were two sets of mechanical arms, facing fore and aft. They protruded from a bubble beneath the seats — if the fighter were a living bird, this would make it look pregnant.

And maybe a little mutated, considering the arms.

Pheonix buckled into the pilot's seat, Steele behind him. They performed the short pre-flight check. At Steele's signal, launch commenced. The small fighter was equipped with motion dampers, as most Ranger equipment was, so Pheonix felt nothing. The blurring of his view outside the windows was his only indication of movement — and that was brief, as the fighter sped along the magnetic rail through the tunnel leading outside.

Space opened up around them. The craft hurtled along its pre-set course, the circular bulk of the battleship and then the much larger bulk of Krasynth III both shrinking behind. Krasynth II was the size of a hominin head in his front view when they came across the first patrol — inefficient and ill-built slaver fighters and the black arrows of dark elf make. They took no notice of the Ranger ship as it shot past; the specialized field generator the ship was equipped with ensured that. Merely an emitter array that mimicked the background of space, it was enough to fool the less-advanced enemy ships as long as they did not tarry.

Coming up to the main body of the fleet itself was more nerve-wracking, however.

Orbiting in lazy arrogance around their prize were the targets. Steele prayed under their breath.

"That's excessive," Pheonix said of the fleet.

The vessel that stood out as the largest was the slaver command ship, a shape Pheonix knew all too well. Two pyramids, one large, one small. The larger sat on what would normally be considered its side, the point facing whatever direction it was traveling in. The smaller sat atop a flat side, rather appearing like a small creature riding a larger one. It wasn't an inaccurate likening; the small pyramid housed the slavers themselves, whereas the other housed 'cargo' (both living and nonliving), to be jettisoned and even detonated in times of need.

Flanking the main slaver ship were four dark elf capitol ships, easily identified by the dark elves' habit of wreathing everything in dark magic, and four pirate battle cruisers, which looked like bubbles stacked together to the nth degree. Stolen from the Koloss, an advanced aquatic peoples and one of the few actively at war with the Rangers, those battle cruisers were worrisome; harboring lasers that were channeled through fold-space engines to achieve massive destructive power, they could cut through even shielded Ranger vessels.

Among these giants were the countless smaller ships that made up the rest of the flotilla.

The fighter carrying Pheonix and Steele weaved its way through, using micro-adjustments from external sensors to belly up to the first objective: the furthest dark elf capitol ship. Pheonix grasped the controls and felt Steele do the same behind him. They only had a few scant seconds to place the mine, a miniature nuke, before the autopilot would engage again.

Each ship got a tiny payload in two places: the bridge and engine. There were a few close calls, where a languishing fighter either got too close or turned towards them, but nevertheless, they made it through safely.

The theory was simple and sound, a tactic as ancient as warfare itself: one small, well-hidden assailant could get through where even a small strike task force would have issues. In a fleet this size, with so much needing to be monitored, the likelihood of discovery was miniscule enough to be worth the severe consequences. Pirates, slavers, and dark elves would not take Rangers as slaves or hostages.

And why have Pheonix and Steele do it instead of a seasoned pilot?

Pheonix needed to be on-ground. They'd given him the mission of engaging the Red Mage Master — he'd proven he could handle red mages with Zu'Resh — and if they were to take Krasynth II back, the Red Mage Master would need to go ASAP. This Red Mage Master, *in his utmost arrogance*, had actually landed his entire ship on the surface of Krasynth II. And it was this ship that was the ultimate destination of Pheonix's mission.

The majority of the evil commanders would remain in space. Evil didn't tend to put high-ranks on the ground; they'd hang around in the relative safety of space. So taking out the ships was essential to winning the ground in more than one way: once the ships started going, and command lost, the ground troops would panic.

Evil were cowards; they'd break and run given the slightest opportunity, and those who fought evil knew well to capitalize on that. Less fighting meant less chance for casualties.

Steele was there partially because it was their reprimand/punishment from the Commanding-General to accompany Pheonix and, once on-ground, secure the FOB. Space around Krasynth II was stuffed. While Steele was not a pilot, between their rudimentary training, the walking Archive that was Pheonix, and the autopilot, it was good odds.

"Objective one complete," Steele said, an edge of relief to their voice. "We have a narrow window between orbital strikes to get down there. Looks like we're ahead of schedule. Unless we want to wait here, which I don't advise, you'll need to take over."

"Affirmative," Pheonix said, and reached up to flick the four switches for manual drive. The viewport lit up in front of his eyes, broadcasting the flightpath to the surface, and he took the control stick.

Like anything, the technical knowledge gained from the Archives was sufficient for basic maneuvering but putting it into context and action was something else, even with practical sim-training. But, true to his nature, Pheonix adapted quickly and was at least decently capable of following the projected flightpath and avoiding obstacles. He wasn't ready to jump into aerial battles, but he could follow simple directions, supported by the ship's VI.

Still, he couldn't blame Steele for the breath they let out when the ship cleared the mess and was angling down to the surface.

"Sixty seconds to next strike," Steele said tightly.

Pheonix steadied the craft's trajectory on the flightpath projection as the upper atmosphere enveloped them, a lightning-like crackling in his viewport, with particles skating along the shields. A red light flashed.

"Commander, I have a heat intensity warning," Pheonix said.

"Flip the coolant switch and nose down by one degree," Steele responded. "Forty-five seconds."

Pheonix accessed to find the switch in question and did as instructed. The warning disappeared.

"Thirty seconds," Steele said hurriedly. "Let the computer take over. Prepare for drop."

Pheonix released the stick and leaned back into the seat. The twin halves of the ejection pod clapped over him, hissing as they sealed. He touched a button on the array set into the arm of his chair, bringing up a readout. The pod lengthened at the feet level, forcing him to stand, and he took note of his direction and goal just as it fired.

No motion dampers on *this* thing. His stomach leapt into his throat and his inner ears told him he was dropping at a significant rate. He braced for the impact, but even so it rattled his teeth.

Last intel pinpointed the Red Mage Master relatively southeast of the FOB. That corresponds, minus two degrees, with the readings I just took.

The straps of his harness cut away, jarred against internal blades by the force of landing. The pod split minutely down its seams as Pheonix drew his hand cannons, then exploded outward, fragmenting into shrapnel at the same moment to render into pink mist anything in the vicinity.

Pheonix found himself alone, though, just outside the FOB. With no time to spare before the incoming orbital strike, he took off running just as bright lights punched behind him. The strike pummeled the FOB's barrier, shaking the ground.

He kept his objective firmly in mind, burning through rocky gullies and past temporary buildings of enemy make. He took targets of opportunity: dark elf spitters (gatling guns firing dark magic), portals, and anyone wearing a red robe or something highly decorated or surrounded by the enslaved. It wasn't hard to tell who the Important People were among these particular groups, as aggressively materialistic and hierarchical as they were.

The groups he took out moved at a snail's pace to his eye — probably not even aware of his presence until death surrounded or took them. He didn't spare time to kill stragglers. It wasn't a slaughter by any means: his priority was movement, and, ultimately, the Red Mage Master. The longer Pheonix took, the longer that bastard would have to finagle a way out.

Halfway to his goal, the panic and chaos he and Steele had caused by their sudden arrival eclipsed him. His targets ran to portals or frantically activated portal crystals, all to no avail. Shots ricocheted off Pheonix's barrier. Magic nullified against his armor. His defense was to be fast. He'd drilled excessively, he knew his route as though it had been mathematically pre-programmed in his head, and he had the element of surprise on his side.

He quickly came across groups that were more organized, attempting to flank or block him entirely, but he did not engage unless necessary. The structures around him became more elaborate and he angled towards the largest of the compounds.

A majority of red mage wealth went to making themselves as comfortable as possible. Even in a warzone, in a red mage-occupied space, one will invariably find lush mansions and every luxury in imagination, prefabricated and dropped as first claim of ownership.

Pheonix's main concern would be at the crown of the biggest palisade, doubtless cocooned in a labyrinth of traps both magical and mundane, a strange mix of paranoia and exorbitance. The buildings pushed in on all sides, byways narrowing and heights climbing well above his head.

He ran into a few minor patrols, avoided or taken out with ease. Bursting out of an alley, he paused a moment to get his bearings. Tents and equipment arrayed out in front of him, parallel to a small ridgeline.

Secondary objective, Pheonix thought as he mounted the ridgeline and pulled the 2-0 caliber out of fold-space.

Below him stretched a good breadth of the army, but more importantly — their six supply portals.

Without hesitation, Pheonix aimed and took out the portals, skipping a few steps back as the explosions from the shots carved huge swaths into the assembled. Those remaining scrambled like ants disturbed from their nest.

Pheonix shook his head at the destruction from just one shot, put the 2-0 caliber back into his fold-space, and continued on.

He came to a large open courtyard, a gigantic statue of a man in robes dominating its center.

He barely had time to sneer before having to dive for cover — the statue being the only option. Crouched, listening to and feeling the angry vibration of rounds impacting behind him, the snark that Pheonix was quickly finding he liked surfaced again: *He had a statue of himself made out of unrefined deutronium? I'm going to kill this asshole.*

The brief glimpse Pheonix got of the Red Mage Master's elite guard was not pretty. Three heavy slaver troops stood on the steps, outfitted in chunky hard-point armor and sleek round helmets. Behind them, perched atop decorative pillars flanking the entrance, were two dark elf Mistresses, harnessed in blood-filled phylacteries. Taking point was a Slavemaster, a power whip in one hand and a firearm in the other.

It was the heavies that kept him pinned behind the statue with a constant barrage of chain-gun fire. He found shortly that not all three were packing the same heat, as a canister burst against his cover and a wash of fire poured between the statue's tree-trunk-thick legs to singe the tips of his wings. Suddenly annoyed, he holstered his guns and reached into fold-space, willing the box of spell crystals to his hand.

They were trying to flush him out, clearly, knowing that if any one of them were to come around the humongous statue, he'd have them in an instant. On the other hand, if he were to emerge into the open, his shields would be down in just as little time and the power whip would carve him into bits. He couldn't die, no, but he also knew he passed out if he pushed his body too far, and they might be able to take him apart and keep him from healing.

He had *some* time — the cowardice ran too strong in them for a full-on assault.

The heat intensified and flames licked to either side of him. He dug through the small wooden box and tossed several crystals in the air. Two shattered to form twin discs that would act like a shield for two long, thin harpoons. He returned the box to fold-space and unholstered one kinetic pistol.

Popping just his upper body past the edge of his cover and trusting his shield to take the fire, he took out one of the chain-gunners. The moment he squeezed the trigger, the four crystals shot past him at blinding speed. He ducked back, realizing several things simultaneously:

A bullet carved a line into the base of the statue at an angle that couldn't have possibly come from any of the foes facing him on the steps. That meant a sniper; and, despite the stereotype, snipers rarely traveled alone, so he could count on at least one more.

In the few seconds he was partially out of cover, his null shield energy reserves had been significantly depleted. There was only so much more he could take of that kind of overwhelming force before it would literally flatten him.

As Pheonix was incapable of fear, the memory of watching himself on the vid feed didn't paralyze him, but his mind did reach for the nearest emotion and came up with anger.

The explosions and hideous screaming from behind him (heard even over the continued fire), meant that his crystal offense had functioned as expected. Though he couldn't see it, he knew the discs had shattered on the magical shields surrounding the Mistresses, dispelling them, and the piercing crystals acted as explosive arrows, detonating any magic devices on the affected person. It was a common tactic among those given permission to carry spell crystals. Even a prepared Ranger could easily fall to a Mistress; and thus, many nasty counter-offenses had been developed.

He took stock of his remaining adversaries.

The Slavemaster: Pheonix had a special plan for him, so if things allowed, he'd be the last to die.

One chain heavy and one grenadier: they needed to go first.

Snipers in unknown locations: although he could extrapolate the position of one based on his shot, any smart sniper would have moved with a quickness after the first shot failed, so he couldn't really count on that. He actually had little time to consider, feeling the pressure of another shot lining up on his head all too soon.

He reached into fold-space again and willed the grenade box to his hand. Digging through it and discarding most options, he came to two spheres with buttons on the face. He stared at them, accessing.

Smart grenades? Chani and her toys.

He had no better options, so he input the time and set them down. They raised up on tiny, spindly metal legs and scuttled off, avoiding the fire pelting him at his six. Still feeling the pressure of the unknown from Schroedinger's snipers, he agonized over every second that passed.

Shouts of warning — a cessation of the incessant hail of rounds — two basso thuds — a tinkling rain of particulate matter and a shrieked expletive.

Now!

Pheonix rolled out of cover, pulling both kinetic pistols in the same practiced motion. The snipers (just as he'd predicted, two, at ten and two o'clock) fired, probably panicking, and were summarily taken out.

They didn't move. What do they teach these idiots?

The dust and noise settled, aside from distant battle sounds from the FOB. Pheonix's radio had been chattering at him, ignored, his entire frenetic trip to the palisade, but a part of his mind was still keeping up with the activity at the front. Ranger drop ships had deposited infantry among and behind enemy lines and were currently engaged with dark elf and slaver forces. Moving forward, but not enough.

The Slavemaster, now alone, squared off with Pheonix, who stayed just out of whip reach. He straightened and slid his pistols back in their holsters, choosing instead to call Malol and Bedaestael to his hands.

The caution on the Slavemaster's face gave way to a grin.

"Really, boy? What do you expect to do with those?"

"Kill you, sa'masser."

Something else flickered in the Slavemaster's eyes. "A slave?" the man asked. "How — "

Pheonix didn't let him finish.

He charged forward. The Slavemaster fired in what was probably a knee-jerk reaction, which missed entirely. The whip cracked forward, and Pheonix caught it with Bedaestael.

"Got you, boy," the slaver smirked — then gave his hand an incredulous look. The power whip, sucked of its life by Bedaestael, fizzled into uselessness.

"Not that kind of sword," Pheonix snapped, and leapt the intervening space.

Malol bit into soft gut, the sharp hunger of the blade slicing through with no resistance. The hilt thudded dully against the Slavemaster's stomach and time stopped.

Through Malol — a sword of Justice — a connection was formed between Pheonix and the Slavemaster.

Into that connection, the man's life poured in a literal storm of imagery — every memory, every emotion, every moment flowing through Malol and into Pheonix. All the horror of the slave pits, he experienced again and again from the side of one who reveled in it. The worst scum of the universe was pierced on the end of his blade, and suddenly it wasn't enough that the man merely die.

As his eyes cleared, an unspeakable rage took Pheonix. Trembling, he jammed Bedaestael with all the force he could muster into the Slavemaster's other side. Pheonix lost his footing and fell atop the slaver, who toppled backwards. The Slavemaster's head hit the ground, eyeballs nearly out of his skull meeting Pheonix's dispassionate gaze.

"*You have been judged,*" Pheonix growled, compelled to say the words that took flight around them like living beings, "*and found lacking.*"

The Slavemaster's befouled soul shattered with that last word. It dispelled, becoming droplets of energy merging back into the greater whole of everything, never to reform.

He wasn't sure how he knew that it was a soul that had been destroyed, but something in him was absolutely certain.

The rage left Pheonix and he was overcome by sickness. Barely managing to crawl off of the corpse, he knelt amongst the rubble, hastily ripped off the gas-exchange mask, and vomited the black bile of what he'd seen. The first tears of his young, hard life poured from his eyes from the force of the expulsion. He wiped his mouth after spitting the final globule of acid to the dusty ground.

Shakily, he stood, Malol and Bedaestael hovering over his shoulders. Already the queasiness was fading, as much as his battered mind tried to hold onto it for study. He took a breath and found, despite the sudden strangeness endured, that he felt fine … more than fine. He scowled, thoroughly confused and not familiar nor happy with the change. The messy kill, the vomiting, the fuzzy sensation of having seen something terrible — why the hell was he buzzing with energy?

Furthermore, it didn't seem he'd needed the mask.

"Justice-zero, Justice-zero, come in Justice-zero, over," Chani's voice came through the radio. He realized she'd been trying to contact him for some time. He made the decision to put the strange thing he'd just experienced out of his mind for the moment.

"Reaper-zero, Justice-zero. Go ahead, over," he replied, trying not to let his lingering turmoil show in his voice.

"Justice-zero, kill that goblin-fucker now. We have no time, portals activating, over."

"Reaper-zero, Justice-zero. On my way, over."

"Reaper-zero, out."

He took off into the black depths of the pyramid's base to find the Red Mage Master, determined to take out his rage on every slaver along the way.

TWENTY-SEVEN
The Agony of Mercy

The dramatic change from harsh starlight to the dimmer interior would have blinded most hominins, but Pheonix's eyes adjusted instantly.

A foyer opened up before him, the space several times again his own height in all directions and opulent beyond any sense or necessity. Burgundy banners embroidered with intricate designs in gold thread hung from the walls and ceiling, marble columns stood as silent sentinels in ordered pace between the entrance and an imperial staircase. Paintings hung between gold-rimmed mirrors. The gold-veined stone floor was covered in burgundy rugs, along with the exotic skins and furs of many animals, whose severed heads bore witness from above. Crystals hovered near the walls, throwing off enough magical light to see by for normal eyes, but probably only barely. Suits of armor and mannequins wearing robes stood next to clear crystal cases enrobing artifacts, gems, and jewelry.

Pheonix's lip curled in a sneer.

Egotistical fuck.

Pheonix moved forward silently, gripping Malol and Bedaestael. It was too quiet, save for an omnipresent sound of flowing liquid that he couldn't quite place.

Past the columns and gilded masturbatory fuckery of the narrow foyer, the space opened up further. Massive cylindrical tanks hung from the ceiling, spotted with glowing-green gauges, dials, button-rich interfaces. The tanks were veritable porcupines, with painfully thin metal tubing sticking out at crazy angles from the bloated metal things, all of which were connected to the ceiling.

As Pheonix approached the center of the space, he noted a door to either side. In front of him, spanning the far wall, were three large doorways that presumably led into other parts of the ship. The center of the three was a balcony over a raised dais, unconnected to anything on either side or below. Jutting from its railing and arcing over the dais below was a giant, gold-plated adder head with a fanged open maw. This center balcony was flanked by twin staircases, each of which arced to a landing and doorway.

The center dais quickly drew his attention as the source of the liquid sound.

Blood continually vomited out of the adder's gaping mouth, falling into a huge, stained basin situated in the floorspace between the double staircases. The smell hit his nose and Pheonix's rage responded as a living thing; he fought to control it, remembering Chani's words.

He swept his gaze quickly to survey the rest of the room. Satellite basins caught even more blood as it rained from the ceiling. The basins overflowed into grooves set into the ground, which carved complex patterns on the floor before disappearing into the walls.

Thus far he had seen no living thing, not so much as a single guard, which had alarmed him until that moment.

In the large center basin, a figure that Pheonix could only describe as 'monster' luxuriated in the stream of blood, head tilted back in ecstasy, mouth open. A bulky thing, it appeared to be made of squared-off muscle groups, but Pheonix could only get the barest general glimpse of its form through the carmine streams covering it. A hot star of magic burned at its core, nurtured by the sick shower.

The monster seemed to realize Pheonix was there, and lowered its head, swallowing visibly. It waded towards him and stepped out of the basin.

What had initially looked to be misshapen musculature was actually armor, as evidenced by stitches along its length. The function of the armor's overly thick form, being several inches off of the monster's body, was beyond Pheonix's comprehension. It looked like it would be both cumbersome and awkward. What lurked beneath the armor was still a mystery.

As blood ran off of the creature, the texture of its armor became more clear. Skin. Ranger clan tattoos ranged up one arm of the horrific armor, stitched haphazardly together. Faces — young faces, frozen twisted into masks of agony and fear — leered from corners of the monster's breastplate.

Pheonix's grip tightened on his weapons. The beast within him begged to be unleashed.

He accessed to see if he could dredge up some information on evil creatures that wore others' skin as armor. He got one result:

Mistresses of the Cult of Blood, one of the quasi-religious organizations propping up dark elf society, wear sapient skin and use a deadly form of osmosis, allowing them to absorb power from blood. The blood of innocents is preferred.

Yes, the description fit.

The Mistress raised her weapon, a double-headed metal spear with a bill hook on one end and a diamond-shaped tip on the other. Pheonix watched, waiting for the first move.

A bolt of power hurtled at him, dragging a wave of blood in its wake from the basin, which splashed onto the floor and quickly spread. Pheonix let the bolt hit him — his inner sight told him it was a weak opening move, meant to test his reactions — but hissed as the blood touched him. It streamed around his feet and unexpectedly burned like fire.

The souls attached to the innocent blood enveloped him in their pain upon contact. He felt it even through his armor.

This blood ... was harvested from children.

And it was now pouring out of the basin and filling the room.

The Mistress came at him with an upswing of the heavy spear-head end of her weapon. Pheonix parried it, but was forced back from the kinetic energy of the strike. The Mistress propelled herself across the blood that quickly became ankle-deep, skating along its surface by magic, zipping around him and striking where she thought she had an advantage.

Pheonix parried, blocked, and sidestepped the spearhead, drifting into a zen-like state of instant awareness, his subconscious overriding thought, muscle memory replacing conscious action. The Mistress appeared to be looking for an opening; he would ensure that she would find none.

Seeing that her tactic was ineffective, she swung her weapon at his legs, intending to knock him on his ass.

Pheonix leapt into the air with all his might, snapping out his malformed wings to hover. The Mistress apparently took this as the opening she'd been seeking.

Sliding closer, she shot the hook-end at him; an extendable, thin metal rod uncoiled from the belly of the shaft. He slashed with Bedaestael, which sliced through the inferior metal. The hook end clattered to the ground, extendable innards retracting. She once again retreated out of range, moving at a pace that was frustratingly hard to keep up with.

As he hovered, he thought quickly. She had superior speed and distance on him, with her ability to skate across the surface of the blood and the fact that he was hampered by it. He *could* pull one of his firearms, but her overall evasiveness would remain a problem. He hadn't trained overly much for shot accuracy against rapidly-moving targets, which was very much a learned skill, an oversight that he was now kicking himself for. And he didn't have enough time to consider the options in his fold-space.

The Mistress seemed exceptionally weak in close combat, which was another reason to avoid using a ranged option. Pheonix was not about to play the enemy's game by the rules they'd set out for him.

So he'd have to neutralize her speed in order to get the advantage.

But — if her speed was based on her contact with liquid …

Making a quick decision, he flattened his wings and slammed down.

All one-thousand pounds of him hit the ground with a deafening thud, cracking the stone floor and violently blowing the blood away from the point of impact. The motion of the ripples overtook the Mistress, shaking her off her feet. She tumbled forward onto her face.

Got you, Phoenix thought acidly.

He leapt toward her while she struggled to recover; but as he drew near, she whipped around, hand out, and shot some kind of fire magic at him.

Oh, shit, he thought in alarm. Not 'some kind of fire magic' — *Nether-flame.*

Ever-hungry, ever-burning, sapient fire closely associated with demons.

With no time to dodge, Pheonix's only option was to throw his cybernetic arm across his face to protect himself and hope for the best.

He pressed forward to close the gap between them, reaching for her with the arm wreathed in Nether-flame, figuring that if it was going to consume him, he damn well wasn't going to go down alone.

His outstretched cybernetic hand slammed into her face.

She fell backwards, Pheonix atop her. He bore down; she tore ineffectually at his arm, legs splashing in the blood in a fear-born flail.

With her pinned, he willed Bedaestael to his other hand, then jammed it into one side of the too-thick armor crafted from stolen flesh. The Mistress jerked, becoming still but for a whole-body trembling.

As with the Slavemaster, a connection was formed between Pheonix and the creature at the end of his blade.

Every muscle tensed to a ripcord, statue-like hardness, the memories of her own misspent life tearing her apart. Pheonix, though he had experienced it once, was not necessarily expecting to go through it again, and so stiffened with the vile invasion of an evil life rushing through his brain. As the memories faded, expectation hung between them, palpably. The Mistress watched Pheonix as if she could sense the words bubbling up from deep within him.

This time, *he* did not speak.

The words boomed in the space around him, in a voice that was not his, with the intensity of spitting hatred.

"You have been judged and found lacking."

Pheonix willed Malol to his mechanical hand.

"Tell your bastard God I have returned."

He stabbed downward viciously.

Pheonix now knew what to expect. As had happened with the Slavemaster, tainted beyond all saving, the Mistress' soul crumpled into its basest components and dissipated.

Pheonix didn't bother to move this time; he let the sickness wash over him and out of him. Vomiting was just another new piece of datum, no more or less unpleasant than anything else he had to deal with. At least as he got to his feet, the sense of having seen something horrible faded quickly and he realized he was brimming with energy again and, for some reason, power.

With his head clear, he abruptly remembered the Nether-flame and looked down at himself. The Nether-flame seemed to be gone. Except …

Licks of purple-red-black flared periodically from between the seams of his cybernetic arm. Judging by appearance, the Nether-flame had somehow inhabited the arm.

The ground buckled under his feet momentarily, the air took up a hum, and he was reminded of more pressing matters. As long as the fire in his arm remained quiescent, he could deal with it later.

"Justice-zero, drop a beacon," Chani's voice crackled through his comm. "The ship's engine is firing up and we need a squad in there now. Sending an engineer to assist with the shutdown."

"Roger, Reaper-zero. Beacon inbound."

Out of fold-space, Pheonix pulled a hexahedron just larger than his clenched fist. One hand on the bottom, one hand on the top, he twisted until runes carved into both halves lined up. He set it on the ground and stepped back. It began to glow, the six points along the equator of the shape pulsing furiously, then shooting out lines of light that anchored themselves to the ground.

A cone of light spilled upwards and fanned out to a vague door shape, through which shadows that became people walked.

A Ranger heavy squad made up of two machine-gunners, two kinetic-gunners, two energy-axers, and two elven legionnaires escorted another man. Half of his skull (including one eye) had been replaced by a multi-tiered, mechanical apparatus with many lenses. One arm was completely cybernetic, but unlike Pheonix's, his was quite bulky, aggressively technical, and bristling with devices and ports. It even had a clear spot for the hand to retract and be replaced by a tool.

Engineer, Pheonix identified.

The engineer pulled out a tube from inside his cybernetic arm, one corner of which he folded back. Out of the tube came ... another tube. He took one tube in each hand and held his arms apart; a screen formed between them and he rotated in one spot, holding the screen up and down. A map formed. Some kind of scanner, then.

"Looks like slave pens to the left," the engineer said to one of the soldiers, a Sergeant by his armor. "Right's where we need to go, that leads into the engine complex."

"You after the Red Mage Master, Commander?" the Sergeant asked Pheonix.

Commander? Pheonix wondered when and how he'd been given rank. "Yes, but what of the slaves?"

"Our priority is the engines, but our backup squad is en route. They'll free the slaves. If you want to take care of it, be our guest. Either case, looks like the big guy himself is three floors up. We'd better be off. Good luck to you."

The engineer nodded to his squad and the whole lot of them took off into the right hallway at a dead run. Pheonix looked after them, but only for a moment. He understood their position. He hesitated, considering his priorities ... then took off resolutely left.

Slaves always came first.

He made his way silently through the twisty, barely lit hallway.

(Warning: mention of implied sexual assault below.)

As Pheonix rounded the corner, the holding area opened up before him. Basically, it was a giant warehouse, stacked floor to ceiling with rough wooden coffins, each big enough to barely hold its horizontal occupant. A rune on each one kept its contents in a stasis slumber. There were more of the coffins than he could count easily or quickly. The central, wide, walking corridor for the guards was a study in the worst of depraved imagination; proudly displayed on the walls were torture devices so bizarre, even Pheonix couldn't discern their uses and didn't want to know.

He spared all of it only the most cursory of glances.

Instead, he focused on a table directly in front of the entrance; on it was a prone body. Around it were three other bodies, standing. Moving. Sounds emanated from the group of flesh.

Malol and Bedaestael jumped to his hands and he leapt at the slavers — blood — screaming, his and theirs — a maelstrom — red, rage — two down, one tried to run — terrified eyes, slack-jawed *worthless waste of resources, undeserving of a molecule of the Creator's light* — blades slicing through flesh over and over, blood and gurgling and sick squelching, he couldn't even scream anymore but the swords fell again and again in Pheonix's mindless need to destroy, until the bodies were mush on the ground, and still it wasn't enough —

Then a hard jar. Malol, in Pheonix's frenzy, bumped one of the boxes. Greedy Malol snatched the energy of the rune. What followed was a cascade of failing runes — every rune in that stack of coffins — all sending their energy, too, into the hungry sword. The electric shock jolted Pheonix out of his all-consuming fury and he stumbled back, panting and trembling.

He wheeled around to meet the half-lidded eyes of the victim, limp on the table.

Pheonix approached, Malol and Bedaestael slipping from his numb hands. Everything in him was crying out to help her.

She was blank. Gone. Physically alive, but her life-spark was flickering and felt weak. It dimmed even as he watched, and he realized what he was seeing: it was trying to separate from the body.

She'd made the decision to die.

He fell to his knees, rested his forehead on the edge of the table, and raged inside that he couldn't even shed a tear or grieve. The swords, cast down, called to him. Silent instructions came from somewhere, which he followed in a daze. He rolled the woman gently onto her back, pulled his weapons to him, and laid them crosswise across her chest.

A white light engulfed her body. Her breath stilled. Her life-spark went dark, and a barely-recognizable breath of wind lifted from her to dissipate quickly into the stagnant and stinking air.

(Continue here.)

Pheonix stood and bitterly looked down at the body.

Is that supposed to comfort me? He thought sickly. *That sometimes all I can do is grant the mercy of death? Is this Justice?*

He let out a sharp breath to steady himself.

Malol and Bedaestael were unusually quiescent as Pheonix recovered them and turned his back on the table — to find himself facing an army of emaciated bodies.

Frightened, starving, beaten sapients of all species were climbing out of the boxes that Malol had stolen the energy from, crowding into the space around Pheonix but never getting too close. Without direction, they milled about in confusion and fear.

He gestured sharply at the door, raw from all he'd experienced in the last hour, but holding himself fiercely in check from taking it out on them. He couldn't squash the slight edge of impatience, though.

"Well? Run! There's a portal outside and a Ranger squad to help."

After a moment's hesitation, a few of them took tentative steps toward the door. Then, in a wave, they poured past him.

"Try not to kill each other on the way out!" he called over the racket of pounding feet. It was a small hallway. Hopefully no one would get trampled.

The omnipresent humming cut off abruptly.

Engine's down. But the bastard probably has an escape route, so I'd better get up there.

From long practice experiencing too much Creator-damned horror, he turned his mind to the next task. The rage and sickness bubbled within him still, but there was no use in focusing on things that had happened and couldn't be changed. He'd have to content himself with taking it out on the Red Mage Master.

The wall between the slave pens and the foyer dissipated, flooding the space with light. The backup squad set about coordinating the retrieval of the formerly enslaved people. By whatever method the backup squad had removed the wall, it was less his concern now than getting up those three flights of stairs.

Rather than trying to squeeze past the fleeing bodies, he jumped over them, using his wings to glide past and into the very small open space behind the second Ranger squad.

Pheonix dashed up the stairs, his long legs easily taking the steps two and three at a time. The staircase curled around a central column, and every fifty steps or so a door opened to his left. Each level was labeled, but he knew his goal was at the top, so he continued upward.

With four doors behind him, the staircase leveled out into a short, narrow hallway, beyond which was a much larger room.

What registered immediately as he reflexively ducked back into the stairs was: *that's a lot of soldiers.*

A barricade of furniture and bodies blocked a final staircase at the far end of the rectangular-shaped room. This was almost the tip of the pyramid, with the room narrowing sharply towards the ceiling. Not to a full point, though; there was still one room above.

But directly ahead lay the Red Mage Master's most elite guards and Pheonix's final obstacle to the master himself.

Barely pulling himself out of sight in time to avoid a barrage of heavy fire (which actually caused him to skip down a few steps to avoid ricochets), Pheonix considered his options. They wouldn't come into the hallway after him, so he had a few moments, but only that — the faint sounds of boots and shouts echoed from below, and he wasn't about to chance that it was reinforcements from one of the doorways he hadn't gone in.

These elite guards and their tactics had been expected, however. And Chani, who had outfitted him, was not nice to the failed mercenaries, exceptionally brutal thuggish slavers and even washout Rangers that tended to populate the inner circle of men like the Red Mage Master. The cruelest of the cruel, but ambitionless, content with scraps tossed at them by their superior as long as it meant they didn't have to do real work and could languish in their own depravity.

Reaching into his fold-space, Pheonix pulled out a very heavy green crystal the size of two of his fists put together. He leaned around the corner, grimacing as a few dozen stray rounds caught his shield, and chucked it. It shattered into a fine mist that hung in the air, catching incoming rounds like a spider's web snagging gnats.

After one last delve into fold-space, out came the 2-0 again.

He waited, listening. First came a high pitched whining, ramping up in energy, like a turbine winding up to full speed. Then a deep, basso *thoom* shook through his very bones as the thousands of rounds that had been suspended in the crystal mist shot back, using their own drained kinetic energy. Handy thing to have for a solo operator against overwhelming odds.

The rounds tore into and through the furniture (and anyone taking cover behind it). Men in thick, hardpoint armor ducked behind marble columns. Most of those standing in the center, about half the total forces, were shredded by their own returned fire. But that wasn't enough to even the odds. Pheonix shot one round of the 2-0 into the small space and leaped down a few steps to avoid the rush of air and debris from the resulting explosion.

He waited for the initial tumult to die down, a mere heartbeat, then ducked into the room. The space was filled with dust and fine pink mist riding on the smoke billowing from multiple fires. Rounds still whined past his head, and studded explosions sounded in parts of the room he couldn't see, some too close for comfort.

Moving with the ease of a shark through water, he took shots at whatever presented itself. His real targets were the heavies, and while most of them were more than likely taken out in the crystal attack, he wasn't about to bank on that. Men groaned and screamed all around him. The choking, thick smoke made it hard to see.

Suddenly, his vision shifted, and he saw blurred shapes of light that stood out in the gloom.

"Null field waning — get in there and stop him from porting out, Justice-zero!" Chani's voice crackled through his comm, hoarse with desperation.

"On it," he replied, incapable of being anything but calm.

His adversaries regrouped, the element of surprise having lost its effect. Shots ricocheted off his shield. Finding cover, he slipped the 2-0 caliber back into fold-space and drew his pistols. He needed mobility, and he wasn't going to get that with the oversized rifle — as satisfying as it would have been to blow the Red Mage Master to smithereens.

A head popped around a corner to his far side, and he blew it off, splattering the brains of its unfortunate owner in an abstract flower across the wall. The decapitated body slumped forward. Staying low to conserve his shield — as low as a seven-foot armored monstrosity with wings could ever be — Pheonix kept on the move to avoid the flank attack he knew he was in for as soon as they got organized.

He kept taking targets of opportunity as he moved. Two men stumbled backwards against the wall in front of him and lost their heads in gouts of blood and bits. Three more ran out from behind them, ready. Their rounds took slivers out of his shield, spun off into walls and piles of debris, spraying him with micro shrapnel.

Before he knew it, he was there.

Adrenaline pumping through his body like a second heartbeat, Pheonix dashed up the final set of stairs.

TWENTY-EIGHT
I'm Done Being Hurt By You

Before he'd even reached the open doorway, he was already taking in his surroundings. As expected, it was a tetrahedron room with mostly transparent walls, making the golden columns studding its length seem out of place. A couple of gilded cages in one corner held slaves lounging on pillows. In fact, there were a lot of pillows, absolutely everywhere. And golden rugs. A lot of gold, and rare materials, and statues, and gems. More pointless, sloppy opulence. Pheonix's brain rejected absorbing any more of it.

The Red Mage Master stood before his newly birthed portal at the far end of the room.

He was a very old human: ashen-skinned, clothed in dark robes (a color achieved with blood, as red mages were so fond of reminding everyone), and wearing enough golden and gemmed accessories to make a dwarf salivate. The mage's long, stringy hair was somehow coiffed with jewels. He was muttering and gesturing with his hands, destroying or tossing small objects as layers of magic settled over him — shields.

Low and quick, Pheonix found cover behind a golden column near the door.

"So, boy, you finally found your way up here," the Red Mage Master drawled without turning to look. "Don't be surprised that I know about you; we all do now. The God Who

Isn't. Amusing, if I do say so myself. Supposedly chosen as a God and yet you can still be crushed; while I have the power of a God and have not been chosen. Well, not yet, anyway."

Pheonix rolled his eyes and holstered one pistol, drawing Bedaestael. He came around the column, aiming steadily with the pistol as he advanced.

A massive fireball caught him on the chest. He walked through the flames unheeding, trailing smoke, and pulled the trigger. The kinetically-propelled round blasted through the portal, disrupting it ... and kept going, through whatever translucent material the walls were crafted from. Crackling energy lanced out from the portal as it catastrophically failed in a detonation of magical power. Nearby pieces of frippery and furniture were blitzed to pieces and carried on the shock-wave that blew Pheonix's hair back from his face.

Something that was impossible to make out in the smoke from the portal hit Pheonix with the force of a small shuttle. He slammed into one of the gilded cages, distantly hearing its occupant shriek. The blow knocked the wind out of him and he saw stars. He caught a glimpse of a long white shape: a marble pillar.

The Red Mage Master grimaced. While not standing close enough to be directly harmed by the aftermath of the portal's destruction, he clearly hadn't been expecting it. He smoothed his ruffled robes.

"Immune to magic, hmm? Well, you certainly aren't immune to objects *conjured* by magic," The Red Mage Master grated, bashing Pheonix about like a rag doll with pillar after pillar, as they shattered on Pheonix's armored body and he conjured new ones. "Wielding elven magical blades, with Ranger armor and technology. I'm flattered that they sent such a precise assassin, but so young. Even I don't press my soldiers into service until they are old enough to squirt."

Pheonix cartwheeled into a pile of pillows, his kinetic shield sparing him the majority of the damage but unable to fully absorb such intense impact. He struggled to stand but was too dizzy. The Red Mage Master didn't give him even a moment to recover — the column came down on him again and again, denting the floor beneath. An incessant beeping sounded in Pheonix's ear, warning that a shield overload was imminent.

Kinetic shields worked by spreading the kinetic energy of an impact across a generated field, but that energy had to go somewhere, so it was converted into power and stored in the generator's battery and secondary tanks. However, there was only so much energy it could absorb before it would need to be released — which the Rangers gleefully worked into the design of the thing.

"What *are* the Rangers doing these days?" the Red Mage Master continued blithely in between the slams, a smile in his voice. "Child labor, unauthorized attacks. I must take it up with the Chosen next time I am in Terelath. This can't be good for the balance."

Mentioning the balance rekindled Pheonix's rage and gave him strength. The column lifted to strike the final blow that would pierce his shield and plaster him all over the floor, and he raised his deutronium arm. Nether-flame licked out of the seams, responding to his fury.

No, Pheonix thought, *I'm done being hurt by you.*

The column came down — and cracked.

Pheonix stumbled out of the rubble, clutching Malol and Bedaestael.

"Well, you certainly live up to your name," the Red Mage Master said calmly, though now his voice held a slight edge.

The mage began conjuring objects and throwing them at Pheonix, who summoned the last of his strength, riding on adrenaline, to break into a full-out run towards the mage. A conjured-and-flung object careened into the doorway behind

Pheonix, bringing a screaming end to the guards finally making their way up from the lower floors.

The Red Mage Master winced. "Oh, no! They were expensive. You brat!"

With the beeping following him like an annoying alarm, Pheonix dodged around the objects that the mage continued to conjure up around him. Flailing his arms, tossing rings, and destroying his immaculate up-do, the mage finally lost his composure.

"*Why — won't — you — let — me — KILL YOU?!*"

Pheonix ducked behind one of the spinning conjurations and released his shield overload. The beeping died off, and the mage (who didn't have sense enough to dodge) took his own conjuration in the face as the stored kinetic force slammed outward. Knocked back by the object, he was then put on his ass by the wave of energy following it.

Pheonix closed in.

Malol burned in hungry anticipation. The Red Mage Master, completely disheveled and consumed by wild fear, had no snide words left as he scrambled backwards with all the grace of a fish floundering on dry land. His mouth flapped but nothing emerged.

Pheonix reared back and, with Malol, speared the mage to a statue of himself. His precious shields were gone in a moment, all magical defenses devoured by the sword, and a keening whine of pain emerged from his contorted face.

Not only did his defenses dissipate into the blade's insatiable hunger, but also his own magic, ripped from his soul. His connection to his patron God, Bast … his connection to the Weave …

Gone.

Pheonix was ready this time, and braced through the storm of imagery — the worst excesses and most deplorable evils. He'd accepted that this was his fate, to relive every moment of every life taken with these swords, regardless of how shitty a life it may have been.

Blank eyes stared into blank eyes as the storm faded — one consumed by a fear beyond sapient comprehension and one as vastly cold as the universe itself.

"You ... you can't do this," the Red Mage Master wheezed finally. "You're just a boy, a false God, you — "

Pheonix had no interest in hearing more of what this thing thought of him.

"*You have been judged,*" Pheonix growled, "*and found lacking.*"

Bedaestael cut upwards underneath the mage's rib cage, shredding his heart; and beyond that, tearing into the deepest reaches of the blackened soul to rend it to nothing.

Leaving the body pinned to the statue of itself, a grisly decoration, Pheonix stumbled away, dry heaving. He bent and vomited black bile, shuddering as it ravaged his body. This was worse than the other two — this time, there were moments when he couldn't think because of the violence of the flood.

When he was finally empty, he straightened and wiped his mouth with a trembling hand. He turned his gaze back to the corpse.

It's over.

"Can you ... let us out?" a timid voice asked from across the room. The slaves in the golden cages, knocked together in the scuffle, were holding hands through the bars. They watched him with terrified eyes.

He took a step toward them and the adrenaline propping him up bled away abruptly, bringing him to his knees. He'd simply taken too much damage, had stretched himself too thin. The world spun, which annoyed him.

The sound of boots reached his ears, muffled and far away. He thought of Malol and Bedaestael, then fumbled for his pistols with hands that felt like putty.

"Oh, Creator," a familiar voice said. "That's ugly."

Me or him? he wanted to ask, but the words wouldn't come out.

Hands pulled at him — he tried to fight them, but he was too weak and couldn't think straight.

"Hey, hang on, kid," the voice said again.

Chani? he thought sluggishly.

"Medic," he managed to slur, then everything went black.

TWENTY-NINE
Farcical Sacrifice

Incessant beeping pulled Pheonix from no-mind.

He'd woken up in his quarters on HQ a little under twenty-four hours after passing out on Krasynth II. He'd still been in one piece, though he'd been sore as all hell. The Nether-flame was still lurking in the cracks of his arm, which wasn't ideal, but it seemed to be quiescent, so he figured he'd deal with it when he could.

Chani had visited shortly after he'd woken up to inform him that he was free to do whatever until the AAR, and it'd been a few days since then.

He sat up and swung his long legs over the edge of his cot, jabbing the comm interface — the source of the beeping — with a forefinger as he did so.

"Pheonix! Let's go! We need to get to the AAR, *now*," Chani's voice belted through. She sounded agitated.

"I'll be out in five," Pheonix said.

The location of the After-Action Review was yet another faceless conference room, and he was apparently the last one to arrive. The Commanding-General was sitting at the head of the long table. The other people at the table were Steele, Chani, a grizzled old Captain who Pheonix didn't recognize, Captain Frendel, and the engineer Pheonix met in the Red

Mage Master's ship. Everyone was sitting, except for Steele. Pheonix took a spot next to Chani as unobtrusively as possible.

"After approximately twenty minutes of hard fighting," Steele was saying, "most hostiles moved away from the FOB, which allowed us to begin pushing the line forward. I remained in place supporting the right flank as the noose was closed around the enemy forces."

The Commanding-General nodded and Steele sat. Around the table, each person stood and spoke in turn, dry information about enemy forces, the flow of battle, munitions, and outcomes. Pheonix logged it but didn't find any need to actively listen.

"Overall, it went off without a hitch," Chani finished off her part with a grin. "Other than one personal transport vessel managing to escape."

Pheonix found everyone's eyes suddenly on him.

After a heartbeat of confusion, he stood. He pulled up a mental checklist from his studies on what to include in an AAR report, and, with that as a guideline, recounted what he'd done on Krasynth II.

He sat again, and there was another moment of silence. It was apparently manufactured to get everyone to look at the Commanding-General, who, when he was certain he had everyone's eyes, brought something from under the table. The 2-0 caliber — floating, held in stasis.

"Care to explain," the Commanding-General began drolly, "Commander Abyssterilon, Special Projects Division, why a security risk was sent to combat without my knowledge?"

"He's Ascended," she said flatly. "Risk assessments are null when Ascendency is in the mix."

The Commanding-General's muzzle twitched. "And the curse?"

"Noneffective on Ascended." Chani sounded bored.

"Regardless, this is a Ranger weapon, and anything to do with the Rangers must still go through me." Chani's brows shot up. Pheonix was thoroughly intrigued by the silent battle of wills happening between Chani and the Commanding-General as they stared each other down in the charged silence.

The Commanding-General finally sighed and gestured that the stasis-bound weapon be taken away, though he didn't look happy about it.

Pheonix watched it go, wondering idly how it had been removed from his fold-space.

The Commanding-General folded his stubby paw-hands in front of him. "Krasynth II has been secured, eighty percent of slaves recovered, et cetera, et cetera. Congratulations on completing the mission without dying."

The comm unit in the middle of the table lit up unexpectedly, instantly drawing everyone's attention.

The Commanding-General activated the interface. "This had better be good," he said. "I'm in a meeting."

"Apologies, sir," the voice on the other end said. "But … uh … it *is* important. The Chosen are calling for Lord Pheonix to be brought before them immediately. On charges of murder."

On the heels of and slightly overlapping this shocking statement, a scuffle could be heard from behind the door. A familiar voice growled something unintelligible — Chani leapt up and the door slid open ahead of her. Pheonix leaned to peek: Sabot had someone in a uniform that Pheonix's implant denoted as belonging to the Conscience Crew, by the throat, dangling off the floor. Pheonix caught an impression of silver half-discs in the person's hand. Null-bands, used as shackles for prisoners.

Sabot had apparently been acting as a choke point by blocking the door, because the person dangling from his fist was not the only one in the hallway.

"Sabot," Chani commanded. "Down."

Sabot instantly released the person, who crumpled to the floor, gagging and coughing. Chani knelt and snatched the null-bands roughly from them.

Pheonix could clearly hear her say threateningly in a low voice, "If you insist on playing this out to its end, we'll be the ones to escort him. *You don't get to touch him.*"

She snapped to her feet and handed the null-bands to Sabot, jerking her head at Pheonix. She didn't look back at him, but the expression on her face promised death.

Sabot approached Pheonix, holding out the null-bands. "Hate to do this to you, kid, but we'll get it worked out," he said, sounding gruff but genuinely regretful.

Pheonix looked between the two of them. He'd been watching thus far distantly interested in the drama, but they were actually serious. They were actually going to bring him up on murder charges. For what? Kills during a legitimate op? Brutality? Anger surged through him, but he held out his wrists for Sabot to secure.

Only one way to find out.

With Chani on one side and Sabot on the other, Pheonix was taken via a long, quiet shuttle ride to the depot. The three of them and their armed escort shuffled into a bug all their own to ride to the surface. Pheonix simmered the whole way, not even caring to look outside.

They landed on the planetside depot and took a crystal to the Seat of the Chosen. Inside the amphitheater was utter chaos. Among the representatives, only a small percentage were self-proclaimed evil-aligned, so the majority of the stands were filled with celebrating people, with a small corner screaming for retribution. And in the center of it all, ranged about the base of the Obelisk, were the Chosen.

The wrongness of the place hit Pheonix the same way it had the last time he'd been in the presence of the Chosen. At this point, he couldn't be sure if his reaction was a flashback or something he legitimately sensed about them.

The escort stopped Pheonix at a small mark on the floor.

"Pheonix," said the same head Chosen who'd ordered him around last time he'd been there. "As a genetic experiment, it is impossible for you to be a God. Though the Obelisk spoke, we believe it was mistaken and misled by your unique, confusing makeup. Given that your Ascended protected status has been revoked, your charges are as follows."

Pheonix shifted his brain to logging mode, putting each asinine accusation — everything he'd done on the three legitimate operations he'd been on, now reframed as crimes to fit the narrative of him being a dangerous murderer — into his memory banks. His conscious mind raced, trying to fit data points together.

The Red Mage Master's words came back to him: *"I must take it up with the Chosen next time I am in Terelath. This can't be good for the balance."*

His gaze settled on each Chosen in turn. None would meet his eye.

They knew what they were doing was wrong.

They knew.

He glanced back at Chani.

*You're planning on just standing there and watching, Commander? These were **your** operations,* he said with his eyes. *Hell, you Rangers **forced** me to go to Krasynth II, unprepared, and then let one of your own try to make me take the downfall. Did I make a mistake in trusting you?*

The furrow of her brow, the flexing of her jaw muscle, the tendons standing out in her neck, and her hands balled into tight fists — all signs that Chani was pissed. Her gaze met his and her mouth tightened into a thin line.

You're saying you have no power here, Pheonix realized, and turned back to the Chosen. *Right. This is part of the system we vowed to destroy. If it was so easy, you'd have done it yourself long ago.*

His eyes traced the Obelisk behind the line of its Chosen, his hatred for it stoking the cold inferno in the pit of his stomach.

The head Chosen prattled on about Pheonix's supposed crimes, but Pheonix no longer cared to take it in as data. He stared at the Obelisk, burning it into his vision while letting himself fall into that icy flame at his core. Hushed, uneasy murmuring from the representative stands reached his ears.

If even the mighty Commander Abyssterilon can't speak up to defend one 'trainee' in this cesspool — the thought was clear despite Pheonix's raging need for retribution — *and no one else in this Creator-damned place will, then fine.*

*Make Justice your farcical sacrifice if you so choose — but that means you're playing by **my** rules.*

"Your sentence is," the head Chosen was saying, "that, as a wrongfully escaped slave, you are still the property of your previous owner. Therefore, you will be returned to E-Pegasi 1 to —"

Having reached the limit of what he could tolerate, Pheonix jerked his arms apart, shattering the null-bands.

Pheonix's hatred and will manifested in a distortion — a ripple of power that arrowed for the Obelisk. Streaking across the ground, it left smoldering cracks of cerulean in its wake, flipped the Chosens' table through pure kinetic force, and slammed into the base of the Obelisk.

The whole Seat of the Chosen rocked with the force of Justice's power colliding with the Obelisk. The representative stands erupted into chaos; people screaming and knocking each other over while attempting to flee. For a heartstopping moment it seemed like the whole place would come down.

The Chosen themselves had gathered, cowering, around the base of the Obelisk as though it would protect them ...

... which proved to be a poor idea in short order.

With a deafening *crack!*, a jagged fissure crawled up the Obelisk and stopped halfway to its tip.

On the heels of the sound, a flash of light emanated from the Obelisk — silhouetting, just for a moment, the twisted shape of a body within.

The rumbling ceased and sudden silence descended. Even the representatives had frozen in place, transfixed.

The Chosen who had been listing Pheonix's crimes straightened as though speared on a rod. Dragged by an invisible tether, he slammed back against the Obelisk. The rest of the Chosen followed on his heels, arranged about the Obelisk and suspended like a fisherman's catch. The silence was only broken by Chani whispering into her comm intently, likely only heard by Pheonix:

"What do you mean the Elders are gone? — Look, I've got a situation here — wait, *what*?"

CRASH!

Three figures created a hole in the domed ceiling of the Seat and came to rest floating around the Obelisk's tip like a living crown.

"I found them," Chani said into her comm shakily.

Pheonix was frozen, fighting the rage that was enveloping him and calling for him to take his swords and *Judge them all.* He was aware of what was happening around him, but had locked himself down. The part of his conscious, calculating mind that rode above the rage felt that if he allowed himself to move, he wouldn't be able to stop himself from calling Malol and Bedaestael to him.

It wasn't time for that yet.

The Chosen opened their mouths and spoke as one.

"*Lord Pheonix is to be made an Executioner,*" they said, "*and afforded all the rights therein. We have spoken.*"

The Availeon Chosen, huddled around its base and tied there by nothing visible, were released none too gently and collapsed in a heap. Most lay unmoving, though some groans could be heard from the pile.

And the Ranger Chosen, those called the Elders, remained floating around the cracked Obelisk's apex.

The Obelisk roared:

HEAR THIS.
LISTEN WELL, AND ABANDON THY FALLACY. BEFORE YE STANDS THE CREATOR-CHOSEN JUSTICE. ACCEPT THESE WORDS, LEST YE BE JUDGED.

The screaming power drained from the Obelisk and it became a silent monument once more. The Elders dropped from their height, landing atop the other Chosen to a chorus of pained grunts.

Chani and Sabot rushed past Pheonix to help the Elders up.

"No, they're at Availeon," Chani said into her comm. "I don't fucking know how they got here! They just came crashing through the ceiling!" She listened for a moment, then said, "The Obelisk, you asshole. Shut up, we'll talk about this when I get back. Damage control."

Pheonix remained rooted to the spot, battling himself. Moment by moment he was gaining control, the tenseness of his muscles settling, the urge to grasp his swords fading. As his mind finally cleared, he gasped in profound relief and dropped to one knee.

"Pheonix."

Pheonix turned.

Chani stood by the bug. For the first time, her gaze on him was guarded. "C'mon."

Pheonix was tense throughout the ride back. Nothing was said until they boarded the shuttle back to Ranger HQ.

"Why didn't you tell me about my genetics?" Pheonix asked.

"I don't know what the hell they're looking at to justify this fucking clown show, but we haven't gotten *anything* useable back from your scans," Chani said so scathingly that it immediately tamed Pheonix's anger. "They *lied*. Though it's true that you were probably created by genetic experimentation, you yourself are not what we would categorize as a true genetic experiment. By all accounts, you aren't possible. If a person created your body, how they did it is beyond me. Though I get the sense the Availeon Chosen know more on that subject than they're letting on."

Chani lifted a brow, looking at the Elders in the shuttle. Pheonix followed her gaze, realizing that this was the first time he'd seen them in person.

"We were not informed," Zeta, one of the Elders, said ominously. "Whatever they found — if, in fact, anything at all — was kept among themselves."

Zeta was a tall, lean Mahji with dark skin, long, neatly pulled back white hair, and a groomed white moustache and beard. He wore Mahji ceremonial clothing and had a royal, commanding air to him. It was no wonder he was the de facto leader for the three Chosen assigned to the Rangers — nicknamed the 'Elders' by the Seconds of Terelath as a subtle indignity, as it was known that to be stationed on Ranger HQ was the equivalent of political exile for anyone serving the Accord.

It didn't take much to guess why these Chosen had ended up 'exiled' to the Rangers, who famously butted heads with the Obelisk at every opportunity. The disdain and anger written across each Elders' face there in that secure shuttle was proof enough.

'Chosen' was not a lightly-given moniker. The Obelisk didn't ask for volunteers. It demanded complete obeisance, and even the freedom of death was denied them.

"We have ways of getting the information we want," dead-eyed, serious Loren said flatly. She was a famously sour-dispositioned elf, sharp and serious, who wore her traditional Lady robes in visible rejection of her role as Chosen. She was fair-skinned, and her dark brown hair was cropped close to her skull.

"The last time something like this happened, the Creator disposed of all Chosen involved as retribution for their iniquity," Chani said.

"The Creator's wrath is none of our concern," Zeta said. "We were not involved in whatever thought process brought the Availeon Chosen to the conclusion that they should try *Justice* for murder."

Chani shook her head and looked out the window, indicating she would not be pursuing it further.

Pheonix accessed:

There is only one time in recorded history that the Chosen were en masse destroyed by the Creator. A trifecta of dark elves, slavers and pirates were allowed to rampage across the entire arm of one galaxy, resulting in thousands of planets subjugated and trillions killed. It has been remembered as the largest genocide known to date. The Chosen of the time facilitated said genocide through political indecision, leaving the trifecta to their own devices, ostensibly to 'preserve the balance' by limiting interference.

The Rangers were held in check, not given the green light to interfere at all until there was an attack on a high elven post orbiting an unstable sun. After suffering a total rout in the resulting space battle, one remaining dark elf ship turned to cowards' tactics. Charging the core with dark energy, the ship suicided into the sun and shattered not only the entire arm of that galaxy but the life-stream and all souls within.

This tragedy later came to be known as 'Battle 451.'

Enraged by their hubris, Spiraea attacked the dark elf home planet, transforming it into a wasteland of poisons and storms. She transported every dark elven soul and all their ships to their newly broken planet and left them there. As punishment for their part in the loss of so many souls, the Creator executed the Chosen involved in the bureaucratic stonewalling — with the notable exception of one.

Ren, the first Chosen instated by the Obelisk and first 'Elder' of the Rangers, had actively lobbied against ignoring the dark elves' actions, but was drowned out by the other Chosen planetside on Availeon.

Pheonix looked at the one Elder who hadn't spoken: Ren.

By all appearances, he was a small hominin child, perhaps a pre-teen. Deathly pale and completely hairless, he had blood-red runes covering all visible skin. His large eyes were of the same color. He was dressed in undecorated robes of a thick fabric and always wore a blank expression, tinged with a ghostly sadness.

As if he'd felt Pheonix's gaze, Ren's eyes flicked up to settle on Pheonix. The tiniest knowing smile curled his small mouth. A sudden intense spell of vertigo forced Pheonix to break eye contact, and by the time he'd recovered and looked back, the boy was staring downward again.

Confusion over the interaction dominated Pheonix's mind for the rest of the journey.

As the shuttle docked at the Ranger HQ, its occupants stood with the anticipation of disembarking. The Elders left immediately, though Chani hung back — as did Sabot, who turned to face Pheonix.

"Everyone will soon know you, if they didn't previously," Sabot said to Pheonix, who blinked in confusion, "which is going to cause you a shitload of trouble very shortly. You've been thrust into the political landscape of a universe that uses politics like a weapon. And, unfortunately, the Rangers are no exception to that. You'll be overrun with clan invites the moment we step off this shuttle, and they won't stop until you've chosen one. So I propose a solution: join Barandor."

Pheonix glanced at Chani, unsure of how to react.

Chani crossed her arms over her chest and sighed. "It's the truth," she said. "And you wouldn't go wrong being a part of Barandor. Frankly, if anyone deserves to have Justice among their ranks, it's them."

Pheonix accessed: *The Barandor clan; a small House, though not a minor one. Barandor is the only clan to have the distinct honor of sitting directly under all three Houses equally, making them somewhat of a major House among minor Houses. The Barandors are known to be honorable and well-respected, with many notable members.*

"That's a bold statement," Pheonix remarked.

"They deserve it. Barandor is the House of our heroes, after all."

"So why aren't you a member?"

Chani made a face and side-eyed him. "Take a guess."

Pheonix could take several, though he wasn't sure which would be correct. Some quick accessing informed him that inclusion in Barandor was invite-only, as opposed to other clans who were open to applications. That meant that Chani had never been asked. As to why she'd never been asked … Pheonix had no clue at all.

I suppose the scion of the Abyssterilon clan couldn't very well up and join another clan, Pheonix thought.

He thought for a moment. "Well, I'd certainly like to avoid as much politicking as I possibly can. Will Barandor shield me from that within the Rangers?"

"If you are recognized as a Barandor," Sabot said, "it will cow all but the most obnoxious of Rangers, who I'm certain you're capable of dealing with on your own. So, in essence, yes."

"I suppose I have no reason to refuse, then," Pheonix said.

The helmeted man held out a hand, and Pheonix grasped his forearm.

"Welcome," Sabot said. He could be mistaken, but Pheonix thought he heard a smile in the voice behind the full helmet.

Chani led Pheonix to her quarters.

The main area was a large, well-lit space decorated in silvers and light blues, with a navy blue carpet. On the far wall was a large L-shaped couch with its back to a wall. In front of it was a small table, and on the opposite wall was a sizeable screen. A faux 'window' displayed a starscape environment, since real portholes or windows were a structural weakness and therefore scarce on Ranger-made vessels.

To Pheonix's right was a small kitchen and dining area with a replicator. Holo-pictures and vids covered the wall between the replicator and the couch. The whole space felt cozy and calm, contrasting with Chani's usual direct and intense energy.

Frankly, he was surprised she'd invited him into her personal space. Maybe this was an expression of trust, an apology for not being able to publicly support him against the Chosen.

The more he thought about it, the less angry he was — with her, at least. Cracking the Obelisk had been immensely satisfying, even if he hadn't exactly done it on purpose. Though he still hated the fucking thing, he'd have to content himself with finishing the job later ... once he had a better grasp on what the consequences of doing so would entail.

He turned to his left to see a long silver table illuminated by many lights, turning the surface virtually shadowless. On it sat various tools, bits of weaponry, metal, and plastics, all scattered between larger, half-finished chunks of Chani's personal tinkering projects.

Among the randomness of the table, a brain in a glass tube with wires trailing out of it particularly caught Pheonix's attention. On the far end of the table was an intricate metal arm bolted to the wall, and a box that Pheonix assumed was a fold-space storage unit by its shape. A lighted glass case (inside which were what appeared to be military awards, commendations, and various other trinkets) stood next to a doorway that led into a dark hallway.

"Hello," a polite mechanical voice said next to him. Pheonix jerked in surprise.

"Hello," Pheonix responded to the general direction of the greeting, not wanting to be rude.

A voc panel hooked to the brain lit up. "Are you a friend of the Commander's? We get so few guests."

"This is Pheonix, Jeeves," Chani said over her shoulder. She'd kicked off her boots by the door and was in the kitchen doing something.

"Oh, it is so good to finally meet you! I've heard so much!" enthused the brain.

"It's nice to meet you too, Jeeves," Pheonix said tiredly. It had been a long day.

"Leave him be for now, Jeeves," Chani said as she turned around again, carrying several bottles and glasses. "You'll have plenty of time to talk later, but I need him for now."

"Roger, Commander!"

She made her way to the couch, which she flumped onto without ceremony. She then poured a liquid that shone with a subtle rainbow luminescence equally into two delicate crystal flutes, curling her long legs underneath her.

"C'mon, kid, make yourself comfortable," she called to Pheonix, who was still hovering by the entryway.

Pheonix took off his boots, leaving them both by hers, and crossed the room to sit next to her.

"This is the same stuff you had at Penny's," she said as he settled, handing him the other crystal flute. "It doesn't travel or keep well when it's removed from the flower and it's hideously expensive, but hey, times like this you gotta get out the good booze."

Pheonix took a sip and let its calming effect wash over him. He needed it.

"So, welcome to mi casa," Chani said after a comfortable silence. "This is the main space, and back there are the bedrooms — mine, my daughter's room, and the spare room that VI-2935 is staying in. Doesn't seem VI is home, though. My daughter's on mission. And you met Jeeves."

Pheonix hadn't known that Chani had a daughter, and didn't know who VI-2935 was, either. As he thought about it, he realized he hardly knew anything about Chani, the person, at all. He knew plenty about 'Commander Abyss.'

"Why are we here?" Pheonix asked.

"Couple reasons: the first being that this is the safest place for you right now," Chani said bluntly. "As you know, you were already a person of interest to a variety of groups across the metacosm, but it's about to get much worse."

"You think they'll attack me on HQ?"

Chani made an unsure noise in the back of her throat as she took a sip from her flute. "After what you did to the Obelisk? Not likely an *attack*, the kind you're familiar with. Even the most arrogant Fug by now would have at least some idea of what you're capable of in combat. I doubt they'd want to take you on, head-to-head. It'd be a waste of resources. But if you make yourself too available, they'll certainly try to back you into a social or political corner, and you're not ready to deal with that shit yet. Hiding beneath my coattails is a good way to avoid it, for the moment." She grinned shamelessly at him.

"I can't argue that. I can't stay under your coat forever, though."

Chani met his eyes with a calculating look, then sighed. "You're not wrong. However, now you also have Barandor, though that only removes most of the Rangers from the playing field. Additionally, the Ascended transcend sapient politics. As you come into that power, you won't have to bother meeting your detractors on their level. Up to you if you want to do your own independent studies on politics — I'll certainly help — but my instinct is that it'll resolve itself soon enough. You're better off focusing on becoming Justice."

Becoming Justice, he thought with a twinge of frustration. *You say that as if it's so simple.*

"What's the other reason?" he asked.

"I invited some friends — don't worry, people you already know — to hang out."

"... Hang out?"

"Okay, fine; we have some things to talk about, but I swear there will be food and drink and maybe even some fun after. It's been nonstop shit for the last few weeks, and we all could use a breather."

"If I'm supposed to rest, I'd rather do it in my own quarters."

"Denied. If I let you go, you'll start working again."

Pheonix stared at her, wondering how much she knew of his investigation, but her expression gave nothing away.

"Ah, speaking of which —" she said, blatantly changing the subject, and dug around under the table in front of the couch. She brought up a datapad and held it out to him. "We should do this before the others arrive. Stick your paw on that."

Pheonix pressed his palm to the screen without taking the datapad from her. It flashed and a list scrolled by as he removed his hand. Chani flipped it around to skim through the list on the screen.

"Hokay, let's see. At the current rate of bounty, with your kills, minus ammo, plus recovered assets, special bonuses …" she rattled off some math that meant nothing without context. "Your total for this last mission is one-point-five million, give or take, added to the one billion and one you already had. Do you need to requisition anything? What was lacking in your last mission? Might as well handle it now while we're accessing your account."

Pheonix thought for a moment. "I had limited ability to engage the enemy at range, especially while under fire. Firearms are great when I can use them, and grenades are effective on groups, but there were several instances where using either was not an option. Also, a more sophisticated form of tracking and enemy movement management would have been helpful, in general." He was briefly annoyed again, remembering the Mistress and her dancing around him.

"So more range, and better target management. Well, the latter is easy; an eye implant and a VI would solve that. For the former … you want range without it being another gun? We've got punch-knives and stunners but they aren't reliably fatal. What about plain old throwing knives? With your eye and strength, I don't think you'd have a problem getting kills with them. They're precisely targetable, can be fatal or nonfatal, and they're silent. Always a bonus. And we can attach them to your wrist for easy access."

"Both sound good. Oh, and can I get solid, non-explosive rounds for that rifle?"

Chani looked up sharply. "You want to keep it after the bitchfit Fuzzy threw?"

"I'm Ascended. You really think he's going to tell me no?"

"Good point. I'll requisition it and your ammo." Chani said with a laugh, then fiddled with the datapad and set it down. "Done. And you have enough left over to buy a small colony if you wanted to."

"Let's not. Speaking of that weapon, how did they get it out of my fold-space?"

"Astra. Personal fold-spaces are connected to the Armory, and through that connection, Astra can access them. That's how requisitioning works; what goes in must come out. It also helps to control our weaponry and keep a tighter rein on it so it doesn't get into hands that would misuse it. It's not a perfect system; people are the weak link, but it's the best we can do right now."

"Oh, and Chani?"

"Yes?"

"Really? Grenades with legs?"

Chani snorted into her drink. "You're lucky I didn't give you the squirrels."

A trilling beep sounded throughout the apartment, emanating from nowhere and everywhere, before Pheonix could question that ridiculous statement.

"Come in," Chani called.

At her voice, the many-layered door peeled back, revealing Tyyrulriathula, carrying a small ornate box.

The elf crossed the room and sat on the couch, his grin threatening to split his face.

"Yo," Chani called from across the room. "How was your trip?"

"Fine, as always," Tyyrulriathula responded casually. "Been a while since I've been here but it never really changes, huh?"

"Not really, no," Chani chuckled.

"Tyyrulriathula," Pheonix said in greeting.

"You made it," Tyyrulriathula said. "Well done. Whole worlds across the galaxies are celebrating the death of the Red Mage Master, Ka'Resh."

Oh, another Resh, Pheonix thought, half-annoyed and half-amused.

"You, on your own, and in such a short time," Tyyrulriathula was saying while Pheonix was briefly lost in thought, "have bought us much relief. Both of the eldest brothers of the deplorable Resh clan are dead by your hand. Justice, indeed. The infighting for a new leader will last years — decades, maybe — since the last brother is in hiding and not likely to return. Now what's this I hear about you pissing off the Obelisk again?"

"No, this time it wasn't him," Chani said. "The Availeon Chosen tried to order an execution."

"Is that what all that chaos was about earlier?" Tyyrulriathula asked incredulously. "The Elders out of nowhere shooting through twelve layers and breaching the damn hull?"

"You heard?"

"Naturally. It was all over every vid feed as soon as it'd happened. Would've caused a panic if Zeta hadn't've gotten a message out — somehow — that they had been called out on an emergency."

"Ugh. Hopefully they learn their lesson *this* time, since we've forgotten our history," Chani muttered into her glass.

"The Elders weren't expecting punishment," Pheonix reminded her.

"No," Chani said. "But they shouldn't. They weren't involved. If the Creator seeks further retribution, it will only be doled out to those who deserve it. The Creator isn't in the habit of making examples unnecessarily." She jerked her head to indicate Tyyrulriathula's box. "What's that?"

"Oh, it's for Pheonix." Tyyrulriathula set the box on Pheonix's lap.

Pheonix stared at it.

"Open it," Tyyrulriathula urged.

Pheonix lifted the lid. Inside, resting on a pillow of soft green moss, was a circlet — a garland of the purest white leaves. It looked so delicate, he hesitated to touch it.

Instantly he knew what it was. The King and Queen of the elves wore something similar. The significance sunk in; the elves were recognizing him as Ascended. He was both one of them and very different.

Pheonix had never been given anything beyond the purely pragmatic: books, weapons, armor. And while he appreciated those things for their usefulness, they were hardly given out of affection. It was necessity. Survival. He understood that, and so he accepted it.

Yet, he felt nothing for that knowledge. Never having anyone care for him meant nothing. Pragmatic gifts meant nothing. This gift … meant nothing.

For the second time, he wished he could feel something, anything. But as he reached for emotions he didn't understand, he came up empty.

"Thank you," he said solemnly.

"It is from all of us," Tyyrulriathula said, his voice thick. "We have been waiting so long for Justice to return." He cleared his throat, flashed a lopsided grin. "Anyway, it's mostly for show right now. You'll see when we head down to Availeon for the Executioner ceremony."

Chani shoved Tyyrulriathula's shoulder. "I hadn't told him yet."

"Oops," said Tyyrulriathula, but he didn't seem very repentant.

"You know how the Chosen called you an Executioner?" Chani asked Pheonix.

"Yeah, what is that?"

"They're a Creator-appointed entity — usually through Metatron — outside any sapient organization and given the backing of the Creator himself. In other words, their authority supersedes the Rangers, the Chosen, the Accord, all of it. So I guess that's something else you can add to your title.

"That it came through the Chosen is really weird — though literally everything else about you is weird, so I guess it fits right in. Anyway, Executioners are taught a very special, very secret ability called 'sliding,' which allows a person to utilize their will to travel through the life-stream and to another location safely. But it can't be done here because of the null field. So, planetside we go. Probably should get that thing looked at before we go, though," Chani said, gesturing at his cybernetic arm. It still burned internally with Nether-flame.

"Yeah, what the hell is that?' Tyyrulriathula asked.

"I took a Nether-flame burst from a Mistress of the Cult of Blood. Somehow, my arm absorbed it."

"I'm afraid to touch it," said Tyyrulriathula.

"I wouldn't."

The trilling sounded again.

"Come in," Chani called for the second time.

Faran strode into the room, looking tired but wearing a slight smile.

"So," Chani drawled, "how's your Laaaaady?"

Faran wrinkled his nose at her but his smile remained. He sat with them. "She is doing well, thank you, Commander. I am glad to hear your mission went well, my Lord," he said to Pheonix. "We are all better for having such an evil soul removed. I also heard of what the Chosen attempted to do. I hope the Creator punishes them beyond the humiliation they already suffered. Even my Lady Spiraea was upset at your treatment."

Pheonix's brain couldn't process an ancient Ascended caring if something happened to him one way or another. It was an uncomfortable reminder of his supposed Ascendency.

Pragmatism. Survival. That had always been Pheonix's modus operandi.

The trilling sounded a third time.

"How many bodies you got comin' to this little soiree, Chani?" Tyyrulriathula asked with a grin.

"This should be the last one," Chani said, "unless we get an unexpected visitor. Sassy. Come in!"

The last guest pounded into the room in a cloud of ash.

"Pheonix!" Theodric yelled and ran up to him.

"Hello, Theodric."

The little, dirty round face smiled up at him from under a cloud of dusty hair. "Hi Pheonix! Gosh, it seems like it's been forever since I've seen you. They've had me training, did you know that? Since I've been all over the place and nobody ever really wanted me around, Mama Chani told me I need to learn a bunch of stuff before I can go anywhere with you, but that's okay with me because everybody here is so nice and I'm having a lot of fun — "

"Jeeves," Chani called, "can you find a place for Theodric to sit please?"

"Of course, Commander," said Jeeves' disembodied voice.

A panel in the wall slid to one side, pushing out a plastic-covered chair.

"I object!" a deep voice growled from nowhere. "A covered chair! This is the absolute last straw! I will not!"

Pheonix scanned the room unconsciously for enemies, finding nothing new or out of the ordinary.

Chani put her head in her hands. "Oh, not this again," she lamented.

Theodric banged his staff casually on the chair. "Stop that, Barnie," he told it as it continued to protest. "You're embarrassing me in front of my friends."

"My name is not Barnie, it is Barnabus, and *I'm* embarrassing *you*? You — you — you — *dreg!* You embarrass me with your continued existence! And you don't have friends! You have the unfortunate fools that tolerate you, but surely even you must know that eventually they will tire of you as everyone else has — "

The staff suddenly engulfed in flame and the rant cut off mid-sentence, replaced with guttural screaming.

Theodric's eyes burned pure white. White-blue veins pulsed under the skin on his face. "*Shut up*," he buzzed, the crackling of flame given words. "How does it feel to know that my Lord chose this *dreg* over you? You're a mistake and I will take back everything you took for yourself. Then I'll finally be *free of you*."

The flame faded and the staff settled into a resentful silence. Theodric blinked away the white glow and shook his head.

"Thank you, Mama Chani, for the seat. I'd hate to mess up your pretty couch." He hopped up onto the chair. "I'm sorry you had to see that, everyone," he said sheepishly. "Sometimes he forgets himself and I have to punish him."

Chani reached over to rub his back, seemingly heedless of the ash that quickly covered her hand and arm. He flashed her a sad smile.

"That was Barnabus," Theodric went on to explain. "He was a demon that tried to usurp my Lord Schieta after he was imbued with the power of flame. Started calling himself the Lord of Fire. So my Lord trapped him in a staff and gave him to me. I'm to take back what he took. Schieta says I have to earn my status as my Lord's right hand at End of Days."

Pheonix's attention was caught by the phrase 'End of Days,' but wasn't given a chance to ask.

"How were you — doing what you were doing, inside the HQ null field?" Faran asked cautiously.

"What, channeling Schieta?" Theodric giggled. "He's Ascended. Your technology doesn't pose any barrier to him. I don't like doing it, though, because it makes Mama Chani upset. And also, it hurts Barnabus."

"Isn't the whole point to hurt him? You are draining him of his life," Tyyrulriathula said.

"But there is a big difference between fading quietly and calmly into oblivion and plummeting there screaming. I *could* be done with him tomorrow if I spent a protracted amount of time channeling, but that's not what my Lord wants. I am his avatar, and that makes me responsible for representing him on the mortal plane. Let Barnie live out the rest of his life and his punishment in peace."

"He doesn't seem very peaceful," Tyyrulriathula said.

"That's mostly his fault," Theodric said. "He won't accept that he did something wrong. Honestly, if he admitted and accepted that he made a very poor choice and truly wanted to do better, Scheita might actually forgive him. But, it is what it is." He shrugged.

"Chani, you've seen this before?" Tyyrulriathula asked.

"He had to do it a couple times during training. Damn near locked down a whole section of HQ because they weren't expecting an avatar to channel right in our laps. We shouldn't have too much trouble with it now, though I might get a call in a few minutes."

"It seems like everyone has been very busy recently," Pheonix commented.

"It's like I've said before, kid," Chani said, "things are changing. And not just for you … or because of you. Weirdness entirely unrelated to you is happening everywhere."

"Yeah, like what happened to the Accord Secretary-General," Tyyrulriathula said offhandedly.

"What?" Pheonix asked.

"Somebody offed him."

Pheonix looked at Chani, brows raised. "Isn't that a big deal?" he asked.

"Not in the way you're thinking," Chani said. "He wasn't the first to go that way and likely won't be the last. Remember the Kings and Queens of the elves who died every one hundred years? You really think that was because of 'bearing the weight of the elven species'?" Chani scoffed. "Rapidly rotating leadership is one of the oldest destabilization tricks. Easiest way to do that is kill 'em, so assassinations and attempted assassinations are just the bread and butter of anyone in a certain political strata. This stays in this room, in confidence, but functionally the Accord has very little actual power. Why do you think we Rangers are known as their fist? There is no 'Accord army' — *we* would be the closest thing to that. But there's only so much firepower we can muster up under the stranglehold that the Chosen and the Seconds have over the political landscape as a whole — even for ourselves, let alone outsiders. No point in legislating if you can't enforce it."

"If they have that little power, why *do* they exist?"

"Well, if our little rebellion succeeds, we can shift power more evenly across the metacosm, and the Accord is a good entity to act as pass-through. Right now, we have a 'seat of the metacosm' from which all decisions come. Ideally, we'd have a meeting place where every faction could come to be recognized and offer their perspective. Rather than unilateral orders going out, we would want input being gathered and processed. As for what they do currently? Mediation, mostly, and public works — in fact, you'll probably get an Accord adoption package, since you don't have any known family and you're a survivor of enslavement. The Accord isn't totally useless, but they're not living up to their potential."

"You said it wasn't a big deal in the way I was thinking — in what way is it a big deal, then?"

"So, sometime either right after or during Krasynth II, the first go-round, it happened ... I guess while everyone was distracted by the shitshow. The Accord held an emergency session — a provision within the Accord's charter allowing them to meet with all species not known to be aligned with evil — and elected a new Secretary-General: a Zzkerin by the name of Sliv Ω Therin. She was the previous Vice Secretary-General, so it's not entirely a surprise that she got the job.

"But what *was* a surprise was that she immediately purged the entire cabinet and legislative body, closed Accord doors to anyone who hadn't explicitly signed the charter — to be more specific, the part of the charter that asserts that the signers will never associate with self-proclaimed evil species — and then, among the survivors, held general open elections for an entirely new body. All Accord-aligned planets were allowed to put forth their own electors and vote. It's been a wild few days, let me tell you."

"Wouldn't that be taken as consolidating power?" Pheonix asked, alarmed. "Or, a ... hostile takeover?"

"By some, it definitely was. Like, the Availeon-side Chosen. Kinda hard to rig over a hundred thousand planets in one general election, two days after taking the job, though. So, clearly, either she spent a lot of time gathering allies, or this was something within the Accord that had been brewing all along."

"Do we need to do anything about it?"

"What is there to do? It's already happened. All we can do is roll with it. Yes, this *level* of political upheaval is unusual, but coups happen all the time, and they're often remarkably calm. Besides, I know Sliv personally. She's good people."

Pheonix *almost* snorted. So that was Chani's real reason for being so chill. "So, in other words, she's aligned with our goal?"

Chani side-eyed him, then said carefully, "She's an ally, yes. You'll see when you meet her. I think you two will get along *famously*." She ended with a chuckle, then clapped unexpectedly. "Alright! Enough politics! It's bad enough I'm still dealing with the fallout from that *and you*."

"To add to the weirdness," Faran said, "our coordinates are shifting. My Lady is complaining that space is changing. She looks for a planet in a place it's always been and it is gone." He chuckled.

Chani waved an arm at him in a, 'See? There you go' type of gesture. "And with that," she said imperiously, "I want to watch my stories. Jeeves, put on Ghurghen Rockwrather, he's my favorite."

"You invited us here to make us watch your stories?" Tyyrulriathula said, returning from the kitchen area with an armful of booze, which he plonked on the table.

"Of course not," Chani scoffed, "but I'm not about to sit here in silence. What do we want to do? Chill and drink? Snacks? Board games?"

"Board games …?" Faran echoed.

THIRTY
Housing the Feral Flame

"I will assist him to his quarters," Faran said, supporting Tyyrulriathula and dodging the drunken Bladesinger's laughing attempts to poke his face. "And then I must meditate on these latest events. My Lord, I will be there for your ceremony on Terelath, and I wish you a safe journey."

Chani stood and stretched. After two hours of various board and drinking games, she was stiff. "Aaah," she said, "unfortunately I've still got backlash from the op and the Obelisk to deal with tonight. The tedious bullshit. You know, my job. What are your plans?"

Pheonix shrugged. "I have sixteen hours until I must be on the shuttle to Terelath. I was going to go back to my quarters and read."

"A suggestion, if I may? Get that thing checked out, *before* you leave," Chani gestured to his fiery cyber-arm. "Arkiolett's shop is the Gleaming Peridot, in Tinkerer's Villa. Input the command 'find' to your map database and you'll get directions."

"I will," Pheonix said.

"What about you, Theo?" Chani asked Theodric.

"Can I come with you, Pheonix? I haven't seen much of Ranger HQ. It sounds like fun."

"Of course, so long as you stay close."

Theodric stood right up next to him and grinned mischievously.

"Oh," Chani called as they were leaving, "don't mind Ellie and Nellie. They'll float around you and try to get you to buy a bunch of useless shit. They're annoying but harmless. As soon as they see that you know Arkiolett, they'll back off."

"Noted," Pheonix said, not sure who 'Ellie' and 'Nellie' were but figuring he'd find out.

He and Theodric said their goodbyes to Chani and the multi-layered door to her quarters closed behind them. A short shuttle ride brought them to the tech district and then to Tinkerer's Villa. Laid out in a grid pattern, shops vied for attention with neon lights, blaring music, holographic effects, robots, and other flashy technological garbage. Pheonix followed his mental map image, listening with half an ear to Theodric's incessant talking — though, he would admit (only to himself) that the oodl's exuberance was soothing. Though Theodric wasn't *actually* a child, despite his appearance and personality, his childlike innocence was a refreshing change of pace from Pheonix's normal routine of battle, gore, death, politics, ego, and frustration.

For the most part, he also ignored the crowds, even when he was stared at openly, or when a gasp or hurried whispering would float in his wake. Ostensibly, it was all over HQ now that this was Lord Justice, and he expected he'd be looked at as something of a celebrity. At least no one had had the temerity to approach him.

Just as the thought crossed his mind, a body blocked his path. He fought down immediate irritation. Some part of him had hoped he'd make it through without being assaulted, but maybe that had been naïve.

The person standing in Pheonix's way turned out to be a hominin man wearing a brown, hooded cloak (which did not cover his face) and brown traveling clothes. A bound sword hung at his waist.

The man bowed. "I am Jeryl, Acolyte of Acolytes of the worshipers of Justice. I apologize for approaching you without a request from you, but I felt that what I had to say was very important."

Pheonix was confused, but not terribly. He'd expected to run into some of the followers of Justice at some point. If he was indeed Justice, it would only be a matter of time, after all … though at the current stage, Pheonix wasn't entirely sure how worship even worked.

"Continue, Jeryl," Pheonix said.

"Thank you, my Lord. What I have to say is twofold: though you were not around, there were always *people* who made sure that Justice was felt, even in the darkest of hours. That will not change. Before you learn of it, I felt it prudent to inform you that some of your most faithful are engaged in battle on Archaic Earth, and we have been unable to extricate them. It may be something that might need your … personal touch."

"I will take that under advisement, and I appreciate your forthrightness."

A smile flickered across Jeryl's hard face and he bowed deeply, lifting one hand with something clenched in between two fingers. Pheonix took it. It was a ring — a thin, simple band made of an opalescent material that gave off a slight glow.

"This was Lazarus'. Aside from his daggers, this was his only possession recovered from Bast's temple." Jeryl mimed spitting after saying the name. "One of our agents was undercover as a temple worker and managed to get it out after Lazarus' passing, though the man died of poison not too long after. It is only right that you should have it."

Pheonix tucked it into his fold-space.

"Thank you," he said.

Jeryl bowed, backed away and disappeared into the crowds.

"I like him," Theodric chirped.

Pheonix shook his head, declining to comment. If he was honest, meeting one of 'his' followers had been awkward. "Come on."

"You know, it's too bad I'm already an avatar of Schieta. Can someone be bound to two Ascended?" Theodric asked as he knocked an annoying robotic copter away from his head with his staff. Barnabus grumbled quietly.

"I don't know, Theodric, but I think that Schieta wouldn't be very happy with that."

Theodric thought about it. "You're probably right. He is pretty possessive."

"You'll have to be content to be my friend," Pheonix said. Theodric beamed and Pheonix felt a small smile tug at his lips.

Theodric naturally moved onto running a commentary on other matters. Anything and everything: his observations of the tech district, his opinions on the things he saw, what he'd eaten for lunch that day and twenty days ago. Pheonix listened with half an ear as they continued walking. They came to a bastion of quiet in the hallway of over-stimulation — a small storefront. An understated, physical sign proclaimed this shop to be the Gleaming Peridot.

"Yes, we're here," Pheonix said in response to the direct question Theodric had surreptitiously slipped into his constant chatter.

"Darn, you *were* listening," Theodric pouted.

"I always listen," Pheonix said mildly, and went through the door as it opened for him.

"Cheater," Theodric muttered behind him, and Pheonix allowed himself a grin.

The noise of the district faded as the doors closed. Gadgets and weaponry (including some mechanical limbs like

Pheonix's arm, but none near so fancy) lined the walls, interspersed with lighted glass cases containing chips for augs and mods.

Pheonix had only a few moments to take in the environment before he was beset upon by a pair of gnomes in floating mech suits. Even with the suits, they broke only three feet, less than half his height. They buzzed around him, rapid-firing suggestions for what he should buy and praising the Gleaming Peridot's superiority, in mechanical voices.

Ah, this must be Ellie and Nellie, he thought.

He reached out to block Theodric's staff as the little mage swung it at one suit that meandered too close — unfortunately, it was with the wrong arm.

The Nether-flame in his cybernetic arm reacted to Barnabus, resulting in a flash that made Ellie and Nellie scatter with cries of fear.

"What was that?" a shrill voice called from the back room. Arkiolett, holding a multi-tool like a weapon, scuttled around the corner. He relaxed when he saw Pheonix.

"Hello, Arkiolett," Pheonix said.

"My Lord Pheonix! What a surprise," he said, then tilted his head in puzzlement. "What was that light just now? Is everything okay?"

Theodric grabbed the wrist of Pheonix's cybernetic arm and the Nether-flame let him, though it reacted like a living thing to the mage's touch. Arkiolett's already-large eyes bulged to see the Nether-flame swimming in the cracks of the deutronium. It flared once more in rebellion against the little mage's scrutiny, but Theodric would not be intimidated.

"Well now look at you," Theodric said in a soothing voice. "How did you get in there? You're angry and scared and far from home. Is Barnabus upsetting you? Okay, okay."

Theodric leaned his staff against the wall across the room, and the Nether-flame settled into its normal smolder.

Seeing it calm, Arkiolett shooed Ellie and Nellie into the back, then approached. He was still holding the multi-tool crosswise over his chest for protection.

"What is that?" he asked reverently.

"Nether-flame," Pheonix said.

"How — how — how —"

"Don't get too close; it's really worked up," Theodric warned.

Arkiolett stopped.

"I'm not even sure how," said Pheonix. "I fought a Mistress of the Cult of Blood on Krasynth II. She fired it at me and the arm took it. That's why I'm here, to have you look at it."

"What?! What did you think *I* could do with that? I can't even get near it!"

"I can keep it calm," Theodric assured.

"Who are you?" Arkiolett asked.

Theodric grinned disarmingly. "My name is Theodric, I'm the avatar of Schieta. *All* flame bows to Lord Schieta, and therefore to me. The Nether-flame is rightfully upset about its situation, but it has agreed not to harm you."

"*A Master of Flame?*" Arkiolett cried incredulously, then ducked his head in respect.

"Um," Theodric said, visibly embarrassed, "please don't do that. Just call me Theodric."

"O-okay, if you insist."

Arkiolett looked at Pheonix for confirmation of Theodric's identity and abilities, and Pheonix nodded. Arkiolett looked between the two of them, then visibly screwed up his courage and came close enough for a detailed inspection.

"Hmm," Arkiolett said after a moment. "I really can't tell what's happening unless I can see past the plating." He looked up at Theodric, pointing at the outline of a panel on Pheonix's bicep, and asked, "Can you open this panel right here for me? Would the Nether-flame allow that?"

Theodric was quiet for a moment, then nodded and flipped the panel open deftly. The Nether-flame flared, then settled into a sullen simmer.

"This is amazing," Arkiolett said, awed. "Without being able to take it apart entirely, it's hard to say exactly what's going on, but it appears that the Nether-flame broke through the deutronium and took residence in the circuitry. I didn't even know that was possible. It destroyed the thorium reactor entirely and now it's powering the arm itself."

Arkiolett stepped back and put a hand on his head, staring into space with a blank look of intense concentration. "Well," he said finally, "the first thing to do is to fix the deutronium. But I can't take it apart, right?"

"I don't think even I could get it to let you do that," Theodric said. "It's taken refuge in his arm to protect itself. Trying to break into its house, essentially, would cause immediate retribution."

Arkiolett sighed and closed his eyes, tapping one foot in concentration. Then he snapped his fingers. "I've got it."

He disappeared into the back room. Ellie and Nellie peeked from around the corner, watching Pheonix and Theodric fearfully.

"Here's what we're going to do," Theodric whispered to the arm. "You can stay there, we won't make you go back to them. You know who I am. You know who he is, what he stands for. That's why you stuck with him. But if you're going to stay there, you need to work with him. You can't be disintegrating anyone he touches. You must listen to him — yes, I know, but he won't hurt you. With him you will get the chance for revenge. Yes, I promise."

Arkiolett returned, carrying a box full of sleek metal plates. He set it down at Pheonix's feet and eyed the arm cautiously.

"Do we have a deal?" Theodric asked sternly.

There was no outward sign of the Nether-flame's decision, but the grin that broke over Theodric's face was indication enough of its answer. He nodded shortly at Arkiolett.

"What's this?" Pheonix asked.

"A kind of a case for the arm to protect the broken deutronium and contain the flame. I had planned on sending this to you as a gift later, but I guess it's serendipitous that you showed up when you did. A lot of serendipitous things surround you," he ended with a giggle.

"Don't I know it," Pheonix said sarcastically.

"Okay, here I go," Arkiolett said.

Clutching the box to his chest, he gulped, and then set his jaw and approached. He settled massive shaded goggles over his eyes, then took from his box a small gun-shaped device, into which he slotted a cylinder of black metal matching the arm. Carefully he placed each piece of the outer casing, then ran the nozzle of the device around its edge, which glowed and sparked and left the piece attached.

The end result was a seamless, black arm with no trace of the fire that lived inside of it. Pheonix flexed his fingers and rotated his shoulder.

"How does it feel?" Arkiolett asked nervously.

"Feels good," Pheonix said. "Smooth. Thanks."

Arkiolett beamed. "Anytime! You've given me some incredible research ideas. Maybe we've been looking at utilizing Nether-flame all wrong. Theodric, do you mind if I contact you later for help when I get full permission? I need your expertise."

"Sounds like fun!" Theodric said, bouncing on his heels, dislodging ash that drifted to the floor as Ellie and Nellie looked on in horror.

Arkiolett scanned the finished arm, then they bid their goodbyes and Pheonix and Theodric left.

Pheonix parted ways with Theodric and headed back to his quarters. After so much activity and being surrounded by people constantly, the solitude of *his* space was comforting. He felt some internal tightness sloughing away.

He had much to do before he had to be on the shuttle to Availeon. His research lay spread across all surfaces of the room.

Neither Chani nor anyone else was aware of what he was working on.

"Astra, you've kept my secret, haven't you?" he said into the empty room.

"Of course, Pheonix," came the AI's voice.

He stood and stared down at the lines of his own mechanically-perfect handwriting, scrawled over hundreds of pages. Complicated graphics drawn over maps, flow-charts and lists of times, dates, names, and shipments.

"I don't need interference. It would ruin everything."

"You are an Executioner. It is against their own law to interfere."

"Chani would. She would think she was helping. I can't have variables I can't fully control; if I am sniffed out, they will flee to the farthest, darkest corners of the universe and burn everything. I may never catch them. These are not stupid men, though they are cunning in their cowardice. I am very close."

Astra was silent. Pheonix followed his previous train of thought to find where he had left off in his research.

He was so close to finishing this puzzle.

The first real clue he'd been given was knowing for certain his body was created via genetic experimentation. That had been a breakthrough, narrowing his required field of research down to a very short list. Genetic experimentation was extremely illegal, and genetic tampering of any kind was only used (under heavy regulation and constant monitoring) within the Rangers to create children between species that had no physical way to procreate (upon request by the potential parents), or to prevent detrimental mutations which would, if left unchecked, cause disease and suffering.

Though, while that was the official statement, it would be naïve to think that there weren't still secret programs utilizing genetic experimentation, probably run by protected, high-ranking individuals (like Chani).

And after many hours of work, spread out in between his intense training sessions and missions, he had a clear flowchart of the last twenty-odd years of activity from all genetic experimentation in the 'verse of his current inhabitation. Luckily, he hadn't had to branch out into other 'verses, as inter-verse travel was governed by the highest authorities in the land. An unauthorized jump (if it didn't kill you) would alert even the Chosen. It was an impossibility, or at least close enough that he didn't have to worry about it.

E-Pegasi 1.

Your sentence is that, as a wrongfully escaped slave, you are still the property of your previous owner. Therefore, you will be returned to E-Pegasi 1, the words rang in his mind. He looked through his latest data points.

E-Pegasi 1: A known slaver coliseum planet, deep in the Dark Sector. His previous owners, apparently. Tracing their activities would be easy but tedious, as E-Pegasi 1 was one of the largest hubs for evil in the known universe. That alone irked him — that such a thing was recognized to exist and not nuked. How many millions died there every day? How many innocents were ripped from their homes and lives, and forced to endure the worst depravities? He couldn't let himself think about it.

Reports reported that all slaves rescued from Krasynth II were from the genetic pits on Tartus 5, meaning that every single one was a modified clone — and cloning or modification couldn't be done without access to genetics research and manipulation. Somehow Krasynth II (and by extension

Ka'Resh and his cohorts) were connected to the genetic experimentation ring (or rings) Pheonix had been chasing. Perhaps Chani's catch phrase of 'I don't believe in coincidences' held more merit than he'd previously given it credit for.

Honestly, at this point he wouldn't be surprised. Pheonix highly suspected the Commander knew *far* more than she let on.

Also, for the first time in three hundred years, humanoid life signs were detected in the atmosphere of the angelic homeworld Assisi, a planet fully engulfed in corruption after a devastating Elysian attack that had left the angels officially extinct. It was a well-known fact that slavers were vultures, preying on destitute or fringe planets to steal whatever biological organisms might remain for the black market. With no scruples or caution, it wouldn't be out of their MO to hide operations in a quarantine zone. Requests for official investigation had been denied (big surprise), but the probability that the activity was slaver in origin was high.

E-Pegasi 1 itself was a little out of his league to tackle, as much as he wanted to test the limits of his newfound 'untouchable' status. He had to be realistic, though. He wasn't ready. And the slaves from Krasynth II were already dealt with; he just needed to keep on top of the reports as they continued to come out.

But Assisi ... that bore further investigation, for multiple reasons.

Decision made, he stretched out on his cot to go no-mind and let things process until the time came to leave.

THIRTY-ONE
Executioner

Pheonix found a small welcoming group awaiting him upon disembarking the shuttle. Chani couldn't join him on-planet, as she was still deeply embroiled in dealing with the backlash from Krasynth II and the situation with the Obelisk, but she had warned him of the dog-and-pony show to come.

However, he hadn't expected Mulahajad.

"Greetings," the old man said with a knowing smile.

"Hello, Mulahajad," Pheonix said tolerantly.

"So have the memories settled yet? How far are you in his journal?"

"Not many, and you're too nosy for your own good."

Mulahajad played at being hurt. "You wound me, my Lord. But perhaps this idle banter should be postponed until we are not blocking traffic?"

Pheonix descended into the main shuttle-port area and the Mahji fell in beside him. The two elven guards accompanying Mulahajad trailed behind, and the four of them made their way into the transpo district proper.

Whatever Pheonix had been expecting, it wasn't this.

A path through the district lined shoulder-to-shoulder with armed elven guards barely made room for them through the multitudes of bodies dancing, singing, and cheering in an overwhelming undulation of sound and movement. Flower petals fell from above, rainbows arced and danced among the clouds, and colorful banners above the throngs drifted in the slight breeze. Even the trees seemed to be swaying in time.

"What is all this? Is this for the death of Ka'Resh?" Pheonix asked Mulahajad.

The Mahji spread his arms. "A party, for you! The four most revered Ascended among the elven pantheon are Spiraea, Lady of the Woods and incarnation of Nature; Law, who has never taken nor been given a name; Life; and Justice, formerly Lazarus, now — you! The people are recognizing that an Ascended is among them."

The walk was long and loud.

Yet over it all, when Mulahajad spoke, Pheonix heard every word clearly. "I hear your investigation is going well."

If it were anyone else, Pheonix would have instantly been on the offensive at such a blithe admission to some rather extreme privacy violations. But Mulahajad was a First, who all seemed to not only know far more about what was going on than any of the later generations, but also didn't seem much inclined to get personally involved.

Information was nothing if you had no intent to use it.

So, Pheonix merely warned him with a look. "I hope you have not shared your awareness of that."

"Of course not."

Pheonix grunted. "There seems to be a conspiracy of my associates doing things without my knowledge."

"And how are you different, hiding your motives and actions from those who might help you?" Mulahajad said sharply, then sighed. "But rest assured, the knowledge of your doings comes from no associate of yours. Although, I do have a question."

"Yes?"

"What is it you seek, oh Lord Justice?"

"For what? My next step? My investigation? My life?"

"Yes."

"You are being deliberately obtuse."

"And I am glad you have learned some humor since last I saw you. Fine, I shall be more direct. Specifically, your investigation. Is it your past you wish to know about?"

"I suppose."

"Which one?"

"If you're referring to Lazarus, my yearning for justice to be enacted on those who mistreat innocents outweighs my interest in a life that may never have been mine."

Mulahajad actually looked surprised. "Never yours? What brought you to that conclusion?"

"Nothing concrete — impressions and instinct, mostly. I feel only a ghost of familiarity to Lazarus, which could easily be explained by our shared tie to Justice. I certainly don't feel like I'm looking into a mirror of any kind."

"My Lord, are you implying that Lazarus was not the Ascended of Justice?"

"I imply nothing. You asked me a question, I answered it."

Mulahajad fell silent, his thick furry brow knitted together in thought. Finally, he sighed and waved a hand as though dispersing something nearby. Then, he said, "On the subject of Justice: do not confuse it with vengeance."

Pheonix glanced at Mulahajad with slitted eyes.

Mulahajad put up his hands in an exaggerated shrug. "I know, but indulge this old man in his attempt at guidance, won't you?"

Pheonix snorted. *Old man, indeed.* "I lack the emotional capacity for vengeance, Mulahajad. I'm sure you know that. The world is data. What was done to me is in the past; but I can and will ensure it never happens to another soul. The Creator bestowed upon me that responsibility."

Mulahajad nodded sagely. "It is good you see it that way."

In short order, a castle loomed in front of them, dwarfed only by the petal of one of Terelath's districts behind it. It was made of a deep, matte green natural crystal, shot through with layers of glittering gold and brown. The base of the crystal was the natural brown of the rock beneath it, growing upwards into the green in places.

The crowd around them thinned and dispersed. Natural formations of this same crystal began to jut up around them the closer to the castle they drew, and eventually met in arches over their heads, forming a corridor.

After a brief walk down this corridor, they entered a massive throne room at the heart of the crystal. Cheering erupted from the Lords, Ladies, elven nobles, priests, Grey Mages, and many other dignitaries Pheonix couldn't quickly identify arranged around the dais.

The King and Queen of the elves stood from their thrones, wearing resplendent white robes that caught the refracted green glow from sunlight filtering through the crystal. A few steps below them stood Tyyrulriathula, dressed in silver Bladesinger chain and breastplate, and holding out before him a black pillow on which rested a black half circlet. Next to him stood Faran. Crosinthusilas floated on the other side of the King and Queen from Tyyrulriathula and Faran. The Prophet, Biarch, and Xenobiarch were arranged around them, as well.

As with the transpo district, a path wound through the assembled, though this one unguarded. Pheonix took to it with Mulahajad behind him. He approached the dais and stopped on the third step, dropping to one knee before the dual thrones of the elven leaders.

The Queen lifted one hand and the noise died down.

"Everyone," said the King. "We welcome you. The crowning of an Executioner is a time to celebrate. Those chosen to wear the black crown are the enforcement of truth and the protection of innocence across the universe. They are the model of righteousness, existing outside of the laws of sapients to uphold the laws of the Creation. It is only fitting that Justice be finally inducted into its ranks."

"Stand, my Lord," the Queen said to Pheonix. "Who speaks for you?"

Pheonix got the sense of hesitancy, so he raised a hand before any could be pressured to come forward.

"I am Justice, and none may speak for me. Though there may be those who wish to, Justice must always stand alone."

The Queen graced him with a beautiful, sad smile. "Executioners are our last line of defense against the sapient-created threats. Executioners must listen to the Creator only, and act on the Creator's will only. To fail as an Executioner means death. Do you accept this burden?"

The words had the tone of ritual, but an edge in the Queen's voice and the intensity in her eyes warned him that there was another meaning to *this* ritual.

Pheonix had done a bit of research before coming to the surface. He wasn't about to allow a title to be attached to his name that he knew nothing about, that was for damn certain.

The Order of Executioners was an association of individuals gathered with the singular pursuit of hunting down criminals who believed they were above the law. He wasn't able to find a lot of information about their structure or leadership, only that they were rumored to be incorruptible. So far, the organization was nothing but red flags.

Frankly, if that meant it was corruption incarnate, Pheonix would delight in tearing it down. If it wasn't, he would use whatever resources it afforded him. Either way, he won.

"I do," Pheonix said firmly.

The Queen gestured Tyyrulriathula forward.

Pheonix had been instructed to wear his new circlet of white leaves for the occasion, which Tyyrulriathula now took from his head and threw to the ground. Its shattering sounded like crystal rain.

Tyyrulriathula raised the black crown.

"So you never forget the vow you have made today," Tyyrulriathula said, his eyes apologizing.

Pheonix put his head down and closed his eyes in acceptance.

Tyyrulriathula jammed the crown on Pheonix's forehead. Spikes set into the inner part of the circlet, not readily visible from the outside, dug into his flesh, sending pain searing through his temples and down his spine, like bolts of electricity that dissipated into his limbs, leaving them buzzing.

"Ow," Pheonix said in his perfect monotone.

"At least he didn't punch me this time," Faran muttered behind Tyyrulriathula.

"A new Executioner has been crowned!" the King and Queen declared together. "Let the fête begin!"

The jubilation from the crowds raised anew, and, slowly, they filed out of the throne room, leaving a small semi-circle of people around Pheonix.

Since Tyyrulriathula was directly in front of him, he spoke first. "You know what this means, right?"

"What?" Pheonix asked.

"You're free. Executioners follow their own rules. You don't have to fear retribution from the Rangers or elves or any other organization, so long as you don't go around committing crimes or killing innocents, which we all know you'd never do."

"Why does any of this matter? I'm Ascended."

Tyyrulriathula made a face. "You are ... but you aren't. You're not like the other Ascended. Executioners don't volunteer: they're chosen by the Creator. I imagine this is the Creator's way of providing a way for you to make your way in this world until you become like them ... if you ever do. Maybe this is your role, to live among us in a way that the other Ascended don't. Who knows? Also to that end, I'm making you General of my Phoenix Legions."

"Why? I know nothing of military operations. Or leading soldiers."

"Pheonix, what are you planning on doing after this?"

"Immediately? Return to HQ, finish up some work there, then learn sliding."

"And after that?"

"I do have plans, yes."

Tyyrulriathula sighed. "Cheeky bastard. Well then, follow me on a hypothetical — what happens if your plans go awry?"

"I will adjust as best as possible."

"What if the situation has spiraled to the point that you can't handle it alone?" Tyyrulriathula pressed.

Pheonix paused. He hadn't considered not being able to do something by himself.

The young elf pointed at Pheonix's face unexpectedly. "That look tells me that you've never even thought about it. That's why we're doing this. What tactical assets does being an Ascended or an Executioner give you beyond what you yourself can accomplish? Things outside your own body?"

After a pause, Pheonix said, "Nothing."

"Remember what we're doing here. Politics is the lifeblood of this accursed place. That means networking, knowing people, knowing the strings to pull, and having the influence to do so. While we don't question that you are Ascended, you don't seem to function the same as the others. And not everyone believes you are Ascended at all, or even cares. I think you know that better than anyone.

"By making you my General, you remain independent, but you also have a recognized connection — me — through which to request aid from either the elves or the Rangers, if necessary. Once you graduate from being a trainee, you become truly independent, and even Chani won't be able to help you unless it's under the table. It doesn't change our relationship, and I won't call you to duty, but it's a way to play at their own game."

"Alright."

"Plus," and Tyyrulriathula grinned, "this means that the threat of Justice on Availeon will always be a word away from one of the most hated Bladesingers. The Seconds will be shitting their pants over it."

Tyyrulriathula went to turn, then stopped. His expression conveyed that something had just popped into his mind. "One more thing: how much have you been reading up on theology and pantheons?"

"Only a bit. My studies are focused mostly elsewhere at the moment."

"You recognize the name Bast?"

"That name brings immediate, deep rage."

"Well, it ought to. He killed Lazarus. He's also the God of murder, the destruction of innocence, and general evil acts."

"I'll add him to the list."

"He's your polar opposite on the spectrum. Fun fact: if you curse using his name, you can cause him pain."

"*Bast*," Pheonix said, then smiled, eliciting a laugh out of Tyyrulriathula.

"Good luck. I'll see you when I see you." Still grinning, the elf gave a jaunty wave, turned, and disappeared into the already-thinning crowd.

The Biarch swiftly took Tyyrulriathula's place. "Congratulations, my Lord."

"Thank you."

The Biarch looked Pheonix over in such a way that it made him feel like he was being appraised for sale. "How are you faring?" he asked. "Your health?"

"You hide your curiosity poorly, Biarch."

The Biarch looked taken aback, then laughed. "Oh, fine. You are impossible, and yet here you are."

"I'm not sure why you think I would have insight into that. You said it yourself: I just am."

The Biarch opened his mouth, then shook his head, dissolving into chuckling. "Children. I of all people should know how much we have to learn from them, and yet my age makes me forget at times. Very well, I will direct my inquiries to those who might know, with your permission. Take care of yourself, boy — ah, my Lord. You are very special."

"Permission granted, and I will try."

The Biarch bowed slightly and was replaced by the ever-energetic Xenobiarch.

"Good job and all that. Heard about your arm. You must tell me more."

Pheonix was already growing weary of the questions and people assaulting him, and the Xenobiarch's brusque manner didn't help his growing irritation, but he gathered his resolve and said, "If you wish to know more, you should seek out Master Tinkerer Arkiolett. It is of his design."

"Yeah, yeah, I know that. The Nether-flame, man!"

Pheonix wasn't going to try to puzzle out how he knew. Apparently certain things got around in certain circles.

"My arm simply absorbed it and converted it to a power source. More than that, I really could not tell you."

The Xenobiarch deflated and huffed like a small child.

"Arkiolett and my associate Theodric, an avatar of Schieta, are working together to research the connection," Pheonix continued, "though they will likely need interested parties to further their analysis."

The Xenobiarch snapped his mechanical fingers and pointed at Pheonix. "Good idea. Bright kid. Knew I liked you."

And off he went.

Next was a person in full teal-and-golden ceremonial plate armor, a full-face helmet, and a long, royal blue cape. Pheonix immediately felt a sort of inexplicable kinship.

"My Lord," came a strong, medium-toned voice, somehow clear despite the helmet. "I will not keep you long. I am the Golden Paladin, pursuant of justice. You likely are aware of me, having spent time on Archaic Earth. I apologize that I know your history without asking, but it does get around."

"I am aware of you, and it is certainly a pleasure to meet you," Pheonix said, and meant it. "The Maester I stayed with taught me much of the history of Archaic Earth and your role in it. It seems we are kindred spirits."

Pheonix got the sense of smiling, though the Golden Paladin's face was hidden.

"Indeed. I only wished to meet you and ask you a question."

"You may."

"Do you have plans to return to Archaic Earth?"

"Not at this time." *Though,* he thought, *there are now several reasons to go. Perhaps I should add it under Assisi in my list of future destinations.*

The Golden Paladin bowed slightly. "Of course, you are in the midst of great change. I ask only that you keep it in mind as you continue your journey."

"I will."

"May the Creator keep you well," the Golden Paladin said and bowed again, turning away.

The Golden Paladin: the de facto ruler of Archaic Earth. The Commander of the Silver Hand, the Order of Paladins that travel literally everywhere to provide succor and protection to places that otherwise might be without. The Golden Paladin united the Kingdoms of Archaic Earth after a war that almost destroyed all life on Archaic Earth in the Third Age, though his history and whereabouts before he got in-

volved with said war remain unknown to the public. He appears to be a particularly devout follower of the Creator, and is known to be a brilliant tactician and fierce warrior.

Why would someone like that come to see him personally?

Pheonix reached up to touch the circlet. It felt immovable, as though welded to his flesh. And it still hurt — a dull sort of ache when he focused on it.

Thankfully, no one else followed the Golden Paladin in wanting a slice of Pheonix's direct attention, though some glances were cast from within the milling groups that warned him that, were he to hang around too long, it'd be taken as an open invitation to more conversation. Swiftly he turned on his heel and made his way into the nearest crystalline tunnel, hoping no one would follow him.

As he walked, he considered his current situation. With the ceremony over, he was free. He needed to eventually report to the training grounds to meet with someone who would teach him sliding, but as far as he was concerned, they could wait.

He found a crystal and used it to get back to the transpo hub and catch the first shuttle back to HQ.

If there was one thing Pheonix had found over the last two years of training and bouncing between emergency mission after emergency mission, it was that he had been incredibly lucky.

He wasn't about to rely on that luck.

His missions in particular had highlighted how green he still was. If he was meant to be Justice, he needed to shave off those green edges as quickly as possible.

Especially if anything were ever to come of the 'rebellion' he'd started over a year ago.

Now that things were calmer, and his training had been handed over to him to coordinate as he saw fit, he was fully ready to dive into it with abandon.

He needed to know more. What evils he'd be facing, what their weaknesses were, what each and every weapon he could get his hands on did, and how they were made and what *their* weaknesses were, and the same for armor. Tactics, history, robotics, tech, and tek. He'd learned all manner of things about the natural world on Terelath; now he needed to shore up his knowledge of sapient-made things, and HQ was the perfect place for that.

THIRTY-TWO
Slide To The Left, Slide To The Right

Half a year passed.

He could spend an entire lifetime learning and not find the end of it — to wit, that was his goal — but after six months of study, he'd reached a point where he was starting to get antsy. Something in him was pulling him back to Terelath; and so, with focus harder and harder to maintain, he made plans and caught a shuttle back to Availeon.

He'd been told to meet his Executioner sliding trainer at the training grounds, but he hadn't been given a bubble coordinate, so from the transpo district he used a crystal to go to the entrance of the training ground itself.

He stopped as a wave of familiarity washed over him. Nostalgia was not an emotion he was capable of, but here was 'safe.' He had pleasant memories here. It was a little odd seeing the training grounds from the outside; he'd always teleported directly in and out of his little bubble. It was its own petal in the giant flower that was Terelath.

With the lighted teleportation pad behind him being the base of the petal, the curve stretched out into impossibly grand distances before him. Consisting of a manicured grassy floor, each individual training zone was contained in its own bubble of magic. It protected the trainee inside from outside view or interference, and kept said trainee from wandering around or being distracted by the outside. Treants — somewhat-humanoid trees — of all shapes and sizes meandered between the uncountable distortions that indicated bubbles. Pheonix descended into the grounds.

The tranquility and seclusion of the walk soothed his nerves, but it wasn't long before someone wanted his attention.

A smallish treant stopped in his perpetual march directly in Pheonix's path.

"Can I help you?" Pheonix asked. He narrowed his eyes, annoyed by a sudden sensation of acquaintance, as though he'd met this creature before. Pain stabbed through his temple and a hazy memory swum into his field of vision of a sapling frolicking around feet that weren't his.

"Have we met?" Pheonix asked again.

"Sort of," the treant responded, painfully slowly.

"I seem to have a vague memory of a sapling. You, I take it. Who are you?"

He got the impression of a smile. The 'face' of the treant was only remotely humanoid, so its expression was difficult to discern.

"My name would take two years to speak. The first Abyssterilon called me Iyalan. Others have as well. I was going to visit you in your training grounds, but here you are."

Iyalan reached into his branches. He pulled out a wooden book and offered it to Pheonix.

Horror froze Pheonix. He took the book with shaking hands and opened it.

Empty.

"This ... this is the Book of Creation," Pheonix said, strained.

He'd studied Creator artifacts with the old man on Archaic Earth — in fact, anything relating to the Creator had been his favorite subjects. The Book of Creation had come up more than once. Though, as with all Creator artifacts, no one knew exactly what the Creator had made it for. Reigning theological theory was that if all of its pages were together and read without knowledge of what the book's true purpose was, it would undo creation.

Memories — mere sensory input with no context — pinwheeled in front of his eyes faster than he could assimilate them. He wavered on his feet and fell to one knee.

"Lazarus was charged by the Creator to protect this book. He gave it to you? *Where are the pages?*" he rasped.

Iyalan dipped down a slender branch, on the end of which was a single purple bloom. A gentle scent calmed Pheonix enough that he could grab on and right himself, though he was still trembling. The treant shook his 'head,' indicating a lack of knowledge. His leaves rustled.

"It was given to me in this condition. No one knows they are missing," the treant said in his lethargic manner. Pheonix barely tolerated the delay in the words. "I was instructed to give it to you … and that you would find them."

Curse you, Lazarus, Pheonix thought in irritation.

He grunted and slid the book into his fold-space. "Thank you," he said, calmer now that the initial shock had worn off.

Iyalan shook his upper half in a sort of bow, and slowly turned away.

Pheonix had no time to consider this shattering development. It would have to be dealt with later. Without the book itself, even if someone were to gather all the pages, they wouldn't get far. He had time.

He only hoped that the last time he had said that — when Arkiolett had been nearly killed by orcs — wouldn't repeat here and now.

Taking a breath to physically calm himself, he continued through the training petal to his designated bubble, the only one to respond to him as he approached.

He passed through the distortion and found himself in even more familiar territory. Cottage, training ring, grass.

Minrathous and a man Pheonix didn't recognize stood side by side on the far end of the open dirt ring.

The man wore the typical Grey Mage robes, but for two differences. A silver chain tied around his waist held censers on long tails, in which burned a material that left the man in a perpetual cloud of oddly-iridescent smoke. His drawn hood revealed the bald head and rune-like tattoos of a Mahji, though with the glowing silver eyes indicative of addiction to thaumium.

Thaumium and Grey Mages, Pheonix accessed. *Thaumium is a magic-infused mineral that Grey Mages 'burn' and inhale the smoke, which increases magical abilities. This is a high level of exposure and causes addiction, whereas low levels of exposure, such as would be used in a tincture to temporarily increase magic, does not. The particular and peculiar structure of thaumium, in an organic creature, creates a temporary latticework throughout the neural pathways of the body and brain that allows for near instantaneous access for electrical signals.*

There was only one Grey Mage that didn't wear a hood: Marcus, the Grey Mage Master.

Pheonix nodded briefly to Minrathous, then met Marcus' eyes steadily, retrieving the empty Book of Creation from fold-space to toss it at his feet. The Grey Mage Master watched it slide to a halt before him, trailing dust.

"Explain this." Pheonix snapped, then went on, not waiting for a response. "Grey Mage Master, the head of one of the groups responsible for making sure *this very shit doesn't happen*. Lazarus left this to you when he went after Bast. Why are its pages missing? Did Lazarus do this? Why did you give it to a *treant*? Speak, man!"

Marcus picked the book up, his eyes wide. He met Pheonix's gaze briefly, with the look of a man about to be hanged, and in another instant he was gone.

"I apologize for that, Druid Minrathous," Pheonix said and bowed to her. Minrathous hid snorted laughter behind a hand.

"No worries. Not that I fully understood what was going on," Minrathous said, "but it seemed important. Ah — well, Marcus *was* here to teach you about Will magic, with my assistance, but I suppose I can rise to the challenge." She pushed her wide sleeves up her arms one at a time for some reason, though they flopped back down immediately.

"You've mentioned Will magic in the past," Pheonix said.

"And now we'll be elaborating on it, as it's a key element to sliding — and, honestly, as an Ascended, you likely already have access to it."

"What makes you say that?"

Minrathous leaned on her staff and tilted her head at him. "Well, let's talk about Krasynth II, the first go-round. When you dashed out there by your lonesome, you startled everyone on ground, which kept them from providing you with immediate support. Lacking that, anyone else would have been *instantly* killed. And I don't say that lightly. Vaporized. Both Marcus and I analyzed, in detail, the vids captured of you on that battlefield, and we determined that one of the many things working in concert to keep you alive was your sheer will to reach that red wizard and destroy him. That is the essence of Will magic."

"You mean to tell me that someone's … mental strength … is enough to, what, cast magic? Change reality?"

"Bluntly, yes."

Pheonix stared at her. She chuckled.

"It's not something we fully understand, so you'll likely grasp it far sooner than even 'masters' of Will magic like Marcus would. But those who use it simply claim to very much want something to happen, and it does. But it's not just the ephemeral Thread of Will that you have access to — as an

Ascended, you literally *can* change reality. Take Spiraea's tantrum on the dark elf homeworld. And we have proof that you can already access this ability, albeit likely only under duress at the moment. But that's why you need this training."

"When did I do that?"

"Krasynth II, the second go-round. Think back to what I've explained about Will magic, and I believe you'll have your answer."

Pheonix's eyes unfocused as he accessed the memories from the battle with Ka'Resh. He almost twitched as the sensations flooded him again: the dizziness and pain from unceasing repeated hits, the constant beeping of his shield overload warning, and that mage's Creator-damned *monologuing*.

Sifting through the memories with 'willing' things to exist in the forefront of his mind, something did stick out —

One clear thought he had made into a declaration: *No, I'm done being hurt by you.*

"Oh," he said aloud.

Minrathous grinned. "You will likely have to manifest a great *desire* to do the thing, which I imagine will be the hardest part for you. But knowing that mastering sliding will allow you, essentially, the ultimate freedom should help forge that desire. So, shall we start small?"

Minrathous sat, and beckoned him closer. "I'll admit, I'm excited, because the Threads were inaccessible to you before, but Will magic bypasses them entirely — or, more accurately, plucks them at the same time? But I'll spare you my musings on advanced theory. In any case, the spells you weren't able to cast the last time you were my student, you should be able to make manifest now; isn't that something? So let's try again." She picked an unfortunate flower from the grass and held it up. "This time, instead of *feeling* anything, or reaching for the Threads, *command* the flower to burn. *Tell* it that *it wants* to become flame."

Pheonix folded his long legs to sit next to her, amused by her exuberance, though not entirely convinced. He focused on the flower. It hadn't escaped him that in the instances when he had supposedly been using Will magic, he had noticed what was happening, but it hadn't exactly connected that *he* was its source. But Minrathous had successfully roused his curiosity. The full weight of his attention settled on the poor little plant, he aligned his thoughts with the incomparable will that had kept him alive and fighting for his entire difficult life, formed the desire to be successful in his head, and commanded the flower to become flame.

Minrathous shrieked and dropped the miniature fireball licking at her fingers, though she shortly dissolved into laughter. "See? See? I told you!"

Pheonix blinked, processing. It had actually worked.

"And *that* is Will magic!" Minrathous continued triumphantly. "The concept is the same no matter what magic you're attempting: shielding, elemental manipulation … or sliding. Marcus will have to elaborate on that whenever he returns from … wherever he went. But," she stood, dusted off her robes, and gestured behind her to the dirt training ring, "that should give you plenty of time to accustom yourself to the practice, using the materials provided over on those tables. I'll be temporarily staying in one of the other cottages while you're in training here, so if you have any questions, come find me."

"Thank you," Pheonix said as he stood. Minrathous flashed him another cheeky grin, and bounced off toward the cottages.

Pheonix swept his gaze across the training area to look for the tables she'd mentioned. There were several set up in the ring as she'd said, with various materials on them, and a set of instructions — or, more accurately, suggestions — on what to do with each object.

Well, he thought and made his way to the tables, *better get to work.*

When Minrathous found him in the morning, he'd been successful in everything on the page of suggestions. Spatial manipulation, activating elemental magic, phase changes, and force application were just some of the Will magic principles he'd mastered overnight. She was beside herself with glee for his quick progress.

"Now we can move onto more advanced practices!" She pointed at the edge of the training bubble. "Distance. This is the true difficulty of sliding, because you'll not only be moving through space, but often to places you either haven't been before or can't physically see. For this exercise, there is a table set outside the bubble with objects on it. You will be moving those objects back and forth between this space and that one. For that, you need to be able to *see* it, and that's the other part of sliding." She lowered her voice, "Which, I guess, I'm also teaching you, since Marcus still isn't here. Thank Spiraea you're brilliant."

Minrathous cleared her throat and continued. "Rather than Willing an effect onto an object, you will be Willing the effect onto *yourself.* Will *yourself* to see the table. You know its general placement, you can imagine what it looks like, you just need to find it."

Pheonix stared blankly at the edge of the bubble, struggling to formulate a plan as to how he'd accomplish what she had tasked him. He closed his eyes and pulled his entire focus as he'd been doing all night, but rather than aiming it at an object, he aimed it at himself. It wasn't as odd as he was expecting, since he often did physical systems-checks during and after battles. This was almost the same process, just more intense. With his focus in his figurative fist, he told his mind to find the table, and bring back a mental picture for him.

While the initial steps were easy to follow, accuracy proved more elusive. He found several tables throughout Terelath before he'd managed to find the one table he was actually looking for.

After that, it was a matter of maintaining focus on two separate objectives: finding a target and performing an action.

By the time the suns were setting, he was drained but had been successful (despite several rather egregious errors). Minrathous enthused congratulations, warned him that things would get more difficult on the morrow, and told him to go to his cottage.

He was honestly glad to flop into his cot. He felt like someone had cracked open his skull and dragged his brain across gravel. With the intensity of his physical training in the past, he hadn't expected mental training to exhaust him, but he'd been wrong. Unfortunately, before he could slip into no-mind, he noticed a new datapad on top of his active research pile. He picked it up. While there was a singular odd report of slaver vessels chasing an energy signature in the Dark Sector, the rest were on slaver activity surrounding the angelic home planet of Assisi: transferral of undocumented, uninitiated individuals by unknown means. A confiscated list of slaver contacts flashed before his eyes and he logged them all mechanically.

That was interesting enough that it pulled his full attention, despite his exhaustion.

Other reports attached to the main ones started to circle tighter around Assisi, and one name he'd seen on the suspected slaver list popped up again and again: Invenes. Whoever that was. There had been a minor trading house of angels with that name on Assisi before the Elysian attack, but there was no way it was related … or was it?

Requests for samples, expeditions, and scans of Assisi had all been denied. It was Ranger SOP to leave a dead planet alone, especially one involving the Elysian, for a minimum of five hundred years. The corruption left behind by the Elysian was not kind and didn't discriminate in what it fouled up.

But someone was evidently interested enough that they kept submitting requests, even though they continued to be summarily rejected.

Why? Oh, he understood why someone would be pressing the issue; the squeaky wheel gets the grease, and all. And slaver activity, especially involving uninitiateds, was a serious issue.

But who would be so interested, and why were they interested? Furthermore, if something within the Rangers had enough interest, even if it went against SOP, it would be kicked to the higher-ups for thorough review. The fact that this hadn't been was suspicious.

More than likely he could thank Astra for these reports. The AI must have been monitoring the direction of his research again. Though he hadn't made any statements about Assisi being his next goal, she may have inferred it.

Although the involvement of others at first had been a bother and a liability, he was beginning to warm to the idea. He snorted, remembering Mulahajad's cheeky reprimand on the subject. It was admittedly useful to have a mind even faster than his own sifting through the billions of pages of dry paperwork submitted into Ranger archives every day. It was beyond him to understand why, since they never *did anything to stop it*, but slaver activity was kept under close watch by the Rangers. Much of what was logged had to do with engagements, raids, and trade. But occasionally, there were unusual gems hidden among the banal day-to-day that were certainly pertinent to someone who handled the unusual, as he did, and he was grateful for the help.

He decided that further research could wait, before laying down in his cot to go no-mind and let everything settle. It had been an eventful day, and he was ready to disconnect.

THIRTY-THREE
Uh-Oh

The blackness of no-mind, interrupted by the sound of booted feet. Immediately suspecting an intruder, he tried to fight — but something held him in thrall.

A door opened, pushed by a hand that was his and wasn't.

Pheonix realized he was dreaming.

She sat on the bed they shared, hunched over her breastplate, which she was scrubbing within an inch of its life. It was her ritual, her comfort. A blue-black pile of curls hid her face from his view, though as he called, "Lady?" she looked up.

A smile broke over her ebony features — the smile she reserved for him, one that warmed a heart gone too cold.

"Lazarus," she said. "You're back. How was the mission?"

Pheonix jerked internally. He recognized her instantly: Life, the woman from the sketch in Lazarus' journal.

The dream shifted; they watched the sunset play liquid fire over the lake near their dwelling, hand in hand. He stole a glance at her profile. Content nestled on her royal features, so utterly absorbed was she in the moment.

He fingered the small box in his pocket. Lazarus' stomach was roiling with an emotion Pheonix had never felt, and therefore couldn't identify, as the sun slowly sank beyond the horizon, a rainbow of colors besieging the new night.

She sighed, and he jumped. She gave him a questioning look, though a smile hovered on her lips. He shook his head shortly, indicating nothing was wrong.

"Come, let's head inside," she said, and turned. She found resistance and faced him again. The young moonlight pulled blue highlights off her skin.

"Lady," he said, and steadied himself, "I am Justice, created to serve one purpose. And in that purpose, though it was what the Creator set forth for me, I have never felt fulfilled. It is only in sharing my life with you that I have ever been whole."

With trembling hands, he pulled the box from his pocket. Light spilled out as he opened it: a small, simple ring made of lumicite, a mysterious phosphorescent material that mimicked the moon's full glow.

The ring that Jeryl had given him.

The shock on her face, illuminated by the ring, could not be discerned as happy or upset. He barreled on.

"Would you do me the honor of becoming my partner?"

Time froze for the brief eternity it took for her to respond. He caught a full-body flurry of gauzy skirt, tears, and woman.

"Yes, Lazarus, yes. For all of eternity, my heart and soul have always been and will always be yours."

Pheonix startled awake, panting. He sat up, shaky and weak. His face was cold; he touched his cheeks and found them wet.

He jumped up from the bed, mind shorting out with the desperate *too much information/not enough information* dichotomy.

That woman's face was burned into his brain, the echoes of emotions he didn't possess ricocheting dangerously among the chaos.

He needed to focus. He needed to regroup. He needed data.

He shuffled through his books, grabbing up Lazarus' journal. Flipping through it, he scanned for any mention of Life, accessing at the same time.

The Ascended of Life. Life was never as close to her worshipers as her sister Spiraea, so was never given a name by the sapients who followed her. She appeared as a dark-skinned elf dressed in the silver-and-gold full plate armor of a paladin, wielding a massive two-handed sword emblazoned with the Great Tree, Yggdrasil.

From the journal, Pheonix got the story on Lazarus and Life. And as he read, hazy memories surfaced.

> Nature was the first Ascended to come into being, though Lazarus wasn't privy to the circumstances of her birth, having not been particularly friendly with Spiraea. Life, Law, and Justice came into being sometime after. Justice and Life, while created at the same time, orbited around each other without ever really interacting until the major sapient species came into their own. Their original purpose, according to Lazarus, aside from embodying their namesake, was to fight the evil Gods and allow the Creation to evolve with as little interference as possible.
>
> In the early days of the sapient species, the Ascended spent much time among them. Justice was given the name Lazarus by the people of Techno-Earth, while Spiraea was similarly bestowed by the elves on Availeon. Law never took a name nor allowed anyone to name him, though he spent as much time with the mages as the other two did with their respective cultures.
>
> Life was the only one of the first four that spent almost no time around the lesser species, and thus,

was also given no name. As the universe rapidly expanded, uncountable new lives drained her and stretched her thin.

She was a serious, stern, meticulous woman. Her rare smile became Lazarus' sun, able to brighten the darkest of days. Beyond the dedication to her duty that they all shared, Life had something else. Love. A share of the Creator's boundless love for Creation. And while it was a great gift, it was also a great burden. Though she'd never asked him to, Lazarus took it upon himself to protect her and do whatever he could to lighten her heart.

He took any mission, any reason to save lives, to spare her the pain of feeling them lost. It became his obsession. But despite all his efforts, Life continually weakened. She could no longer fight or even pick up her greatsword. After accepting his partnership, they held a ceremony in Godholme, in front of the Creator, to seal their bond.

Lazarus redoubled his effort, blind to the reason for his beloved's rapid decline.

Bast, his opposite, was using his followers to drain her, purposely causing mass genocide and destruction to steal the life out of the universe — and keeping it from returning.

Lazarus berserked when he discovered the underhanded attack. Despite warnings, he assaulted Bast's temple by himself, and fell victim to an ambush. The foyer of the temple sealed and flooded with Nether-flame, consuming him. There was no escape from Nether-flame, even for Ascended.

Lazarus' journal ended on a hastily scribbled note of rage explaining Bast's involvement and claiming Lazarus' intentions.

Pheonix sat back, mind working.

His previous dream-memory surfaced. That must have been Lazarus' final moments. But in those moments, Lazarus had reached out to the Creator — and found silence.

Why?

Lazarus hadn't known what had happened to Life. The only thing Pheonix knew about her for sure was that she hadn't manifested in Ages. But that was true of all Ascended in the most recent Ages: they tended not to manifest, for reasons unknown to sapients. The elves assumed that Life was still around, but was refusing to manifest. While there were some sects of individuals that believed their Ascended were dead, neither side had proof for or against their theories. There just wasn't enough known about the Ascended. The whole situation caused strife and arguments among the sapients, forming schisms in religion and culture.

The only death that was widely known was Lazarus', because Bast had crowed about it from the highest tower as proof of his own Godhood, and moles in his temple had witnessed it.

A tentative knock on his cottage door distracted Pheonix from his research. He glanced out the window; the suns were just rising.

Emerging from the cottage, Pheonix found Marcus standing next to Minrathous, hands tucked into his wide sleeves. He looked haggard.

"My Lord," Marcus said immediately as Pheonix neared. "I apologize about my abrupt departure, and the length of my absence. You took me by surprise, and I thought it best to find answers posthaste."

"And did you?"

Marcus took his hands out of his sleeves, revealing the book, which he returned to Pheonix.

Pheonix opened it to find one page. "This is all you could retrieve?"

"It was the only page the Congress kept. You see, after Lazarus' death, the Congress of Mages convened to make a decision on what should be done with the book. This is one of the most dangerous artifacts known to them. Only Justice was worthy of its protection. The temptation would be too much for any sapient, and the other Ascended already had their charges and none would claim it."

"How did you come to possess it?" Pheonix asked.

Marcus hesitated. "Lazarus entrusted it to the Congress, before he left to confront Bast, as you already know. So when news of his death reached them, they made the decision to tear it apart and hide the pages, so that none could use them."

"That's ridiculous," Pheonix said. "History proves that tactic ineffective."

"Be that as it may, you must understand how it shook the universe to have Justice killed. Many thought it was the end of days. They did what they thought was best at the time."

"Is there any record of where the pages were sent?" Pheonix asked.

"No, my Lord. The thought was that even if one entity were to collect them all, the book would be useless without the page kept by the Congress. And to reduce the possibility of traitors from within, none of the Congress know where the rest ended up. I, as the Grey Mage Master, kept the book's shell as an extra layer of protection."

"Then why did you give it to a *treant*?"

"A 'find magic' spell doesn't work around beings of magic. And since treants are pure Nature magic, the book would be essentially undetectable in the care of one. And there are billions of them in Terelath. Even if you somehow knew that the book was being held by a treant, you'd have to physically search each and every one to find it."

Pheonix covered his face with one hand out of exasperation.

Well, at least his reasoning is sound. But now it falls upon me to rectify their hasty mistake, Phoenix thought, but kept it inside. The logic of it made sense in context, as much as it was an inconvenience. What other choice did they feel they had?

Didn't mean he was happy about it, though.

"What do you wish us to do?" Marcus asked. "I can reconvene the Congress, start an investigation — "

He quieted at Phoenix's raised hand.

"I will handle it. One individual can go undetected where many would invite disaster. Send me any information you have through Austraelus — logs, vids, reports. Be discreet."

"As you wish," Marcus said tiredly, and bowed. "Shall we continue with your training? Minrathous has updated me on your progress, which is honestly astonishing, considering the timeframe."

"I thought I was supposed to have an Executioner trainer for this." Pheonix said.

It was Minrathous who answered, her normally cheery face clouded. "That person became indisposed."

Glancing between the two of them, Pheonix got the distinct impression that there was something they weren't telling him, but decided to accept it. Executioners were a busy lot — the person who had originally been slated for his training probably had had something come up.

"You've grasped the basic and advanced principles," Marcus said. "Suffice it to say, you probably have guessed your next and final step."

"Moving myself."

"Correct. There isn't much to elaborate on that subject. It is merely taking everything else you've already learned and putting it into practice; but we will be present to ensure your safety if you find yourself stuck."

Pheonix couldn't have guessed that Marcus meant *literally* stuck, until one of the morning's string of failed slide attempts had him sideways with his feet in a tree — as in, his feet were *inside* the tree.

While Marcus hadn't been incorrect in saying that the principles were exactly the same, execution of them was a whole different beast. In the same way he'd struggled with tuning his focus for the 'seeing' portion, he was struggling with the level of precision needed to move his own body. It didn't help that the dream from the night before dogged his thought process at every step.

As the day went on, though, sliding did get easier. He appeared less inside of things, though there was one close call with Marcus — Pheonix materialized less than an inch from him.

During the midday break, he sat in the grass with the sun warming his back, with the intention of going no-mind to regain some energy. However, intruding thoughts kept him from being able to drop into that state. For some reason, he couldn't shake himself of Life's visage. The dream kept replaying over and over again in his head, unprompted and unwelcome.

Disgusted with his own lack of concentration, he stood and initiated another slide — only realizing his mistake too late.

The beautiful elven woman was still burned in his mind's eye.

EPILOGUE

Klaxons and alarms rattled through HQ at high decibels, accompanied by flashing red lights.

Chani's wrist-comm trilled and she ducked out into the hallway to take the call.

"What the hell is going on?" Chani said into her wrist-comm.

"Commander, the trace has gone dark," came Jeeves' voice.

Chani froze. "I understand," she said, more calmly than she felt, and returned to the conference room.

Oh, the shit had hit the fan this time.

Glossary

Accessing - *Term* - When Pheonix pulls information from one of his internal sources (most commonly an implant).

Accord space - *Location* - The sectors of space mapped, regulated, patrolled, and with infrastructure put up and maintained by the Accord and related groups.

Age/Ages - *Term* - A measure of time. Generally about one-hundred-thousand True Years, though more accurately bookended by major events. The Age in which the events of *Everdark* take place is the Sixth Age.

AI - *Technology* - Rather than the weird shit that technobro humans here on Earth use, this refers to actual Artificial Intelligence: a sapient mind housed in and spawned by a machine base.

Anders Rivios (*Ann*-durrs *Rih*-vee-ose) - *Character* - Captain of the Battle Cruiser Chevalier. A highly proud woman who only cares about her reputation and rank.

Andural (Ann-*du*-rahl) - *Character* - Elven First. Legendary Bladesinger-smith who forged the superstructure of Terelath, the elven garlands, and many elven artifacts. Believed to be long dead.

Archaic Earth - *Location* - An Earth with several Kingdoms united under the rule of the follower of the Creator, the Golden Paladin. One of the most endemically magical places in the known metacosm that isn't straight-up deadly. The predominant society eschews technology for convenience and uses it primarily when more mundane options aren't available, or are inefficient.

Arkiolett (*Are*-kee-oh-let) - *Character* - Gnomish Master tinkerer currently running a shop in the Tinkerer's Villa on Ranger HQ. Wears his heart on his sleeve. Kind, but a little blunt.

Arkitekt - *Species* - A mysterious species that, in the distant past, spread gene-seeds and artifacts throughout the metacosm, apparently at the behest of the Creator, then disappeared utterly. No one currently knows why, or what became of them.

Ascended - *Group* - The Creator's direct influencing forces within the metacosm, representing elements and concepts.

Ascendent beings - *Group* - Individuals just below the Ascended in power and ability. This designation contains the Firsts, Ethers, etc.

Assisi (Ah-*see*-see) - *Location* - The angelic homeworld. Razed by Elysian 300 years prior to the events of *Everdark* and *The Fractured Balance*.

Aunrielthalassa and Aolenthalassa (Ahn-ree-el-thaa-*lah*-ssa and Aa-oh-len-thaa-*lah*-ssa) - *Characters* - The elven Seconds. When an elf/someone with knowledge of elven politics says "the Seconds," they almost always are referring to these two weasels. Regardless of what the official statements are, these are the two elves who almost single-handedly control the actions of the elves and, by extension, most of the metacosm.

Austraelus/Astra (Ah-*stray*-lee-uss/*A*ss-tra) - *Character* - The organotek AI of Ranger HQ. Cheeky, polite, faelike.

Availeon (Ah-*vay*-lee-uhn): The elven homeworld. Orbited by Ranger HQ.

Bedaestael (Beh-*day*-stay-ell) - *Character* - One of Pheonix's swords. Crackling lightning. Talkative and whiny.

Biarch - *Character* - An elven First and the Prime elven Healer, head of the elven Healers. The penultimate kind soul, unbothered, moisturized, happy, in his lane, focused, flourishing.

Bladesingers - *Group* - An elven Calling, the chosen of the Ascended of Law who are gifted Lawblades. At present, only male elves can become Bladesingers.

Bladesong - *Phenomena* - A Song (mixture of magic, sound, and quantum) allowing a Lawblade to suspend in the air and spawn multiple other, magical blades. The Bladesong controls the movement of all the blades in a complex composition.

Bladestorm - *Phenomena* - When a Bladesinger's emotions run too hot, he has the chance of losing control of his Lawblade, which will create a feedback loop that spawns thousands upon thousands of blades to destroy his target and anything in the vicinity ... including himself.

Blood magic - *Term* - A highly illegal type of magic fueled by the mana inherent in an individual's life essence. Practitioners of this type of magic are called red or blood mages.

Chani Abyssterilon (*Sha*-nee Ah-biss-*tear*-ih-lawn) - *Character* - Race of Man. Special Projects Commander for the Rangers. Competent, cunning, parental. Knows far more than she lets on.

Chosen - *Group* - Beings tethered to the Obelisk; a political body meant to communicate the Creator's wishes to the metacosm. They answer to the Obelisk and the balance.

Commanding-General - *Character* - Highest rank in the Rangers, below the Elders. Currently held by an Akeela who is gruff, straightforward, intimidating, with a bit of a temper.

Congress of Mages - *Group* - The only organization made up entirely of magi. Established in the Second Age, the Congress is made up of some of the pre-eminent names in magic. They make and enforce the rules on the utilization of magic in the metacosm. Watched closely by the Accord.

'Creator's Light' - *Term* - A reference either to the literal light of the Creator (meaning the Creator's direct energy/power) or the more euphemistic love or attention from the Creator.

Crosinthusilas (Crow-sihn-*thoo*-sih-lahs) - *Character* - An elven First and the Prime Lady. One of Pheonix's trainers on Terelath. Slightly unhinged, icy and sharp, with a love of storytelling and history.

Cybernetic augmentation - *Technology* - Physical technology-based augmentation, a step up from implants. Usually only used to replace a limb or other major body part.

Dark elf - *Species* - A subspecies of elf that split away from the others for wont of power. They are often seen associating with slavers (or are slavers themselves).

Demon - *Species* - An evil species that came from 'the Nether' (though it's not known what/where that is). Grotesque and hungering only for domination and death, it took a sacrifice of unrivaled proportion to stop them during the Great Demon War. The metacosm is constantly on the lookout for demon portals or signs of demon activity.

Deutronium - *Term* - The hardest known ore in the metacosm. An incredibly valuable resource, as only its discovery made long-term spaceflight and space stations possible.

Drakkan (Dra-*cahn*) - *Species* - Hominid/dragon mix. Agile, intelligent, withdrawn.

Dwarf - *Species* - A species of rock hominids created by the Forgemaster. Boisterous, aggressive, single-minded about their interests (which mostly include minerals).

Elf - *Species* - A First species; immortal and magically-inclined, tied to nature and the elements. They believe emotions are for the 'lesser species' and that they've risen above them.

Elven Council - *Group* - One of the governmental bodies of Accord space made up of mostly elven Seconds. Based in Terelath, they work closely with the Chosen and, to a lesser extent, the Rangers and Accord.

Elven Seconds through Sevenths - *Groups* - Elven generations based on birth order by Age and, though less important, parentage.

Elysian (Eh-*lee*-see-ann) - *Species* - Space-faring species of 'false Gods' made quickly legendary for their cruelty and power. Unknown provenance.

Evil - *Group* - Due to 'the balance' being the accepted ethos of much of the upper echelon of political power in the metacosm, evil has claimed legitimacy by way of the Creator's will. Evil people and organizations (such as sapient traffickers, thieves, poachers, raiders, etc.) have no need to hide their activities, as they are openly the 'balancing' factors of the metacosm.

Executioners - *Group* - An organization formed by ancient elven leadership and unleashed onto the metacosm, gifted special garlands that give them authority superseding any other governmental body. Known for their staunch dedication to Justice.

Faranthalassa/Faran (Fah-rahn-tha-*lah*ssa/Fah-*rahn*) - *Character* - An elven Ranger with way too many titles, one of which is the Master of Propriety. One of Pheonix's trainers on Terelath. Somewhat uptight, but steadfastly dedicated to his principles.

Firsts - *Group* - The initial individuals of a species brought into existence directly by the Creator. They are older than Time itself and are often nearly on-par with Ascended in both knowledge and power. Very few are known of in the Sixth Age, though where they went is a common topic of debate among academics and citizens alike.

Fold-space - *Technology* - Ranger tek allowing an individual to store items within a space that is accessible only by this tek and by certain quantum-minded individuals.

Fug (Commander Fug) - *Character/Term* - A Ranger Commander whose exploits became so legendary among the Rangers that his name ended up synonymous with bad decisions and is often used as an expletive. (As in: "For Fug's sake.")

Garland (elven) - *Term* - A circlet worn by most elves. Said to be forged en masse as gifts to his people by Andural.

Gnome - *Species* - A diminutive species created by the Forgemaster. The most technologically-savvy species in the known metacosm, who prize the ability to tinker above all things.

Goblin - *Species* - An evil species known for their disregard of life and close-to-gnomelike obsession with technology. Enemies of the dwarves.

Godholme - *Location* - Quantum space at the center of all the multiverses. Said to be where the Creator and Ascended live. Takes on the appearance of a small planet covered in constantly moving, intricately-interlocking, filigreed metal plates.

Grey Mages - *Group* - The only class of mages that use Will magic, a sect of whom serve Law as peacekeepers on Availeon.

Healers - *Group* - Individuals with the power to Heal without technological means.

Hominin - *Term* - A species group relating to humans and Race of Man, among others. Many of this group were created by the Creator. Generally characterized by their shorter life-spans and tempestuous natures. Excludes those of primate genetics.

Implant - *Technology* - Bio-nanotech that bonds with a body's systems to enhance it in some way from the inside (e.g. translation, communication, or access to archived information).

Initiated/uninitiated - *Term* - To be initiated is to be aware that other species exist outside of a society's planet/current knowledge. Most initiated societies are expected to be contributing to or participating in metacosmic society in some way. Most uninitiated planets are left that way for a reason.

Jae Steele - *Character* - Race of Man. Vanguard Fleet Commander and Ranger liaison to the Accord. A chill and capable person whose easy smile makes them friends wherever they go.

Krasynth II (*Cray*-sinth two) - *Location* - Barely a planet, a rocky wasteland with minimal atmosphere. Rich in deutronium.

Ladies (elven) - *Group* - An elven Calling, the chosen of Celestial, Ascended of the Weave, who are gifted with direct access to the Weave. At present, only female elves can become Ladies.

Law - *Ascended* - No name known. The rarely-seen enforcer of Law in the metacosm. Gifts Lawblades to Bladesingers.

Lazarus (*Lah*-zah-russ) - *Ascended* - The previous Ascended of Justice. Killed in the Second Age by Bast, evil God of Murder.

Life - *Ascended* - The Ascended of Life. No name given. Distant but kind and welcoming.

Life-spark - *Term* - A light within every individual that denotes their species. Can indicate other things too, like health status. Can only be 'read' or seen by certain species/individuals.

Loren (*Loh*-ren) - *Character* - Elf, former Lady, and Chosen. An 'Elder' of the Rangers. Sour, and openly hates being a Chosen, but supports the Rangers to the best of her ability.

Magitek - *Technology* - Often shortened to 'tek.' Different from 'technology' or 'tech,' which is purely science-based, magitek combines physical sciences and the Weave through complex processes that produce some of the most terrifying and powerful things in the metacosm.

Mahji (Maa-*jye*) - *Species* - An inherently magical First species of hominins. In fact, they are so attuned to the Weave that it often kills them, sometimes in infancy.

Mana - *Term* - A byproduct of the Weave's interaction with other domains and realms, fuel for the complex quantum calculations that make up the effect known as 'spells.'

Malol (Maa-*loll*) - *Character* - One of Pheonix's swords. Burning red. Grumpy, quiet, hungry.

Minrathous (Min-*wrath*-uss) - *Character* - A human druid. One of Pheonix's trainers on Terelath. Honest and kind, if a little cheeky. A person to whom serving Nature is second nature.

Mulahajad (Moo-*lah*-ha-jahd) - *Character* - Mahji First and High Mahji. Quirky, rule-bending action-taker outside any system.

Multiverse/'verse' - *Term* - Separate complete universes next to each other. The barriers between verses can be crossed, but it is a dangerous and highly-controlled thing.

Nether-flame - *Term* - A sapient heavy flame, though not much is known about it other than that. Seemingly antagonistic to organics, with infectious properties. Utilized — brutally — by demons during the Great Demon War.

No-mind - *Term* - A skill specific to Pheonix. He can essentially switch the computing processes of his conscious and subconscious minds, putting his conscious mind, external senses, and body 'to sleep' (in the language of computers, not organics), which allows him to consciously access and analyze stored information with frightening depth.

Oodl - *Species* - Also called the 'Genetically Diversified Collective' (mostly by the Rangers) and by the slur 'dreg' (mostly by assholes). Individuals of highly varied genetic construction.

Orc - *Species* - An evil species known for their worship of the God of Pestilence. They drink 'pustulence,' a substance made by their Elders and their God, to prove their devotion — but it also rots them from the inside out.

Pheonix (*Fee*-nix) - *Character* - (Yes, it is 'PhEOnix,' not 'PhOEnix.') Genetic experiment who was raised by slavers. Has few emotions and an obsession with Justice.

Penny - *Character* - The flamboyant hominin owner of the famous bar Penny's on Terelath. They always know what drink you need. Trust the Master. Close to Chani.

Ranger HQ - *Location* - The most advanced spacefaring vessel in the metacosm. A planet-sized sphere made up of multi-layered rings surrounding a gravitic core. Most Ranger operations happen out of this location.

Rangers - *Group* - A militarized, space-faring society working closely with the Universal Accord to attempt to keep peace and protect innocents within Accord space. The mitigating factor to 'evil,' and, although not blatantly contemptuous of evil (for the sake of 'the balance'), then subtly so.

Rangers (elven) - *Group* - Personal servants of Spiraea. Known for being able to thrive in the wildest of Nature. Many are bow-users.

Ranger Great clans — Abyssterilon, Rivios, and Akamatsu - *Groups* - The Rangers were formed in the First Age by John Abyssterilon and Damien Rivios, whose families then went on to solidify the resulting political structure around themselves, creating the first two Great clans of Abyssterilon and Rivios. Lesser families (like Barandor and Beowulf) then aligned themselves with a Great clan to vie for political power. Akamatsu was a later addition to the Great clan structure.

Rec-suit - *Technology* - A universal biological recovery suit developed by the Rangers. Worn by nearly every Ranger under their armor. Has multiple iterations, uses, and designs.

Refresher - *Technology* - Combination shower/toilet/changing room. The hygiene functions are achieved through sonic waves tuned to oscillate across surfaces and shake loose oil, dirt, etc.

Ren - *Character* - Hominin-appearing (though his true species is unknown) and Chosen. An 'Elder' of the Rangers. Rarely seen, rarely speaks when he is. A mystery.

Replicator - *Technology* - A terminal that specializes in making edible matter, which it does through a self-replicating mycelial colony with added aminos and water as needed. It's not gonna make a five-star meal, but it's better than nutrient pills or starvation.

Resh Brothers - *Characters* - Two of the brothers, Zu'Resh and Ka'Resh, are Red Mage Masters and evil bastards both. The third brother is in hiding.

Sabot (*Say*-bow) - *Character* - Indeterminate species. The poster boy for the perfect soldier. Curt. "No one is more professional than I" embodied. One of Chani's personal Team Sergeants.

Sapient - *Term* - A being with higher thought processes and a soul. (The Accord has an entire checklist to determine whether or not an individual/species is sapient. Note: sapient is different from sentient.)

Shahharath Aaldur (*Shah*-hah-wroth Ahl-*duur*) - *Character* - The elven Iyavesti (Ee-yah-*vess*-tee) or 'forever-teacher,' the living well of knowledge to which all elven minds are connected. Sleeping underground in Terelath in the Vault of the Firsts.

Shielding technology - *Technology* - Generally comes in two types: generators and personal belts. Shield generators are massive and massively powerful, but can only produce one kind of shield (kinetic, null, magic, etc). Shield belts closely layer a field over an individual's body and can be tuned to shield the user from multiple sources of affective properties.

Slavers - *Group* - Evil merchants focusing on sapient trafficking.

Song - *Term* - Generally used by elves and angels to refer to the Creator's Song, the background music to the metacosm that only certain species and individuals can hear.

Space pirates - *Group* - Evil scavengers made up of a motley assortment of societal rejects from all across the metacosm.

Spiraea (Spih-*ray*-uh) - *Ascended* - "Lady of the Woods." Ascended of Nature. Fierce, moody, enigmatic. Patron of the elves and Availeon.

Stasis - *Technology* - A generated flow or field that almost totally suspends molecular movement. Since full suspension is impossible, the mechanism providing the stasis effect (be it a spell or a generator) will re-fire every time it detects movement. It is the closest thing to 'freezing time' possible in a physical universe.

Temperjoke - *Ascended* - Ascended of Chaos. Personality and actions 'dictated by Chaos.'

Terelath (*Teh*-reh-lath) - *Location* - The main city of the elven homeworld of Availeon. Seat of the Chosen.

Terminal - *Technology* - A boxy piece of every-technology, used for anything from creating food to dispensing knowledge.

The balance - *Term* - The belief espoused by those in power (such as the Chosen and the elven Council) that evil was created by the Creator and is meant to remain in balance with non-evil — that finding harmony between the two is the Creator's greatest wish of its creations.

The Creator - *Character* - An omniscient, omnipotent being who is said to have created the metacosm and everything in it.

The Dark Sector - *Location* - The sector of unmapped space (that which is outside of Accord space) known to be controlled by evil interests.

The Man In Black/The Death Dealer - *Character* - An enigmatic evil entity who repeatedly showed up in Pheonix's early life and acted like he knew something about Pheonix. Whenever he appeared, he left a trail of mass death.

The Metacosm/Creation - *Term/Location* - Everything that was, will be, is, might be, ought to be, and shouldn't have been. A universe and its shadows.

The Obelisk of Time/"The Obelisk" - *Term/Character* - A Creator artifact that claims to be the origination of laws that the sapient species should follow. Speaks through its Chosen.

"The Old Man"/Maester - *Character* - A mysterious old hominin man on Archaic Earth who took Pheonix in and taught him about many things.

Theodric (Thi-*ah*-drick) - *Character* - Oodl. The Kaehin deis Ohd: chosen avatar of Schieta, Elemental Lord of Flame. Carries a staff named 'Barnie.' Childlike, innocent, talks way too much.

Thread (of the Weave) - *Term* - Individual strands of the Weave, each attuned to a different magical element.

Tyyrulriathula (Tee-rule-ree-*aath*-you-laa) - *Character* - Elven Seventh. Bladesinger and apprentice smith. One of Pheonix's trainers on Terelath. Flippant, honest, emotional. Pheonix's best friend.

Universal Accord ("The Accord") - *Group* - A political entity consisting of every initiated non-evil species. They work closely with the Rangers to keep peace and support civilians of all shapes and origins — not just in Accord space, but beyond it as well.

Unit - *Term* - A base ten measurement system (milliunits, centiunits, units, etc.) primarily used by the Rangers.

VI - *Technology* - Virtual Intelligence. Nonsapient advanced machine-based algorithms usually used to assist sapients (both organic and otherwise).

War-Bladesingers - *Group* - Bladesingers who threaten a Bladestorm. They are specially trained, taught to harness the Bladestorm.

War-Ladies - *Group* - Ladies who threaten a Spellstorm (similar to a Bladestorm). They are specially trained, and gifted with phylacteries that absorb the intense excessive mana they exude.

Weave-user - *Group* - A person capable of manipulating the Weave and mana. These people go by *many* names: magus, Weaver, spell-caster, spell-user, etc.

Weave - *Term* - A mesh of 'threads' that makes up one of the major base supports of the metacosm. These threads and the Weave itself can be called on to use magic in the physical domain.

Will magic - *Term* - A mysterious and rare type of magic. Those who use it claim to 'will' things to happen.

Xenobiarch (*Zee*-no-bye-ark) - *Character* - An elven First and the Prime Augmentor, head of the elven xeno-mechanics. ADHD personified. Even speaking full sentences is too slow for him at times; he has places to be, you know.

Zasfioretaeula (Zass-fee-*oh*-ray-tay-*ee*-uu-lah) - *Character* - Elven First. Prime War-Bladesinger. Cool, unreadable, professional.
Zeta (*Zey*-ta) - *Character* - Mahji and Chosen. An Elder of the Rangers. Strict, cutting, skilled.

About The Prime Speakers

What is a Prime Speaker, you may be asking?

Well, others may refer to our profession as 'author.' We Speak for the Metacosm, and bring its stories to this reality.

A is an opinionated intellectual with a penchant for theology, psychology, politics, hard sciences, and mathematics. They are a combat veteran with severe complex PTSD and bipolar. They've traveled all over the world and enjoy video games. The majority of the Metacosm was crafted by them over several decades, influenced by *Dungeons & Dragons*, real and emerging science, world observations, video games, and books.

N is a neurodivergent (autistic and ADHD) creative magpie. While writing fantastical stories and drawing the characters from them was something she'd done since she was a child, it was discovering anime (specifically, *Pokemon* and *Sailor Moon*) that led N into the arts seriously. Her long list of creative interests include photography, 3D, illustration, videography, fashion design, character design, and, of course, writing. N has the rare genetic connective tissue disorder Ehlers Danlos Syndrome and a myriad of fun comorbidities.

All things Metacosm:
http://metacosmchronicles.com

Milton Keynes UK
Ingram Content Group UK Ltd.
UKHW041116061224
452240UK00005B/272

9 798991 187411